PRINCESS IN LINGERIE

Lingerie #12

PENELOPE SKY

Hartwick Publishing

Princess in Lingerie

Copyright © 2018 by Penelope Sky

All rights reserved.

Contents

ONE

Carter

_____

Now that Mia was firm in her decision to murder me, I had to chain her up.

I wasn't happy about it.

Neither was she.

Just like when she first came into my captivity, I cuffed her ankles to the bed so she could only reach the bathroom when she needed it. Her bedroom was stripped bare, so only the essentials remained behind. Without access to anything, there was nothing she could use to plot against me.

But now she would have to live her last few days this way.

Like a prisoner.

She sat on the bed and stared at me with hatred. Like I was the biggest asshole on the planet, she despised me. But that hatred was nothing compared to her disappointment. There was a point in time when she'd actually liked me, enjoyed fucking me. There was affection between us, delicate kisses between two lovers. She even said I was a good man. But now, all of that was gone.

She hated me again.

"Let me know if you need anything." I pocketed the key and walked out of the room.

"Fuck off, Carter."

I kept my back to her but paused on the threshold. Insults never bothered me, but hers did.

She had a son.

I shut the door and locked it behind me before I walked into my office.

She had a son.

I couldn't believe it.

An eight-year-old boy was out there somewhere, without a mother or a father. He would never know how strong his mother was, how hard she fought to get back to him. Instead of giving in to the temptation of suicide, she continued to persevere in the hope she would be free someday.

She was brave.

Far braver than I was.

Most people would have given in to the temptation and prayed their child would understand. But her spirit gave her the strength to keep moving forward, to accept Egor's punishments in the hope she might escape someday. That was probably the reason why Egor chose her to begin with—she wouldn't take her life like all the others.

Could I really give her back?

Did I want to be that man?

If I didn't have a family to protect, I would consider it. If I could keep this war for myself, I might take the plunge. I cared about this woman and not just because I was attracted to her. It was because I respected her. She reminded me of my sister, of the strong Barsetti women who didn't put up with bullshit.

I felt like shit.

Worse than shit.

I already didn't want to do this, but I didn't want to do it even more, knowing she had a little boy.

What if this were my mother? I couldn't picture my life without my mother, the woman who stayed home with me every single day and raised me. I was a grown man who didn't need anything anymore, but I would always need her. I would do anything for her. Mia was an exceptional woman who had already lost the last three years. Why should she lose more time? And we both knew Egor would kill her eventually.

Her son would lose her for good.

Could I stand by and let that travesty happen?

Did I want to?

I sat in the leather chair behind my desk and stared across the room at the bookshelf. I used this room for paperwork, but it was unnecessary. I had so many luxuries I didn't even need, like this huge house. Mia didn't even have her freedom.

I went over it in my head again and again. Even if I wanted to save Mia, it wasn't possible. Egor paid me a hundred and fifty million to get her out of the Underground. Regardless of how rich he was, that was a lot of dough for a single person. That meant she was extremely valuable to him.

The idea of just letting her go without a fight seemed unlikely.

Even if I wired the money back to him, he still wouldn't be happy about it.

I needed to ask the Barsetti clan for advice, but I couldn't ask Conway. His wife was about to go into labor at any moment. I didn't want to ruin this special time with him with my problem. I didn't want to bother my father either, not when it would stress him out. That meant there was only one person I could turn to.

I called Vanessa.

She answered right away, despite the late hour. "Carter?" She panicked into the phone. "Everything okay?" I hardly ever called her, and if I did, it wasn't this late at night.

"Yeah, everything is fine. I'm sorry to call you so late. I was actually wondering if I could talk to Griffin…" I didn't have his number, and I didn't want to bother Conway by asking for it.

"Oh…sure." The phone became muffled as she made the handoff.

Griffin answered the phone in his deep voice. "Carter. How can I help you?"

We'd never really talked one-on-one before. I always hovered in the background, letting my father and uncle decide how to handle him. But after he saved my family, all of that hatred had faded away. He was accepted into the Barsetti clan. I dropped my dislike along with everyone else. "Can I speak to you in private? Vanessa can't know about this conversation."

"Alright." His movements turned audible as he excused himself from her presence. They were probably in bed together at this time of night. It was nearly a full minute before he addressed me again. "This should be interesting…"

"I apologize for bothering you. But I have no one else to turn to."

"That doesn't sound good," he said with a chuckle. "We just declared peace with the Skull Kings, and now something else comes up…"

"It went well?"

"Yes. We made the exchange and buried the hatchet." His baritone reverberated over the line. "They were pleased by the money and the little speech your uncle gave. We parted on good terms. I'm glad that shit is over."

And I was about to stir up more. "Good to hear."

"I'm sure your father was going to call you in the morning. He's probably still talking to Crow right now."

"In our family, no news is good news."

He paused a while before he spoke. "What can I do for you, Carter?"

Just because the issue with the Skull Kings was completed didn't mean saving Mia was a good idea. But it did make it a little easier. "Fuck…it's a long story."

His smile was obvious over the phone. "Those are the best kind."

"So…I did one more deal a month ago. Some guy offered me an insane amount of money to buy a woman from the Underground. Claimed he was her brother. I was greedy and stupid and took the deal."

"This doesn't sound good."

"The woman is beautiful, smart, sassy…very much like a Barsetti."

"Yep," Griffin said. "I see exactly where this is going."

"I realized this man isn't her brother. He's her old master. She ran away from him and got captured by the Skull Kings, and he wants her back. He's a psychopath. The more I've gotten to know this woman—"

"And fuck her."

I didn't deny it. "The more I've come to care for her. She didn't know I was giving her back to Egor until she overhead my conversation. Of course, she got angry. Felt like I betrayed her…which I did."

"She thought she was just getting a free vacation with a nice master?" he asked incredulously.

"She was skeptical at first…but eventually believed that."

"Poor girl," he whispered.

"Anyway…I told her I had to give her back even though I didn't want to. I don't want a war with this guy, not after all the wars my family has already fought. My father and uncle just want peace. I can't do that to them…"

"I've only dated Vanessa a short while, but I've noticed a pattern with the Barsettis. They get themselves caught up in a lot of bullshit."

I didn't rise to the insult, knowing he didn't mean it in an offensive way.

"So, what are you asking me, Carter?"

I didn't give him the last piece of information until now. "I'd already made my decision to give her back even though I didn't want to…until she told me something else. It makes me sick to my stomach. It fills me with so much guilt, I can barely breathe."

"What is it?" he asked quietly.

"She has a son…"

Griffin was silent.

"He's eight. There's no father in the picture."

He was quiet longer, obviously at a loss for words.

"I have no idea where the kid is right now. If she knows, she didn't tell me. But when she told me that…I lost all my nerve. I already didn't want to give her back, but now…Fuck. All I can do is think about my mom and how devastated I would be if I ever lost her—" I knew I'd shoved my foot in my mouth, but it was too late to undo the damage. I'd forgotten that Griffin has lost his mother…and his father.

"Yeah…it's pretty shitty."

"I apologize, Griffin… I wasn't thinking."

"No." He spoke with a firm voice. "No need to be delicate, Carter. I'm not a delicate man. And you're right, losing a mother isn't easy. This kid reminds me a lot of myself. His mother is a slave to men, and there's nothing he can do to help her. I was very young when my mother was killed. I barely remember her face. But I could never forget her spirit."

I fell silent, unsure what to say to that.

"It's a pretty fucked-up situation you're in, Carter."

"What do you think I should do?"

"I can't answer that."

"You've gotta have some advice, Griffin."

He sighed into the phone. "If this were Vanessa, I'd murder every man in Italy to get her back. I'd risk my life a million times to give her the life she deserves. I wouldn't even need to think about it. The fact that you have to think about it tells me she's not Vanessa to you."

"I don't love her…if that's what you're asking."

"But you care about her enough to think about risking everything to help her."

"I guess…"

"Sounds complicated."

I chuckled with pain in my heart. "You're telling me. I was trying to think of a plan to get what I want and avoid the war. Maybe I could save her and save my family at the same time."

"What's your idea?"

"There's only one possibility—fake her death."

Griffin was quiet as he considered what I said.

"If I can make Egor believe she killed herself, then he could forget about her. I could wire the money he paid me, and that would be the end of it."

"She could never really be free, though," he said. "Because if he spots her somewhere, it could destroy your entire plan."

"Well...she offered me something if I saved her."

Griffin's grin was obvious over the line. "I think I know what it is."

"So she would be with me anyway. I guess her kid would be too. I would probably sell this place and move to Tuscany, start over in a new place."

"The plan is plausible. But if Egor is an egomaniac, he's not going to let you make him look like a fool. He's going to want to see the body for proof—so he won't be outsmarted."

"That's what I was worried about."

"And if this woman is as alluring as you make her seem...then he'll probably be suspicious of you."

"Agreed. So the only way I could accomplish this is with another body...but that's not going to happen."

Bones was quiet for a long time before he spoke. "I can make that happen."

"What?" I blurted. "You have a body?"

"I know a guy."

"Who just has dead bodies lying around?"

"Something like that," he said vaguely.

"But the corpse would have to look identical to her. She would have to be decomposed at the perfect amount."

"I realize that," he said. "But if we tell him that Mia died in a fire, it could ruin her features enough to make her indistinguishable."

"She killed herself by burning herself alive? That sounds extreme."

"Tell him she did it after she overheard your conversation. The idea of going back to him was so disturbing that she killed herself. You kept her locked up in her room, so the only option was to burn herself alive."

"Why would she be exposed to fire?"

"She could have had a candle in her room. Lit the drapes on fire. Then the room caught on fire…and the flames engulfed her. By the time you got there and put it out, she was dead."

"Sounds extreme…"

"It's the only option you have."

It seemed like a plan that could easily go wrong. "And then what? Hide her forever?"

"He'll forget about her eventually. But it'll take a few years for that to happen. She'll have to stay close to you for a while. Private property where he can't even see through the gates."

"Yeah…" The idea of her and her son living with me didn't bother me, surprisingly. Especially with the offer she'd given me, that would be the ideal situation. A part of me knew I should help her because it was the right thing to do and not make her uphold her end of the bargain.

But I wasn't that kind of man.

If I was going to take this kind of risk, I wanted something out of it.

I wanted her.

Griffin spoke again. "So, what are you going to do?"

"Fuck…I don't know."

"You've got to decide soon. When are you supposed to give her back?"

"Friday."

"Shit. You need to decide now. Because you're going to have to catch that room on fire and put it out again, just in case he checks."

"I'm gonna have to burn my own house?" I asked incredulously.

"A controlled fire."

"Sorry, don't have much experience with that."

"I'll help you."

"You know a lot about this stuff…"

He chuckled over the phone. "I've seen a lot of shit in my young life. Does that mean you're in?"

It seemed like too much work for one woman, but I

knew handing her over would haunt me for the rest of my life. She was a good person. Her only crime was being in the wrong place at the wrong time. Her freedom was taken from her as if she'd never had it in the first place. If she hadn't gone to that bar with her friends, her life would have been completely different. She was beautiful and exceptional. She deserved to be with her son, to have a man she wanted to be with.

But all of that was stolen from her.

I shouldn't want to help her, but I'd grown fond of her over the last month.

Doing nothing didn't seem like an option.

"Carter?" Griffin's voice interrupted my thoughts. "You need to decide now."

I kept thinking about the tears in her eyes, the way she spoke about her son. Her heart was on her sleeve, and she showed her resilience when she threatened to kill me. She slashed me with that knife, willing to do anything to escape. There was nothing that could keep her from her son…from raising him to be a man.

I was her last chance. If I handed her over, that would be it.

She would never escape.

"Alright," I said. "I'm in."

I WENT BACK into her bedroom a few hours later. She was lying on the bed with a pillow under her head, her ankles still attached to the foot of the bed. She had a small blanket on top of her, and she was still in the clothes she wore earlier. Her eyes immediately cracked open when the door opened. Prepared to be dragged away, she sat up instantly, like I was about to haul her back to Egor.

I came to her side of the bed and sat on the edge, my weight making the mattress dip slightly. I hated the way she looked at me, prepared to fight me with every-thing she had. There was no hesitation on her part. It didn't matter that she'd slept with me and enjoyed me. When it came to her son, I didn't matter anymore. It made me admire her even more. "I've changed my mind. I'll help you."

She froze in place, her eyes widening noticeably.

"I talked to a friend of mine, and I think I have a plan." I continued to watch her, to see her brown eyes turn warm like hot coffee. The beauty of her soft features became more noticeable. Like her eyes were made of deep pools, they began to water. "It's going to be—"

The chains didn't hold her back as she launched herself into me, moving into my chest and wrapping her arms around my neck. She clung to me as the metal of the chains clanked together. She gripped me hard, her face burrowing into my neck. She cried audibly, her chest colliding with mine with every deep breath she took.

My arms circled around her waist, and I held her,

feeling so warm inside. This plan would bring me nothing but stress, but it also brought me peace. Feeling this woman thank me with her tears made it all worth it.

"Carter…thank you so much." She pulled her face away from my shoulder and held my gaze, her eyes leaking with tears. She wasn't ashamed of her emotion, not when her gaze was so steady. She cupped my cheek with one hand. "You're a good man. I always knew you were." She brought her lips to mine and kissed me. It wasn't full of gratitude, but something deeper. She kissed me like she meant it, like she'd given me her heart as well as the rest of her body. Her hand moved to my shoulder, and she gripped me, her tear-soaked lips devouring mine.

I cupped the back of her head and returned her deep embraces, getting lost in the chemistry that had been there since the moment I'd laid eyes on her. Something about her made me weak. Something about her made me question who I was.

When she pulled her lips away, her hands continued to cling to me. Her tears were on my lips now. She looked at me with those beautiful, warm eyes, the gratitude deep inside. "Thank you…"

"Before you thank me, you should know that I expect something in return." I held her gaze with authority, wanting her to understand that my decision wasn't made based on the goodness of my heart. I had other motivations to risk everything for her. She was asking me to make a huge sacrifice, and I wanted my actions to be rewarded. "Do you understand me?"

Her eyes shifted back and forth as she held my gaze. "Whatever you want, Carter. If you give me back my son…I will gladly submit to you."

Hearing her say that word made me melt on the spot. Submit. I wanted to fulfill my desires, and I wanted it to be consensual. I would finally get what I wanted—without the guilt. "Then we have a deal."

Her eyes emitted more tears. "Thank you…I don't know if I'll ever say it enough times. I dream about my son all the time. I wonder if he's having a good birthday. I wonder if he thinks about me. I miss him…miss him so much." Both of her hands gripped mine on my thigh. "The idea of seeing him again…gives me so much joy."

I stared at our joined hands. "If this works, both of you will have to live with me for a while. I'll be moving to Tuscany where we can have more privacy. It'll be at least a year before the two of you can go off on your own…just in case Egor's watching."

She nodded. "I understand. Wherever you call home, we'll call home. I'll make you a home and give you whatever you need, Carter. As long as I can raise my son, I don't care where we are. I used to read a story to him every night before he went to sleep… I'm looking forward to doing that again."

Hearing these confessions made me hate myself more. I should have helped her a long time ago.

"What's your plan?"

I told her everything I'd discussed with Griffin.

"You're right," she said. "Egor will want to see that I'm dead with his own eyes. You have to make sure you find someone as similar to me as possible…not sure how you're going to do that."

"I have a guy."

"That doesn't mean you're going to kill someone, right…?"

"No, of course not." I never asked Griffin, but I didn't need to. He would never do that, especially with Vanessa in his life.

"Okay. When are we going to do this?"

"Tomorrow."

"When are you supposed to give me back, again?"

"Friday."

She nodded. "We don't have much time left."

"No, we don't."

"You think he'll believe you?" she whispered.

"I hope so. Sometimes fear of something is worse than the actual thing itself. So knowing you have to go back to him might have been enough for you to take your own life. You realized there was never any hope that you would escape and find your son, so you just ended it. It's believable."

"True. And you'll give him back the money?"

"I'll wire it after I discover your body."

She gripped my hands tighter. "How long do I have to wait to see my son?"

"Do you know where he is?"

She nodded. "An orphanage in Milan."

"Egor knows about him?"

"Yes."

"I'll have to pay someone to adopt him, someone not connected to me. That way Egor won't know we took him."

"Yes…that's smart."

"It'll take me a few weeks to get that taken care of."

"Okay," she whispered. "I've waited this long. I can wait a little longer."

"And I'll need to hide you somewhere when Egor comes snooping around. I'll hand you off to my friend Griffin. There's nowhere safer in the world than by his side."

"You think we can trust him…?" Fear entered her eyes. Mia had only one kind of experience with men. It was impossible for her not to assume Griffin would do the same thing every other man did.

"Absolutely. He's one of the best guys I know. He's in love with my cousin Vanessa. He won't even touch you. I promise. And you'll love Vanessa. She's pretty amazing."

"Oh, okay," she said in relief. "Then that should be fine. When will I be with you again?"

Did she want to be with me? "After I buy the house in Tuscany. I'll move you there in the middle of the night."

"Okay. So…we start this plan tomorrow?"

I nodded. "Tomorrow."

She sighed then cupped both of her cheeks. "God, I hope this works. Just thinking about my son brings tears to my eyes. I never thought I would see him again, and now I'm so close…it terrifies me."

I watched this strong woman break down right in front of me, her son being her only vulnerability. "It's really happening, sweetheart. I'll get him back for you…I promise."

GRIFFIN SHOWED up the next day, bags under his eyes and exhaustion in his limbs. It didn't seem like he'd slept much the night before. He stepped inside the house, and we got straight to work. He had the equipment we needed to burn the bedroom, along with the candle that started it all.

We carried everything to the bedroom and set it on the ground.

He was in a particularly sour mood. "The fire will have to originate near the nightstand. Just in case he hires men to really check everything."

"Didn't sleep much last night?"

He looked me dead in the eye. "I had to pick up the body."

"You found one that quickly?"

"My guy is good." When he stood to his full height, we reached the same level. He was thicker than I was, having more muscles than any other man I'd met in real life. His tattoos made him innately formidable. With sleeves of black ink, he seemed like a difficult man. Mia might have a hard time leaving with him.

"You didn't kill anyone, right?"

"No," he said with a dark chuckle. "Vanessa would leave me if I did."

Thank god for that. "What the description?"

"Brunette, same age, same body description. The face is charred pretty bad, so her features will be nearly impossible to decipher. I'm not gonna find anyone better on such short notice. This girl was supposed to be cremated. Her family will get animal remains."

I felt guilty for lying to a family, but since I was saving someone else, I could justify it. "Alright."

Footsteps sounded down the hallway, and then Mia walked into the room. Her long hair was pulled into a braid, and she was wearing jeans and a t-shirt. She'd slept in my bed with me last night, even though we didn't have sex. She took one look at Griffin and immediately flinched, terrified of his dangerous appearance.

His eyes flicked to her, not the least bit surprised by her reaction. "Griffin."

"Uh…Mia." She immediately turned to me, showing fear for one of the first times. Even in the face of danger, she didn't back down. But this time, she was visibly affected by his terrifying appearance. In her defense, he did look like a member of a drug cartel. "Is Vanessa here?"

"No," Griffin said. "She needed to work today. And I haven't told her what's going on…yet."

"You didn't tell her?" I asked incredulously.

"Sorry," he snapped. "I was busy finding a dead body in the middle of the night and getting all this shit for you."

He had a point. "Alright. Fair enough." My arm moved around Mia. "I know Griffin looks like a murderer, but he's not. Trust me. He's a good guy."

"Well, I am a murderer." Griffin crossed his arms over his chest. "It's what I do for a living, actually. But I've never been into hurting women. So we won't have a problem." As if nothing had happened, he picked up the flame gun and carried it to the corner.

When Mia and I had some privacy, I spoke to her again. "He would never hurt you. I promise you."

She looked into my eyes for reassurance. "I was just hoping Vanessa would be here…"

"You don't need her to be here. He won't even touch you. This guy has a done a lot for my family because he's so in love with my cousin. I understand why you're scared because of what you've been through. But trust me on this."

She found comfort in my gaze before she nodded. "Alright."

"You should go downstairs so we can get to work."

"Okay." She rose on her tiptoes and cupped my face so she could kiss me. Whether she was fulfilling her end of the bargain or she actually meant it didn't matter to me. As long as her lips were on mine, I was happy. She gave me a soft kiss then a smile before she walked out.

I turned back to Griffin, who was staring at me with a wicked grin.

"What?"

He shook his head then got to work. "Nothing."

I WALKED Mia to the truck.

Griffin was already behind the wheel, waiting for her to join him. The engine was on, and he was scrolling through his phone to keep himself busy.

She looked up at me, her hands resting against my chest. "Are you sure you want to do this? It's not too late…"

It was too late. I'd given her so much hope, and I couldn't take it away now. "Yes."

Her eyes softened. "I'll see you soon, right?"

"In about a week or so."

"You'll call me?"

"When I can."

She hooked her arms around my neck and hugged me, her luscious body pressed against mine.

My chin rested on her head, and I secured my arms around her waist. I'd be lying if I said I wasn't afraid of Egor's wrath. There was a real possibility he might not believe me. He might come to the house and find something that contradicted the lie I'd made up. I'd be risking everything, my life and my family.

But I had to try.

"Thank you, Carter. I can't wait to see you again…" She tilted her chin up and looked at me again, the sincerity in her eyes. She squeezed my arms tightly before she leaned in and kissed me.

My hands cupped her cheeks again, and I kissed her, finding strength in the embrace. Her affection offset the terror in my heart. And a part of me believed that my family would be proud I was saving a young woman so she could be with her son. This wasn't about the money anymore. It was about doing the right thing…even though I wanted something in return. "I'll miss you too, sweetheart." I squeezed her arms before I opened the passenger door and helped her inside.

Griffin kept staring straight ahead, indifferent to our interaction.

"Tell Vanessa I said hi."

Mia stared at me with a prominent look of affection, like there were no words to describe how she felt toward me. She'd told me she hated me, that I wasn't a good man. But now she looked at me like I was some kind of superhero. "I will."

It was hard to shut the door and walk away. It was hard to do this on my own, to know she wouldn't be in my bed that night to chase away the stress. If I could get lost between her legs, it wouldn't be so bad. But I had to wait until this was over before I could finally get what I wanted.

I SAT in my office and stared at my phone, taking my time before I made the phone call. Egor was a psychopath. I didn't know much about him, but I knew he wasn't an enemy I wanted to make.

But this was the decision I had made.

I had to follow through with it.

I was worried about the grief this would bring my family, but I had to remember that I was a terrifying opponent as well. The Barsettis were loyal to one another, and that's what made us ruthless. We would stop at nothing to protect each other. A paid army was only loyal for the paycheck, but soldiers bound by love were a completely different story. My family had allies in many places, and now that Griffin was a part of our family, we were even more powerful. Egor had probably heard about the attack on Conway in Milan—and how we wiped out an entire team within minutes.

He didn't want to fight me either.

I finally made the call.

Egor answered almost immediately. "Carter. I wasn't expecting to speak to you until Friday. Hope this conversation brings good news." His voice was slightly cheery, probably because he was expecting to get his main source of entertainment back. "I'm exhausted from my business meetings. I'm looking forward to becoming reacquainted with her."

I wanted to throw my phone against the wall and destroy it, not out of jealousy, but pure hatred. "She's the reason I'm calling. We have a problem on our hands."

"What kind of problem?" He immediately turned serious, slightly hostile.

"When you called me the other night, she eaves-dropped. She figured out I was handing her back to you."

He chuckled. "I imagine that didn't make her too happy."

"No…it didn't. I had to chain her up again because she tried to kill me with a kitchen knife."

He laughed into the phone. "That sounds like her. I thought we could make this transition smooth, but perhaps we can't. You'll have to drug her first…even though I would love to see the look on her face when we make the transfer."

Now I just wanted to kill this guy, to stab him in the neck and watch him bleed to death. "There won't be any transfer, Egor. I woke up in the middle of the night to the sound of the fire alarm. The fire was coming from her room, and by the time I got there, the place was in flames."

"What?" he snapped. "What the fuck happened?"

"She had a candle on her nightstand. I think she set

the drapes on fire so the flames would spread… I think it was suicide."

Egor was silent.

"She wouldn't talk to me after she heard the phone call. She stayed in her room the entire time, chained to the bed. I didn't think this was even a possibility. Otherwise, I would have kept an eye on her. I've already wired the money back to you since this happened while she was in my possession."

He still didn't speak.

I leaned back in my chair and stared my bookshelf, unsure what his reaction would be. He was probably so angry, he didn't know what to say.

"I didn't think she was at risk for suicide. She didn't display any of the signs."

He finally said something. "No, she never did…"

"Maybe it was an accident, but I don't think it was. She didn't scream."

"Then what happened?" he asked, his voice coarse.

"I ran in there and put out the fire. She was on the bed, burned pretty bad."

"When did this happen?"

"Just now…" I sighed into the phone. "That whole bedroom is ruined. It'll have to be restored. I wanted to know what you wanted me to do with the body. I have a guy who can get rid of it, but I wasn't sure if you wanted it."

Egor was quiet again.

It was impossible to gauge his reaction over the

phone, not through his silence or carefully chosen words.

"You better not be fucking with me, Carter."

My blood turned ice-cold. "I'm not. You think I wanted to lose a hundred and fifty million dollars?"

"We both know she's worth more than a hundred and fifty million dollars, Carter."

I didn't deny it since that would make me look like a liar. "Get out here and look for yourself. I don't appreciate being called a liar, not when I've always been an ethical businessman. It's not my fault your slave hated you so much that she killed herself the second she realized she was going back to you. Not my problem, Egor."

He returned to his palpable silence.

I wasn't going to be a pushover because that would just make me look guilty. "She's just a woman. You can replace her in a heartbeat. If you treat them that badly, they're a dime a dozen. Now, what do you want me to do with the body? I left it in the bedroom, but I don't want it sitting there longer than necessary."

Egor growled into the phone. "My men and I will be there in a few hours."

Click.

I CALLED GRIFFIN.

He picked up right away. "How'd it go?"

"I'm not sure. He's on his way to look at the body."

"That doesn't surprise me." The sound of the engine was in the background since they were only halfway to Florence. "But our job is spotless. He'll be forced to accept it. And make sure to be an asshole. The more of an asshole you are, the more believable you are."

"That shouldn't be difficult…since I am an asshole."

He chuckled. "At least you're honest about it."

"He told me I better not be fucking with him."

"He'd be stupid not to be suspicious."

"But I made it seem plausible that she killed herself, since I said she did it right after our conversation."

"It'll be fine," Griffin said. "There's no evidence to the contrary. He might watch you for a while, but even then, he won't find anything. Eventually, he'll find someone else and forget about her. It's the circle of life for criminals like him."

"Yeah, probably. How's Mia?"

"She fell asleep about an hour ago."

"Oh, good…she must be comfortable around you, then."

"Vanessa called me on the drive home, and Mia heard everything. Probably realized there's nothing more unthreatening than a guy who's pussy-whipped."

"Did you just call yourself pussy-whipped?" I asked with an eyebrow raised.

"So?" he countered. "You think you aren't? You

called me in the middle of the night to find a burned corpse and help set fire to your house."

He had me by the balls.

"That's what I thought. Let me know what happens with Egor." He hung up.

An hour later, the black Escalade pulled up into my driveway. Undoubtedly, there were four armed men with him. I didn't have a chance, but I brought my loaded gun anyway. I stuffed it into the back of my jeans, and I walked outside to greet my guests.

Or my enemies.

Egor got out of the car first. I assumed it was him because he was the only one in a suit, navy blue with a black tie. He was not quite six feet tall. With typically Russian looks, he approached me as he buttoned the front of his jacket. He had blond hair and blue eyes, and he was a man in his early forties. He stared at me coldly, not issuing a greeting.

"Egor." I stood with my hands in my pockets, unflinching in his presence.

He continued to watch me.

"Do your dogs follow you everywhere? Or is it just the two of us?" I headed back to the house, turning my back on him as a sign of strength. I was either stupid or arrogant. There was no way to know which one.

Egor followed me, his armed men remaining outside.

I stepped inside and took the stairs, aware of him behind me. I didn't make small talk as I guided him to the bedroom where she'd stayed. I stepped inside first then moved to the side, the smell of smoke still heavy in the air. It was almost impossible to breathe.

Egor stepped into the room then slid his hands down the front of his jacket, as if he was afraid of the effect of the smoke on the fine material of his clothes. His biggest obsession was dead, but he cared more about his expensive suit.

It was disgusting.

He examined the room, the signs of smoke and ash everywhere. The bed had burned into dust, along with the nightstand. Some of the wall had been burned away, exposing the insulation. There were signs of the fire extinguisher we'd used when we controlled the burn. He stopped over her body, which was on the floor. Half of her hair had been burned off, and her previous features had been wiped away by the flames. He kneeled down to examine her further.

I made sure that the corpse matched everything on Mia's body, from the scars on her back to the noticeable freckle on her hip. Griffin helped me with the cosmetics, mutilating the corpse further before it was fully prepared.

Egor pulled on white gloves before he turned the girl over, looking for all the scars she had accumulated in his captivity. He examined her back, her right wrist, and searched for the large freckle on her hip.

He found them all.

He stood up again and pulled off his gloves, tossing

them on the ground beside her. "My men will take care of the body. I'll put her at the bottom of the ocean where she belongs."

I hid the relief on my face.

"You received the money, right?"

He pulled out his phone and checked the account. "You're fifty million short."

"That's what I paid for her at the Underground. I'm not eating that cost." Griffin said I needed to keep being an asshole. That was exactly what I was going to do. If I wasn't guilty, I shouldn't act like it.

He gave me a cold stare before he put his phone away. "Fine."

I maintained my stoic expression, but a parade was marching in my heart.

"We'll wrap her up and leave." He came toward me but didn't extend his hand. "I hope you enjoyed her while you could."

"Only when she didn't behave." Pretending I'd never slept with her would be unrealistic. Admitting I'd been with her wouldn't give me motivation to plan this whole charade, but lying about it would be worse.

"I will miss her," he said with a sigh. "But knowing she'd rather die than come back to me is a reward in itself. I loved torturing that woman…but I'll find someone else to torture instead."

His words made me sick to my stomach, made me want to hurl all over his fine suit. If Mia wasn't the victim, it would just be someone else. I had to remind myself there was nothing I could do about it. There were other men just like Egor all over the world. Even if I did kill him, someone else would take his place. But it didn't stop me from wanting to murder him, from wanting to punish him for what he did to Mia. He ripped a family apart…just for his own amusement. It took all my strength to speak the words out loud. "I'm sure you will."

TWO

Mia

———

Griffin took me to a small apartment in Florence, a one-story place right above an art gallery. He was the kind of man that didn't say much, focusing on the road ahead of him without asking me any questions. He seemed disinterested in my existence altogether, and he didn't have a perverted vibe humming around him. Most men I met were sick, wanting to hurt me for their own pleasure.

He looked at me with complete indifference.

His presence was innately dangerous, like he could yank a tree directly out of the ground. His muscled arms were covered with endless ink from his tattoos, and he seemed like a man from the streets.

But the second he spoke to Vanessa, he was a different man altogether.

Sweet, gentle, and obviously in love.

That's when I finally let my guard down.

He didn't care about me because he had someone special to care about.

Griffin walked into the apartment first, where he was greeted with a loving kiss from a petite brunette. She wrapped her arms around his neck and rose onto her tiptoes to feel his mouth. His powerful arms wrapped around her slender waist and squeezed her tightly.

Their affection made me think of Carter.

I wished he were there now.

Griffin seemed like a strong man capable of anything, but Carter put me at ease like no one else. He'd proved his loyalty to me, proved that he had a heart under the rock-hard chest. His dark eyes made my body flush with heat.

When Vanessa finished greeting her lover, she turned to me. "It's so nice to meet you, Mia." Instead of shaking my hand, she hugged me. It was full of affection and friendship. "I'm glad you're here. I hope you don't mind taking the couch. We only have one bedroom."

"And we need the privacy." Bones carried his bag down the hallway into the bedroom.

Despite her olive skin, she blushed slightly. "That's why I rarely take him anywhere."

"I think it's sweet."

She smiled. "So you guys got along okay on the drive? I know he's a bit intimidating."

"He was wonderful. Didn't say a word to me or look

at me. It was really nice." It was nice to be treated like a regular person, not some beautiful woman with sex between her legs. There was no attraction on his part. It was nice to be viewed as a person instead of an object.

She raised an eyebrow. "Sounds like he was pretty rude."

"No, not at all." I stepped farther inside the apartment and looked at the couch. "Thanks for letting me stay here. I didn't mean to get you two involved in this."

"Don't worry about it. There's nowhere safer in the world than right here, with that guard dog down the hallway."

I took a seat on the couch. "Seems that way. But I still feel bad getting you mixed up in this."

"Don't." She sat beside me. "If a Barsetti asks for a favor, you do it. Carter needed us, and of course, we were there. I have to admit I was surprised when Griffin told me everything, but…I guess I'm not surprised at the same time."

"It's not how it seems. Carter is a good man." I didn't want his family to think he was a bad person. After the sacrifice he'd made, he was nothing of the sort. Egor was the evil one.

"I never thought otherwise." She got up again. "Something to drink? Eat?"

Griffin came back into the room. "How about I make us something? So you don't make the poor girl sick."

She narrowed her eyes at him. "Want me to slap you?"

"Ooh." He smacked her ass as he walked by. "I hope you do, baby." He opened the fridge and pulled out a few ingredients.

It seemed like I'd walked into a house of newlyweds. "Water is fine."

"Coming right up." Vanessa poured me a glass and returned to me as Griffin started to cook in the kitchen. She set the glass beside me on the coffee table.

"You guys are really cute together."

Vanessa smiled but didn't reply to what I said.

I took a drink. "I hope Carter is okay. I wish I could call him."

"He'll call when he can." Griffin didn't look up from the pans on the stove. "I'm sure he's fine."

"Carter is a really smart guy," Vanessa said. "He's the smartest Barsetti, actually. All through school, he had unusually high marks. His parents thought he was cheating because they didn't know where his intelligence came from. He went to school for engineering and started his car company right away. Really impressive."

"Yeah…it is." He also knew a lot about the female anatomy, how to make me come without even trying. Was that skill? Or was I just that hot for him?

"I work in the gallery during the day, so you can join me if you'd like. Or stay here. It's up to you."

"Sure. That would be great." I liked the way

Vanessa and Griffin treated me like a normal person,
not some poor victim who'd just endured a lot of pain.
I'd been a prisoner for so long, and this was the first
time I'd ever truly been free. If I really wanted to, I
could walk out the front door and go to the coffee shop
down the road. I could hop in a taxi and go anywhere.
It was the greatest feeling. "I'm not sure what else to do
with my time except sit here and wait for him to call."

"Been there, done that," Vanessa said. "It's no fun."

Griffin glanced at her from his spot in the kitchen,
catching the look on her face before he returned to
his work.

"Well, maybe you can tell me some stories about
Carter," I said.

"Like, embarrassing ones?" she asked with a smile.

"Yes. Especially embarrassing ones."

"Get comfy," she said. "Because I have quite
the list."

THE NEXT DAY, Carter called Griffin.

Griffin was sitting on the couch with the TV on
while Vanessa and I played checkers at the coffee table.
He took the call, his muscular arms practically ripping
through his t-shirt. "Carter, what happened?"

I was about to put down my piece when I heard
what Griffin said. "Is he okay?"

"What happened?" Vanessa said. "Did Egor leave?"

Griffin held up his hand before he put the phone on speaker and set it on the table. "Hey, I put you on speakerphone because the women were pestering me with a million questions."

"The women?" Vanessa asked.

"You are women, aren't you?" Griffin asked with a straight face.

She narrowed her eyes with menace, but there was a note of affection in the look.

"Carter," I said. "Everything okay?" I wished I could speak to him privately, but this would do.

"Yes, sweetheart," he said, speaking to me in the same tone he always did. "I'm fine."

Vanessa's face turned back to the phone, her eyebrow raised.

"Did he believe you?" I asked, slightly afraid of the answer.

"Yeah, I think he did," Carter said. "He was suspicious in the beginning. Came into the house and examined the body himself. But he seemed to find what he was looking for. Said he wanted to bury the corpse at the sea because he refused to bury you properly. We parted on decent terms."

"So, you think it's over?" I couldn't let myself believe it unless it was actually true. I would hate to be that happy only for my hopes to come crumbling down again.

"It would be stupid to assume that, but I think so. I'll keep laying low for a bit. I'll have the house repaired while my real estate agent finds me a place in Tuscany. I've also found someone to adopt your son and take him out of the orphanage."

Even though I was sitting with two complete strangers, I became overwhelmed with emotion. The tears sprung to my eyes. I didn't care that Carter asked me to bed him in exchange for my freedom. It seemed like more than fair after what he'd done for me. "Oh my god…"

Vanessa stared at me, her eyes softening.

"I'll just need his name so I can get started on the paperwork," Carter said.

"Okay," I whispered. "Luca Moretti…" I hadn't said my son's name out loud in so long. It felt so good to feel that name on my tongue, to picture his beautiful face. I missed holding him in my arms, missed taking him to the park to play with his friends. I missed everything about being a mom.

"Alright," Carter said. "I'll get started on all of that. I'll check in when I can. Thanks, Griffin and Vanessa. I appreciate what you're doing for me."

"No problem," Vanessa said. "Mia is lovely."

"Let us know if you need anything," Griffin said.

"Alright," Carter said. "We'll talk later."

"Wait." I didn't want him to hang up, not yet.

"What's up, Mia?" Carter asked.

I grabbed the phone and took it off speakerphone. "Excuse me for a second…" I took the phone out the door to the staircase. I sat down at the top and held the phone against my ear. "I just wanted to talk to you…alone."

"You alright?"

"Yes, your family has been wonderful to me. I really like Vanessa."

"She's pretty cool. I thought you two would get along well."

I sat in silence with him, just appreciating his presence. After he'd decided to help me, my feelings for him had changed. They immediately deepened into something much heavier. I saw him as a hero, as the man who saved me. "All of this doesn't seem real…the idea of seeing Luca again…doesn't seem real."

"I know, sweetheart. But it is real."

"Because of you…all because of you."

He was quiet.

"Carter, thank you."

"You shouldn't thank me," he whispered. "I'm getting something out of this. My hands aren't clean."

"I don't care about that. Doesn't change my opinion of you."

"It should."

It didn't. He would always be kind to me. He would always listen to me. He would give my son and me a life we couldn't have had before. I was broke, without a single penny to my name. I had no way to provide for my son…without Carter. "I'll never be able to repay you for what you did. I miss you so much."

"Miss me?" he whispered. "I didn't think you could

miss me, not after what I did to you."

"I do miss you. I wish you were here now."

He sighed into the phone. "It's strange…what those words do to me. Because I miss you too. I wish you were in my bed tonight."

"Me too…and not just for sleeping."

He sighed again, like I was pushing his buttons.

"When can I see you? Vanessa and Griffin are in their newlywed phase. I don't want to burden them more than necessary."

"Maybe a week," he said. "Depends on how quickly the real estate agent moves."

"Okay…"

"But it won't be much longer than that."

"And my son?"

"That will be a little longer. The paperwork always moves slowly for those sorts of things. They'll have to do a background check and a bunch of other stuff before he's released."

"Okay…"

"But it'll be soon. I promise."

"I know."

After a long pause of silence, he spoke. "I'll talk to you later, sweetheart."

"Alright, Carter."

"Good night."

I didn't want to say good night to him. I didn't want to get off the phone. But I let him go, knowing I needed to be patient. "Good night."

THREE

Carter

After a few days passed, I finally got a call from my real estate agent. He told me he'd found the perfect place, a three-story home on ten acres of land. With a long driveway and cobblestone walls that surrounded the property, it fit my bill of privacy. With the lush landscape and tall trees, it hid most of the house from view.

It was perfect.

He sent me pictures, and I was immediately sold.

Without even looking at the place, I took it. It was already furnished, which was even better. I didn't care about decorating. I decided to buy it under my corporation so it wouldn't be traced back to me, just in case Egor was looking into my whereabouts. It seemed like he genuinely believed me, but there was no way to really know.

Griffin called me. "When are you coming to get her?"

"Uh, hello to you too."

"Hi." He spoke with a deep tone, full of irritation. "When the fuck are you coming to get her?"

"Is she being difficult or something?" Mia was a bit sassy, but she was also lovely. I couldn't picture her being rude or obnoxious to her hosts.

"No. She's great," he said in annoyance. "She and Vanessa are two peas in a pod."

I chuckled when I understood the source of his frustration. "Oh…now I get it."

"She's cockblocking me."

"Not likely."

"She and Vanessa spend all afternoon at the gallery, and when they're finished there, they go out. Vanessa has been showing her around Florence, taking her shopping and out to eat. It's a fucking pain in the ass. So when the hell are you getting this woman out of my house?"

I laughed because I knew he was being dead serious. He didn't like to share Vanessa with anyone this long.

"I left for a mission for three days, and then I had to do some work for Crow. I just got home, and then I had to help you. The madness never stops. I want some time with my woman. The Barsetti bullshit is getting old."

"Well, I hope you get used to it. It never ends."

He growled.

"I just talked to my real estate agent. I'm in the process of buying a place in Tuscany. It's big and private."

"Great. Let me know when you're having the house-warming party," he said sarcastically.

I ignored the jab. "I'm working on Luca right now. Things seem to be going smoothly, but it's just a lot of paperwork."

"Well, that should be irrelevant right now. When you get the keys to the place, you'll fetch your woman?"

My woman. I'd never called her that before or thought of her in that way. But I did save her in exchange for ownership. She was mine. The thought made my spine tighten, made me miss those pretty brown eyes. I'd been sleeping alone every night, thinking about her and also preparing for another confrontation with Egor. Workmen had begun repairing the damage done to the house, and once that was finished, I would be putting it on the market. "Yes."

"Good. Because I feel like I don't have a woman anymore."

"I apologize," I said sarcastically.

"No, you don't, asshole. If I didn't love Vanessa so much, I wouldn't put up with your bullshit."

"Good thing you do."

"By the way, I think we need to tell Crow about all of this."

I'd planned on keeping it a secret from my family as long as possible. "Why? I thought you hated him anyway."

It was the first time Griffin was silent. He took a long time to ponder before he spoke. "He's not so bad."

Wow. That was the first time I'd heard him say something nice about my uncle. "Did something happen?"

"I think we buried the hatchet. That's all you need to know."

"That's good to hear. My father told me how much my uncle stressed about you."

Griffin sidestepped the subject. "It feels wrong keeping this a secret. I helped you because there wasn't time to think of anything else. But now that the mission is complete, we need to think about how we're going to handle this."

"My family has dissolved the issue with the Skull Kings. There's no issue on that front."

"But Egor could become an issue."

"Unlikely," I answered.

"Alright, even if that's true, how are you going to explain Mia?"

I shrugged even though he couldn't see me. "My family doesn't really ask about my personal life. Sometimes my mom pesters me about kids, but her questions don't go too deep."

"But they've never seen you with someone, right?"

"I suppose."

"And you won't be able to hide Mia forever. Since she has a kid, that's even more suspicious."

I hadn't thought that far in advance. "I could tell them she needed work, so I decided to help her out."

"Out of the goodness of your heart?" he asked incredulously.

"What?" I demanded. "Crow has a butler. My parents had a butler, but now they just have a maid. It's not that strange."

"But Mia is young and beautiful."

"Maybe I sleep with her once in a while. So?"

He chuckled. "You're getting awfully defensive, man."

"I just don't think I need to explain her purpose. Not when I'm not even sure what her purpose is."

He sighed into the phone. "Conway's wife was basically a slave to him for a while. Seems to be a Barsetti trait."

"Just because Conway did that doesn't mean the rest of the Barsetti men have."

He was so quiet it seemed like he'd hung up.

"Griffin?"

"Just giving you some friendly advice. You're right, everything is probably fine. The dust has finally settled, and peace should reign. But Crow butted into my relationship without mercy, and with your family being so close, I think it'll happen to you as well. And since you did go to the Underground again…your family might have the right to know."

When my father had confronted me about it, I told him I wouldn't return. I felt bad for lying to him, even after the problem had been fixed. Sometimes my father was difficult to talk to because he was so aggressive and

emotional. Ironically, my mother was the more prag-
matic one. I loved my father, but I'd always been closer
to my mother. "I see what you're saying."

"I think they're going to find out anyway. May as
well be the one to tell them."

"And if I don't, will you?"

He scoffed into the phone, clearly insulted. "I'm no
snitch."

"That's not what I meant—"

"I may come from the streets, but I'm not a rat. I'll
take your secret to the grave—because I'm a man. But
you're lucky enough to have a compassionate and loyal
family. They'll understand a lot better than you think
they will."

"I can't even picture that conversation…"

"You can spin it a little," he said with a chuckle.
"Don't mention she's stuck in indentured servitude. You
can skim over that part."

"Alright. I'll take care of it once I'm out there."

"Good. And that better be soon. I don't like sharing
Vanessa with anyone. I've paid for her with my blood
and sacrifice. The only reason why I'm on my best
behavior is because Mia seems like a nice person who's
been through a lot. But trust me, my sympathy won't
last long."

"I believe it."

He hung up without saying goodbye.

It was the most extensive conversation I'd had with
Griffin, and I realized we'd bonded—in a strange way.

It was the most interaction I'd had with him, and it was obvious he was just as loyal as Vanessa claimed he was. He'd dropped everything to help me, despite the crazy circumstance. He'd already proven himself, so he didn't need to prove himself further. He did it because he wanted to—because he was part of the Barsetti family.

ONCE THE MONEY had been transferred, the house was officially mine. The movers packed my essentials, and I drove to Tuscany in one of my million-dollar rides. On the drive, I called Griffin through the speaker system.

"Coming to get her?" he blurted, cutting right to the chase.

"Yes."

"Thank fucking god. They went to get their nails and have lunch."

"That sounds nice. Girl time."

"Girl time means not Griffin time."

I chuckled. "Man, you sound like an egomaniac. It's not like you don't see Vanessa."

All I got was a growl in response.

"Anyway, I'm on my way. I was wondering if I could talk to Mia."

"Like I said, she's out with Vanessa."

"I'll call Vanessa, then."

He hung up without saying a word, just like yesterday.

I called Vanessa next. Mia answered right away, knowing she was the person I wanted to speak to. "Hey." Her voice was always soft when she spoke to me, not filled with the sass and hate like when we first met. It was brimming with affection, like she'd been thinking about me constantly, waiting for this phone call to take place.

"Hey, sweetheart. Griffin tells me the two of you have been having fun."

"Oh my god…there are no words." She turned cheery instantly. "We've been to restaurants, coffee shops, art galleries, clothing stores…everything. I haven't been outside like this in years. It's so nice."

I was grateful Vanessa had taken the time to show her around, especially when Griffin was breathing down the back of her neck. "I'm happy to hear that."

"Your cousin is so nice. I love her."

"Yeah…she's pretty cool."

"I understand why you love your family so much. Griffin is a little tense, but he's great too."

"He's just possessive of Vanessa."

She chuckled. "I noticed that. So…when am I going to see you?"

She should hate me for the deal I made with her. I only gave her freedom in exchange for her submission. I wasn't willing to risk everything just for her. No, only when I got something in return. In business, that was fine. But this wasn't business…because she was a human being. I could make it right by letting her go, but I didn't want that. I wanted her to fulfill her end of the bargain. "Today."

"Today?" she asked happily.

"Yes. In a few hours."

"Really? Did you get the house?"'

"I did. It's about thirty minutes outside Florence. Close to my family but not too close."

"I'm sure it's lovely."

"I'm gonna swing by and drop off my things with the movers. Then I'll come get you."

"That's great," she said. "I've loved staying here, but I want Griffin and Vanessa to have their privacy back. They're so in love, and I feel like I'm getting in the way."

I didn't tell her about Griffin's frustration. He was like a caveman who could only speak in anger and nothing else. "They've enjoyed having you. But I'll enjoy having you more." After this time apart, I was eager to be with her again. I'd risked everything for this woman, and I wanted to cash in my reward.

Mia didn't say anything to that. "Any update on Luca?"

"Still doing paperwork. It'll be at least a week before I can pick him up."

"One more week," she said under her breath. "I can go one more week…"

I knew Luca was the main thought in her mind

right now. Maybe she did miss me, but her affection for me would never compare to her need for her son. I understood that. "It'll be over soon, sweetheart."

"I know…thanks to you."

I drove with one hand on the wheel, my eyes focused on the road ahead of me. The fields passed on either side of me, and I hung on the line even though there was nothing else to say.

"I'll let you go, Carter. I'll see you in a few hours."

"Alright, sweetheart." I hung up.

I considered calling my father to tell him the truth. It was something I should man up and do, but it seemed wrong to do it over the phone. A face-to-face conversation was a lot more respectable. I called him anyway, to tell him something else.

He answered right away. "Son. What are you doing?" He breathed heavily over the line, like he was in the middle of moving something massive at work. He growled when he set something down then turned his attention to me completely. "I just finished loading the barrels into the truck."

"Are you at the main winery?"

"Yep. What are you doing?"

"Driving."

"To Tuscany, I hope?"

"Actually, yes."

He paused, his happiness becoming palpable. "You're staying with us for a visit?" My father was usually abrasive and difficult, but when I was coming to stay, he became audibly happy. "Your mother will be so thrilled. How long will you be staying?"

"Actually, I won't be staying with you guys."

"If you think you're gonna stay at a—"

"I bought a place. It's about fifteen minutes away from you and Mom."

Speechless, he sat on the line.

"I've decided to make the move. I do most of my business virtually anyway."

He still struggled to find the right words to say. "Carter…I don't even know what to say. You have no idea how thrilled I am. I miss you so much…" My father didn't get sentimental often, so when he showed his emotion, it was profound. "I see Carmen a lot more often, but the idea of having both of you here… It's a dream come true."

I was only moving there because it was easier to hide Mia, so I felt bad for letting him think I was doing it to be closer to family. "I got a great deal on a house that I couldn't pass up. I'm a few hours away."

"I can't wait to tell your mother. I'm gonna tell your uncle first because he's standing right here, but I'll call her next. We'll have to get together to celebrate."

"Absolutely," I said. "Maybe tomorrow. I still have a long drive and have to move my stuff in."

"Of course," he said. "The timing is perfect because Sapphire is about to pop at any moment."

The thought of Conway made me feel better about this move. I used to see him all the time, and now we hardly spoke. I would get to spend time with him again, even when he was a father. "I'm excited to see what the new Barsetti is gonna be. Hope it's a girl since it'll drive Conway crazy."

Father chuckled. "Yeah. Raising a daughter isn't easy…and when she's an adult, it's even harder."

When I was growing up, all my guy friends would tell me how hot my sister was. She was a hot commodity—still was since she was single. I knew my father hated dealing with it, just the way my uncle hated dealing with Vanessa.

"So, tell me about your house," Father said.

"You know that place with the iron gates and cobblestone wall?"

"The one that's ten acres and three stories?" he asked in surprise.

"Yep. That one."

He whistled. "That's one fine piece of real estate… and a little big for one man."

"I'll have a maid."

He chuckled. "Not what I meant, and you know it."

I smirked but didn't address it. "I'll talk to you tomorrow, Father. I should concentrate on the road."

"Alright, son. Love you."

"Love you too."

WHEN I FINISHED PUTTING my stuff away at the

house, I drove to Florence to retrieve Mia. I parked in front of the gallery behind Griffin's truck, then walked to the front door of the apartment. I knocked and was greeted by Griffin.

It was the first time he looked genuinely happy to see me. "Good, you're here." He grabbed the bag off the floor and handed it to me. "It's got all her stuff inside it. It's pretty heavy…they did a lot of shopping."

I felt the weight on my shoulder. "And they bought a lot of shoes, I can tell."

"Yep."

"I'll send you a check for everything."

He brushed it off. "Don't worry about it."

"No, I will. She's my woman. I'll buy her clothes."

He grinned, his arms across his chest. "Your woman, huh?"

"You know what I mean." I stepped farther into the apartment and saw Mia come toward me. She used to stare at me with disgust, her eyes full of raging flames. But now, the look was totally different. She came to me like she'd been waiting for me to walk through that door all day. She moved into my chest, her small body perfectly fitting against mine. She was over a foot shorter than me, and her hair smelled different because she'd been using a different shampoo. My hand cupped the back of her neck, and I felt the softness of the strands, remembering how they felt against my thighs and stomach when her lips were sealed around my dick.

My other arm circled her body, resting in the deep

curve of her lower back. I squeezed her against me, having missed her more than I realized. There was a connection between us now, a loyalty both of us felt.

She stayed against me for a long time, sinking into my body like it was as comfortable as a pillow. "I'm so glad you're here." She tilted her chin back to look at me, and she rose on her tiptoes to kiss me on the mouth.

I kissed her back, embracing her soft lips. My arm tightened around her waist as I squeezed her against me, and my fingers dived deeper into her hair. I nearly forgot my cousin was standing there with Griffin because Mia's kiss did crazy things to me. When I pulled away, I saw Vanessa grinning at me, like she was getting a lot of enjoyment out of this. "You ready to go, sweetheart?"

"Yeah." She pressed her lips tightly together to absorb my kiss then hugged Vanessa. "Thank you for everything. I really appreciate it."

"We loved having you," Vanessa said. "If you ever need a break from Carter, you have my number."

When she turned to Griffin next, all she got was a nod from him. "We're always here if you need anything."

"Thanks." Mia came back to me, not expecting any more from Griffin.

Griffin wasn't an affectionate guy, but I suspected he purposely didn't touch Mia. Maybe it was because she had been a slave for so long. Or maybe he just didn't touch any women besides Vanessa. Vanessa wasn't the jealous type, so that didn't make sense.

"Thanks again." I hugged Vanessa before I shook Griffin's hand. "You always have my back, and I appreciate it."

"That's what Barsettis do," Vanessa said. "Griffin told me about your conversation. I hope that means you'll be speaking to your father?"

"I will," I said. "It's a conversation that needs to happen in person."

She nodded in agreement. "Understandable."

I guided Mia out of the apartment and to my car at the curb. After the bag was dropped in the trunk, we got into the car and started the engine.

She looked around at the buttons in the car, along with the glowing lights. "I won't jump out of the car this time."

I chuckled. "I wouldn't mind chasing you down again if you did." I pulled onto the street, and we made our way out of Florence. There was a lot of traffic, so I couldn't push the gas as much as I wanted to, but once we broke free of the city, I pushed the engine hard.

She looked out the window with a slight smile on her lips, gazing at the sky as the sun set over the horizon. The lights were a mixture of purple, blue, and pink, the perfect colors of a distant sunset.

After spending a week apart, we were together again, but I didn't have anything to say. It was nice just to sit with her, to embrace what was going to happen next. Maybe all of our problems were really behind us. Or maybe they were lurking around the corner. Either way, we'd made our decision.

I approached the front gate and hit the clicker in the car. The large metal gates swung inward to allow my car inside. I took the long drive farther onto the property, moving through the trees and alongside the perfectly manicured grass. The gate closed behind me, the cobblestone wall encompassing the property as the ivy grew over the walls. When Conway realized I bought one of the best pieces of property in Tuscany, he'd be pissed he didn't beat me to the punch.

When the house came into view, Mia gasped under her breath. "You've got to be kidding me…"

I shouldn't care about impressing her with my money, but I did. I wanted her to feel like royalty, to know she didn't belong to just a random man. She was owned by one of the richest men in Italy, a descendant of one of the noblest Italian families.

"You bought this place?"

"Yes." I pulled into the garage and closed the door behind me before I killed the engine.

"Just like that?" she asked incredulously.

I snapped my fingers. "Just like that."

She looked at me with new eyes, as if she didn't understand how powerful I truly was.

I grabbed her bag from the trunk and carried it inside.

She followed behind me then took in the house, a mansion that was far too big for a single man. She examined the hardwood floors, the plaster walls, and the Italian craftsmanship that made this house strong despite its decades of age. She explored it on her own, admiring the double grand staircase and the different living rooms. The dining room itself could accommodate twenty guests.

I set my wallet and keys on the entryway table then scrolled through the emails on my phone. There was a text message from Conway.

Heard you moved to Tuscany. You need to get a life and stop following me.

I grinned then wrote back. *What can I say? I missed you.*

I missed you too, asshole.

Conway was practically a brother to me, and having him close by was just another perk to making the move. I slid the phone back into my pocket when Mia met me in the living room.

"This place has three floors. Did you know that?"

I tried not to grin at her ignorance. "Yes. I noticed that when I bought it."

She held up three fingers. "Three."

I nodded. "The top floor gives great views of the countryside."

"It's unbelievable," she said. "I've never seen anything so beautiful." She crossed her arms over her chest and looked around the living room, admiring the

PENELOPE SKY

carefully designed furniture and the large flat-screen TV.

My home was beautiful, but it didn't compare to the woman in front of me.

She turned around and came back to me. "So… how is this going to work?"

I upheld my end of the deal and liberated her from the hands of a psychopath. Now we were five hours away, enclosed behind a thick wall in a mansion. Mia was officially mine—because I'd paid for her with my sacrifice. "It's your job to make a home. I expect this place to be clean at all times. I want home-cooked meals throughout the day. According to my friends and family, you're the maid of my estate. Do we understand each other?"

"What about Vanessa and Griffin?"

"They know otherwise."

"But you still want me to fill that role?"

"Yes." They would keep the secret to themselves. No one else needed to know the extent of the relationship. I might tell Conway…or he might figure it out on his own. He could read me pretty well. "I have to tell my parents what really happened…since they deserve to know the truth. But I'm going to tell them I gave you a job because you had nowhere else to go. And that's the extent of our relationship."

She watched me with observant eyes. "Alright. What about when Luca gets here?"

"You guys can have the west side of the second

60

floor. He can have his own room, and you can have yours. I don't mind letting him live here, but I want him to stay out of my way. I'm not going to lie, I have no experience with kids. Know nothing about them."

"I understand, Carter."

"There's another living room up there, so you guys will have plenty of space. The third floor is mine and off-limits to him. When I want you, that's where we'll meet."

"Do you think it would be better if Luca and I lived somewhere else?" she asked. "Because I can work here during the day, drop him off at school, go home after work, and be with him. When he goes to sleep, I can come back…"

I wanted her underneath my nose at all times, to make sure Egor didn't take her away without me knowing about it. And when Luca was at school, she would be available throughout the day. "No. I want you here."

"You're sure you want to share your space like that?"

"I said the third floor is off-limits. So I won't have to share my space."

She didn't react to my cold demands. She'd vowed she would be obedient and grateful, and she kept her word.

I wondered if it would continue that way. "The room next to my bedroom has everything we'll need for our relationship." I leaned against the counter and watched her expression, wondering if I would see fear or hesitation.

She didn't show either.

"Do we understand each other?" I asked quietly. "Those are my terms. I expect you to fulfill them."

"And I will."

"Sir."

Her eyes flashed slightly. "Sir."

I felt my dick harden in my jeans when I watched this sassy woman respond to me so easily. She was the same woman who jumped out of a car, who tried to kill me with a knife. She cut a tracker out of her own ankle just to get away from me. But now, she submitted to me, giving in to my cruelty without objection.

I backed her up into the wall of the living room, my size outmatching hers. When her small frame hit the wall, I gripped both of her wrists and pinned them above her head. I squeezed her hands tightly as I looked down into her face. I felt her pulse increase against my fingertips, watched her chest rise and fall harder as my proximity made her squirm. She was in a V-neck t-shirt and jeans, and I stared down her top to the delicious cleavage line between her swollen breasts. The last time I'd fucked her, I didn't know she had a child. Now that I knew, I looked at her in a new way. Her body had given life, and that made me respect her figure even more. I couldn't tell that a little person grew inside her, that she'd survived one of the most challenging events in life.

It turned me on.

Her eyes met mine, the brown color sexy against her soft skin. Her slightly parted lips were ready for mine. She was absolutely still as I cornered her against the wall. "Carter."

"I didn't tell you to talk."

Her eyes flashed in momentary revolt, but she covered up the anger quickly, remembering her place.

I wanted to enjoy this moment, enjoy the toy I'd just secured. She was mine as long as I wanted to keep her. She wouldn't run, not after what I did for her. She would behave because it was the sacrifice she made.

I stared at her soft lips as I squeezed her hands further, feeling her pulse spike as I touched her. Ever since she came into my possession, I'd wanted to dominate her. I wanted to hurt her the way Egor did. No other woman turned me into this kind of man, the kind of man that wanted to control a woman rather than enjoy her. She was a good woman who deserved a good man, but something about her didn't turn me into a good man...quite the contrary. "I'm not sure what I want to do first." I brought her wrists together above her head with a single hand so my free palm could dig into her hair. I secured my fingers in her strands and tugged down, bringing her gaze directly onto me.

"Can I suggest something...sir?"

I moaned under my breath, loving the way she called me sir, the way she asked to speak. I was harder than I'd ever been, getting off on this woman's submission. She wasn't the kind of woman that allowed a man to conquer her…but she gave me permission. "Yes, sweetheart."

"I want you…the way you've taken me before. I want it slow and good. A man has never made me feel that way before. I just got you back, and I miss it… I missed it for the past week."

Listening to a woman ask you to fuck her was the sexiest thing in the world, especially when Mia was that woman. She wasn't afraid to tell me exactly what she wanted, even though I was the one in charge. "It doesn't matter what you want. It matters what I want."

"I know…but I know you like it when I want you."

My spine shivered at her words because she was right.

She didn't fight against my hold, but her breathing increased as she waited for my answer. "Once in a while. I'm not sure how much I'm going to like what you want to do to me…and it would be nice to have something I want."

"Again, it's not about you."

"But I know you like feeling me come."

She was right. I got off on it.

"It doesn't hurt to ask, right?" she whispered. "Because I do enjoy being with you. And if this is how the rest of my life is going to be, I would like to be satisfied sometimes."

"What makes you think I won't satisfy you? Even when we do things I want to do?"

"Because that's how the last three years of my life have been…and I didn't enjoy it at all."

I pressed my mouth closer to hers so my lips barely touched hers. "You'll enjoy it with me."

"I don't know…"

"You will, sweetheart. And just so you understand, no other men allowed. I own you."

"Do I own you?"

I held her gaze, my hostility obvious in my look.

Her eyes filled with disappointment when she got her answer.

There'd better not be any objection to it because this relationship had never been romantic. It had always been physical. It had always been about ownership. The only goodness I would show her was rescuing her from Egor and getting her son back. She'd better not ask for anything else.

And she didn't.

I released her hands then gripped her slender waist with both hands, my fingers underneath her shirt and directly against her soft skin. My mouth moved to hers, and I kissed her, greeted by her warm breaths and her reciprocation. My embrace started off as soft, and within minutes, it turned hot and heavy. The sounds our moving lips made filled the room, and I could hear it reverberate back at me. I could feel her breaths turn to pants. Her hands slid up my back, and she clawed at my shoulders, the pressure of her small fingertips digging through my t-shirt. Her chin was tilted up she could access my complete mouth, so I took her tongue as she gave it.

I had all of her now.

I could take her as slowly as I wanted. I could take her as quickly as I wanted. This woman was officially mine, belonged to me in a way she never belonged to Egor. She was there out of devotion and loyalty, not fear. She kissed me because she wanted to.

My hands slid farther up her shirt, and I unclasped her bra in the back so I could feel her tits. I squeezed both of them and flicked my thumbs across the nipples, making them pebble and harden. I breathed into her mouth as I felt her tits harden in my palms. I could feel her arousal absorb directly into my skin, feel our heat mix together and create an inferno.

And we were only kissing.

I couldn't wait to sink my hard dick inside her, to feel the pussy that ignited my obsession. I wanted to take it slow, to fill her inch by inch and watch her reaction to me. I wanted to see the gratitude in her eyes as I fucked her, to be thankful I was fucking her instead of Egor. Then I wanted to watch her come, to watch her come for her master.

Me.

She spoke against my mouth. "Fuck me, Carter. I miss it…"

I paused against her mouth, taking an involuntary breath when she said the words. The fact that she wasn't saying them for my benefit only made it better. I lifted her in my arms and carried her up the stairs. I already knew my way around, so I kissed her as I carried her to the third floor. Lighter than air, she was like a feather in my arms. I got harder in my jeans because I knew I was finally about to have her.

I stepped into the master bedroom and dropped her on the bed. My hands went to her jeans right away, and I pulled them down her legs at the foot of the bed. Her panties came next, and I felt a rush of adrenaline when I saw how soaked they were. The slick residue was shiny, fresh from her cunt. When I got them off her ankles, I laid them on the bed beside her, so I could look at them as I fucked her. My hands moved for her shirt next, leaving her naked and beautiful.

I undressed slowly, taking my time as I removed my shirt and jeans.

Mia watched me with the same arousal. Just as I felt when I saw the moisture in her panties, I could tell her eyes adored the way the tip of my cock drooled for her.

I wrapped my hand around my length and smeared the residue over the head of my cock, to lubricate myself before I slipped inside. I wanted that cunt so much, hadn't stopped thinking about it since the last time I saw her.

I stood at the edge of the bed and positioned two pillows under her head. I wanted her perfectly angled to look at me, to watch me fuck her. My hands hooked behind her knees and spread her wide apart before the head of my cock found her entrance. Like it had a mind of its own, it knew exactly where to go. I slipped inside her, pushed through her tightness, and slowly sank deeper and deeper.

Mia moaned when she felt me, bit her bottom lip in the sexiest way. She held on to my forearms while her knees were pressed into her waist. "Carter…this feels even better than I remember."

I wasn't even fully inside her yet. My sensitive tip could feel her tightness and wetness. She wasn't kidding when she said she missed me. She didn't want me to chain her and whip her, not right away. She wanted to enjoy me first. When she gave an erotic performance like this, I didn't mind in the least.

I pushed until I was all the way inside, balls deep and completely sheathed in her arousal. This pussy was better than the others I'd had before. It was so tight and so slick. Despite giving birth to a son and being raped by a monster, she felt like a virgin I hadn't popped yet. I squeezed the backs of her thighs with my fingertips and felt my cock attempt to twitch inside her. It was tempting to come then and there, to dump my come inside her since it'd been so long since the last time I did it.

With her mouth open and her teeth visible, she breathed loudly through the pleasure, stuffed with a big dick that stretched her just right. Her nails cut into me, and she looked so sexy with her legs open for me like that. Her tits looked perfect, and her pretty hair was sprawled across the pillow around her. "God…Carter."

Jesus.

I scooped my hands around her thighs and pulled her toward me as I started to thrust. With slow and even strokes, I shoved my length entirely inside her and pulled out again, feeling her soft flesh around me from tip to base.

Her eyes were on me the entire time, steaming like hot espresso. She licked her lips. Sometimes she would bite her lower lip. Her nails would carve into my skin. Like she was enjoying it even more than I was, she came apart right before my eyes.

How the fuck would I last?

I pulled my dick out of her and saw the glistening smear of arousal that covered me. Clear and shiny, it was all her, along with the cream that already built up at the head of my cock. A long thread of sticky slickness stretched between the head of my cock and her pussy. She was so drenched, we were connected even when we were apart. "Jesus Christ, sweetheart." I shoved myself back inside her with a hard thrust, hitting her deep and making her wince slightly but moan at the same time.

I moved into her hard and fast, wanting to push her to a climax as quickly as possible. A women's pleasure wasn't a challenge for me, but right now, it seemed to be the most difficult thing in the world. I knew she wanted those powerful orgasms I'd given her before, and I had to deliver before I enjoyed mine.

She grabbed the edge of the bed underneath her ass so she could pull herself into me, meet my thrusts with her own. Her tits shook with her movements, her nipples hard and stimulated. Her moans turned to screams, and my name flew out of her mouth more times than I could count.

"Come, sweetheart." I was a man who could usually last longer than this, but right now, that seemed impossible. I rubbed her clit vigorously while I slammed into her, determined to push her over the edge and give her the climax she'd been craving.

Thankfully, she did. Her eyes closed and her mouth flew open as she bucked her hips and enjoyed the orgasm my cock unleashed. She yanked herself farther into me, taking more of my length as I rubbed her clit continuously. Her pussy clenched around me with the grip of a warrior, and more of her slickness flooded my length. I was soaked from tip to base, drenched in this woman's pleasure.

Her orgasms seemed to last forever, but maybe that was just because every second she enjoyed one was a second I had to hold back. But being the gentleman that I was, I kept my shit together, kept my dick hard and penetrating. I slammed into her with my thumb circling her clit, milking every single second of goodness out of the climax.

When her hips stopped bucking and the momentum passed, her eyes opened again and settled on me. Her pleasure had been powerful, but she looked at me like she wanted more, like that was only the beginning. Her hands reached for my chest as her pussy slowly softened around me. "Please come inside me…sir."

My cock naturally twitched at her choice of words. Anytime a woman wanted my come it was hot, but she put a special spin on it.

"I want it…so much."

Jesus. Christ. I gripped her by the neck and stared into her face as I finished, giving my final pumps before release. With my eyes fixed on hers like a hunter and its prey, I pounded into her pussy before I felt the explosion from the head of my dick. I ruptured inside her, filled her with so much come that it moved up my dick as I kept thrusting into her. Her little cunt couldn't take it all. It never could. I moaned as I enjoyed the pleasure that circulated in every single vein. I could feel the heat all the way in my gut, feel the aftershocks of goodness ripple through me. It was a good climax, better than normal. Every time this woman made me come, it was better than the last time.

"That's exactly what I wanted…" Sweat gleamed in the valley between her tits even though I was the one who did all the fucking. Her hands felt my chiseled stomach as I continued to throb inside her, my dick slowly beginning to soften. "And I want it again…please."

I loved hearing that word from her mouth.

Please.

Like she had to beg me.

"Please, sir," I corrected.

Her nipples hardened, and the skin of her cheeks flushed crimson. "Please, sir."

I WOKE up the next morning with Mia beside me. Naked and beautiful, she had her hair spread all over my pillow. She smelled like a woman who had been thoroughly fucked the night before. I pressed a kiss to the back of her shoulder when I woke up, aroused by the sight of her beside me.

This was real.

My fantasy was real.

She stirred when she felt me kiss her. She turned over slightly, the sheets slipping below her chest to reveal her beautiful tits. "Morning."

"Morning." I trailed kisses from the back of her neck all the way down her spine. I kept moving when I reached the top of her ass, and I knew she didn't expect me to keep going. When I did, her skin covered in bumps, and she tensed noticeably. I moved right between her cheeks, over her asshole, and down to her pussy. I kissed her there, tasting our fluids mixed together from the night before.

She was absolutely still, her breathing nonexistent and her eyes closed. Her hard nipples told me she liked it.

I knew I liked it.

I kissed the back of her shoulder again. "I want

breakfast in forty-five minutes, after my workout." I kicked the sheets back and hopped out of bed. I pulled out my gym shorts and t-shirt without looking back at her.

She didn't mouth a single protest, knowing she had to earn her keep. She didn't get to live in a beautiful home like this for free. She got up and pulled on the t-shirt I'd discarded the night before on the floor. "What would you like, sir?"

As much as it turned me on to hear her call me that, she didn't need to say it all the time. "Use sir after dinner. Carter is fine for now."

"What would like, Carter?"

"Egg whites and veggies."

"Do we have any groceries?"

"No. Take the car to the store. Keys are in the entryway. I turned off the thumbprint activation for you."

Both of her eyebrows rose. "You're going to let me drive your car?"

"For now. I'll get you something else soon."

"But you're going to let me drive *your* car?" she repeated. "It's like a million-dollar car."

My fingers moved underneath her chin. The second I touched her, she softened. "You're the strongest woman I know. You can handle it, sweetheart." I kissed her on the lips before I turned away.

I headed to my private gym, did a rigorous workout, then took a quick shower before I arrived downstairs.

The dining room had a nice view of the front of the estate. I sat there in my sweatpants with my laptop and got to work on emails and setting up meetings.

Exactly as I wanted, Mia brought my morning coffee and served breakfast—in silence.

I took various phone calls and had difficult schematics shipped. I had to make full sketches and send those images to the engineers in my lab. Even though I had some of the brightest minds working for me, I still had to delegate everything personally. That was the only way things ran smoothly.

Hours passed, and before I knew it, it was lunchtime. Mia approached me at the table where I'd been sitting all morning. "Let me know when you want lunch, Carter."

I looked at the time on my computer, realizing it was past one. "I'll take it now. And I want you to eat with me, sweetheart."

"Alright." She returned twenty minutes later with salads and sandwiches for us both, along with freshly brewed iced tea. When she took the seat perpendicular to me, I shut my laptop and put my phone aside. "You don't have to stop working because of me."

"I'm aware." I drank my iced tea as I looked at her, seeing the beautiful woman who never wore a drop of makeup. With soft brown hair that framed her face and coffee-colored her eyes, she was a sight to behold. "Lunch is good. Thank you."

A slight smile formed on her lips. "Thanks."

I turned my gaze back out the window, seeing the perfectly manicured gardens that hid the gates from view. With a state-of-the-art security system on the grounds, it would be difficult to cross my path without me knowing about it.

"So…any news on Luca?"

"Still working on it, sweetheart. They're running the background report on my guy. When they're done, they should release Luca. We'll make the exchange right away."

"Alright." She looked into her iced tea, her eyes downcast. "I'm just anxious. I'm happy to be here. I'm happy that I'm free from Egor. I just—"

"I understand, sweetheart."

She turned back to me, sighing quietly. "What if he doesn't remember me…?"

"That's crazy. Of course, he will."

"He was only five when I didn't come home… living in that orphanage for three years must have been a nightmare for him. He had no idea what was going on. He didn't know what happened to me. It's just… I hate Egor for what he did. Rape and torture are nothing compared to taking my son away from me."

It broke my heart to listen to this. It made me want to kill Egor.

"And now, I can't have any more children…which is just as hard. I've always wanted three kids."

"It's not impossible, sweetheart."

"But unlikely," she whispered. "I should be grateful I have at least one——"

"No. What Egor did was unacceptable. He should die for what he did to you."

Her eyes shone with gentleness. "I hate him…never hated someone so much in my life."

"And you should."

"I always promised myself I would kill him some-day…but now that I'm getting Luca back, I should just let it go."

I wanted to take care of it for her, but I knew vengeance wouldn't be smart. We should just be thankful we were both able to get away without inciting his wrath. "Yes. You should concentrate on your son."

"I will," she whispered.

I had a few questions for her, but they were all personal. She was my property now, but I didn't have the right to ask her about her past. Anything that happened before me was none of my business. That didn't stop my curiosity. "Can I ask about Luca's father?"

"Sure." She looked me in the eye. "There's not much to tell."

"Were you married?" I shouldn't feel jealousy over someone I didn't care about. If I did care about her, I would just let her go for good. She was a slave to me now. In some ways, I wasn't better than Egor. But the idea of her loving a man made the veins in my body burn. The idea of her making love to someone every night while looking him in the eye made my blood boil. Professing to love him for the rest of her life just made it worse.

Shit, what if she was married now?

I was standing between her and her husband.

Fuck.

After she finished drinking her iced tea, she answered my question. "No. Never been married."

Thank fucking god. "Can I ask what happened?" The father obviously wasn't in the picture at all. Otherwise, Luca wouldn't be in an orphanage.

"I got pregnant with Luca very young. I had him when I was eighteen."

If he was eight, that meant she was twenty-six now. So she was a bit younger than I was.

"The father said he was too young to be a dad and didn't want the responsibility. Told me to get an abortion. I had no interest in that, so I kept the baby. It was really hard to raise a son at that age. I didn't have any support and I was broke, but I worked two jobs and put myself through college. When I graduated with a clinical lab science degree, I moved to Italy for my first job. I was the lead scientist for a large winery, overseeing the fermentation process. I was making decent money and giving Luca a good life. Mastering two languages at once, he was a bilingual kid. Then I made the mistake of going to a bar with some friends…a decision that ruined my life. That's how I ended up here…"

I stared at her, dumbfounded. Her life journey

hadn't been easy, and just when she finally found stability for her son, some asshole took it away from her. She didn't need a man to take care of her, not when she could hustle on her own. "Have you spoken to the father since you were pregnant?"

She shook her head. "No. The last time we spoke, he said he wanted me to get an abortion."

Coward. "So he has no idea all of this happened to you?"

"No. And I had a hard life growing up, the product of a drug-addicted mother. I was taken away from her at a young age after my father died and put into foster care. But that didn't stop me from thriving, from getting good grades in school and getting a full scholarship to college."

"Badass."

She flinched at my words.

"You're self-made. That's really impressive."

"Well, that's sweet to say. But look where I am…"

"You're a survivor. That's what I see. Not a victim."

She shrugged. "I wouldn't have made it this far without you, Carter."

"You wouldn't have made it this far without your-self. Anyone else would have taken their own life. You never did…because you had Luca to live for."

She turned her gaze away, like she was on the verge of tears.

"When your son is old enough, he'll be very proud to call you his mother."

"Like I would ever tell him about all of this."

"I don't know…if he was an adult, I don't see why not."

"No child wants to hear that about their mother," she whispered. "I would never hurt him like that."

That was for her to decide, not me. "Either way, he'll be proud of you. It's difficult to be a single parent."

"You know…it never really was. I loved every second of it. Sure, it was hard sometimes, but it was all worth it. I wouldn't trade it for anything. Even if I could go back in time and make better decisions, I would still do everything the same. Luca is everything to me."

It reminded me of the way my parents spoke about Carmen and me. We were the light of their lives. They never spared their love or affection. "I look forward to meeting him. I wonder how much he looks like you."

"He looks a lot like his father. But he has my eyes."

"I love your eyes." I blurted out the words without thinking.

She smiled slightly. "He's very sweet. Very bright. But then, it's been three years…and I wonder how much he's changed."

"I'm sure he's the same sweet boy you remember."

"I hope so, Carter. I hate to think of how those people treated him."

My hand moved to hers. "If he's as strong as his mother, he did just fine."

FOUR

Mia

All I could think about was Luca.

Running my hands through his soft strands, seeing the kindness in his eyes that he inherited from me, touching those small hands and bringing them to my lips. A lot could change in three years. In the five years that I'd been with him, he grew so fast. Now I couldn't imagine how much taller he was, how much stronger he was.

I hoped he would remember me.

I hoped he wouldn't hate me for leaving him.

Maybe one day, he would understand. When he got older, he would want an explanation of where I ran off to. The last thing I wanted him to think was I left voluntarily, that I'd been a coward like his father and disappeared. The only reason I was gone was because someone forced me.

Otherwise, I would never have left his side.

Living in the new mansion was a dream come true. With a beautiful landscape and high walls, it was a realm of peace and quiet. The customized furniture filled out the home well, and my bedroom on the second floor immediately felt like home. Luca would have the room beside mine, but I imagined I would want to sleep with him for a while.

Egor was rich as well, but I never could take advantage of his luxuries. I was always starved and beaten. With Carter, I could make this place my home. I had a good degree that had allowed me to have a stable job, but that salary never would put me up in a place like this. I wasn't sure how long Carter wanted the two of us to stay here, but Luca had a lot more resources staying here than he did if we were on our own.

Truth be told, I wanted to be free. I wanted to have a little apartment with my son, to put our lives back together. I used to be a strong and fearless woman, but those days were over. Being a prisoner for so long had changed my mentality. Carter was the only man who could have possibly gotten me out of that situation. The idea of being on my own again, being unprotected, gave me a jolt of anxiety. If I stayed here, I would have a man who could protect my son as well as me.

It was a weak thought to have. I'd never depended on a man before, and I didn't want to start now. But the truth was in my heart. It was undeniable. With these powerful walls surrounding the house, along with Carter's presence, no one could touch me. He asked me to submit to him in return, and that seemed like a reasonable price to pay.

I kept the house in tip-top shape and prepared all of Carter's meals. I'd learned what he liked and didn't like, and I tried to make new things so he wouldn't get tired of my cooking. The house was so big that I had to clean the other floors just so they wouldn't get dusty.

My bedroom on the second floor had its own bathroom and a nice balcony that overlooked the yard. I had a private living room with a TV and a fireplace. It would be a perfect place for me to spend time with Luca. I sat on the couch and visualized my son playing with his toys on the ground.

I didn't have any toys for him. I didn't have any clothes. I didn't have anything for my son. Without a penny to my name and no assets, I wasn't sure how I would give him what he needed. I refused to ask Carter for money. I had more pride than that.

Carter tapped his knuckles against my bedroom door.

I lifted my chin to look at the door, to listen to the sound that shattered my eardrums. It was hard to believe I had so many rights. He didn't just barge in here. He knocked, approaching my space with respect. The little things like that made me tear up. My life with Egor had been torture. I couldn't even use the bathroom without someone watching me. Carter gave me a completely different life, one where I felt safe and respected.

He knocked again when I didn't answer. "Sweetheart?"

"Come in, Carter." I rose from the couch and slid my hands into my back pockets.

He stepped inside, wearing jeans and a black t-shirt. His muscular arms stretched out the fabric, and his powerful chest filled out the clothing well. His wide shoulders led to narrow hips, and just above that was his chiseled eight-pack. If I saw Carter across the room somewhere in public, I wouldn't be able to leave without making a pass at him. He was beautiful, sexy with classic Italian features. I'd buy him a drink in the hope of getting his number. Now I was living with this beautiful man, and I was sleeping with him too. To the best of my knowledge, there hadn't been another woman in his life in the meantime. I was the only one. It wasn't exactly the way I wanted to start a romance, but if I had to be in this situation, I'm glad it was with him. If I had to do this for the rest of my life, never get married or have more children, it wouldn't be so bad. At least the man I was bedding was the sexiest man I'd ever seen.

He stopped in front of me, his head tilted slightly as he regarded me. Concern came into his expression, his dark eyes flashing with intensity. "Everything alright, sweetheart?" He invaded my personal space, stepping toward me and sliding his fingers up my arm. His fingertips were callused from gripping a pen while he worked. They were probably also worn from typing on the keyboard all the time, maybe from working on cars too.

"Yeah, I'm fine." I cleared my throat. "It's just… never mind." My head tilted toward the floor, seeing his waistline and long legs.

His fingers moved under my chin, and he forced me to look at him. "No, not never mind. Tell me." His brown eyes were comforting to look into, to see the pool of chocolate that was innately peaceful and intense at the same time. "I never want to hear you say never mind again." The backs of his fingers brushed against my cheek before they moved into my hair.

My body warmed until it became so hot I started to melt. The tender affection reminded me of the lovers of my past, of being a participant in an intimate moment. But the touches Carter gave were different, packed with possession and a new level of desire. It made my fingers tingle, my stomach tighten. To top it off, it made me feel safe. When I first met him, I thought he was a monster like Egor. But he turned out to be quite different…in every good way possible. There was no confusion as to who he was. He was transparent, telling me he wanted to hurt me like Egor, but giving me freedom at the same time. There were lines he never crossed.

"Sweetheart?" he pressed.

"It's nice hearing you knock…" My eyes shifted back to his face again, seeing those pretty eyes set in a hard face. He didn't shave so his beard was coming in, but the hair couldn't disguise the sharp lines of his jaw.

"I never had those kinds of freedoms before. Now I do…"

His eyes fell in sadness as his hand moved to the back of my head. He pulled me in for a kiss, giving me a soft embrace on my lips. He felt me for an instant, his mouth taking the lead as he guided me into a deep kiss.

All thought ceased to exist in my mind.

He pulled away, affection in his look. "A woman like you shouldn't have to be grateful for that." He tucked my hair behind my ear then moved his hand to my waist. He'd been busy working the last couple of days, taking care of a new model that he was releasing. He went into his office, and I didn't see him much.

"I know." I shouldn't be grateful. I shouldn't be grateful that Carter saved my life in exchange for my sexual servitude. But since I liked sleeping with him anyway, it seemed like I was getting a great deal.

His powerful arms circled my waist and rested in the steep curve of my back. His large hands gripped the fabric of my shirt and squeezed me. He held me like I was his lover, not his slave.

I wondered when he'd want me to fulfill my end of the bargain. So far, he'd given me full rein to do whatever I wanted. And when we were in bed together, it was always the kind of sex I liked.

"I wanted to ask if we should start picking up things for Luca. I'm not gonna sugarcoat it—I don't know shit about kids. But he probably needs a new bedroom set and toys. Some school supplies too."

I wouldn't ask Carter for anything. Luca was my son, not his. "You don't need to do any of that. He has a place to sleep and food. We don't need anything else." I didn't want him to spend a dime on us, not when he risked his life to get me away from Egor.

"I want you two to make yourselves at home. Do as I ask and pick up whatever Luca needs." His tone turned harsher, wanting me to obey him without question. "You pay your way around here every day—and every night." He squeezed my waist before he kissed me again, this time a lot more aggressively. He sucked my bottom lip into his mouth and gave it a nibble before he released it. He gave me a final look before he turned away, a warning in his gaze. "Pick up what you need. You'll pay for it tonight."

I SPENT the whole day shopping in Florence. I got Luca clothes and supplies for school, and I got him new decorations for his bedroom. The last thing he liked before I left were dinosaurs, so I picked up toys and a new duvet. I put everything on the credit card Carter gave me, feeling guilty for spending his money like it was my own.

But I knew tonight he would make me pay for it.

I carried everything into the house and set up Luca's bedroom. I washed the new sheets and duvet before I made up his bed, and then I put his toy chest in the corner along with everything I bought him. A new backpack and school supplies sat on the desk. With a few changes, I'd turned the elegant bedroom into a child's haven.

I stared at the bed before I sat on the edge of it. My weight sank into the mattress, and I brought my hands into my lap. My eyes scanned the room, the place where my eight-year-old would live right next door. Tears burned in my eyes, and before I knew it, I started to sob.

The tears were mixed with both sadness and happiness. I had lost so much time with my son, and I feared how difficult his life must have been without me. I was afraid his teachers were mean to him, that other kids picked on him. I was afraid he wouldn't remember me, that he wouldn't forgive me for leaving him. But I was happy that he would be in my arms again soon, that I could cry into his shoulder and feel his little body in my embrace. We were a family, and I was finally getting the other half of my soul back. I'd never loved any man the way I loved Luca. There wasn't any room in my heart for someone else. I'd dated on and off, but nothing ever stuck. The only man I'd ever felt any real affection for was Carter.

But the rest of my heart belonged to my son.

The bedroom door opened, and Carter looked at me with sadness in his eyes. He was in his sweatpants, bare-chested and barefoot. He was getting ready for bed and probably came to retrieve me. Once he heard my sobs on the other side of the door, he probably didn't have the patience to knock. Wordlessly, he joined me on the bed and wrapped his arm around my shoulder. He comforted me, knowing exactly why I broke down into tears.

I turned my face into his shoulder and closed my eyes, letting my tears smear against his warm skin. My hand moved against his chest, and I felt the impressive muscle under my fingertips. I felt safe for a moment, knowing nothing could hurt me when this powerful man was beside me.

"He'll be here before you know it, sweetheart."

"I know…I miss him so much."

Carter moved his fingers through my hair, gently consoling me while he let me cry into his chest. "He misses you too."

"I can't wait to hold him, to talk to him. I've never loved anyone the way I love him. I can't even explain it."

"You don't need to." He lifted my gaze so I would look him in the eye. "My mom still loves me like crazy, and I'm a grown man. I'm successful and strong, and she still brings me soup when I get sick. I'm not a parent, but I understand the way you feel about your son…because it's the way my mother feels about me."

Despite Carter's rigidness and aggression, he was sweet underneath all that muscle. He was caring, sympathetic, and compassionate. "Your mom sounds lovely." I wiped away the moisture from the corners of my eyes, making the tears stop.

"You'll probably meet her eventually."

"Really? I thought you would hide me from your family."

He shook his head. "That will be impossible. I'll tell them you're the maid and nothing more."

"And Luca?"

"You come as a set." He rested his hand against the back of my neck then pressed his lips to my forehead. "I know you're anxious, but he'll be here soon. My guy told me he's in perfect health and he's a happy boy."

"Really?" I whispered.

"Yes."

I moved my cheek against his shoulder again. "That makes me happy."

"And you'll be even happier when he's here."

SINCE I WAS UPSET the night before, Carter gave me the night to relax. I slept in his bed by his side, but there was no sex that evening. He spooned me from behind and kept me warm in the middle of the night.

The following day, his patience had worn out. After he worked all day and had dinner, he wanted to cash in on his reward. I already knew it was coming because he didn't want tame sex forever. The first time we slept together, that was what he had in mind. But he caved and gave me what I wanted since it was better than nothing at all.

I walked into my bedroom and found a white box with a black ribbon around it. Carefully tied into the perfect bow, the material was made of fine lace. I gently tugged on it so the material would come apart and reveal the logo on the box.

Barsetti Lingerie.

I recognized Carter's last name and also the brand. I'd never put the two together before. I opened the lid and saw the black ensemble sitting inside. Stitched with real diamonds, it was sexy and classy at the same time. I felt the material in my hands, touched the soft lace in my fingertips. Partially see-through, it would cover most of my skin while revealing it at the same time. It was two-pieces, a push-up bra and a G-string that hardly covered anything. There was a note on top, so I unfolded it and read.

SWEETHEART,

Put this on. Come to my bedroom. Kneel.

HIS INSTRUCTIONS WERE simple and to the point. It didn't surprise me in the least. He'd had me wear lingerie before, but he'd never bossed me around so aggressively. The last instruction was difficult for me to accept, but I knew I had to obey.

Kneel.

He wanted me on my knees in front of him, submitting to him completely. He wanted all the power, the authority to hurt me, fuck me, and do whatever he wished. Like all other men, he wanted to dominate a woman, to treat her like a slave instead of a person. After being degraded by Egor, I never wanted to be in that position again. I wanted a man who would treat me right.

But I owed Carter a debt I could never repay. I would hate every moment of this, but it was my duty. And I also wanted to make him feel good, to enjoy me the way he wanted. He had a dark side, but that didn't make him an evil man.

He did the right thing when it mattered.

I pulled the lingerie out of the box and changed. It fit me perfectly, like he'd measured my body before he picked it out. I kept myself barefoot since I would be removing my heels anyway. I fixed my hair and then climbed the stairs to the third floor where he would be waiting for me. My heart was pounding with adrenaline, fearful of the pain about to come my way. I would have more bruises and scars on my canvas. I would be the object of cruelty and punishment. I anticipated the pain with fear, but I knew I needed to suck it up. It wouldn't always be this way. There would be nights when Carter would take me slowly and gently, making me come as I lay on my back and enjoyed him.

I arrived at his bedroom and walked inside. The

second I stepped into the room, I saw him standing at the foot of his bed. In his black boxers and with a hard expression on his face, he didn't look like the man who comforted me yesterday.

He looked like he didn't possess an ounce of compassion.

Fueled by testosterone and muscle, his hard-on was outlined in his shorts. The muscles of his chest and stomach were tight in anticipation, like he wanted to rush me and pin me to the ground. His arms were crossed over his chest, the muscles of his biceps flexed with power.

I was caught off guard looking at him, detecting his carnal mood the second I was in his presence. He'd given his direction very clearly, so I obeyed and lowered myself to my knees in front of him, sitting on the rug in front of his bed.

He stared at me with a mixture of carnal desire and ferocity. His eyes trailed over my body, appreciating the way the lingerie cupped my tits and formed a deep cleavage line. He lowered his hands to his sides and straightened. "Eyes down."

I moved my gaze to the floor, obeying the command without question.

He watched me for a full minute, the silence stretching between us. He'd probably anticipated my resistance since I'd always been a bit sassy. But now that he gave me back my son, I was loyal to him completely.

He probably got hard from it, aroused by the sight of my complete submission.

He pushed his boxers down and let them fall to the floor. Then he walked toward me, his large feet thudding against the rug as he approached. Only his legs were visible to me, his muscled calves and thighs impressive as he moved. He stopped in front of me, standing over me. "Suck me off." His fingers moved under my chin, and he lifted my gaze to meet his. His throbbing cock was tinted red from all the blood that moved into the thick length. He grabbed his dick and positioned it down, prepared to slide it into my mouth.

I opened my mouth, ready to take him.

But he didn't close the distance between us. He flashed a look of anger. "Yes, sir."

I brought my lips to the head of his cock and kissed it. "Yes, sir," I said quietly.

His intense gaze deepened when he heard those words. His hand moved to the back of my head and kept me in place as he inserted his dick all the way to the back of my throat. During our nights together, he was always gentle and slow, taking his time like he was in no rush. But now he was quick and hostile, thrusting himself into my throat without gentleness. "Wider."

I opened my mouth farther so I could take his length deeper and harder. He was moving so fast, it was difficult for me to breathe. I had to time my inhalation with his thrusts to keep myself breathing. I flattened my tongue and tasted the goodness that oozed out of his tip. His desire was obvious in his taste, in the way he thickened even more than usual. I moved with him and took him as deep as I could go without gagging.

"Look at me."

My eyes landed on his, and I watched the hardness of his jaw, the way his eyes burned with angry desire. It was like he'd never wanted to fuck a woman so much, but also had never hated someone more. It was an intense and terrifying experience because he'd been so different that morning.

"You look beautiful with my cock in your mouth." He gripped my neck and thrust himself a little harder, hitting me even deeper.

I kept my mouth open and refused to gag, knowing that would ruin his pleasure. His cock was bigger than my mouth could handle, but I kept up with him, doing my best to be what he wanted. When I saw how much he enjoyed it, it made me enjoy it too. I could feel the moisture seep into my thong and weigh it down. Saliva spilled over my lips and dripped down my chin and to the rug beneath my knees. My hands gripped his thighs for balance, and tears burned in my eyes because my throat was being rubbed until it was raw. I kept going anyway, letting him fuck my throat without mercy.

Ten minutes passed, and he kept going, his cock thick but not on the verge of exploding inside my mouth. He obviously had other plans that night, and coming in my mouth wouldn't be the finale.

He finally pulled his dick out of my mouth, and the saliva dripped off his length and onto the floor. "Up."

I moved to my feet, unsure what he wanted next. Egor did a lot of twisted things to me, but I suspected Carter would never take it that far. Perhaps he had a taste for the darker things in life, but not the evil things.

We stepped into the room across the hall, a bedroom with a four-poster bed and walls that were different from the rest of the house. Judging by the thickness, these walls were probably soundproof. I wiped away the spit that dripped down my chin, his taste still on my tongue. The bed in this room was completely black, along with the rest of the furniture. There was an assortment of whips, chains, and cuffs. But there were no knives or fire…to my relief.

"Bend over." Uttering commands with the least number of words as possible, Carter turned into a dictator with one thing on his mind. He wasn't the man who comforted me yesterday, who told me I deserved a better life. Now we'd been reduced to a man and a woman, stripped down to our basest purposes.

I didn't look at him before I moved to the edge of the bed and leaned over it, my torso propped on my elbows while my feet remained on the ground. My ass stuck out, and the curve in my back deepened. The bed was a little high, so I had to move onto my tiptoes to be elevated enough.

Carter came up behind me, pressing his dick right in between my cheeks. His hands started at my shoulders and slowly migrated down, feeling the small muscles of my back as he moved down to my ass.

I closed my eyes as I felt his touch, felt his cock in between my cheeks. Hot and throbbing, it ached for me. Once it felt the moisture I produced for him, he would fuck me even harder in pleasure.

Carter opened the nightstand beside the bed and pulled out a few things. A little bottle of lube and a small butt plug. I'd never used one before, but I recognized what it was. Carter didn't seem like he was into any of those things, but perhaps I was wrong.

He peeled my thong down to my thighs then squirted the lube over my ass cheeks. His large palm rubbed the liquid into my skin, making me smooth everywhere. Then he pressed two fingers inside me, pushing into my entrance before I had a chance to prepare for it.

I took a deep breath but didn't wince.

His fingers explored me while his breathing turned deep and heavy. He pulsed inside me, feeling my asshole relax as I got used to his probing fingers. When he removed himself, he inserted the butt plug in his place.

I tensed when I felt it stretch me apart, but I knew I had to relax. His cock was much bigger than that, so I had to prepare for it. If I couldn't handle this, handling that would be so much more difficult.

He pressed his cock in between my cheeks again as he stood right against me. His palm moved across my cheeks before it stopped on the right side of my ass.

Without warning, he struck me, hitting me so hard I jerked forward.

"God…" I gripped the sheets of the bed and breathed through the unexpected pain. I felt the device inside me with the momentum, felt it stretch me even more.

Carter rubbed the mark he'd made before he hit me again.

I jerked forward but remained silent this time, prepared for the blow.

Again, he hit me, striking me as hard as last time. He didn't start off gentle, hitting me with the full force he could unleash. His palm slapped against my ass and made a loud echo in the room. Skin on skin, the hit stung and made the area throb. I felt the blood rushing to the surface, felt the bruise before it even appeared.

When he hit me again, I felt his cock throb against me. With the sound of his heavy breathing, it was obvious how much he enjoyed this, how much he got off on hurting me.

His arousal turned me on in a twisted way. If hurting me made him feel good, then I enjoyed it in some way. But every strike hurt more than the last, and I couldn't keep my whimpers at bay. My moans started off as whines and grew into something deeper and louder. Soon, tears spilled down my cheeks, and my voice cracked with my pain. It was better than the painful whips I'd received from Egor, but this still hurt.

When Carter heard me cry, he stopped. He rubbed

the area with remorse as he listened to me get my breathing under control. He leaned over me as he continued to rub the area, his forehead against the back of my head. "I'm sorry, sweetheart. But I love hurting you...I really do." He turned my face so he could look at me, see the tears himself. The arousal in his eyes only intensified at my pain. He kissed one tear away before he pulled back and positioned himself against my ass. He pulled the plug out of my ass then quickly slipped his massive length in, stretching me apart as he inched his way farther. My body resisted him, never having had anything that large inside me before.

His hands pressed against the mattress on either side of me as he rested his forehead against the back of my head. He sank deeper, showing gentleness for the first time that evening. When I was on my knees, he shoved himself hard inside my mouth. When he spanked me, he never slowed his twitching palm. But now, he entered me as delicately as possible. When he was as deep as he could go, he stopped and breathed against me. "Jesus..."

I breathed through the pain, felt the immense stretch inside my ass. Carter was much bigger than Egor was, and I could feel the difference every time he was inside me. Tears welled up in my eyes again as I fought the pain down below.

He breathed into my ear as he started to move, his hot breaths packed with arousal. He could feel me shake underneath him, could listen to the sound of my muffled tears. Everything turned him on, especially the power he had over me. He fucked me in the ass like he owned me—because he did own me. "Your ass feels even better than your pussy."

If I didn't find Carter so attractive, this would be a different situation. But since I found his looks as appealing as his soul, I enjoyed feeling him enjoy me. I liked being the object of his fantasy, even if that involved being uncomfortable. When he was turned on, I was turned on.

He grabbed my neck with his large hand and squeezed me as he fucked me harder, slamming his enormous dick deep in my ass. He moaned as he pumped, losing himself completely.

I whimpered at the pain but loved the way he enjoyed it. I could feel his cock thicken a little more, feel him hit the threshold of his pleasure. I knew he was about to come inside me, knew he was about to finish. "Come in my ass."

He paused and moaned at the same time, aroused by what I'd just said. "Sweetheart…not without you."

Carter made me enjoy sex when I didn't think that was possible. After what Egor put me through, I thought I would swear off men for the rest of my life. But Carter rekindled a fire inside of me that continued to burn bright. Sex wasn't only enjoyable…but amazing. It was the kind of sex I thought was only depicted in movies. I'd never had that kind of passion with any of my lovers, but then again, maybe the men I'd been with weren't as experienced. But right now, I didn't think I could climax with this huge dick in my ass. "It hurts…"

"I know, sweetheart. Why do you think I'm enjoying it so much?" He moved his hand underneath my belly and snaked his way to my clit. His hand found the wet area, his fingers getting covered in the moisture that leaked from my slit. "Seems to me like you're enjoying it," he whispered into my ear.

"I'm enjoying you enjoying me…"

He rubbed his fingers hard against my clit, moving in a circular pattern to stimulate me as much as possible. His face hovered near mine, and he breathed hard as he thrust inside me, his cock continuing to hit me deep.

The second his fingers touched my aching nub, I felt the fire in my belly. I was wet from feeling him enjoy me, and now that he touching me even better than I touched myself, I felt my body prepare for the climax.

I couldn't believe it. His enormous dick was practically ripping me apart, but that didn't stop me from teetering on the edge. My body swayed closer to the finish line as his fingers worked. Coupled with his hot breaths in my ear, the effect was immediate. "I'm gonna come…"

He moaned in my ear as he pounded his dick into me without mercy, taking me even harder than he did before. He shoved himself deep inside for the finish, coming far inside my ass while his fingers kept up the action against my clit.

I came the second I felt him thicken and explode inside me. I couldn't feel his come like I could in my pussy, but knowing he was filling me made my climax even stronger. The pain somehow made the pleasure even better, made my previous orgasms seem like nothing in comparison.

"Fuck." He growled in my ear as he finished, his cock twitching as he dumped every drop of his seed inside me. His hand stayed on my neck until he was completely done. When he started to soften inside me, he rested his face against the back of my shoulder, breathing heavily as he recovered from the pleasure we'd both experienced.

My eyes were red and puffy from the tears I'd shed. Now that the sex was over, the pain from his spankings came back to me. The skin stung because of his powerful palm. My ass started to relax as his cock became smaller. Despite the pain I'd just endured, it ended with a climax that matched the intensity.

He slowly pulled out of me. "Alright, sweetheart?"

"I think so…"

He walked away into the bathroom, and a moment later, the water was running. He came back to me and took me by the hand before we both stepped under the warm shower together. Once he was satisfied, he turned back into the man I knew, the gentle one with a kind soul. He grabbed the soap and rubbed it into my skin, showing me the right gentleness to balance out the harsh way he handled me before. Carter seemed to be two different men, one who cared and respected women, and another who wanted to be a tormentor.

He faced me, the water dripping down his hard chin until it fell to the tile beneath our feet. "I'm sorry for being what I am. I'm sorry for getting off on your tears. A part of me is ashamed. Another part of me wants nothing more than to do it again." He held my gaze like he wanted me to say something in response, as if he'd posed a question.

I looked into his dark eyes and didn't see a monster. Egor broke my bones and tortured me to a psychotic degree. Carter's actions were tame compared to my former master. But I didn't say that, not when it would only hurt him. "You don't owe me an explanation, Carter. You told me what you wanted, and I accept that. You've shown me your good side. When I said no, you listened. When I asked you to help me, you did. After what you've given to me, I can give this to you."

He pressed his forehead to mine and closed his eyes. "I'm glad you don't hate me."

"I could never hate you."

"A real man shouldn't enjoy listening to his woman cry…"

"You don't. When I cried over Luca, you were there for me. You didn't enjoy it. It's a different situation."

"I've never been this way before. I've never wanted to hurt a woman before." He lifted his gaze to look at me again. "When I saw the scars on your back…it started all of this. There's something about you that makes me into a different man."

"A better man, I think."

He cocked his head, his eyes narrowing on my face. "How so?"

"Look at everything you've done for me, Carter."

"I should do that out of the goodness of my heart, not for something in return."

"And you did," I whispered. "I know I could say no at any time. You never told me that, but I know it's true. I submit because I want to, because it makes you feel good. I enjoy turning you on, regardless of how sinister it is."

He closed his eyes for a moment, my words affecting him somehow.

"What did I say?"

He opened his eyes again. "Hearing you say you submit because you want to…is very sexy. You're obeying me because you want to. You're listening to me because you choose to. Makes me feel like less of an ass."

I moved into his chest and rested my forehead against his powerful body. The water rained down on both of us, the drops cleaning our skin and washing away the past. It was difficult to see Carter as anything but my champion. Without him, I wouldn't have the freedom I was enjoying that very moment. "I want half and half. I'll give you exactly what you want if you give me what I want."

"What is that, sweetheart?"

I lifted my gaze to look at him. "The slow sex…"

"You want me to make love to you."

"Yes." It was exactly how I liked it, slow, deep, and gentle. I liked the kissing and the touching. I liked taking our time, my legs spread as he sank me into the mattress. It was the best sex I'd ever had in my life, having this powerful man on top of me. "You give me what I want, and I'll always give you what you want."

"That sounds fair." He rubbed his nose against mine.

I rubbed mine back. "Yeah. I think it is."

FIVE

Carter

———

When I opened the front door, I was greeted by Conway's arrogant smirk.

In jeans and a t-shirt, he was dressed casually since he was working from home a lot more often. He stepped inside without being invited and surveyed the large entryway with the double staircase. He whistled under his breath. "Of course, you buy the hottest piece of property in Tuscany when I'm trying to buy a place for my family."

"You shouldn't have dragged your feet." I shut the door behind him and followed him into the house.

He continued to look around, impressed with the place. "This place is nearly the same size as my parents' place."

"Still get lost."

"Why did you need such a big place? Got some kids I don't know about?" He chuckled before he walked into the kitchen and helped himself to a drink from the bar.

I would have a kid there very soon. "I bought it for the privacy. It has the large gate in the front, and the house is quite a distance from the road." I grabbed a glass and filled it when he was finished.

He took a drink as he stood with me at the kitchen island. "So what happened to your little pet? Egor picked her up?"

I hadn't mentioned this to him. He'd been busy lately, so we hadn't talked about it. I swirled my drink before I brought it to my lips.

Conway stared at me, his eyebrow slowly rising. "Carter?"

I swallowed the liquor down my throat then rubbed my lips together. "It's a long story…"

"Alright." He kept his focus on me, his black wedding band sitting on his left hand.

"I didn't give her back to Egor. In fact, she lives with me now."

His eyebrow inched even higher off his face. "What?"

"I couldn't give her back, Conway. Just couldn't do it." It would have haunted me for the rest of my life, especially knowing her son was alone because of my decision.

"Did you kill him, then?" he demanded. "Or are we going to get shot at any moment?"

"No, I didn't kill him. I faked her death… It was an

ordeal." I told him about the operation Griffin and I did together. "Egor bought it. Took the body with him. Then it was over. That was a few weeks ago."

Conway was clearly pissed, but he didn't explode. "How are you sure?"

"He took the body and hasn't said anything. It seemed like he believed me."

"What if he sees her somewhere?"

"Why do you think I moved way out here?"

He slowly nodded his head in understanding. "I should have known…"

"I just couldn't do it, Conway. If I gave her back, I never would have stopped thinking about it. The guy is a psychopath."

"Well, if you're in love with her, what other choice did you have?"

"I'm not in love with her," I said quickly.

He turned back to me, the anger emerging again. "You risked your life and the rest of the Barsettis for a woman you aren't in love with?"

"She has a son," I snapped. "When she told me that…I couldn't go through with it." I knew the mention of a child would calm Conway down since he was about to be a father. "It would have been wrong. Everything worked out fine, so it doesn't matter."

"It better have."

"The Skull Kings have been taken care of, and Egor has more important things to do. If I keep her hidden for a while, we'll definitely be in the clear."

"So, what's the plan? Her kid is just gonna live here?"

"Yes."

He chuckled. "You're kidding me. You're gonna live with a kid?"

"The place is three stories," I said coldly. "I told her to keep him out of my way."

"But still," he said. "I haven't even had my kid yet, and I'm freaking out about it."

"Well, I'm not going to be a father. The kid is her problem, not mine."

He kept up his hostile stare, looking me in the eye like he saw something.

"What?"

"And you think you aren't in love with this woman?"

"I'm not."

"Right…"

"I'm really not," I hissed. "I brought her for my own reasons."

"What reasons are those?" He finished his glass then crossed his arms over his chest.

"Not that it's any of your business…but I have a special kind of relationship with her. A relationship that involves whips and chains…"

He nodded slightly in understanding. "So you rescued her from that asshole so you could replace him?"

"Not exactly…but yes."

"Must be one hell of a woman."

"She is," I blurted, picturing that brown hair and beautiful skin. "So, how're Sapphire and the baby?"

"We aren't done talking about you, asshole." He slammed his glass onto the counter. "You've gotta tell your dad or my dad what's going on. They just cleaned up our mess, and they have the right to know if there's another potential situation on the horizon."

I didn't want to bring my father into my personal life, but due to the events of the past, it would be the right thing. "I'm going to talk to my father when I see him."

"Good. Thought I would have to argue with you more."

"Griffin already made his case. Said I needed to do it."

He nodded in approval. "I used to hate that guy. But now…he fits right in."

"Yeah, he does," I said in agreement. "He was the one who helped me, got the body to replace Mia. Burned the house for me…did everything."

Conway leaned against the counter and crossed his arms over his chest. "You can say this woman doesn't mean anything to you, but you put everything on the line for her. I didn't tell Sapphire I loved her until much later, but the moment I paid a hundred million dollars for her, I should have known. This is no different, Carter."

"I didn't drop any money for her," I countered.

"But you put a dead body in your house and burned

a bedroom. The damages alone are gonna cost a hundred grand."

"You think a hundred grand means anything to me?"

"It's still inconvenient."

Mia had a significant impact on me, made me feel things I'd never felt before. I'd never wanted to fuck a woman the way I did with her. I pounded into her ass last night and enjoyed every single second. I'd never gotten that much pleasure out of someone before. I wasn't sure what to make of it. "She's a good person. It was the least I could do. I bought women in the past with the intention of saving them, not giving them to their tormentors."

"So, what's the plan? Just let her live here?"

"She cooks and cleans. She's basically the maid."

"Who you screw at night."

I shrugged, not sure what else to say. "We'll see what happens…"

"I'm not sure what our parents will think about this."

"It's my life, so I don't really care what they think."

He narrowed his eyes on my face. "Cut the shit, Carter. We both care. When I told my father the truth about Sapphire, I was fucking terrified. Not scared of him punching me, but of him being disappointed in me. He's made a few comments to me in the past…and they always make me feel like shit. Don't expect your parents to be happy about this. They'll probably be livid, honestly."

I didn't want to admit that I put our family in danger, especially after everything that happened to us. But I didn't want to live by their opinions either. What was done was done. I couldn't go back and change it.

"And they aren't going to be fine knowing you have a slave."

"She's not a slave," I countered. "It's not like that."

"That's not what you said to me earlier…"

"She's treated well, and she has nowhere else to go."

"She said that?" he asked.

"No…but I can tell." She'd been a prisoner for three years, and she was just getting her son back. After everything she'd been through, she wouldn't be able to just go back to work like nothing happened. She had to focus on her relationship with her son. And the schools in the area were some of the best in the country. "One day I'll get tired of her, and she'll leave. And if she never wants to leave, I need a maid anyway."

Conway kept looking at me, the judgment in his eyes.

"And you think you're any better?" I asked incredulously. "You did the exact same thing with Sapphire."

"And I fell in love with her. Sounds like the same thing is happening to you."

I refilled my glass so I would have a reason to break eye contact for a moment. "If I felt that way, I would just say it. But I don't. My livelihood doesn't depend on my sex life, so whether I'm monogamous or not, it doesn't matter. I'm not interested in being a stepfather, and I'm not interested in love either. I care about her…a lot."

"Enough to put everything on the line."

I ignored his jab. "But I don't love her. Think whatever you want, Con. That's the truth."

He kept his arms crossed over his chest, watching me like he didn't take me seriously. "Whatever you say, Carter." A slight grin came over his face, like he couldn't wait to tell me I was wrong when the time was right.

"Can we talk about your wife now?"

His grin became wider. "Yes, my pregnant wife… she's doing alright. She's about to pop any moment, so she's a bit…how do I put this politely…difficult. She can't sleep, has a hard time eating, she's not in the mood for sex anymore…"

"Maybe that's because of you, not the pregnancy."

That wiped the smirk right off his face. "It's the pregnancy, trust me."

"Seem a little defensive about that."

"Shut the hell up, Carter."

"If she's about to pop, what are you doing over here?"

"Came to check out your new place. Seems like we haven't talked in a while, and obviously we haven't because your life has been pretty damn interesting the last few weeks."

"Exceptionally." After last night, my life got even better. Something about Mia drove me crazy, made me into a different man. I'd never been into dominance or anything kinky, but now I wanted to tie her up and fuck her like a psychopath. "Got names picked out?"

"Yes."

"What are they?"

"Not gonna say until the baby gets here. Depends on if it's a boy or a girl."

"I'm excited," I said. "We have another Barsetti on the way."

"I'm excited too. But also fucking terrified." On the surface, he seemed so calm and self-assured. It was a great poker face, his professional expression that kept all of his models and employees calm right before a show. "All this time, I've been focused on making sure Sapphire is safe, comfortable, and healthy…but now the baby is actually coming. I have a whole other person to worry about every single day."

"You do great with Sapphire, so I'm sure you'll be fine, man. If anyone can hit this out of the park, it's you."

He gave me a slight nod. "Thanks, man. I'm glad we've decided to move here since my parents will always be around to help out. They're pretty excited about it. My mom wants another baby around the house."

"Where are you guys going to live since you don't have a place? You guys are welcome to stay here if you want. Staying with your parents for the past month must be taking its toll."

"We found a place we like, and now we're in the process of purchasing it. But it's not gonna be done until after the baby comes. No need to rush at this point. So we're gonna stay with my parents. There's no possible way that my mom would ever let us stay with anyone else. She wants to be part of everything. I think it'll be good for Sapphire anyway. It'll let her relax while we have an experienced parent take care of the baby. Sapphire can sleep, and I can get some work done."

"So, free babysitters?"

"Yes," he said with a chuckle. "But good babysitters. Vanessa and I turned out alright."

"She turned out alright. You…I'm not so sure about."

He rolled his eyes. "Asshole."

"Yeah, I know." I refilled our glasses. "I miss this."

"I know," he said as he looked into his glass. "We used to see each other all the time. Now, we hardly talk."

"That should all change now that I'm living here. We're only a few miles apart."

"True. It better change." He took a drink before he pulled out his phone to check the screen. When he didn't see anything, he slid it back into his pocket. "Paranoid that I'm gonna miss a call from her."

"If she knows you're here, she would just call me next. Chill."

He chuckled. "When you have a pregnant wife, I'll tell you to chill."

Footsteps sounded behind us, and then Mia entered the room. In a red sundress that she bought at the store yesterday, she was beautiful. Blending in perfectly with the hot summer in Tuscany, she looked ready to bask beside the pool. She flinched slightly when she realized I had company. An instant of panic came over her face before she recovered, like she wasn't sure what to do. "I hope I'm not interrupting anything. I'm Mia." She walked up to my cousin and extended her hand. "You must be Carter's cousin Conway."

After Conway looked at her, he turned his expression on me, that knowing smile on his lips. Then he turned back to her and shook her hand. "Yes, I'm Conway. And it's lovely to meet you, Mia. Carter has told me a lot about you. That dress is beautiful, by the way."

"Thanks," she said, a soft smile coming onto her lips at his compliment.

I tried not to care that he was being charming with my woman, but it was difficult. Conway was a good-looking Barsetti just the way I was. I didn't want Mia to find him attractive, not that I should care.

"Carter told me you're his new roommate," Conway said. "If he's being an asshole to you, just give me a call and I'll straighten him out. He's a bit stubborn sometimes."

"A bit?" she teased. "He's more than a bit."

Conway laughed. "I like her, Carter. Any woman who talks shit about you is okay in my book."

She turned to me and placed her hand on my arm. "He may be stubborn, but he's also very sweet, selfless, and kind. He's been extremely generous to me, and I could never repay him for what he's done for me." She gave me a quick squeeze before she dropped her embrace. "Can I get you guys anything? Make dinner for the two of you?"

The touch was so simple, but it sent chills all the way down my spine. I wanted to yank her back toward me and kiss her. I wanted to lift her onto the kitchen island and pound into her right then and there. She teased me, but she also showed her affection at the same time. She was loyal to me, showing me that I was the only man on her mind.

"No, thank you," Conway said. "I just stopped by to say hello. I should get back to my wife."

"She's having your baby soon, right?" Mia asked.

"Yes," Conway said with a smile. "It's good to know Carter talks about me."

"I don't," I countered. "I just talk about your wife."

He chuckled. "Can't say I blame you. She's pretty great."

"Still not sure how you got her," I said. "Oh wait, that's right. You bought her."

"You wanna die, asshole?" Conway couldn't keep a straight face, the trace of a smile on his lips. We hadn't joked around with each other in forever, and now the insults were rolling out one by one.

"We don't have time for that. Your wife is about to go into labor."

"You're lucky for that." He finished his drink and left the glass on the counter. "By the way, you should talk to your father soon. Once the baby comes, there won't be much time for that sort of thing."

"That's a good point."

"And if he's pissed at you, the baby will soften him up." He clapped my shoulder as he left the kitchen. "It was nice to meet you, Mia."

"You too, Conway." She gave him a wave as he walked out.

When he left the house and shut the door behind him, I turned back to Mia.

She smiled in a guilty way. "I'm sorry, I wouldn't have come down here if I knew you had company."

"Don't be ridiculous." I came around the kitchen island toward her. "You live here, Mia. You can do whatever you want."

My specific choice of words made her flinch. The carefree smile on her face immediately faded away when she digested the words I spoke. I didn't think twice about them, but she was still sensitive about her newfound freedom. "Can do whatever I want…"

"Because you can do whatever you want, sweetheart."

Her eyes shifted away from my face, and she inhaled

a deep breath. "I know this doesn't make any sense, but I always feel bad when I realize how much I have now. I compare it to how it was before, and the memory catches me off-balance."

I wasn't a therapist or someone who was capable of understanding such intense emotions. I wished I could help her, but I just couldn't. "I can only imagine."

She lifted her gaze to look at me again, and when she didn't have anything else to say on the subject, she mentioned Conway. "Your cousin is nice."

"So is his lingerie." It was worth every penny because it made her slutty and classy at the same time. A beautiful woman like her deserved to be covered in diamonds and lace.

"Are all the Barsettis extremely successful?"

I shrugged. "Seems that way."

"Must be something in the water."

"Or something in the blood." My hand cupped her cheek, and my thumb brushed across her bottom lip. I'd never been threatened by Conway when we picked up women. He was just as handsome as I was, and even a little more famous. But the idea of Mia finding him attractive made me a little jealous. I wanted to be the center of her focus, wanted her eyes to be obedient to my worship.

She chuckled. "Guess so. That's exciting that you'll have a second cousin."

"I feel like they'll be more of a niece or nephew. Conway has always been a brother to me."

"That's sweet."

"Do you have any siblings?" I'd never asked before.

"No, I don't. Just me," she said with a sigh. "When I see the closeness you share, it makes me wish I had the same thing."

I never took for granted how lucky I was, to have an expansive family that was always loyal to each other. I never felt alone in the world, not even when I was five hours away in a different city. "You do. With Luca."

A soft smile appeared on her mouth. "Yes, with Luca. I've always wanted to give him a sibling. But now I need to let that dream go."

"I don't see why that dream isn't possible."

"It's very complicated to reverse the procedure."

"But not impossible," I said. "And even if it were, there are other ways to have children. Don't let Egor stomp on your dream to grow your family. You'll make it happen." Encouraging her didn't make a lot of sense since she was my prisoner. I told her other men weren't allowed in her life. There was only room for one man between her legs. Since I wasn't looking for a wife or a family, I couldn't be what she needed. Since I couldn't give her what she wanted, this arrangement had an expiration date. I couldn't keep her forever, and I knew that. Perhaps I'd get tired of her in a year or two, and I could release her back into the wild.

"You're right, Carter. You always know what to say." Her hand moved to my arm again, and she squeezed it.

I loved it when she touched me. The movement was

kind, but it meant more to me. She comforted me, reminded me that I was the man she held deep affection for. And I was the man who chased her fears away. Now that Conway wasn't here, my hands went to her hips, and I backed her up into the counter. My lips pressed against hers, and I kissed her slowly, our lips moving together with precise gentleness. Every kiss was purposeful, full of warm breaths and quiet moans. My hands were in her hair, and her hands were glued to my chest. I cradled the back of her head so I could deepen the embrace, devour her with my mouth and tongue. I'd kissed her many times, but that didn't satisfy my hunger. I'd just fucked her mercilessly the night before, and now I was touching her tenderly, like she was my wife rather than my slave. She did strange things to me, turned me into two very different men. Sometimes I was evil, and sometimes I was kind.

The windows were open and the sunlight shone through, but that didn't stop me from undoing my jeans and pushing them down with my boxers. I yanked my shirt over my head and tossed it onto the tile before I moved to her pants next. Her jeans and panties were gone before I lifted her onto the counter.

Her arms hooked around my neck, and she folded herself against my body, moving into position so I could have her right then and there. Her fingers dug into my hair, and she gave an abrupt moan when she felt my cock slide in hard. "Carter…I love it when you take me like this."

I rested my face against hers as I enjoyed the sweetness of her pussy. "Like what, sweetheart?" I wasn't tying her up and making her submit. We were just two lovers in the heat of the moment. It all started with a simple touch to my arm, an act of possession in front of my cousin.

"Like nothing can stop you from having me."

MY FATHER CALLED ME. "Hey, your uncle told me Conway stopped by yesterday. Said you had a fancy place."

"Yeah." I sat at the dining table with my laptop in front of me. My second cup of coffee was at my side. I'd finished breakfast a few hours ago, and now it was some time past noon. "He stopped by for a few minutes before he returned to Sapphire."

"Since you're taking visitors, how about your mother and I stop by for lunch?"

Normally, I would love that idea. But with Mia around, I didn't think that would be a good idea. I wanted to speak to my father in private about the situation. "Uh, you know…how about just you?"

He paused for a long time, sensing something was off. "Why just me?"

"Because…I need to talk to you about something."

It was a silence of disappointment.

I could feel his anger over the phone.

"What the fuck did you do, Carter Barsetti?"

"Just come over, alright? Leave Mom behind, for now."

"Your mother misses you, Carter."

"I know…but I don't want to talk to her about this right now." My mother would be far more disappointed in me than my father would. I couldn't handle that. I hated being shunned by her. I hated it when I gave her a broken heart. "It needs to just be you."

"I'm coming." He hung up.

I set my phone down and waited, knowing I would be able to feel my father's wrath before he even arrived at the door.

Mia walked inside, looking cute in a pink apron. "Everything alright, Carter?"

Normally, I would fuck her on the dining table to get my mind off the situation, but since the war was coming to my front doorstep, that wasn't an option. "My father is coming by right now. I have to tell him about you."

"Oh…I see. Should I stay out of the way, then?"

"I think that would be best."

She moved her hand to my shoulder and rubbed the muscle. "Let me know if you need anything."

I grabbed her hand and brought it to my lips, pressing a kiss to the curve of her palm. "I will, sweetheart." I released her hand and watched her walk away. My father must have been close by since he arrived five minutes later.

Even his knock sounded angry.

I walked to the front of the house and opened the door, revealing my angry father on the doorstep. His tanned skin was tight across his face and arms, showing chiseled muscles and the hard lines of his jaw. Even though they were a different color, his eyes were just like mine, and his dark hair and Italian features were like mine too. I had slightly softer features, my mother's legacy. But I possessed his height and his musculature. "Come in." I stepped out of the way so he could walk into the entryway.

He didn't make a comment about the house or the grounds. He marched inside, his hostility obvious in the movements of his body. "What is it, Carter? I had to lie to your mother, and I hate doing that."

"I didn't ask you to lie to her."

His eyes flashed with annoyance. "How else would I get over here without bringing her? All she can talk about is the new baby and your place. She's so excited that you live here now, and she wants to come see you."

"And I want to see her too." I led the way into the kitchen, that way our voices wouldn't echo off the vaulted ceilings and the wooden staircases. "But I have to get this out of the way first."

"Get what out of the way?" He followed behind me and stopped at the kitchen island. "Your uncle just cleaned up the Skull Kings mess. This better not be another mess to clean up, alright? We've got a new Barsetti on the way. We can't fuck it up for them."

"Yeah, I know," I said. "And no, there's not another mess." I truly believed I'd tricked Egor into thinking that corpse belonged to Mia. With his temperament, he would have made an attack by now. There was no way he still had the body because it would have decomposed. He must have dropped it in the ocean over a week ago.

He looked visibly relieved. "Then what is it, son?"

I looked into my father's face, seeing the way he relaxed when he assumed the situation wasn't that bad. I didn't know how to break the truth to him, to tell him I disobeyed him because of a large pile of money. He would be disappointed in me. I knew he would be. I could take responsibility for my mistakes, but watching my father disapprove of my decisions hurt.

I didn't know where to begin, how to start, so I just blurted things out. "About two months ago, I got a strange phone call from a man named Egor—"

"Oh, this isn't good…" He crossed his arms over his chest.

"Asked me to bid on his sister at the Underground. I told him I wasn't in the business anymore."

"Good. Because you shouldn't be."

I dropped my gaze for an instant. "Every time I said no, he offered more money. When there was a hundred and fifty million dollars on the table, I caved. I thought this man was admirable for not giving up on his sister. If Carmen were in a bad situation—"

"She would never be in a bad situation because I raised her better than that."

"Anyway…I went to the Underground and bought her."

My father's eyes narrowed, bursts of fire igniting in his gaze. His jaw tightened noticeably as he pressed his lips tightly together. Even the muscles of his arms flexed. His wrath was about to unleash as a bolt of lightning. "Jesus Christ…"

"When I brought her back to the house, she wasn't like the other women I bought. She was daring, brave, and a bit crazy. She jumped out of my car when I driving sixty kilometers an hour, and she came at me with a knife."

"Looks like her father raised her right…"

"After talking with Egor, I realized he wasn't really her brother. It became obvious that he was her former master…that he tortured her and raped her for years. Now he wanted her back, and he was willing to do anything to make that happen."

Both of his hands tightened into fists. "This story just gets worse and worse…"

"I was supposed to make the trade four weeks after I bought her. I kept my distance from her and didn't get attached to her. But it was inevitable that she gained my respect. And before I made the trade, she told me something I couldn't shake off. She told me she had a young son…"

My father didn't show any pity. "This is why the

Skull Kings came after Conway. All this shit was your fault."

I took the insult like a man. "Conway and I aren't sure, but we think so."

He gripped his skull and started to pace in the kitchen. "You risked all of us for some woman?"

"I didn't know any of this was going to happen. And for the record, Conway didn't know anything, not until after I bought her."

"So that just makes it worse," he hissed. "My son is the reason all of this bullshit happened. My brother walked into the lion's den and could have been killed, Carter. I talk shit about your uncle all the time, but make no mistake, I couldn't live without him." He got in my face, his hand pushing against my chest. "That man is everything to me. He's my brother—he's my blood." He threw his arms down. "And I could have lost him because of your stupidity."

I bowed my head, ashamed. "I know…I'm sorry."

"You're sorry?" he snapped. "I told you not to go back there, and you did it anyway."

"I know…"

"You're practically a billionaire, Carter. Why the fuck did you need more money?"

"Because I'm weak, alright? I'd gotten away with it for years. I thought I could do it one more time."

He shook his head and started to pace, furious. "Then what the hell happened? Did you give her back?"

I didn't want to give my answer. "No."

He halted and gave me a fiery look. "You've got to be kidding me."

"Griffin helped me. I told Egor she killed herself by catching on fire. We found a corpse to replace her, made him believe it was her, and then it ended. I moved out here to have more privacy so he wouldn't spot her somewhere."

"Jesus fucking Christ."

"He believed it, Father. It's been weeks, and I haven't heard from him. He's temperamental, so he would have done something by now."

He gripped his skull again. "I should beat the shit out of you right now."

"Yeah…you should." I deserved a punch to the face. "But I had to do it. I've bought dozens of women before and got them to safety. I couldn't just hand over this innocent woman to her tormentor, especially when she had an eight-year-old son. I couldn't do it."

"But you could put us at risk?"

"We aren't a risk. I covered my tracks."

He shook his head. "Tracks get old, but they never disappear entirely. You'll always be looking over your shoulder."

"He doesn't live here. He's Russian. I gave him the corpse so he could drop it in the ocean. He obviously did that. Otherwise, he would have a decomposing body on his hands. All the evidence to contradict my story was on the body, so he clearly didn't notice anything. I even burned my own house to make the story more believable. It's done—and it's been taken care of."

He stopped pacing and leaned against the counter again. "Thank god your mother isn't here."

Yes. Her disappointment would be worse.

"You're always going to be looking over your shoulder, Carter."

"I know…but he'll find someone else eventually and forget about Mia."

"Mia?" he whispered. "She's got a name, huh?"

"Yes."

"And what did you do with her?" He turned his hard stare on me, burning me alive with his disappointment.

"I brought her here."

"In the house?" he asked, dumbfounded.

"Yes…she lives with me."

He turned away and gave a slight nod, like he understood something that was never said. "Now I get it…you love this woman." He rubbed the back of his neck and sighed, frustrated but no longer angry. He turned back to me, his eyes a little less hostile.

"No, I don't love her. I just wanted to help her."

"Then why is she living here?"

"She needed somewhere to go. She cooks, cleans, takes care of the house—"

"And fucks you at your command." His voice rose,

bouncing off the walls of the kitchen and becoming louder.

I held his gaze, unsure how to circumvent the accusation.

"Don't lie to me again." The muscles of his body tensed all over again. It seemed like he wanted to grab me by the neck and choke me. "Because I will beat the shit out of you if you do it again. Men don't lie, and they definitely don't lie to their fathers. So what kind of man do you want to be, Carter? A liar? Or a piece of shit?"

I didn't flinch as I held his gaze, feeling the pain in my chest. A son's worst fear was his father's disappointment. I wasn't a child anymore, but I lived for his approval. He told me he was proud of me for everything that I accomplished. I was a self-made man, and when he told me how happy he was, he had tears in his eyes. Now all of that was in the past. I was letting him down in the present.

"That's why she's here? You're her new master?"

I held his gaze because it would be pathetic to look away. I didn't want to admit the truth to my father. I was hoping to avoid this subject altogether since my father never mentioned my personal life. That was a boundary he respected. "Yes."

He clenched his jaw and looked away.

"But I did want to help her as well."

"Sure, Carter." He dragged his hand down his face, sighing in frustration. "This is a fucking nightmare."

"There is no nightmare," I said. "I took care of Egor."

"Let's hope so. The things of the past have a way of returning…in the way you least suspect. We thought Bones was long gone, but then he had a son who infiltrated our ranks. Sure, he likes him now, but there was no way any of us could have anticipated that."

We could argue in circles for weeks. "The decisions have already been made. She lives here now, and that's the end of the story."

"How long?"

"I don't know. Maybe a year or two."

"And then you'll let her go?"

"If she ever really wanted to leave, she could walk away. She knows that."

"Because you've told her?" he demanded.

"No…but she knows me. She knows I'm not a monster. She knows I'll take care of her and her son. She knows she's comfortable and safe here, hidden away from the real monsters outside these walls. She's not a prisoner, and I'm not a master. We're friends. We care about each other. There's more here than that…"

"But you don't love her?" he countered.

"Love isn't something I'm looking for."

"I've heard that before."

I leaned against the refrigerator so we could face each other.

"Now what?" he asked.

"I don't know."

"Is her son here?"

"No. I had a guy get him out of the orphanage. He'll be here next week."

"And you're okay living with a kid?" he asked incredulously. "For a man not looking for love, it seems like you're trying to settle down."

I didn't want to be a father. I didn't want to be a husband. I just wanted to be Carter, the successful car designer. "I made it clear he needs to stay out of my way. They live on the second floor. I live on the third. He's not allowed up there."

"You obviously don't know shit about kids. They don't just listen."

"Mia seems like a pretty authoritative person."

"Mia...pretty name." The rage slowly left his eyes, but the disappointment was still there. "You can have any woman you want, Carter. Why bother with this one?"

It was a good question, and I didn't have a good answer to match it. I'd been with lots of beautiful women who were lovely and interesting. Mia was different in ways I couldn't explain. She'd been raped and beaten, but I didn't see her as a victim. I didn't care that the last guy who fucked her did it by force. I didn't view her as damaged goods, but as a powerful woman who didn't give up, no matter the odds. "I don't know... I really don't."

"You know, I would be a lot more supportive of this if you did love her. If you fell in love and this was the one woman you wanted to spend your life with, I could be on board. I could understand. But the fact that you're doing all of this for a woman who doesn't mean that much to you…just annoys me."

I bowed my head, hurt by his harsh words. "I saved an innocent woman. That doesn't make you proud?"

"You only did it so you could fuck her."

"That wasn't the only reason."

"Say whatever you want, Carter. No matter what you have, you always want more. I don't get it."

I raised my head again, feeling sick because of his coldness. "Where do we go from here?"

He shrugged. "I don't have a fucking clue, Carter."

I hated it when he called me by my first name. It meant he was angry. Otherwise, he called me son. "I don't want Mom to know." She was the strongest woman I knew. She was always vocal about her opinions, and she put my father in his place so easily. She was a fierce disciplinarian, pushing Carmen and me as far as she could to make us good people. Raising me wasn't easy, and I respected her for doing such a good job.

"Normally, I would make you tell her yourself. But I agree…she shouldn't know about this. Only Conway knows?"

I nodded.

"Then we'll keep this between us. No reason to upset her, especially if nothing bad ever happens."

"Agreed."

"So, Mia will just be your maid. That's the story."

I nodded.

He searched around the kitchen, like she would pop out at any moment. "Can I meet this girl?"

"You want to?"

"Absolutely. Need to have a few words with her."

I walked into the other room where another staircase was. "Sweetheart, could you come down here?" I never called her by anything else besides sweetheart, so the action was involuntary. If I'd been thinking more clearly, I would have called her Mia in front of my father. I walked back toward him and heard her footsteps on the stairs.

She emerged a moment later, the apron gone. In a yellow sundress with her long hair pulled back in a ponytail, she was more beautiful than a sunflower. She livened up my new home, bringing the sunlight directly into the house. She smiled as she looked at me and my father. Slowly, she approached and extended her hand to the man who raised me. "It's so nice to meet you, Mr. Barsetti. I'm Mia."

My father didn't take her hand. Instead, he wrapped his arms around her and gave her a fatherly hug. He patted her on the back, embracing her the way he did with Carmen. "Pleasure to meet you. I'm Cane." He stepped back and dropped his touch, wearing a friendly expression in his eyes that he hadn't shown me during our conversation. "My son just told me everything, not by choice, but by force. I want you to know that you can come to me if you need anything. If my son doesn't treat you right, I have no problem beating him into the ground. He won't fight back, so it'll be an easy match. He may be a confident man, but when it comes to me, all he knows is fear. So if you ever want to leave, you're free to do so. Let me know, and I'll make it happen."

She opened her mouth, but no words came out. Utterly speechless, she didn't know what to say. "That's very kind of you…. Her eyes shifted to me before she looked at him again. "Honestly, your son is very good to me. I wouldn't be here right now if it weren't for him. He has a good heart. He makes me feel safe, makes me feel beautiful. I know evil because I've seen it with my own eyes…and he's not it."

When my father looked at me again, all the hostility was gone. Something about her words softened his resolve. "Good…I'm glad to hear that." He stepped back from her and slid his hands into his pockets. "We're going to keep this from his mother since…I don't think she would take it well. So this will stay between the three of us…and Conway."

Mia looked at me, the affection and sincerity in her eyes. She wore her heart on her sleeve when it came to me. She obviously respected me, and there wasn't a hint of fear coming from her. When I'd first captured her, she was constantly timid around me, so I noticed the difference in her behavior. Now she was comfortable and relaxed, knowing she had far more freedoms here than she would have anywhere else. "I understand."

After a bout of silence, my father spoke again. "Well, I should get going."

"I'll walk you to the door." I escorted him through the kitchen and back to the entryway. I thought he would stay for lunch and I would show him around the house, but he clearly wasn't interested in that.

We walked outside into the hot sun where his black car was parked.

"Thanks for not telling Mom."

"If Mia isn't going to be here forever, I don't see why we should. If this were the woman you loved…that would be a different story."

I cared about Mia a lot, would do almost anything for her, but love wasn't on my radar. She was the longest relationship I'd ever had because most of my flings were just a few weeks. I respected her story, respected her resilience. "I'm sorry I disappointed you, Father. I hate it when that happens…makes me feel like shit."

He looked into my face, his expression unreadable. His gaze flicked away for a moment, and he sighed quietly. When he looked at me again, there a small sign of affection. "No matter how much you disappoint me, it doesn't change the way I feel about you. You're my son, and I love you with everything that I have. I'm still proud of the man you've become and everything you've accomplished. I'm not perfect, so it's unrealistic for me to expect you to be perfect…but I want you to be better than me. That's all a father wants… for his son to be better." He moved his hand to my shoulder and gave me a squeeze.

I lived for those squeezes, lived for my father's praise. I looked up to him in many ways, had always wanted to be a strong man like him. Sometimes he was irrational and emotional, but he was still the smartest guy I knew. Everything I learned, I learned from him. "Thanks, Father."

He gave a slight nod before he dropped his hand and walked away. "Invite us over for dinner. Your mother wants to see you before Sapphire goes into labor."

"Alright. I will." I stood in front of the house and watched him leave the property and drive out of the gates. They closed behind him automatically. I heard the engine of his car as he sped away, and when the sounds stopped, I knew he was gone.

Now that he had left, I questioned everything about myself. I'd put everything on the line for a woman I didn't love. I was having her son live with us when I knew nothing about kids. I didn't even want kids myself. My whole world was changing to accommodate this woman. I didn't consider myself to be a hero, so it wasn't in my nature to help someone like this.

But I wanted to give this woman everything…everything she deserved.

SIX

Bones

We stood together in the doorway of the apartment. My black bag was over my shoulder, and Vanessa was staring at me with eyes full of tears. Last time I left, she was stronger. But this time, all of her strength had disappeared. She'd been pushed too far, her heart beaten too severely.

It hurt me so much that I considered calling the whole thing off.

But I couldn't do that to my boys. I could never betray my family. They had my back, and I had theirs —end of story. I just had to make it through one more time. When this was over, I would never hurt her again.

Vanessa sniffled then wiped her tears away. "Sapphire is going to go into labor at any moment."

"I know."

"You can't miss that."

"The timing is shitty. But there's nothing I can do, baby. I have to do my job."

Fresh tears fell down her face.

I hated it. Fucking hated it. I held up a single finger. "One more time."

"One time too many," she whispered. She covered her face with her hands for an instant, giving her a second to control her quivering lip. "Doesn't matter if it's the last time. What you're doing is still dangerous. You could still get killed—"

"Not gonna happen, baby." Any other man would get fed up with her disapproval, but I was better than that. If I was going to make her cry, then I was going to be the one to listen to it. I would stand there as long as she needed me to, go in this circle as many times as it took before she could let me go. "I promise you."

"You never know…"

"Ask any Barsetti, and they'll tell you I'm the strongest man they've ever met."

"Even the strongest regimes fall…"

"Not me, baby. I'm not doing this for the money anymore. I'm doing this job right because I have to get back to you. I have something to live for, not something to die for."

She tilted her gaze to the floor, her tears glistening in the light. "Griffin, I'm never going to be okay with this… I don't want you to leave."

"I have to. The sooner I leave, the sooner I come back."

"What if you don't come back at all?"

I dropped the bag on the floor then moved my hands to her hips. "Baby, look at me."

She kept her chin angled toward the floor, her eyes closed.

"Baby." I could redirect her gaze with my hand, but I didn't want to. I wanted her to look at me when she was ready, to obey me when she felt like it.

After thirty seconds, she finally looked into my eyes.

My hand wrapped around the back of her neck, keeping her in place as I spoke to her. "I will come back, baby. You can do this. This is the last time, and it's over forever. Instead of worrying about me, be happy that you never have to do this again. This will be the last time. I promise you. Even if Max comes to me and asks for a favor, I will say no. I made it clear these would be my last jobs. That was the deal we made. I won't change my mind. When I return, we'll be starting a new life together. I have no idea what I'm going to do, but I will find something. So spend time picking out what house you want. When I get back, we'll buy it."

"I want to do that with you…"

"Then pick your favorites, and we'll visit them together."

She rested her palms against my chest, her breathing a little less shaky. The tears stopped falling, but her eyes were still wet. "Okay…"

I rested my forehead against hers. "Have faith in me, baby. Remember who I am. Remember what I'm

141

capable of. You shouldn't be worried about me, but all the men who face me."

"I don't care how strong you are, Griffin. My fear comes from love. Love makes me irrational, makes me paranoid. I'm so scared of losing you that even a one percent chance is too high."

"It's not even one percent, baby." I pressed my lips to her forehead. "I want that list of houses when I get back. And hopefully I return before Sapphire goes into labor. But if I don't…tell them congratulations for me."

"I will."

I rubbed my nose against hers. "I love you, baby."

She started to cry again. "I love you too…"

I kissed her tears away before I turned my back on her and grabbed my bag. I walked out the front door without looking over my shoulder, unable to watch her cry as I left her. The only thing keeping me going was the fact that this was my last mission before permanent retirement. After this, it would be a quiet life of…I wasn't even sure. I would have to find something to keep me busy. If Vanessa was working in the gallery all the time, I couldn't hover over her and distract her. And I certainly couldn't work out all the time. When this mission was complete, I would give it more serious thought.

I got on the way and headed to the airport. I called Max through my headset.

"On the road?" he asked.

"Ten minutes from the airport."

"Alright. The guy will meet you in Morocco. Before you take the trip to the mountain, he'll meet you with the artillery."

"Good to know."

"Bad mood, huh?" he asked.

"Vanessa…"

"Gives you shit every time you leave?"

"I wouldn't phrase it like that. It's just difficult for her. I keep telling her it's my last mission, but that doesn't make her feel better."

Max was quiet for a while. "So, you haven't changed your mind, then?"

There was no possibility of continuing this profession. If Vanessa and I had to go through this every single time, we wouldn't last. She would resent me in time and eventually leave me. And if we had kids, that would be even worse. If I wanted her to be my wife, I had to be the husband she wanted. That meant my job was to protect her, to protect our children, and be exactly what she needed. Vanessa was the perfect woman. She could replace me in a heartbeat if she wanted. "No. And I won't, Max."

He sighed. "That's a shame."

"It's time for me to move on. I'm sure you understand that, even if you don't agree with it."

"I suppose. It just won't be the same without you."

"You guys are just as capable as I am. You don't need me."

"That's not why, man," he said quietly. "Now that

you've moved and settled down…we don't talk as much anymore."

I'd been so busy with my own life that I hadn't even noticed. I couldn't remember the last time I spent time with the guys. After Vanessa and I got back together, they weren't a priority anymore. "I'm sorry, that's my fault."

"Damn right, it is."

"Things will be different, especially when I get married. It'll be even more different when I start a family. But I will always make time for you guys. You're my family. I'll never forget that."

"Whoa, a family?" he asked incredulously. "Since when did this happen?"

"Vanessa gave me an ultimatum. If I want to marry her, I have to give her a family."

"And you agreed?"

"We both know I can't live without her."

"That's some serious shit. When are you gonna propose?"

"I don't know," I answered. "There's a lot going on right now. Her brother is having a baby in the next few days, so not anytime soon. And I have this mission, and I didn't want to ask her to marry me before I left. Would just make it harder for her. I don't even have a ring."

"I don't think you need one, man. Vanessa doesn't seem like the kind of woman that cares."

"I care. I want her wearing a fat diamond everywhere she goes, so every asshole out there can see me on her hand even if I'm not with her."

He laughed. "Of course you do."

We spent the next ten minutes talking, and I pulled up to the airport. "I'm here, so I should get going."

"Alright, man. I'm glad we had this talk. Made me feel a little better about the whole thing."

"Yeah, me too." I didn't have these kinds of conversations with the guys, but this one was necessary. It was okay to wear your heart on your sleeve sometimes. I loved my boys, and I knew they loved me too. "I'll call you when I land."

"Alright. Bye."

"Bye."

MOROCCO WAS a place filled with snake charmers, fire dancers, and a town square full of belly dancers, jewelry sellers, and stands with pots and pans. It was an innately poor country, but it still possessed so much beauty in the valley of the village and the mountains surrounding the area.

With my fair skin, I didn't fit in. So I covered myself with a long-sleeved black shirt and a hoodie. I met with the arms dealer, grabbed my artillery, and then took the Jeep to the Atlas Mountains.

The man I was looking for lived in a palace at the top, isolated from the rest of the world. Men who lived on the outskirts of the city were always easy targets. The men along the perimeter were easy to take out, and there was no time for any backup to assist.

It was like shooting fish in a barrel.

It was under the cover of darkness when I emerged. I could see the fires from the city below, the thousands of people gathered in the town square for shopping and nightlife. I left my Jeep hidden under a tree then infiltrated the palace.

The man I was looking for was an impostor. He made deals in intelligence but fed the wrong information to important groups. As a result, he manipulated events to suit his specific desires. It affected nations as well as thugs. Taking him out would make the world a better place—literally.

I snuck up on the perimeter, snapped a few necks of the men who got in my way, and then made it inside the palace. The servants were on the bottom floor, but since they were innocent slaves forced into a life of servitude, I tied them up and shoved them into the closet.

I moved to the next floor with Max in my ear. He'd acquired a schematic of the place, so I knew exactly where to go. I didn't need to make this death look like an accident, not when the man had so many enemies. It would be impossible to figure out who was behind his death.

I found him on the third floor, watching TV while he smoked his cigar and enjoyed his booze. The entire room was full of smoke because he inhaled the cigars on an hourly basis. The white color permeated the room, and it was difficult to breathe. I enjoyed a cigar once in a while, but that habit died when Vanessa made it forbidden.

I watched him for a moment, finding it ironic that his drapes were closed to secure his privacy. If they had been open, his guards would have been able to see what was happening. I had to get in and out of there as quickly as possible, so I approached him from behind with my blade drawn. Before he even realized what was happening, the knife was against his throat, and I slit it with one quick move.

He fell to the couch, dead in seconds.

I wiped the blade on the couch before I sheathed it in my belt. It was a quick kill, and now my only job was to get home. I moved back down the hallway toward the stairs, and that's when I came face-to-face with someone who shouldn't have been there.

His son.

Twenty-five and next in line for the throne, he stared at me with his ferocious brown eyes. He was unarmed, but he had something worse. A large horn that could be heard throughout the entire palace.

I pulled out my pistol and shot him.

But not before he hit the button and made a loud noise that shook the walls.

My bullet pierced him in the chest, and he was down.

But the damage of the horn was irreparable. Men were shouting and footsteps were pounding.

I had to get out of there—now.

I MADE it out of the palace and back into the mountains. There were too many men chasing me, so I drove the Jeep over a cliff and moved on foot, getting deeper into the mountains and into a location they wouldn't be able to find unless they were on foot too.

The trail was dangerous, and I hugged the rocky outcropping until I was completely on the other side of the mountain. In the pitch darkness, it was dangerous. It was far more dangerous than murdering a powerful man.

When I made it to the other side, I called Max.

"What happened?" he asked immediately.

"His son saw me and sounded the alarm. They chased me for a while. But I ditched the Jeep into a gorge and climbed the mountain until I found a place where they can't follow me. I mean, they can, but it's unlikely."

"Shit. I'll send in a chopper."

"Wait until morning. They'll be looking for me all night, and if they see a chopper, it'll be easy to figure out where I am."

"It'll be even easier during the daylight."

"They'll probably give up by then."

Max listened to what I said and debated to himself for a moment. "It's too risky, Bones. I've got to get you out of there."

"It's too risky for the pilot. You need to wait until tomorrow night."

"That will put you back in the schedule by an entire day."

"It's the safest move—for everyone." I would have to stay on the mountain for an entire twenty-four-hour period, but I could tough it out. I had water and food. It'd be cold, but I'd been in worse situations.

"The target is dead?"

"Yes."

"What about the son?"

"Got him too."

"Alright. We'll do it your way. I have your coordinates on GPS. I'll use the satellite feed to keep track of the people around you. If anyone comes close, I'll know about it." His fingertips typed against the keyboard in the background.

"Thanks, man."

"Sleep if you need it. I'll be awake."

"Alright." I wasn't sure if I could sleep right now, not when all this adrenaline was pumping in my veins. "You need to tell Vanessa. But emphasize that I'm alright. I'm still coming back. It'll just be a little longer than we planned."

"Do you want me to tell her what happened?"

I didn't want to lie to her. Lying wasn't in my

nature. And I didn't want to mislead the woman I loved. But knowing her, it would kill her inside. She would panic and break down. "No. Don't tell her. Just tell her that my target moved so we had to make a new plan before we went in."

"You're sure?" he asked, knowing I never lied to anyone.

"She'll lose her mind, man."

"Yeah, I know. It's probably the best idea."

"Then do it."

"Alright. Will do."

SEVEN

Conway

────────────

It was impossible to sleep when Sapphire was tossing
and turning all night. Left to right then right to left, she
moved back and forth, unable to get comfortable
because her stomach was so large. The baby had been
kicking a lot lately, keeping her up all night and in pain
during the day. There was nothing I could do to help
except stay quiet and not complain about my lack
of sleep.

That would be an asshole thing to do.

When she turned again and sighed, I knew she was
losing her mind.

"Muse." I turned toward her and placed my hand
over her distended stomach. "Everything alright?"

Sweat sprinkled her forehead, and she took a deep
breath. "I just want this baby out…"

I rubbed her stomach and then placed a kiss to her
shoulder. "It's coming, Muse. Any day now."

"But I want it out now…" She gritted her teeth and breathed through the pain. "Don't get me wrong, I love our baby. But I would love our baby a lot more if it was in my arms, not my uterus."

I pulled up her shirt to reveal her bare belly. My hand glided along the mound, feeling the life under my palm. "The baby doesn't want to leave because you've made such a nice home for them. They love you already."

She relaxed slightly at my words. "I love them too… a part of me will miss being pregnant. But right now, I'm tired of being pregnant."

"I wish I could help you, Muse."

"You are…" She rested her hand on mine. "You're helping me right now."

I leaned down and kissed her forehead. "I love you."

"I love you too," she whispered.

When I pulled away, I saw the sweat mark in the valley between her tits. They'd gotten bigger with her pregnancy, preparing to feed my son or daughter. But right now, they were still mine to enjoy. "You know, there are a few things that help initiate labor…" I'd been trying to get laid for the last week, but she'd been so self-conscious and uncomfortable that she wasn't in the mood.

"We're about to have our baby, and all you can think about is sex."

"Remember how you got pregnant in the first place." I moved to my knees then pulled her panties down her legs. I was relieved when she didn't object and try to cover her stomach. No matter how many times I told her how much her belly turned me on, she didn't believe me. If only she knew how sexy she was, pregnant because I'd knocked her up. I put a pillow underneath her back then slid myself inside.

Damn, it felt good.

This might be one of the last times I would be able to get sex from her until the baby was here. She would need at least a month to heal if the birth was natural. Now that I was in between her legs, I didn't want to leave. Sex was so good, whether she was nine months pregnant or back to her petite size. That was because I loved her, loved her more than anything else.

I kept her legs apart with my arms and held myself on top of her, my stomach grazing against her enlarged belly. I thrust into her hard, unable to control myself before it felt so good. Fucking my pregnant wife was one of my biggest fantasies, even if she wasn't in my lingerie. I was the one who got her pregnant in the first place, and I was oddly proud of that.

She got into it minutes later, her nails clawing at me. She moaned with my thrusts, her enormous tits shaking with my movements. The headboard tapped against the wall, but my parents were an entire floor above us, so the noise didn't matter.

I was going to give my wife an orgasm before she gave birth to my baby. It was the least I could do, knowing the extensive trauma she was about to experience. I wanted to come right in the beginning, to fill her with more come, but I held on, knowing I had to do this right.

Thankfully, she came. She managed to find her release despite how uncomfortable she was. She dragged her nails down my back as she screamed, her beautiful face tinting red with arousal. "Conway…"

I came seconds later, ready to release now that I'd finished my job. I pumped deep inside her, filling her with my seed with a satisfying moan. I'd been wanting this pleasure for over a week. Now that I finally had it, I enjoyed every second. "Fuck…I'm gonna miss you being pregnant."

"Then you'll have to get me pregnant again."

I leaned down and kissed her. "I will." I slowly pulled out of her then leaned down to kiss her stomach, to love my woman and the baby we made together. I had no idea if I was about to have a daughter or a son, but as long as they were healthy, I was happy. I kissed her belly button and everywhere the baby might be, and when I felt a large kick, I pulled away. "They're ready to come out, baby." That was when I felt the moisture soak into the sheets directly under my knees. It took me a second to understand what happened because I'd never experienced anything like it.

"What?" Sapphire asked, noticing my hesitation.

"Your water just broke."

"It did?" She jolted upright and felt the sheets

underneath her, which were damp from the pool she'd just released. "Oh my god…"

"It's alright, Muse. It's time to get you to the hospital." I hopped out of bed, pulled on the clothes I kept laid out for the occasion, and then got her outfit out of the dresser.

She continued to lie there as she gripped her stomach. "Oh my god…I'm having a baby. Jesus, I'm having a baby…" She started to breathe hard, gasping for breath as she began to panic. "I've gotta go to the hospital… I've gotta push a football out of my vagina…"

I grabbed the bag with supplies and set it on the bed. "Alright, let's get you dressed."

She stayed still. "Conway, I can't do it. I just can't…"

I grabbed both of her wrists and pulled her up. I kneeled on the floor at her feet so we could be eye level. "Muse, I know this is scary, but you can do this. If anyone can do this, it's you."

"It just won't fit." Her breathing increased as her panic became worse. "The first time we had sex, you barely fit—"

"Muse, just breathe." I grabbed both of her wrists and squeezed them. "This is natural. Women do it every day. I'll be there the whole time. You aren't doing this alone."

"You aren't pushing anything out of your—"

"Don't think about the process. Think about what we're getting at the end. Our little boy or little girl will be here. We're starting our family, Muse. That is the most beautiful thing in the world. You grew this little person inside you. Do you understand how amazing that is? Now it's time to meet them."

She slowly nodded, her breathing slowing down.

"You're the strongest woman I know. You can do this."

She nodded again. "Okay."

"Now, let's get you dressed and get going." I gently pulled her to her feet and helped her change out of her pajamas into the new clothes. I stripped the sheets off the bed and left them on the floor so they wouldn't soak into the mattress. "Just sit here for a second, and I'll get my parents."

"Alright." She lowered herself into the chair and breathed, her hands on her stomach.

I ran up the stairs to the third floor and knocked on my parents' bedroom door. I hadn't done this since I was still living in the house as a teen.

"Coming." My father's deep voice sounded completely awake even though it was the middle of the night. He was always prepared for anything. He opened the door, shirtless in just his sweatpants. "Is it time?"

"Her water just broke."

He grinned, fully awake at three a.m. "That's great. Your mother and I will get dressed and meet you downstairs." He started to shut the door.

"Wait."

"What?" He opened the door wider and looked at

me, his chiseled physique still tight and strong for a man in his late fifties. His muscular arms led to a powerful chest, and the veins bulged across the surface.

"I just… I'm gonna be a father."

He grinned slowly. "It's not as scary as you think it's gonna be."

"I don't know anything about being a father."

"I didn't know anything either. You and Vanessa grew up just fine."

I ran my hand through my hair, still nervous. "My whole life, it's just been me. Now, I've got a wife and a kid… This isn't where I thought I would be a year ago."

"Life is crazy in its unpredictability. But that's what makes it wonderful. I promise you, being a parent is the most rewarding thing you'll ever do in your life, even more rewarding than starting your own company. Trust me on that."

Muse had her breakdown when her water broke, and now that she wasn't around, I was having mine.

My father continued to grin while he watched me. "I have no doubt you'll be a great father."

"How so?"

"Because you're a great husband."

"I haven't been married long…"

"Doesn't matter. You took care of her right from the beginning. You'll do the same with your kid."

I stared at him, feeling a little better.

"Your mother and I need to get dressed, son. And you should be down there with your wife."

"You're right…absolutely right. I just needed—"

"A little pep talk. I understand. I wish my father had been there to give me one when I had you." He wrapped his arms around me and gave me a hug. He patted me hard on the back. "You'll do great, Conway. I really believe that. Now go have your baby."

MUSE WAS in labor for ten hours before anything happened.

I held her hand and let her squeeze mine through every contraction. As the hours passed, the pain increased, and so did the bruising to my hand. Even though I needed my hands for work, I let my wife do whatever she wanted.

She was giving birth to my baby, after all.

Covered in sweat and exhausted, Muse struggled the entire time. It was the most gruesome day she'd ever experienced, and the baby hadn't even started to descend to her opening.

I wished I could do this for her.

I ran my fingers through her hair and kissed her forehead. "They'll be here any moment, Muse. It'll be over soon. When we get home, I'll take care of the baby so you can rest as much as you want. And you can eat whatever you want."

"Can I get that in writing?"

I chuckled and kissed her again.

When another contraction hit, it was the worst one she'd ever felt. She screamed so loud that the nurse ran into the room to check on her. After lifting the sheet and examining her dilated entrance, the nurse told us it was time to start pushing. "I'll grab the doctor. That baby is coming now."

"Thank god," Muse said. "Finally…"

"You've just got to do some pushing and the baby will be here, Muse. Now push hard. It'll be over sooner."

"Alright." She squeezed my hand and got ready.

The doctor came in, pulled on his gloves, and then it began.

I watched Muse do something impossible, push a living person out of her body. She pushed her body to the limit, screaming, crying, and giving all her energy to the effort. Dripping with sweat and exhausted, she had times when she wanted to stop, but she didn't. She kept going, determined to get our baby out.

"The baby's crowning," the doctor said. "Just a few more pushes."

When Muse knew she was almost done, she pushed even harder. She gave it her all and pushed until our baby was finally out.

When I heard the baby cry, I finally felt relief. High-pitched and loud, the cries echoed off the walls of the hospital room, but it was also the most beautiful noise I'd ever heard in my life. Muse sat up to see the baby for the first time, to see the life she grew with her body.

The doctor held up the baby, using both hands to hold the small person wiggling around in his arms. "Congratulations. You have a son."

"Oh my god…" Muse covered her cheeks with her palms as the tears emerged. "We have a boy."

I stared at the little person in the doctor's arms, the boy who was screaming at the top of his lungs because he'd been ripped from the warmth of his mother into the cold world. All I wanted to do was protect him, to wrap him in my arms and give him the comfort he craved. I was shocked to see my son for the first time, to realize I would be a father to a son. My father raised me to be a man, and now I would do the same for him.

The nurse cleaned off our son and wrapped him in a warm blanket before she approached us. More than anything, I wanted to take that baby from her arms and cradle him against my chest, the same thing I did to Muse when she was scared. But I knew Muse deserved to be the first one to hold our son, after everything she'd just been through to bring him into this world.

The nurse slipped him into her arms, and immediately, he stopped crying.

I couldn't believe it.

Muse looked into our son's face, crying even harder as she saw him up close. "He stopped crying…"

"Because he knows who you are." I placed my hand underneath her arm, helping her support our boy. He hadn't opened his eyes yet, taking his time as he got used to this new world he'd just been pushed into. With his little fingers and little toes, it was hard to believe he would grow into a man my size someday. I imagined my parents experiencing this same moment with me, holding me in their arms, not knowing I would grow to over six feet tall.

Muse kissed his forehead, her tears leaving her chin and landing on his face.

That's when he opened his eyes. His green eyes.

He looked right at me, staring at me like he wasn't sure what he was seeing.

"He has your eyes…" Muse continued to cry, entranced by our son the way I was.

I looked into those eyes, seeing my own genes staring back at me. I inherited my eyes from my father, as did Vanessa. That tradition seemed to keep going with my son. He possessed the Barsetti green eyes.

That was when this all felt real.

This was my son. And I was his father.

EIGHT

Vanessa

I was sitting in the waiting room with my parents, waiting for the delivery to be over. I was anxious to meet my niece or nephew, the first member of the next generation. My parents would be grandparents, and the entire family was excited for the new addition.

I only wished Bones were here to share the moment with me.

Because this new baby would be his niece or nephew too.

I didn't know when he would ask to marry me, and it really didn't matter when that time came. Even if he never asked me, that would still be fine. I would always see him as the man I'd spend my life with. Even if we were husband and wife, it didn't do our connection justice. It was even deeper than matrimony.

My phone rang, and Max's name appeared on the screen.

I was sitting next to my father, and I answered the call instantly as I stepped away to take it. "Hey, is Griffin okay?" Max usually called me to check in, so I shouldn't assume there was any bad news to share. But I'd been waiting for this stupid mission to end—once and for all.

"Yes. He's totally fine. But we did have a bit of a hiccup in our planning. The target isn't where we thought he was going to be, so we had to go with a new plan. So he'll be gone an extra day."

I had to wait a whole extra day for him to come back? "But he's fine, right? Nothing has happened to him?"

"Vanessa, he's fine," he said with a sigh, as if Bones had warned him I would behave this way. "I just wanted to let you know so you wouldn't worry when he didn't return home on time."

I crossed my arms over my chest and stared at the checkered tile of the waiting room. "Thanks for letting me know. My stomach is tied up in knots, and there's stitch in my chest every time I breathe."

"I get it. Cynthia goes through this too."

"I'm so glad this is the last one. I can't keep doing this."

"He mentioned this was difficult for you."

I didn't care if everyone thought I was overreacting. Normally, I was a logical person and had a good attitude about a lot of things. But when Bones was gone and there was nothing I could do to help him, it gave

me the worst bout of anxiety. I turned into an overpro-
tective, obsessive girlfriend.

"All I'll say is, Bones is my best guy. I've never seen
him come across something he couldn't handle. To be
honest, it's far more likely that something would happen
to you instead of something happening to him."

That shouldn't make me feel better, but it did.
"Thanks."

"Just relax, Vanessa. He's given up everything for
you. There's nothing that's gonna stop him from
coming back to you."

"I know, Max."

"So, your brother is having a baby, right?"

"As we speak. I'm in the waiting room."

"Well, congratulations. And enjoy this wonderful
time. Don't worry about Bones."

"I'll try…"

"Talk to you later, Vanessa."

"Okay. Bye." I hung up and held the phone in my
hand. I didn't turn back to my parents because I was
still on the verge of tears. Even though Bones was okay,
the idea of waiting an extra day for him to come home
killed me. I couldn't wait for the moment when he
walked into the house with that bag over his shoulder. It
would be over for good—and we would never have to
worry about it again.

"*Tesoro*, everything alright?"

I turned around to see the concerned expression on
my father's face. "Yeah. Max just called and said Griffin

would be gone an extra day. Had to move something around. Didn't really explain why."

Even though today was an exciting day for my father, his face immediately mirrored my own. The sadness crept into his expression, and he moved his hands into his pockets with slumped shoulders. "I'm sorry, *tesoro*."

"I know I shouldn't worry, but it's not hard not to."

"I understand the feeling more than you know." He released a sigh, the corner of his mouth rising in a sarcastic smile. "It's what I've been doing on an almost daily basis since I had the two of you. I constantly worry about everything. Now you know how it feels."

"If this is how it feels, I'm very sorry," I said with a weak chuckle.

"Apology accepted." He moved his hand to my shoulder and gave me a gentle pat. "Don't worry about it, *tesoro*. I've seen that man in action, and there's nothing to worry about. He's not only fast and power-ful, but he's smart. If he can't fight his way out of a situ-ation, he'll think his way out of it."

Except for the time when the men came to his apartment and almost blew his brains out. If I hadn't been there, he would have died. What if that situation happened again? What if I wasn't there to help him? "I know you're probably right…but my heart isn't going to slow down until he comes back. He promised me this would be the last time. I know he keeps his promises."

"He will, *tesoro*. He'll come back."

"I just have this feeling in the back of my mind that something's wrong."

"What do you mean?"

"Griffin is always so meticulous with everything. If a plan doesn't work, he takes his time figuring out what to do next. He doesn't just change course without thinking it through. He's not careless."

"You may be overthinking it. Maybe he saw a good opportunity to do something else."

"And what if he didn't…?"

He moved his arm around my shoulders and lowered his voice. "This is my advice. Don't worry about something until there's something to worry about. If Max says he's fine, then let it go. If you get a phone call that says otherwise, then start to panic."

It was another life lesson my father taught. "Alright."

He rubbed my back before he released me. "Do you think it's a boy or a girl?"

"I don't know…what did you want when you had Conway?"

"A boy," he said immediately.

I raised an eyebrow, offended by the answer. "You said that pretty fast."

He grinned and placed his hands in his pockets. "I wanted a boy because I was so protective of your mother. Imagine having a young, beautiful version of her running around. It was a scary thought. But then you came…and you were stronger and smarter than your brother. I raised you to be tough and fearless, and that's what I got. I never had to worry about you, *tesoro*. I thought having a daughter would kill me, but it was the best thing that ever happened to me. You have good instincts…and make good decisions."

My father's approval meant the world to me. His words made me feel warm inside, made my confidence grow even more. I always wanted to be strong like my mother and wise like my father. It seemed like I'd accomplished those things.

We moved back to the chairs, and I sat beside my mom.

"Everything alright?" she asked, her hand moving to my thigh.

"Yeah, just worried about Griffin," I said.

"You don't need to worry about him," Mama said. "He's a capable young man."

"Yeah, that's what Father said."

"And you should listen to him." Mama pulled her hand away and looked at the TV in the waiting room. "He knows a thing or two." She glanced at her watch then sighed. "She's been in labor a long time…hope everything is alright."

"Everything is fine," Father said. "Sapphire is a Barsetti. She's got this."

I smiled, loving the way my father accepted Sapphire so easily. She'd become a member of our family before she took the Barsetti name. I wished he'd been as accepting toward Griffin, but I'd made my peace with the past.

The nurse finally came into the waiting room.

All the Barsettis stood up, taking up half the waiting room with our numbers alone.

My father moved forward. "Everything went alright? Is Sapphire okay?"

"She's more than okay," the nurse said. "She gave birth to a son about twenty minutes ago. They've been spending some time with him, but they would like to see the rest of you. Just a few people at a time."

"A boy?" my father blurted.

Mama moved into Father and hugged him tightly, her face against his chest. "We have a grandson…"

My father hugged her back, his chin resting on her head. "We do, Button. Can't wait to see him."

I watched my parents, my eyes getting slightly teary. My parents still loved each other after all these years, and I knew Bones and I would be that way too. He hadn't wanted children until I told him it was a requirement if he wanted to be with me, but I had no doubt he would be a good father…just like my father. "I have a nephew."

Father kissed Mama on the forehead before he released her. "Let's meet him."

Uncle Cane and Aunt Adelina remained behind with Carter and Carmen so we could go inside first. We walked into the hospital room, seeing Sapphire sit up in her bed with the baby in her arms. She didn't look like she'd just given birth. There wasn't any sweat on her forehead, and her hair was done. And she smiled brighter than the sun as she looked down at her son.

"Oh my god…" I approached the bed, unable to believe that the new Barsetti was really there. I moved into my brother's side and hugged him hard, sharing a rare moment of affection with the man I usually teased.

He hugged me back. "Sis, I'd like you meet your nephew."

I stared at the little baby in her arms, seeing the slightly tanned skin and the beautiful features of a baby boy. When he opened his eyes, I saw the startling green color I possessed. "He has your eyes."

Mama and Father moved to the other side of the bed to get a good look. Mama immediately sniffled as the tears watered in her gaze. She covered her mouth with her hand, stifling the emotion that took over her body.

Father kept his arm around her, maintaining a stoic expression but visibly touched by the newest member of the family. "He's so beautiful, Sapphire. He has Barsetti eyes."

Sapphire turned her torso so she could hand the baby off to my father. "Here. Meet your grandson."

"I'd love to. But I think his grandma should go first." Father stepped aside so Mama could scoop her arms underneath him and pull him to her chest. She held him close, and when she felt him in her arms, she started to cry harder.

My mother hardly ever cried, and right now, those tears seemed to be of joy. "He's perfect…"

The baby was quiet as he stared up at my mother, seeing his grandmother for the first time.

Father kept his arm around her waist, looking into the face of his first grandson. "Do we have a name?"

"Yes," Conway said. "Reid. Reid Barsetti."

"Reid…" Mama continued to stare at her grandson. "It's nice to meet you, Reid."

"I like it," Father whispered.

Mama handed Reid over to Father so he could hold him next. Once Father had Reid in his arms, he softened even more. He smiled as he looked at his grandson, displaying emotion just the way he did when he spoke to me. "I love him already."

Conway kept his arm around my shoulders, showing me more affection than usual because he was in a good mood. "Sapphire was amazing. She was in labor for so long, but she got our son out. She was a badass."

Sapphire shook her head. "Stop it…I was so scared."

"I was scared too," Mama said. "Childbirth isn't easy."

"And now we have an amazing son," Conway said proudly. "He's perfect. Healthy. Beautiful." He took a deep breath and sighed, his joy palpable.

"I'm happy for you, Conway," I said. "It's the happiest day of your life."

"Yeah, it is." He looked down at his wife. "No offense, honey."

She smiled. "None taken."

My father walked around the bed and handed Reid to me. "Here's your aunt."

I scooped him into my arms and looked into the face I would love for the rest of my life. My nephew was perfect. With a beautiful face and gorgeous eyes, he was an adorable baby. "He's so cute." He stared at me like he was just as fascinated with me as I was with him. "I can't wait to spoil you and piss off your father."

"Be careful," Conway warned. "Because when you have kids, I'll get my revenge."

The thought of kids made me think of Bones, who couldn't be here to share this moment. "Griffin had to work…"

Conway patted my back. "That's okay. The two of you will come by the house when he's back, and you can spend the whole day with him. I'm sure Reid would love to meet his uncle."

I smiled at the way my brother included the man I loved, even though he wasn't my husband. "Thanks."

We spent the next while passing Reid around, taking turns holding him. When an hour passed, Father looked at the clock. "We would love to stay, but I know your uncle is anxious to meet the new Barsetti too. We'll be in the waiting room. How long will you guys be staying?"

"Until tomorrow morning," Conway answered.

"Alright," Father said. "We'll make the final arrangements for the baby's arrival at home."

"Thanks," Conway said. "We appreciate it." He hugged all of us and then shared a special moment with our father. "Thanks for everything, Father. Now that I have a son, it really hit me how much you've done for me...how much you love me."

Father cupped the back of his head and kissed him on the forehead. "I know, son. As your love grows every single day, you'll understand it more and more."

NINE

Bones

———————

I stayed in the mountain overnight, feeling the freezing temperatures as the night deepened. If my muscles weren't so thick, I could have been in serious danger. Max continued to talk in my ear every few hours, assuring me there was no one approaching me through the satellite feed.

I had a lot of time to sit there and think. And of course, I thought about Vanessa.

I wasn't in any serious danger, but if she knew what was going on right now, it would kill her. I felt like shit for putting myself in this situation, for risking what we had for money. My loyalty to Max had trapped me in the situation, but that didn't change anything. It was still horrible. I was sitting in the mountains surrounded by snow, and I was waiting until the following evening to finally make my escape.

When I came clean about it, she would kill me.

The hours passed until morning arrived. I stayed hydrated and snacked on the emergency food supply I'd brought. It was nothing but protein bars, not nearly enough to fuel my size, but it was all I had.

That night, Max spoke in my ear. "Chopper is moving in."

"What about the men?"

"They've pulled back. They searched the mountain and the path to the town square, but they started to disperse when nothing happened. Since the chopper can't get to your location, you need to move down to the flat surface."

"Got it." I packed up my gear and moved out, taking the quickest way down to the flat section of land. I wanted to get out of there as quickly as possible, to end this final mission and put it behind me. I wanted my money and my retirement. "I'm in position."

"Alright." Max was quiet for a minute while he worked with the pilot.

Ten minutes later, I heard the sound of the rotors. All the lights were off, making it impossible to see. It could only be heard if you were close enough. The wind swept through my hair as the chopper landed on the sand, and once it was on the ground, I hopped inside.

The chopper rose into the air and flew away. The lights from the square were noticeable from this height, and as I watched the country slowly disappear, my heart rate started to slow down. I'd never been scared during a mission. I didn't fear death or pain.

But I feared Vanessa.

That mission didn't go as smoothly as all the others. On top of that, I lied to her.

I fucking lied.

But I didn't have any other choice. If I'd told her the truth, she would have had a serious breakdown. Max told me Sapphire went into labor, and I couldn't ruin this beautiful time in Vanessa's life. I knew I'd made the right decision.

But she would tear into me anyway...as she should.

I put the headset on and relaxed when the sight of Morocco was no longer visible. Max spoke in my ear. "You alright, man?"

"I'm fine."

"Need any medical attention or anything? Dehydrated?"

"I'm fine," I repeated. "Just get me home. Tell Vanessa I'm on my way."

I REFUELED my body on the plane, eating the enormous meal I bought at the airport. I drank water by the gallon, and after a few hours, I started to feel better. I slept the rest of the way, finally relaxing after four days in Morocco.

When the plane touched down on the ground, it

was a bumpy entry, and the movement stirred me from sleep. I wiped the sleep from my eyes and felt the relief circulate in my bloodstream. I was officially back in Florence.

I got off the plane, grabbed my bag at the terminal, and finally drove home.

Vanessa would be there. Max gave her my flight information, and even though she had a new nephew to visit, she wouldn't miss seeing me when I walked through the door. She would drop everything to see me, to make sure there weren't any bullet holes in my flesh.

I parked my truck at the curb then took the stairs to the small apartment I shared with her. The sun had just gone down, but the late summer heat was undeniable. The front door wasn't locked, so I stepped inside.

She was standing there, waiting for me. She was my t-shirt with puffy eyes, her hair stretched down her chest. She didn't look happy to see me, just emotional that the turmoil was finally over. "Thank god…" She moved into my chest and hugged me, her face resting against my beating heart. "It's over… I'm so happy it's over."

I rubbed her back while my chin rested on the top of her head. "Me too."

"Never again?" she whispered.

"Never."

"Promise me?"

"I promise, baby. Never." Even if Max asked again, I would deny him. I finished my term because he asked, but we were even now. After what happened in Morocco, I could never do this to Vanessa again. I had no regrets about my decision. Work used to be my life, but now this woman was my life. I would gladly give it up to make her happy. "It's over now. You never have to worry about it again. I'll sleep by your side every single night as long as we live. I'm ready to give you the quiet life I promised."

She stayed against me, clinging to the moment like she never wanted it to escape. She must be feeling so many things at once, relief as well as joy. She kept her hands around my waist and rested against me, using me as a crutch to support herself. She didn't need me for anything, and that made her love even more pure. She loved me because she wanted to, because she had to.

I gave her all the time she needed to let the past go. She was probably still resentful she had to go through that turmoil for so long. It must be difficult to accept the fact that it was truly over, that it would never return again.

My hand moved into the hair at the nape of her neck, and I gently caressed her, my fingers tinging once I embraced my woman. Being on that cold mountain made me long for her even more, long for the bed we shared together. I warmed the sheets throughout the night, and she hugged me like I was her favorite teddy bear.

When she was finally ready, she lifted her gaze to look at me. "You're right…it's over. It's us now. At last."

"Yes." I leaned down and kissed her on the forehead. My lips burned the second I felt her, and the guilt inside my chest started to boil. My moral compass had never pointed north, but lying had always been something I despised. It stripped my credibility as a man. A man who lied wasn't a man at all, because he feared the consequences of his actions. That wasn't me. I could look her father in the eye and tell him things he didn't want to hear. But that was still better than pretending to be something I wasn't.

"My brother had his baby. He's so—"

"I have to tell you something. I want to get it over with before we change the subject."

She stilled at the interruption and slowly backed up. "Okay…what is it?" She pulled away and crossed her arms over her chest.

I hated the instant she moved away from me. I hated the space between us, the divide that kept us apart. It just made me want to get this over with even more. "I lied to you."

Her eyes widened in surprise.

"I did it because I had to. But I promise you, I'll never do it again."

"What did you lie about?" Her voice turned firm, her hostility slowly rising.

"The reason why I stayed in Morocco an extra day was because something went wrong."

She immediately started to breathe hard, the terror moving into her gaze. Her hand moved over her chest, like she was massaging away a dull pain that formed in her heart.

"I took out the target, but his son caught me. He set the alarm, and I had to run. There were too many men on my tail, and Max couldn't evacuate me. I ditched the car in the mountains then moved on foot. I hiked to a place where they couldn't find me and waited it out. I was there for about twenty-four hours, waiting for the men to move their search elsewhere. That's when Max sent the chopper and got me out of there."

She rubbed her chest, her eyes filled with pain.

"I told Max not to tell you the truth at the time because it would destroy you. There was nothing you could do to help me, and there was no point in worrying. I wasn't in any serious danger. I just had to be patient before I made my move. I was cautious on purpose. If I didn't have you, I probably would have had the chopper pick me up right away. But I took my time, knowing I couldn't take any chances."

She covered her face with her palms, sighed, and then dragged them down her face. "Not take any chances, huh?" Her cold sarcasm filled the apartment. "A bit ironic…since every time you leave, you're taking a chance."

I knew she would be pissed. But there was nothing I could do about it except face it like a man. "It's over, Vanessa. That was the last one."

"Like I said, all it takes is one time, and you're dead."

"But I'm not dead, baby. I'm home—right now."

She crossed her arms over her chest again. "I can't believe you lied to me. You told me you never lie."

"I know…I didn't feel good about it."

"Oh, that makes it better," she hissed.

I knew she wasn't really angry about the lie, just the fact that I was ever compromised. "Baby, let it go."

"You could have died!"

"I wasn't anywhere close to that. There was just a bump in the road. Big difference."

She threw her arms down. "Shut up, Griffin."

My eyes narrowed. "I'm gonna let that comment go because of the context. But don't ever tell me to shut up again. I love you, baby. But I don't put up with shit from anyone—including you."

She averted her gaze, taking my words to heart.

"I'm sorry that I lied. I didn't know what else to do."

She tucked her hair behind her ear, her breathing still rapid. "I know…"

"I never want to lie, especially to you. It's not who I am. I never want to be that kind of man. I despise those kinds of men. But I had to protect you. Your nephew was just born, and I didn't want to distract you from that, especially when there was nothing you could do anyway."

"My father could have helped you."

"And I would rather die than accept his help."

Her eyes flashed in pain.

"Because I would never want you to risk losing your father. I'm not worth it."

"Griffin…"

"Can we put this behind us?" I said quietly. "I won't lie again."

"I know you won't."

"Then you forgive me?"

She rolled her eyes. "Griffin, you don't even need to ask that. I'm sorry I'm acting this way right now. I just…want you safe. I want you home. I just…it kills me inside. Everything is over now, so I need to let it go… put it behind us."

"I agree."

She raised her gaze and looked at me, her eyes watering with emotion. "Let's forget it."

I knew she would forgive me. She knew I wasn't a liar. My decision to mislead her didn't change her opinion of me. Now, those green eyes were on me, the gateways to her beautiful soul. Now that I was home, I didn't care about the mission I'd just completed or the money wired into my account. It was the last time I would walk through the door from work. That part of my life was officially over. "It's forgotten." My hands were in her hair next, and my mouth was on hers.

Her slender hands wrapped around my wrists, and she gripped me as I kissed her, breathing into my mouth with arousal. She gave me her tongue first, her nails slowly digging deeper into me.

I didn't bother carrying her down the hall to the

bedroom. Instead, I pushed her thong over her luscious ass until it fell down her slender thighs and hit the floor. Once my jeans and boxers were pushed past my balls, I lifted her into my arms and pressed her against the wall. My large hands gripped her ass cheeks, and I angled her against the wall so I could shove myself inside her.

Her arms wrapped around my neck, and she pulled her knees against her chest, folding her body closer so I could fit deeper inside her. Her face was level with mine, and she held my gaze as I started to thrust into her. "Griffin…"

I was buried between her legs, exactly where I should be. Her pussy was warm after the freezing cold of the mountain, so slick and wet that my cock was surrounded by my woman's desire. There was no place I'd rather be, no other woman I would rather be fucking. We were connected at all times, but when I was deep inside her, it was a different story. Our hearts beat as one, and our souls intertwined. Love was a myth until I met this woman, and now it looked me in the face every single day. Full of passion, loyalty, and trust, we had something no one else could comprehend. We beat the odds to be together, made endless sacrifices so we could have this for the rest of our lives. I'd been shot a dozen times, but I had far more scars from keeping this relationship together.

But it was all worth it.

I SLEPT in that morning because I was exhausted from the mission I'd completed. It was almost nine when I opened my eyes, on my back with Vanessa pressed into my side. Her arm rested across my hard stomach, and her sexy leg was tucked between mine. She must have been exhausted too, unable to sleep while I'd been away.

I ran my fingers through my hair then wiped the sleep from my eyes as I took in the morning light that filtered through the bedroom. It heated the room, lifting it several degrees as the summer sun rose higher in the sky.

Vanessa must have already been awake because she sat up when she knew I wasn't asleep anymore. Her hair was pulled over one shoulder, and when she woke up first thing in the morning, she was even more beautiful than usual. Her eyes glowed a little brighter after a full night of rest, and the olive skin of her face seemed more relaxed. As she slowly moved on top of me, the sheets fell, showing her perky tits and endless curves.

I lay back and enjoyed it.

She straddled my hips then pressed her palms against my chest for balance. "Now it's time for you to give me morning sex."

My hands moved to her tits, and I groped them as she sat on top of me, her lovely figure looking perfect in the morning light. My thumbs flicked over her nipples, and my cock twitched when I felt her. "I'm all yours, baby." The only reason why I fucked her every morning when she was barely awake was because I needed her. Had to have her in order to function normally. How could a man lie next to a woman like her every morning and do nothing about it? I got to keep her for the rest of my life, and that was a great perk of monogamy. I could fuck her whenever I wanted—no explanation necessary.

She ground against my length, smearing her slick arousal from my tip to the middle of my shaft. Her body was wet because it was used to getting sex at this time of day every single morning.

My hands gripped her waist, my fingers meeting across her back because she was so petite and my hands were so big. If I pressed my thumbs into her stomach, I could crush her. She was small but not delicate. Even if I were twice her size and ten times her strength, she would still beat me somehow. That's what turned me on about her. She was resourceful and determined.

She lifted herself up and pointed my cock at her entrance. Slowly, she slid down, putting my thickness inside her. It was never easy for me to shove myself inside her with a quick thrust. Her pussy was still tight, still needed a few seconds to prepare for my size. She moaned as she slid all the way down, taking in my most of my length like a real woman.

I wanted to roll her over onto her back and fuck her hard like I did every morning, but I decided to lie still and let her do all the work. If she wanted to fuck me, she was more than welcome.

She pressed her weight into her palms against my

chest and rolled her hips, pulling her pussy down over my length repeatedly. She moaned right away, like she'd been wanting to do this for the past hour. The signs of arousal crept onto her face, and she let her pretty mouth open with the endless moans that came belting out. Her fingers dug into my chest as she fucked me harder, getting off on my fat dick.

I thrust my hips up to meet her cunt, to shove myself inside as she lowered her body at the same time. I could feel her racing heartbeat under my fingertips, feel her sexy muscles shift and flex as she worked hard to fuck me.

Fuck, this felt good.

My hands gripped her tits again, loving the way they shook right in my line of sight. I wanted to come, but I would let her finish first. She deserved a powerful climax after the way she fucked me so good.

She moved her hands to either side of my head, her hair falling down around me. "I love you, Griffin…" Spoken in a whisper but packed with the passion of a lover, it was one of the sexiest things she'd ever said. I was buried deep inside her, feeling her as intimately as possible, and she wanted me there every day for the rest of our lives. This woman could have any man she wanted. All she had to do was flash a smile and snap her fingers, and she could capture all the hearts around her. But I was the only man she wanted, the only man who was good enough for her. I was the only man she wanted to ride like this.

I propped myself up on my elbow so I could be closer to her. My hand moved to her hair, and I cradled her face against mine, feeling that pussy surround me over and over. "I know, baby. I can feel it." I brought her forehead against mine while my fingers continued to stroke the silky strands of hair. The sound of our moving bodies was loud in the room. Her wetness increased, making it echo noisily and turn both of us on even more. There was so much slickness between her legs that it built up around my balls. I listened to her breathing, listened to it grow deeper and heavier. I didn't kiss her because being pressed together like this seemed even more intimate. All I wanted to do was feel her, listen to her, and enjoy her.

Her hips bucked against me harder, and she started to scream. "Oh god…" She took my dick harder, pounding it inside her as she drove herself to a climax.

"Yes, baby. Come all over me."

She grabbed on to my shoulder as she finished, breathing in my face and moaning at the same time. "Yes…"

I felt her tighten around me, crushing me with the strength of an anaconda. This pussy was unbelievable, better than anything else I'd ever had. This was the only place I wanted to be for the rest of my life. I never missed the promiscuity of my old life. Why would I, when I had the perfect woman to fuck every single day? "My turn." I sat up and wrapped my arm around her waist, my other hand keeping me propped up. I guided her against me as my mouth moved with hers. When we were pressed together this tightly, I could feel her at a much deeper angle. My full length was buried inside, covered in the come she just gave me. She was tighter than before, her climax making her cunt constrict more profoundly. Every time I came inside her, the same look of pleasure entered her gaze. She got off on my orgasms, loved watching me dump my come inside her. "Here it comes, baby."

"Give it to me." Her arms hooked around my neck, and she breathed unevenly, her pussy so slick and warm. Her soft flesh was perfect against my dick, the home I never wanted to leave.

I pumped inside her three more times before I hit my trigger. I burst, dumping mounds of come deep inside that gorgeous pussy. I kept thrusting hard, moaning under my breath and digging my fingers into her skin. "Fuck…" I never got tired of this, never got tired of enjoying this woman. "Baby." My lips moved to the corner of her mouth, and I kissed her, enjoying the aftershocks of my climax. I put my come exactly where it belonged—deep inside my woman. I moved my face in between her tits, loving the trickle of sweat that formed there. For a petite woman, she had a sexy bust. Her tits weren't big, but they were perfect. I licked the sweat away then felt her heartbeat against my mouth. Her body didn't just belong to me, but her heart and soul as well. I had all of her because I earned her.

She rested her face in my neck, hugging me as she

felt my cock soften inside her. "I want you again." She spoke against my ear, her gentle voice innately sexy.

I was satisfied, but if my woman wanted something from me, I delivered. "Yes, baby."

I POURED myself a cup of coffee then sat at the kitchen table. It was almost ten, and I was barely getting my day started. This kind of laziness wasn't normal for me, but since I'd spent the last hour fucking my woman, I didn't punish myself for it.

After all, I was officially retired.

Vanessa walked into the room wearing the shirt I had on the night before. It moved past her ass and almost touched her knees. "You want me to make you something?" She poured herself a cup of coffee.

"Define make." I drank my coffee, looking over the mug to stare at her.

"As in, pour some cereal into a bowl and add a splash of milk."

I couldn't eat that shit, complex carbs along with all the sugars in the milk. "That's not making anything." I liked to tease her. If I got her angry enough, we ended up having sex right on the kitchen table.

"It is to me." She pulled a bowl out of the cupboard. "So, do you want some or what?"

"Do I ever eat cereal?"

"No. But if you want me to make you breakfast, you'll have to compromise."

"That's a compromise I'll never make." It didn't matter to me that Vanessa couldn't cook. I wasn't in love with her because of the food she made. I was in love with her because of her other extraordinary qualities, like the fact that she shot me without hesitation. Those were the traits I cared about. But it would be nice if she made something once in a while. "What are you going to make our kids?"

She'd just finished pouring the milk into the bowl when she paused. "Our kids?"

"Yes. Our kids."

She turned to me, the emotion in her eyes.

"What did I say?" She'd said she wanted kids. This shouldn't be surprising.

"I just…never heard you say that before." She carried the bowl to the table beside me but didn't take a bite.

"I'm officially retired. We can talk about that stuff now." I'd made the sacrifices she'd asked me to make. All of that shit was in the past now. If she wanted to start a family, all she had to do was tell me when. My only job would be to fuck her—which I did anyway.

"I guess we can… So you want to have a family with me?"

I wasn't a patient or compassionate man, but I was a man deeply in love with a woman. "You gave me an ultimatum, Vanessa. I agreed to it."

"But you don't actually want kids?" She watched me hesitantly.

"I want what you want."

Her eyes fell in sadness. "I don't want to make you do something you don't want to do."

"I didn't want to fall in love with you, but that happened anyway. I didn't want to be monogamous with someone, but that happened anyway. I didn't want to be part of the Barsettis, but that happened anyway. All the things I didn't want to happen happened…and I wouldn't change any of it. I'm sure having a family will be the exact same way. It's not something I'm interested in right now, but when that time comes, I'm sure I'll change my mind like all the other times in the past."

The sadness slowly disappeared from her face.

"And like I said, you're going to make cereal for the kids?"

Finally, she smiled, shaking off her sorrow completely. "I guess you're right."

"I'm always right."

"I wouldn't take it that far…" She picked up her spoon and started to eat.

We hadn't done much talking since I came home, so I asked about the obvious event in her life. "How's Conway and Sapphire?"

"Oh yeah." She dropped her spoon back into the bowl. "They had a boy and named him Reid. He's so cute." She pulled up a picture on her phone. It was an image of her holding the baby in her arms. "Look. He has Barsetti eyes."

I looked at the baby in her arms. I didn't care about babies, but he seemed healthy and happy. He was staring at Vanessa, transfixed by his aunt. "Nice."

She pulled the phone away. "Sapphire was in labor for like twelve hours before Reid came. She was so tired. She went home yesterday. But Conway was so happy. I could see it on his face. He was never the fatherly type, and then when his son arrived, he turned into a different person. And my parents are so happy. I haven't seen them this excited in a long time."

"I'm glad everyone is doing well." In situations like this, I didn't know what to say. I'd never known anyone who'd had a kid or been a part of a family like this. It didn't seem like a big deal to me, but it was a big deal to Vanessa, so I had to pretend I cared.

"You have a nephew. I can't wait for you to meet him. I wish you were there…"

I felt guilty for not being by her side when it was important to her, but at least I would never miss anything again. Now I would be by her side every single day. "My nephew?"

"Yeah, of course." She looked at me with surprise. "Whether we're married or not, you're family, Griffin. You're his uncle. Conway said the same thing to me in the hospital. He wished you were there to meet his son."

Her words were jarring because my hatred for the Barsettis had lasted so long. Now they considered me to be family, making me an uncle to their nephew. I wasn't sure how to process those feelings. I'd only been part of a family for a short time, and it didn't last long enough for me to really remember it.

Vanessa continued to watch me, as if she could read my thoughts like they were words that appeared on my face. "Yes, Griffin. You're an uncle." She turned back to her cereal, which had gotten mushy since she'd spent so much time talking to me. She probably looked the other way to give me a moment to process my thoughts.

I went back to drinking my coffee when my phone rang. If it was Max, I didn't want to talk about the business anymore since I was no longer a part of the group. I just got home and wanted to devote all my time to Vanessa since I'd left her for four days. I fished the phone out of my pocket and saw Crow's name.

I answered. "Crow, what's up?" I used to answer his calls with silence, but since I'd dropped our feud, I spoke to him like a normal person. Letting go of my hate helped me relax. It took a lot more work to hate someone rather than to just accept them.

"I know you got in late last night. Just wanted to see how you were doing. Everything good?"

Was he calling to check up on me? When my eyes darted to Vanessa's face, she was grinning so wide, like she couldn't control it. "Yeah, everything's fine. Why?"

"Vanessa told me you had to stay an extra day. Just wanted to make sure everything was okay."

I'd never had someone check on me before. It was a

little strange. "Yeah. I did the job then came home." I'd never had anyone look over my shoulder. Vanessa was the only one who was obsessed with my well-being.

Vanessa grabbed her phone and wrote a message on it before she pushed it in front of me. *He's checking on you the way he checks on me.*

I read the words and finally understood what was happening.

"Take any damage?" Crow asked.

"Not a scratch. Just a little tired."

"I can imagine. Conway and Sapphire are staying with us for a while until the house is ready and they've recuperated. The two of you should come by and see Reid. Conway and Sapphire really want you to meet him."

A lifetime of loneliness and solitude had hardened my heart so much that it was still difficult to thaw. Vanessa was my first love, my first passion in life. She showed me all the things I'd been missing, giving me the life I used to envy. I'd hated her because she had everything that should have been mine, but despite what I'd done to her, she was willing to share it with me. "I'll talk to Vanessa about it."

"Great. So, how does retirement feel?"

"Not sure yet. I'm too young to retire."

"I agree. I have a proposition for you. We'll talk about it when you come by."

I wanted to reject his idea right away, but since I was working on my manners, I let it be. "Alright."

"Tell my daughter hi for me."

"I will."

He hung up.

I put the phone down, surprised I'd just had a normal conversation with Crow. He was a man I'd despised for a long time. Now he was a strange mixture of a friend and my girlfriend's father.

"So, you want to drive out there?" Vanessa asked, having heard every single word of the conversation.

I wanted to spend the day with her, preferably in bed. But when I saw her eyes light up in excitement at the thought of both of us visiting her family, I didn't put up a fight. I could be selfish, but with Vanessa, I didn't want to be. "Sure."

"Great. I bought Reid this cute little outfit, and I want to give it to him. He's too small to wear it right now, but in a few months, it'll fit him perfectly." She carried the half-eaten bowl to the sink and left it sitting there. "I'm so excited."

I watched her move around the kitchen, her happiness infectious. I'd traded in my dangerous lifestyle for a simple one in Florence. My days would be filled with the Barsettis, but since that made Vanessa so happy, it didn't sound so bad.

Not at all.

WE WALKED in the door and were greeted by her parents.

It was the first time I'd set foot inside that house since I forgave Crow. It had been impossible for me to sit through dinner when I kept thinking about that shotgun pointed at me. But now it was a new beginning, a clean slate.

I had to forget all that stuff.

Pearl hugged me before she kissed me on the cheek. "How are you, honey? So glad you're home—for good this time." Pearl gave me her motherly affection, looking at me with love and treating me like a son. She was the person who had suffered the most in this family, and it was remarkable that she could welcome me so easily. She must see my father when she looked into my face…sometimes.

"I'm glad to be home too. So is Vanessa."

Pearl squeezed my arms affectionately before she let me go. "I hated seeing my daughter go through that. I can't count the number of times my husband left me to go fight some war. I'm happy to know that's over for good. It means a lot to both of us that you made that sacrifice."

"It's my job to protect her. How can I do that when I'm somewhere else?" I was never worried about not coming home. But now I was worried about leaving my woman unguarded. If I wanted to be her husband, she would have to be my first priority. I couldn't have it both ways.

"Excellent point." She smiled and stepped aside so Crow could greet me.

He skipped the handshake and embraced me the way he embraced Conway—minus the kiss on the forehead. "It's good to see you, Griffin. You look well. No gunshot wounds anywhere." He patted my shoulder as he stepped back. "That's always a good sign."

"Yes, Mr. Barsetti."

Crow flinched at the use of the name, as did Pearl. His eyes softened at the sign of respect I gave him. "Call me Crow. Please." He patted me on the back, embracing me as a father embraced his son.

Vanessa had tears in her eyes. The second she blinked, they dripped down her cheeks. She quickly wiped them away, but not quick enough for us not to notice the emotional moment she was experiencing.

Her parents didn't greet her the way they greeted me and chose to dismiss themselves from the entryway, giving her a moment to compose herself.

I stared at her, watching her combat the emotion that she couldn't resist. Since this was her parents' house, I wanted to refrain from my usual affection because it seemed inappropriate, but then I remembered I'd never cared before. I'd always been transparent about my feelings and thoughts. I was easy to read, like an open book. "Baby." I moved into her and cupped her cheeks so I could focus her stare on mine. Over a foot shorter than me, she was tiny in comparison to my size, but all woman just the same. I kept her gaze on me, knowing my expression would calm her in a way nothing else could.

"I'm sorry… I've wanted this for so long."

"I know." I wiped away her tears with the pads of my thumbs.

"I never thought it would happen."

"It did happen. You should be happy, not sad."

"I am happy…" When she took a deep breath, she stopped the tears that pooled in her eyes. "Ever since I was a little girl, I imagined bringing my future husband to meet my family. I imagined him being close with my father, having their own relationship. My father is my best friend…and I wanted my future husband to be my father's best friend too. For so long it didn't seem possible. But now…" Her voice broke, and she didn't finish what she was saying.

Now I felt guilty for hating her father for so long. I should have given this to her a long time ago. "I don't know about the best friend part, but I respect your father. I respect him for raising you. Where would I be if he hadn't done that? Where would I be if I didn't have you?" I pressed my forehead to hers and closed my eyes, treasuring the single most important thing in the world.

"Griffin…"

The only time I'd ever shed tears was when I walked away from Vanessa. I'd kissed her goodbye and left the house, knowing I would lose her forever. Every step I took put the distance between us, and that made the tears grow bigger and bigger. It was the only instance in my adult life when I felt something so strong that it broke through my callous soul. I felt something similar now, but fainter. "Look at me." I opened my eyes and stared at her face, seeing the way she kept her eyes closed as I held her.

She opened her eyes, the surface of those green gems still shiny.

"We have everything we want now, baby. Be happy."

"I am happy…that's the problem." She chuckled and blinked her eyes quickly, trying to dispel the moisture.

I kissed the corner of each eye, getting the salt on my tongue. "Let's visit your nephew now." My hand cupped her cheek, my fingers reaching into her hairline. There was something arousing about comforting her, taking care of her. I'd never loved someone so much, not like this. I loved my boys and I loved my mother, but this was different. I'd trade my life for hers in a heart-beat—without even thinking about it. Her tears were my tears. Her pain was my pain.

"Okay."

I kissed her on the mouth, a simple kiss that was soft and sensual.

When she pulled away, she rubbed her nose against mine. "I love you."

I moved my lips to her forehead and kissed her, embracing her in a way I never embraced any other woman. "I love you." My arm moved around her waist, and I guided her to the sitting room near the back of the house.

When we stepped inside, Sapphire was comfortable on the couch, wearing a long dress that was loose around her stomach. Her hair was pulled back, and she looked exhausted, like motherhood was just as hard as people described. But she also glowed even though she was no longer pregnant. She watched Conway cradle their son in a single arm, Reid wrapped up in a blue blanket. A quiet coo came from the bundle, and a small hand rose to reach for Conway's face.

Sapphire smiled. "He loves you already, Con."

"He does," Conway said in agreement. "But he loves you more...and I'm okay with it."

Carter turned to me first. "Hey, man. Glad you're back." He greeted me with a handshake, behaving like I hadn't just helped him pull off a crazy stunt. Together, we found a corpse to replace Mia so we could get her away from Egor. No big deal.

"Thanks." I shook his hand firmly before I turned to Carmen. I considered giving her a one-armed hug, but since her father was there, I just gave her a gentle pat on the shoulder. "How are you, Carmen?"

She made a disgusted face. "What the hell was that?"

"What?" I asked, dead serious.

"This weird thing..." She patted me on the

shoulder awkwardly. "Come on, you can do better than that."

A restrained grin came across my face.

She moved in and hugged me, squeezing me hard like we were family. She hugged me when we saw each other in Florence, but since her father wasn't watching every little move I made at those times, I was a lot more comfortable. Things were going really well with the Barsetti family, and I didn't want to cross a line and fuck everything up again. "This is how you hug family, Griffin. Learn from your mistake."

I chuckled. "Alright, I will." Carmen was still my favorite Barsetti. Her blunt candor was refreshing. When she smiled, it was sincere. She talked to me like a friend when she didn't even know me. She was the only Barsetti to give me a real chance, to trust Vanessa's instincts and accept me.

Cane came next. A guilty look was in his eyes, like he knew that whole charade was because of him. "Heard everything went well. Glad you're back home." He gave me a one-armed hug then patted me on the back. "My daughter tells me you walk her home all the time?"

After we went out for drinks or dinner, I always did. "Yeah."

Cane gave me a look of gratitude—and remorse. "Thanks, man. That means a lot to me."

"She doesn't need me to walk her home," I said in Carmen's defense. "I just do it because I like her."

Carmen nodded in approval. "And that's why I let you." She turned her angry look on her father. "I told you that you were wrong about him. I'm always right, but you never admit it."

Cane sidestepped the comment by bringing his wife over. "I don't think the two of you have properly met. This is my wife, Adelina."

Adelina hugged me right away. She was beautiful like her daughter, with soft brown hair and pretty eyes. She smiled when she greeted me, reminding me of Pearl. "Nice to meet you, Griffin."

"You too," I answered.

Conway rose to his feet then came toward me, his son cradled in his arms. "Reid, it's time for you to meet your uncle Griffin." He turned his arms toward me so I could get a good look at the baby's face.

The green eyes were apparent, the same ones that Vanessa had. With olive skin like the rest of the Barsettis, Reid seemed to follow in his family's footsteps right away. He was quiet, kicking his feet gently as he stared at me in fascination.

Conway prepared to hand him over to me. "Here, hold him."

I'd never held a baby in my life, and I didn't want to do it now. "No."

Conway stilled at my harshness; everyone did.

It was touching that Conway trusted me enough to hold his son, so I knew I had to backpedal. "I've just never held a baby before…"

"Neither had I," Conway said. "Let me show you."

"No," I repeated, stepping back.

Vanessa turned her look on me. "Griffin, just hold your nephew." She looked at me with annoyance, not letting me get my way this time. "You're making it a bigger deal than it needs to be."

"This is someone's kid, Vanessa."

"No," she hissed. "This is your nephew. Now, suck it up and do it."

I looked around at her entire family, who were all patiently waiting for me to do what she asked. Maybe I was the one overreacting, but holding a kid seemed like a terrifying burden. I didn't want to drop him or do something wrong. My livelihood depended on me being careful, shooting with perfect aim and getting myself out of difficult situations. Holding a child shouldn't be hard. "Alright."

Conway moved Reid into my arms and pulled away when his son was secure. "I was scared the first time too. But it's not so bad." He pulled away, not the least bit afraid that I would let his son hit the ground.

I stood there with Reid in my arms, the small baby that weighed practically nothing. He looked up at me with his big green eyes, fascinated by my eyes just the way I was fascinated by his. He fit perfectly in the crook of my arm, his length not spanning farther than the length of my forearm. I held Vanessa every day with ease. Not sure why I thought holding a baby would be any different. Now that I was actually doing it, it didn't seem so difficult. All the stress faded away, and the little boy in my arms actually brought me peace.

"Aww," Vanessa whispered beside me. "Two peas in a pod."

Conway turned his back on me and joined his wife on the couch, perfectly comfortable leaving his son across the room with me. He grabbed his wife's shoulders and massaged the tension out of her back, taking care of her once he was done taking care of Reid.

Crow came to my side and looked down into his grandson's face. "Pearl and I have been on night duty, taking care of Reid when he cries. I haven't done that since Vanessa was a baby. It's tiring, but I enjoy it."

"That's nice of you," I said, still looking at Reid.

"He's a bit of a crier. He's usually loud more often than when he's quiet. Seems to like you."

"Not sure why he would."

He patted me on the back. "He feels safe with you, Griffin. As we all do."

———

AFTER WE HAD DINNER TOGETHER, people gathered for drinks in the living room. Everyone took turns holding Reid, and whenever he started to cry, Sapphire would either feed him or Pearl would change him.

Crow pulled me off to the side to speak to me in private. "Let me give you a tour of the house."

It was three floors of luxury, so I was not sure what he wanted to show me. "Alright."

He took me up the stairs to the second floor. "There's mostly spare bedrooms here, along with a small gym. When the kids were young, this was their territory. Lars's old bedroom was down this hallway too. He's on the first floor now since the stairs are a little hard for him."

"He's been working here for a long time."

"He's been in the family since I was born," Crow said proudly. "He started to slow down about a year ago. He does stuff around the house to keep busy, but he relaxes most of the time now."

"That's generous of you to keep him here."

"Generous?" he asked. "He's been a loyal servant to my family since the beginning. Actually, he is family. This is where he belongs." He guided me to an open bedroom door. "I wanted to show you Vanessa's room."

I followed him inside and saw the queen-size bed against the wall. Everything was decorated in tones of champagne pink and white. Classy and elegant, it fit her style perfectly. Her vanity held an old jewelry box, and there was a scarf hanging up on the back of her door. This was where she slept when we spoke on the phone last Christmas. It had been too dark for me to see her surroundings clearly, but now the image was easy to picture. I wasn't sure what Crow wanted me to say about it, so I said nothing.

"From when she was in a crib until she left for

university, this was where she stayed. I watched her grow from a little girl to a very impressive young woman. Now she's a professional success…couldn't be prouder." He walked to the nightstand and picked up a picture frame. "This is the three of us at her first art camp when she was in high school." He showed me the picture, Crow and Pearl on either side of Vanessa. Vanessa was visibly younger, maybe seventeen at the time. She had a spot of paint on her nose and on her apron. She always got paint on her nose, and now I knew it was because she rubbed her nose with her arm when it itched. I only knew that because I watched her all the time. He sighed as he looked at the photo. "She's a dream come true. Even through the difficult times, she was nothing short of lovely. When Pearl was pregnant with her, I was hoping for a boy. I never wanted to raise a girl. And then she came…a fierce spitfire. I knew I didn't have anything to worry about. She's just like her mother, a titan."

I stared at the picture for another moment before he put it back. I wanted to ask why he was showing me things, but I thought that would be rude. Of course, I found all of it interesting. It just seemed like something Vanessa would share with me instead.

"The reason I'm telling you all of this is because…this is what I imagined I would do when a man came to ask for my permission to marry my daughter." He came back to my side, his hands in his pockets. He wasn't the silent and hostile enemy he used to be before. Since we'd buried the hatchet, he'd only shown his vulnerable side to me. Just as he was with the rest of his family, that was how he was with me. "I would want to share these things with him since he's the only other man who will love her as much as I do." He looked out the window into the darkness beyond. "I know she'll always be my daughter, but I know things will be different now. I know I have to let her go…and that revelation has been very difficult for me."

I turned to look at him, to see the pain on his face. "You never have to let her go, Crow. I don't want you to."

"That's nice of you to say…but I understand it can't be the same. And it shouldn't be the same anyway. You're the man replacing me…and she couldn't have picked anyone better."

It was the nicest compliment he'd ever given me. "I haven't asked for your permission yet."

He looked around her bedroom and settled on the painting on the nightstand. He took a deep breath before he spoke. "But I know it's coming." He moved his hand to the center of my back and rested it there. "And I'm happy about it. Really, I am." He patted me before he dropped his arm.

I could feel the pain in his touch, feel a father grieve like he was losing his daughter forever. "Crow, Conway married Sapphire. Now that he has a wife, it seems like he's closer to you than he was before. They moved here to be closer to family—because they want more of you and Pearl."

He didn't say anything, his eyes still on the picture.

"And Vanessa has told me how much she wants to be close to you. It wasn't an ultimatum, but she didn't sugarcoat what she wanted. It was a compromise I was willing to make, to move to Tuscany so we can be ten minutes apart. You say you're losing your daughter… but you aren't. I love her more than anything in this world. There's nothing I wouldn't do for her. But I can share you with her… I want to share her."

He smiled slightly, the emotion in his eyes. "That's very kind of you to say."

"I've never wanted to come between you. I just wanted…to be accepted among you."

"And you are now." He clapped my shoulder again. "You're a Barsetti with a different name."

"Things may be changing, but they will stay the same. You can help us with our kids the way you help Conway. You can be the grandparents who watch them while Vanessa and I are at work. You can be in our lives as much as you want."

He chuckled. "Be careful what you say. You won't be able to get rid of us."

"I knew from the beginning that I would have to share Vanessa with all of you. I'm happy to do that."

He sighed. "You're a good man, Griffin. Truly. And since you mention work…that's what I wanted to talk to you about."

"I'm not sure what I'm going to be doing with my time, but don't worry, I won't be getting into anything remotely illegal. I'll find honest work. I'll just have to find something that interests me. I've accumulated enough wealth over the past decade that I don't need an income anymore. Vanessa will be well taken care of. But I'm too young to stop working. I need to keep busy…or I'll go crazy."

"I couldn't agree more. That's what brings me to my proposition…"

"With all due respect, Crow, I don't need you to find me work." I was capable of finding something on my own. Maybe I would start a business, a gym or a personal training facility. I was in amazing shape, and men would pay a lot of money to have me get them into their prime condition.

"My idea sort of falls under that category, but not quite."

"Then what's your idea?"

"As you know, Conway has his own billion-dollar company that he runs. His wife and children will inherit it someday. Vanessa has her artwork. Carter runs his own car company, and Carmen is a florist. Cane and I always assumed that at least one of our kids would want to take over the winery eventually, but it doesn't seem like that's gonna happen. So…how about you?"

I stared at him with a blank look on my face, unsure what he was asking me, exactly. "I don't know shit about wine, Crow."

"And you can't learn?" He raised an eyebrow. "When Cane and I retire, we don't want to sell it. If it comes down to that, we will. But it's another legacy that can live on after us. It's our dream to hand it down from generation to generation. We really want to keep it in the family, and since you're family…we wondered if you'd be interested."

I kept looking at him, unsure how to respond to the offer. I wasn't even his son, and he was giving me something he'd worked on his entire life. It was incredibly generous. "I don't know…"

"What don't you know about?" he asked, clearly disappointed with my answer. "You walked away from your old life for my daughter. Instead of doing something else to keep busy, be part of this. When you have your own children, you can share it with them. It's more than just a business, it's deep in our blood. Plus, the two of us will spend a lot more time together working side by side. Cane and I aren't planning to retire anytime soon. We've both got at least a decade left in us. But when we start to wind down, it would be nice to know everything is ready to go, that you'll be there to step up."

I still didn't know what to say. When I left the killing business, I figured I would spend the next six months trying to find something entertaining. I didn't ever expect to be given this kind of offer.

"You told me you never wanted to come between my daughter and me. If you work for me, we'll be even closer. I'll see her even more. And more importantly, I'll see you. You know how happy Vanessa would be."

She would probably cry again.

"You're moving to Tuscany anyway, so it won't be a far commute."

"The commute isn't my hesitance."

"Then what is?" he asked, crossing his arms over his chest.

"Maybe you should talk to your kids and Cane's kids first. They should get a say in it."

He nodded. "I already did."

I raised an eyebrow. "They were fine with letting me take over?"

"I told you, they don't want it. They all have their own dreams and pursuits, not that I'm complaining. I'm very proud that Cane's and my kids have all chosen their own path in life. My dream used to be having my son work with me every single day…but that's okay. I couldn't be prouder of who he's become."

That touched me even more, that Conway, Carter, and Carmen were completely fine with letting me take over the family business. They really did see me as family even though I hadn't married Vanessa yet. "I don't know what to say, Crow. Your generosity…leaves me speechless."

"I'm not being generous. You're doing me a favor."

I knew he was lying. He was just saying whatever needed to be said to get me to agree.

"It stays in the family this way. That's what we all

want. Your old profession seemed to be solely based on money. It doesn't seem like you're passionate about anything else."

Except Vanessa.

"So the winery is perfect for you."

"I suppose…"

"If you really aren't interested, there's no hard feelings. But I would like you to seriously consider it."

"If I do, I have a stipulation."

"Let's hear it," Crow said.

"You can't pay me."

He tilted his head slightly, surprised by what I said. "What?"

"I don't want your money. I'll work there for free."

"I don't feel comfortable with that."

"And I don't feel comfortable taking a dime from you. I can take care of Vanessa on my own. I'm not taking her father's money."

He sighed. "That's not how it is—"

"When you and Cane retire, I'll start taking a cut. But not before."

He held my gaze, his arms crossed tightly over his chest. He didn't like that offer at all, but he didn't know how to circumvent it.

"I have no need for money. I own real estate, investments, all kinds of things. Honestly, the last thing I need is money. Vanessa can live out the rest of her life as a queen if she wants to. I worked hard for those earnings, and I'm proud of it—regardless of how I earned it. I'm a self-made man, going from living on the streets to living in mansions. Taking your money would undermine all of that."

He shook his head slightly. "I don't agree with that at all, but I respect your opinion."

"Those are my terms. Take them or leave them."

"So when we retire, you'll start keeping the profits?"

I nodded. "When the two of you are really ready to let it go, then yes. But mainly because that money is Vanessa's. It's her inheritance that I will take care of. And when we have our own children, I'll pass it on to them…from their grandfather."

The second I spoke my last sentence, his eyes watered noticeably. Legacy was obviously important to him, leaving behind something for a future generation. All he wanted was to protect his family, selflessly. "That's exactly what I want."

"Then do we have a deal?" I extended my hand.

He glanced at it before he took it, a soft smile stretching across his lips. "Yes. We have a deal."

TEN

Carter

My family came over for dinner that night, my parents and Carmen.

Mom walked into the house first and squeezed me so hard, she seemed to possess Father's strength. "I've barely stepped inside, and I love it already. The landscaping is beautiful. The ivy on the wall…gorgeous." She pulled back and cupped my cheeks, looking at me with the same fondness in her eyes that was always there. "It's perfect. I don't even need to see anything else."

I chuckled. "Thanks, Mama."

She kissed me on the cheek before she let me go. "But I definitely want a tour anyway."

My father embraced me next, a slight look of disapproval in his eyes. He resented me for lying to my mother—and for bringing him into the lie. "Carter." He patted my back then stepped off to the side.

"Father…"

Carmen came next, wearing a long blue skirt and a ruffled white top. Her hair was in long curls, and her eyelashes were thick with mascara. She always looked like a beauty queen. When we were growing up and she didn't wear makeup, she still had a natural beauty that couldn't be denied. She whistled under her breath as she looked around. "Jesus, this place is fancy. The Queen of England could live here."

"I don't think she would like it very much."

"Because you'd be here?" she teased, wearing an arrogant smirk.

"So glad you're here…"

She chuckled then patted me on the back. "Seriously, I love it. When we pulled up to the gates, I screamed a little bit. And the drive up to the house is like something from a movie. Mama was freaking out the whole time because she was so excited. She might move in."

"Not gonna happen."

I showed them the downstairs living room, the backyard with the pool, and the bedrooms and personal gym on the first floor. I didn't bother taking them up the stairs since it was more of the same. I took them into the kitchen next. "This is the kitchen and dining area." When we stepped inside, Mia was working at the kitchen island in her apron. With her hair pulled back in a nice ponytail, her pretty face was revealed. She wore heels and a blue dress, looking more like a housewife than a maid. Ever since she'd moved in with me, she'd started wearing nice clothes and did her makeup. She didn't seem like a woman who would try to impress a man, so I assumed she did it just because she wanted to. "Good evening, sir. Dinner will be ready shortly."

The second she called me sir, I felt a stir in my pants. Now I associated that title with sex, and it was impossible not to.

"Who's this?" Mom asked, approaching Mia at the island. "And what smells so good?"

Mia quickly washed her hands before she shook hands with my mother. "Mrs. Barsetti, it's a pleasure to meet you. I'm Carter's maid." Her eyes focused on my mother's features, probably looking for the similarities I shared with her. Mia wore a pretty smile, and the makeup on her face made her glow even brighter than usual. Instead of looking like the help, she looked like a supermodel working in my kitchen. "I hope you're hungry. Carter asked me to make his favorite dish."

Mom was slightly startled by Mia, staring at her like she couldn't believe that my maid was so beautiful. She finished the handshake before she recovered. "I could eat lasagna any time."

"Damn, you're hot." Carmen, the big mouth of the family, blurted out those words without thinking twice about it.

I rolled my eyes. "Carmen, come on."

"What?" Carmen said innocently. "She is. Look at her. Can I borrow that dress?"

Mia's cheeks blushed slightly, and she smiled in a way I'd never seen before, like she was actually uncomfortable. She always kept her composure around me, even when I was the bad guy. "Yeah, sure. We look about the same size."

Carmen walked up to her and greeted her with a hug. "I can't believe my brother has a maid. I guess that's a good thing because he didn't know how to do his own laundry until he was twenty."

"Carmen." I wrapped my arm around my sister's shoulders and slowly steered her away from Mia. "Why don't you go set the table?" I gave her a gentle push, getting her out of the kitchen and away from Mia.

Mia smiled, like she didn't seem bothered with the conversation. "Nice to see you again, Mr. Barsetti." She shook my father's hand.

He did the same. "Likewise. Need any help?"

"Absolutely not," she said. "Take a seat in the dining room, and I'll get the drinks started. A scotch, neat for the gentlemen and a glass of wine for the lady?"

Mom smiled. "That would be nice."

Carmen walked back into the room. "I'll take a scotch too—make it a double."

I lowered my voice so only Mia could hear. "Don't make it a double…"

Mia chuckled. "Alright, sir."

We moved into the dining room and sat down at the table. I was relieved the introductions were over. Now we could talk about something else other than my hot maid. But judging by the excitement in Carmen's eyes, she couldn't stop thinking about it. "Did you hire a model to be your maid?"

I ignored my sister's question, not wanting to talk about how hot Mia was in front of my parents, especially when my father knew I was sleeping with her. "She's good at what she does—regardless of her looks."

"Or her looks make her better at what she does…" Carmen wore a playful grin.

"Anyway…" I tapped my fingers against the table. "I'm glad you guys could stop by and see the place. I'm liking it so far."

"What about work?" Mom asked. "You're doing everything over the phone?"

"Yeah, pretty much. But I'll have to talk some trips here and there. That's the nice thing about having Mia around. She can keep it looking nice while I'm away, make sure the gardeners take care of the yard. Stuff like that."

Carmen narrowed her eyes on my face, not buying my story for a second.

"Your father and I are very happy you decided to move back," Mom said, beaming with pride. "When Conway decided to move back, we were pretty jealous. But now all the kids are together again. It's really wonderful."

"Yeah, I missed seeing Conway all the time." I used to see him every weekend when we were both in Milan. We drank and fucked around, spent the nights on the

town. But his bachelor days were long behind
him now.

Mia walked into the room and put the drinks out for
all of us. She handled everything like it wasn't her first
time waiting on people. Maybe Egor had her do something similar when she was in his captivity. "Dinner will
be right out. Anything else I can get in the meantime?"

"No, we're okay," I said. "Thank you, Mia."

She smiled then walked out again.

Carmen shifted her gaze back to me, suspicion
written all over her face.

I ignored her look, knowing exactly what she was
thinking. If I provoked her, she would accuse me of a
lot of things I didn't want to be accused of. "So Reid is
pretty—"

"There's no way that woman just works for you,"
Carmen blurted. "You're telling me this gorgeous model
waits on you, and you keep it professional?"

I used to want to strangle my sister a lot. This was
one of those times when I really wanted to strangle her.
"My professionalism is none of your business, brat.
Now be a mature adult and behave."

"So, she isn't just your maid," Carmen said with
victory. "I knew that wasn't possible."

"Mind your own business, Carmen. Every time you
talk to a guy, I don't assume anything."

Carmen laughed loudly, like I made some kind of
joke. "Anytime a guy comes anywhere near me, you
treat him like a criminal."

"Because he probably is," I countered. "You don't have good taste in men."

"Excuse me?" she hissed. "When have you ever seen a guy I've dated."

"I don't need to."

Mom sighed at our bickering. "Knock it off. We're all together now, and we should be happy. We have so much to be grateful for. We have a new Barsetti, and Carter is going to be close by from now on."

I never thought I would be happy to have my mother intervene. It reminded me of our childhood. Carmen and I didn't bicker very much anymore, but then again, we weren't around each other a lot. She was headstrong and opinionated, never afraid to speak her mind regardless of who she angered. It was one of the things I loved about her…but also hated. "Well said, Mama."

Carmen rolled her eyes when our parents weren't looking.

Mia brought dinner a moment later, and once everything was set on the table, she returned to the kitchen to start the dishes.

We talked about Reid most of the time, along with Vanessa and Griffin.

"I like Griffin a lot," Mom said. "He's got a dark side to him, but most men do. It's natural."

"I like him too," Carmen said. "I've never seen Vanessa happier. She's dated a few guys but never anyone who's made her fly so high. I can tell he really loves her. Whenever we go out, I see the way he looks at her. I hope I find a man who will look at me the same way."

I didn't want to deal with that day when it arrived. Dealing with Griffin was already a pain in the ass. When it was my own sister, it would be even worse. I knew exactly what kind of monsters were out there. The last thing I wanted was for my sister to end up with one of them.

"I have no doubt you will," Mom said. "When you find the right one."

"Nunneries are cool too…" I suggested, half joking and half serious.

She rolled her eyes. "Should I tell Mia the same thing? Bet you wouldn't like that…"

No, I wouldn't. That was the only pussy I was screwing these days. When I tried to recall the last woman I'd been with, I couldn't even remember a name. It was over two months ago now. It was hard to believe I'd been with the same woman that long.

"Mia is very pretty," Mom said. "Where did you find her?"

Father and I agreed to keep up the lie, but now that Mom was asking me for details, I felt shitty for making up a story. "I asked a friend for a recommendation, and her name popped up. She's good at taking care of the house, but she's also loyal. I wanted someone I could trust."

"She seems very nice," Mom continued. "Does she live at the house, or does she drive home?"

Carmen watched me, interested in my answers.

I didn't want to lie about all the details. It would just bite me in the ass later. "Yes. She lives here."

"So you live with that hot piece of ass?" Carmen asked. "All the time?"

I glared at her. "Don't call her that."

"It was complimentary," Carmen said. "She's drop-dead gorgeous. Like, why is she a maid when she could be a model for Conway?"

"Not all women want to parade around in their underwear," I snapped.

"Is there something wrong with women wanting to model lingerie?" She tilted her head to the side, cornering me into an argument on purpose. She was too smart for her own good and knew how to spin the narrative. If she got tired of being a florist, she could easily be a lawyer.

"That's not what I said," I argued. "Mia likes her job."

"I can't imagine anyone would want to wait on you," my sister responded. "Mom did it for eighteen years and hated it."

"I did not hate it," Mom said with a chuckle. "I miss it, actually."

"Why are you hung up on my maid?" I asked. "Do you want to date her? Because I can put it in a good word for you."

Carmen narrowed her eyes on my face. "I'm sure she's too busy with you."

Father drank his scotch, doing his best to ignore both of us.

"Anyway," Mom said. "Dinner was delicious, so she seems like a good addition to the house."

"She is," I said. "She also has a son who's going to be staying here."

"A son?" Mom asked in surprise.

"Really?" Carmen asked. "How old is he?"

"Eight," I answered. "I haven't met him, but he sounds like a good kid."

"They're both going to live here?" Carmen asked in surprise.

"Yes." I held her gaze as I spoke. "Mia's had a difficult life, not that it's any of your business. I'm trying to help her out."

Father sighed quietly then downed the rest of his scotch.

"That's nice of you, Carter." Mom placed her hand on my arm. "To help someone like that."

"Like I said, she's a great addition to the house." I held my glass without taking a drink. "I enjoy having her around. The place is too big for one person, and it's too big for me to take care of all the time. I need someone handling it full time." If I hired a man or an older woman, none of these questions would have been asked. But since Mia was exceptionally beautiful, especially in that cute dress she wore, all my family could do was fixate on was her looks. I guess I couldn't blame them…since I'd done the same thing since I met her. "Now, if we're finished talking about her, I'll give you a tour of the rest of the place."

———

I SAID goodbye to my family on the doorstep.

Father clapped me on the shoulder. "Come by the winery for lunch sometime."

"Sounds like a plan." I said goodbye to my sister next. "See you later." I hugged her, despite how much she annoyed me over dinner.

She returned the embrace then spoke to me with a smile on her face. "Look, all I'm saying is, that woman is not only gorgeous…but she can cook like a chef. She knows how to make a mean drink, and she keeps the house spotless. If I were you…I would be all up in that." She kissed me on the cheek then walked out with Father.

I ignored what she said and turned to Mom. "Sometimes I wish I were an only child."

"No, you don't," she said with a chuckle. "Your father and I would obsess over you even more."

"True."

She hugged me around the waist, over a foot shorter than me just the way Mia was. "But she does have a good point. You could have a maid do that for you…or have a wife do that for you." She rubbed my back before she pulled away and looked at me. "I try not to ask you too much about your personal life. Your father gets angry at me. But I don't want you to get caught up in work and luxury and forget there's more out there. Money and looks will fade…but love never dies. Your father was just like you when we first met, but once he settled down and had a family, he became a much happier version of himself. That's the only advice I want to give you."

"And you want me to marry Mia?" I asked incredulously. "You met her one time and tried her cooking. I don't think that's enough interaction for an arranged marriage."

"Of course not," she said. "But when I saw her, I hoped that…it doesn't matter." She patted my chest with her palm before she stepped back. "Just keep an open mind, Carter. The only time a soul is complete is when it finds its second half." She walked out toward my father, who wrapped his arm around her waist as they headed to the car. He opened the door for her, got her inside, and then they drove off with Carmen in the back seat.

I headed back to the kitchen and saw Mia shut the dishwasher before she turned it on. The place was spotless like it was before she started dinner. The leftovers were placed in the fridge, and the counters had been cleaned off. "Where did you learn to cook?"

She turned around at the sound of my voice. "The internet."

"My family really enjoyed it. Mom was impressed."

"Well, that's flattering." She washed her hands in the sink, scrubbing them with soap before she patted them dry with a kitchen towel. "I was a bit nervous to see your family. Wasn't sure how they would be. But they're lovely…like you." She hung the towel on the hook then turned back to me, looking beautiful in the dress she wore. The apron was gone, and her high ponytail kept her hair out of her pretty face.

"I'm sorry about my sister. She's a weirdo."

She chuckled, her cheeks blushing. "No, her candor was refreshing. Besides, who doesn't like a compliment?"

"And she's straight by the way. I would understand why that would be a surprise to you."

"Come on, Carter. She was just being nice." She placed her hand on my biceps and gave me a gentle rub.

The second she touched me, my body hummed to life. I loved feeling those fingertips, loved feeling that womanly touch. The embrace was innocent, practically meaningless, but those little touches made my entire body feel warm.

"She reminds me of Vanessa. Honest, transparent, refreshing. I really liked her. I liked everyone, truly. Remember that the past three years of my life were unbearable. Before that, I never had a place to call home. It's nice being around a family, being part of something normal."

Since she was serving us, it didn't seem like she was part of the family dynamic, but she obviously didn't see it that way.

"It makes me miss Luca, though." She crossed her arms over her chest and sighed.

"Less than a week now, sweetheart."

"So, what did you tell them about me?"

"That you were the maid. That's it. But obviously, Carmen can't seem to believe that."

"In her defense, she's right on the money." She smiled in a beautiful and sexy way.

"My mom likes you too. But she had a little talk with me in the doorway, basically told me she wanted me to settle down."

"With me?" she asked in surprise.

"Not necessarily. I think seeing me with an attractive woman, who's cooking in my kitchen, made her think of the kind of life she wants for her son. She wants me to have a wife and a pack of kids."

"Well, there's nothing better than being a parent, so I agree with her."

"I don't have anything against kids. I just don't want to be a father."

"It's not as difficult as you think it is, Carter."

"I would have to make a lot of sacrifices."

"But those sacrifices come with immense rewards." She tilted her head slightly as she looked at me. "Not everyone is meant to have children, and if someone doesn't want a family, that's perfectly fine. But I don't think you fall into that category, Carter. I see the way you are with your family."

I didn't know what to say to that since she was absolutely right. I loved my family. I loved the Barsetti clan. It was an honor to be part of a family so noble and respected. We were loyal to each other—to all ends.

"Have you ever introduced a woman to your parents before?"

"No," I blurted, finding the question comical. "Never."

"You've never had a girlfriend?" she asked, her eyebrow raised.

I shook my head. "The girlfriend thing has never interested me. I've never needed a romantic relationship with someone, not when I'm satisfied by other things, like sex, work, and family."

"Then it's no surprise that your mother and sister were so surprised to see me, since they've never seen you with a woman in any capacity."

"I guess."

"You told them I'm living here?"

I nodded.

"Did you tell them about my son?"

I nodded again. "They find the situation strange. They probably think there's something romantic going on between us. But I'm not going to correct my mother and tell her we're just fucking. I might be able to have that kind of conversation with my father, but not my mother."

"Understandable."

"I'm sure they'll get used to as time goes on and they realize nothing is gonna happen."

She held my gaze without reacting, but there was a hint of sorrow in her eyes. I wasn't sure why my words would matter to her. There didn't seem to be anything between us, at least nothing romantic. "What?"

"That makes me sad."

My heart started to race, the sweat forming on my palms. I stared at her beautiful face and felt the trepidation in my chest. I didn't blink as I stared at her, and she didn't blink as she stared back. Did our closeness develop into something more right under my nose without my realizing it? Did she want me, despite everything I'd done to her? My heart started to beat faster, and instead of rejecting her honesty, I wanted to push her against the counter and kiss her…even though I didn't understand why. "Why?" My voice came out as a whisper because that was as loud as I could make myself speak.

Her hand moved over her hair, and she tucked the brown strands that had come loose behind her ear. "I don't want you to be alone, Carter. I understand a man's need to remain free as long as possible, but always being alone…sounds depressing. I know commitment sounds horrifying to a man like you, a man who can have anything that he wants. But I promise you, it'll be the best thing you'll ever do. So don't say it's never gonna happen. Keep the door open."

When I heard her explanation, I realized she'd misinterpreted what I said. She wasn't referring to herself specifically, but to women in general. My heart rate didn't slow down even though her intent was clear. She spoke of me being with someone else so easily, like the possibility of us didn't even cross her mind. That should be a good thing, exactly what I wanted. But I found myself disappointed by her dismissal. It made absolutely no sense. "I'll think about it."

"Good." Her radiant smile returned. "When you meet Luca, I think it'll really change your mind."

"I don't know anything about kids, sweetheart."

"You don't need to. They'll teach you everything you need to know." She moved closer to me, slowly inching her way into my body. She stopped in front of me, her palms moving to my chest. She rubbed me lightly, her luscious lips just inches from mine. "Can I ask you for something?"

When she was this close to me, smelling like roses and looking beautiful as ever, I was immobile. All I wanted to do was stare at her, devour her with my eyes. Every time she rushed me, she gave me a thrill no other woman could match. "Anything." I'd already risked my life for her, risked my family for her. But now I was offering myself to her again.

Her hands slid up my chest until her arms hooked around my neck. She moved closer to me, embracing me like a lover. With her nose almost touching mine, she whispered against my lips, "Can we make love tonight? You know…the way I like?"

This beautiful woman was asking me to please her, to cover her body with mine and sink her into the mattress. After years of rape and torture, her body came to life for me. She wanted sex the way I gave it to her, wanted me to please her in a way no other man did. I wanted rough sex, to chain her up and make her cry, but when she asked me for this, I wouldn't deny her. I loved pleasing her as much as I loved hurting her. "Yes."

HER HANDS EXPLORED MY PHYSIQUE, starting with my shoulders and making their way down my chest and stomach. Her hands wrapped around me, and she gripped my ass, pulling on it so I could move inside her faster. Sexy moans and pants came from her slightly parted lips, sounding like a woman being thoroughly pleased. Her ankles dug into my ass, and she rocked with me, ready to come for the second time.

My hand reached into her hair, and I yanked on the band keeping the strands secured in a ponytail. As I tugged, it snapped free, letting her beautiful locks move across the pillow. I fisted it next, gripping it as tightly as the band. My cock was met with her abundant arousal, the slickness between her legs that I'd come to worship.

Most of my sexual escapades were muffled by a condom, but with Mia, it was just the two of us. Skin on skin, man and woman. The only reason I'd lasted this long was because she'd asked me to please her in such a seductive way. This strong woman wasn't afraid to ask for what she wanted, and I wanted to deliver so she would ask me time and time again.

"Carter…" Her nails ran up my back until they dug into my shoulders. She sliced the skin accidentally, gripping me so tightly she wasn't aware of what she was doing.

That was fine by me.

Her lips brushed against mine as she spoke into my mouth. "I'm gonna come again."

I could feel the way her pussy tightened around me, the beginning of her pleasure. "I know." I could feel her body as intimately as she could feel mine. I'd been sleeping with her long enough to understand every movement she made. From her change in breathing to the way she dug her nails into my body, I knew every move. My cock slid through her soaked arousal, and I could feel the tightness increase, feel her approach the cliff she was about to fly over.

Her hand moved into the back of my hair, and she fisted the strands as she kissed me. With quivering lips and sexy breaths, she made love to my mouth the way I made love to her body. She kissed me like she needed me, like the affection would push her over the edge and give her a climax she wouldn't forget.

As I felt that moment approach, my cock hardened noticeably, ready to join her when that moment arrived. I was buried so deep inside that pussy, and I couldn't wait to give her everything I had, to make her pussy full with my seed. I loved coming inside her, felt even more pleasure every time I did it. Our sex was vanilla, plain and simple, but she enjoyed me so much that it became the best I'd ever had.

She suddenly gripped me tightly as she hit her threshold. More moisture pooled around my length as her spirit sailed into the heavens. She fisted my hair and moaned against my mouth, coming all over my dick. Her kisses stopped as she moaned harder, her ankles digging deep into my ass. "Oh my god…"

I'd never got so much pleasure making love to a woman. It didn't matter how slow and easy it was, it always felt good. I already saved Mia and planned to bring her son back to her, so I didn't owe her anything. But nonetheless, I wanted to please her—because I enjoyed it. I came when she was almost finished, my big cock pressing deep inside her as I exploded. My entire body felt numb as I released, the pleasure so over-whelming my body couldn't absorb it all. Once I filled her, the goodness was so great I forgot to breathe. Releasing inside her was the sexiest feeling I'd ever encountered. I was on fire, burning all the way down to the bone. I loved filling her with my come, erasing Egor from existence. I claimed this woman, keeping her in my bed because she was mine to enjoy. "Fuck…" My climaxes were better with Mia, probably because I got off on how much she enjoyed me. I loved being deep inside her as she spread her legs like that, begging me without saying a single word.

My cock kept throbbing until I was completely finished. Once the waves of erotic pleasure died away, my cock slowly softened inside her. Surrounded by her cream and my come, my cock could stay there forever, but I pulled out slowly.

She kept her legs around my waist and hugged me tightly, like she wasn't done with me. She gave me a kiss so hot it made me stay. Our lips moved together aggressively, our breaths filling each other's lungs. It was like I hadn't pleased her at all, just made her want me more. Her ankles eventually released from my ass, and she ended our kiss.

I turned over and lay on my back, my wet dick slowly softening more. Exhausted and satisfied, I lay in the dark with her beside me. My chest was slick with sweat, and my ass was sore because I'd been thrusting into her for so long.

She was warm too, but that didn't stop her from cuddling into my side. The sheets were pushed to the bottom of the bed, but neither one of us wanted them. We lay together, a tangled mass of two sweaty bodies.

Her hand rubbed my chest gently, her hair touching my neck and shoulder.

I stared down at her curvy figure, loving her slender waistline and wide hips. She didn't have any stretch marks, so I wouldn't have even known she'd had a baby. But even if she had, it wouldn't have changed how much I wanted her.

The scars on her front were limited. Egor seemed to keep them on her back, using it as a billboard for his cruelty. Every time he looked at her rear, he was reminded of the power he had over her. When I looked at her scars, I didn't think about him. I thought of her strength inside. He might have beaten her to the ground, but she was the one who got up again.

"Can I tell you something?" she whispered, her hand freezing against my chest.

"Yes."

"I've never had sex like that all my life. I've been with a few guys, some were better than others, but with you…it's so good."

Like she didn't compliment me enough, she did it again, this time with enthusiasm.

"Are you like that with all women? Or is it just me?"

I didn't know how to answer her question because I didn't like to compare her to the rest of my lovers. "I don't know. It's different every time."

"Do you enjoy me as much as I enjoy you?"

I stared at the ceiling, smelling a mixture of sex and her perfume. "That answer is obvious, sweetheart. I love being buried between your legs every chance I get. You can lie there and do nothing, and it's still damn good. Your pussy is like a drug to me."

"I've never had a man describe it that way before…"

"Then you haven't been with the right man." I didn't like to think about the men she bedded before me. I didn't like to think about the man who knocked her up and left her behind. I didn't like to think about anyone enjoying her but me.

"No, I haven't." She kissed my shoulder, her soft lips pressing hard against my skin. "But now I have."

I WAS dead asleep when Mia started kicking me.

"Stop!" She threw her arms hard against me, punching me right in the stomach.

My eyes flashed open, and I prepared for danger, my mind immediately awake and prepared for battle. I spotted Mia beside me, her eyes shut. There was no one else in the room. Two seconds later, I realized she was having a nightmare. "Sweetheart." I grabbed her wrists so she would stop punching me. Tears streamed down her face, and she whimpered in pain, the nightmare torturing her. "Wake up." I shook her hard, trying to get her to snap out of it.

She finally stopped fighting me, her eyes snapping open and her breathing deep and irregular. She yanked her wrists away from my grasp and immediately sat up, her eyes looking around the bedroom for her assailant. She gripped her chest and felt her own heartbeat against her palm. "Oh my god…" Bathed in sweat with messy hair, it seemed like she just finished a real battle.

"Sweetheart, it's me. It's just the two of us." I kept my hands to myself, giving her a second to realize her surroundings. There were tears in her eyes, and they weren't the kind of tears I liked to see. "It's just a dream."

"A dream…"

"Yes." My hand moved into her hair, and I pushed the strands back, revealing her tear-stained cheeks. "I'm here. Nothing is going to happen to you while I'm here. You're safe." I didn't need to ask what her nightmare was about. There was only one person who ever tortured her. She was free from him, but her trauma would be there for a long time.

"Okay…" She wiped her tears with her fingertips and sniffled. She stayed still for a long time, slowly making sense of what just happened. She breathed deep and hard until her breathing returned to normal.

My hand rested on hers, reminding her I was there if she wanted to talk about it.

It didn't seem like she did. "I'm sorry. I didn't mean to—"

"Don't apologize." I gently tugged on her arm and brought her back toward me.

She moved into my chest and hugged me, cuddling into my body for protection. "The nightmares started after you rescued me. I know he's gone, but…I guess I haven't moved on yet."

"It'll take a long time before that happens."

She rested against me, and the longer I held her, the calmer she seemed to be.

I didn't want to be like Egor. I didn't want to torture this woman and give her nightmares. Mia was a beautiful woman who deserved more than that. "I know I said I would save you if you did something for me in return. But, Mia, you don't have to stay. You're free to leave whenever you want." I wanted to keep her as long as I wanted, to tie her up and whip her on the nights I was in the mood for something darker. But I'd grown to care about this woman, and I wanted her to have what she deserved—freedom. I didn't want to be like Egor. I wanted to be better than him.

"I already knew that, Carter." She sat back so she could look into my face. "But to be honest, I feel safe here. I want to stay here. When I was your prisoner at your other place, the idea of staying with you forever sounded tempting. The only reason I continued to fight was because of Luca. But now that he's coming here... there's nothing else for me out there. Luca's father left me because he was selfish—"

"Pathetic," I said. "The word you're looking for is pathetic." If I ever knocked up a woman, I would never turn my back on her. Even if it was a one-night stand that I didn't even like, it wouldn't make a difference.

Her eyes softened. "And then Egor ripped me away from my son and destroyed me...you're the first good man I've ever met. All I want is a quiet life for Luca and me. I just want to work and make sure he goes to a good school and becomes a man I'll be proud of. There's nothing better out there, Carter. I want to stay here. I want to be with a man who can protect us. If it were just me, it would be a different story, but since I have a son…I need a man to keep him safe." She took a deep breath, her eyes watering. "Because obviously, I can't. I failed him. I left him in an orphanage without an explanation…"

"Don't do that," I whispered. "You're rewriting history. That's not what happened, Mia."

"But that's how he'll see it."

I shook my head. "No, he won't. He loves you."

"I don't know…I hope so."

I squeezed her hand. "I know so. There's nothing my mother could ever do to make me stop loving her. I'm a grown man who doesn't need her anymore, but my respect for her will never change. You and Luca are welcome to live here as long as you want. If you're looking for protection, I fit the bill."

"You're so sweet, Carter. I feel like I'm getting the most out of the situation. I get to have my life back, I get to sleep with a beautiful man who's kind, and I get to focus on raising my son. I can't picture myself ever dating again, so having good sex with a friend is a dream come true for me. Until you meet someone you fall in love with, of course. If that day ever comes, you don't have to worry about us. We'll get out of your hair."

I couldn't picture that day ever coming. I couldn't picture myself falling in love with a woman I met at a bar. I'd never had a deep connection with anyone—except Mia. She spoke of a purely physical relationship and a friendship, like that was all she wanted. Unlike other women who wanted more from me, Mia never did. There was a twinge of disappointment, but it didn't make any sense because I wouldn't want it to be any different between us. After what I did to her in the beginning of our relationship, it shouldn't be surprising. Why would she want me? I chained her up to a wall and treated her like a slave for weeks. I was going to beat her and rape her until she talked me out of it. Maybe I was good to her now, but it hadn't always been that way.

"Did I say something?" she whispered, her eyes shifting back and forth as she looked into mine.

I hadn't realized how far I'd drifted away with my thoughts. "No."

"Okay." She smiled before she moved into my chest again. "I'm sorry I woke you."

"No need to be sorry." I kissed her forehead. "You never have to be sorry."

ELEVEN

Mia

—————

I counted down the days until Luca would be in my arms.

I almost couldn't believe it.

He was eight years old now. Three birthdays had come and gone. I missed all of them. I missed his first day of school too. I didn't take a picture of him before he walked out the door with his backpack. I didn't get to hear about his friends and his schoolwork.

That had been taken away from me.

I still wanted to kill Egor for what he did to my son and me. But I had to let the vengeance go and find peace without murdering him. He deserved to die, but it was unrealistic to think I could pull it off. Carter was the only one who could, but I refused to ask him to do that for me. He'd already done enough.

My life in Carter's home was simple and peaceful. I took regular trips to the store and the market to prepare our meals, and I cleaned the enormous house and made sure there wasn't a spot of dust anywhere.

It was nice.

At night, Carter fulfilled my fantasies, and I fulfilled his.

There was nothing more I could ask for.

I wasn't sure how I got so lucky. My life could have been quite different. As I aged, Egor would have gotten tired of me and replaced me with a younger version. At that point, he would have killed me since I had no other purpose to fulfill. My son would have been an orphan for the rest of his life, and I would have turned into fish food.

But then Carter came into my life—and gave me a second chance.

I would never be able to repay him for what he had done for me. Being spanked and whipped at night was the least I could do. The night before, he had me on my back while he fucked me in the ass. It hurt because he was so big, and he got off on the sight of my tears, but I still did it anyway because that was what he liked.

To fuck me in kinky ways.

That morning, Carter worked out and then met me in the kitchen with a bag over his shoulder.

"Are you going somewhere?" I blurted.

"I need to do some work in Milan. We've worked on a new schematic, but we need to fine-tune the details. I'll only be gone for about two days. I'll fly there and back. Easier than driving, as much as I enjoy driving my cars."

I stared at him blankly, unable to process what he'd said. "So…I'm going to be here alone?"

"You'll be fine, sweetheart. I've got an alarm system and a few guns. I told my father you would be here alone, so he'll keep an eye on things."

It would be the first time I was completely on my own. Even when I had Luca, I was never alone. Now I would be in an enormous house with no company. Before Egor, I would have been fine, but now everything was different. With Carter around, I always felt safe. But if he was five hours away, anything could happen.

Carter must have seen the terror on my face. "Sweetheart?"

"Can I come with you?"

"Back to Milan?" he asked incredulously. "That's not a good idea. I can't risk anyone spotting you."

I'd forgotten about that.

"I know you can handle this, sweetheart. You're tough."

I didn't want to be weak, but now that I had the luxury of a man like Carter, it was hard to picture my life without him. "I'm sorry…I just don't like it. You'll be five hours away, and that scares me. Anything can happen. What if someone tries to break in?"

"You shoot them in the face," he said seriously. "But that's not gonna happen. The walls are fourteen feet high, and the front gate has surveillance."

"An alarm system isn't going to stop someone like Egor. He'll just snatch me before the cops arrive. We're out in the middle of nowhere. It'll take at least twenty minutes before help arrives."

"Which is why I asked my father to keep an eye on you."

That wasn't good enough. "He's not you."

He sighed and set his bag on the floor. "I don't know what to tell you. I have to go."

I didn't want to be difficult, but the idea of him being gone was terrifying. He was my savior, and without him I was helpless.

"You cut a tracker out of your ankle, sweetheart. Even though I was in the house, you managed to get my alarm code and take one of my cars. You actually jumped out of my car when I first got you. You aren't the kind of woman that scares easy."

"That was when I had nothing to lose, Carter. Now that I have everything, the game has changed. The only time I've ever been safe in my life is when I've been with you. Now that you're leaving…it's like the rug is being pulled from underneath me."

He dropped his confident gaze and released a quiet sigh. "I have to head to work. I'm the owner and face of this company."

"I understand that."

"I'm going to have to go to work often."

"I know…"

"So this is something you're going to have to get used to."

"What if I stayed with Griffin and Vanessa again?" Griffin seemed like a powerful man whom no one would cross.

"I don't want to bother them, Mia. The only option we have is if you stayed with my parents, but I'm sure—"

"I would do that."

Surprise entered his gaze. "You want to stay with my parents?"

"Your father knows the truth, so he'll understand why I'm nervous. He seems strong and smart. I know he lives close to your uncle and cousin. Staying there sounds a lot better than staying here alone."

"You're serious."

"Yes." I wouldn't be able to sleep at all here, not until Carter walked through the door again.

"Well, I'm sure they would be fine with it. I'm just surprised you would want to stay with them for two nights."

"They were lovely people, Carter."

"I know that," he said. "But you hardly know them."

"Your dad showed me what kind of man he is. I trust him."

Carter rubbed the back of his neck as he considered it. He sighed then lowered his hand. "Alright. Pack your stuff."

I WASN'T sure what Carter's parents said over the phone, but they must have agreed because he dropped me off on his way to the airport. Like a gentleman, he carried my bag to the door and greeted his parents. "Thanks for letting Mia stay with you for a few days. The house is too big for one person."

"It's no problem at all." His father smiled at me before giving me a one-armed hug. "We've got a lot of space, and we love to fill it with people."

"You're always welcome here," his mother said. "Let me take your bag. We'll have a few guest bedrooms upstairs."

The place was two stories. It wasn't as big as Carter's place, but it was still a palace by my standards. They had a few acres of land, a private vineyard, and a pool out back. Their home was decorated with luxury items, from custom paintings to Italian-crafted furniture. "That's very generous. Thank you."

Carter pulled up his sleeve to look at his watch. "I've gotta catch my flight. Love you guys." He turned to me, about to kiss me right in front of his parents. He quickly hid his intention, giving me an awkward pat on the shoulder. "I'll pick you up on the way home. See you later."

"Bye." I wished I could hug him before he went, tell him it meant a lot to me that he'd left me in good hands. But since I would always be the maid in front of his family, I kept up my indifference and said goodbye with a quick wave.

When Carter left, his mother took me upstairs to the guest bedroom. It was large for a visitor, having a private bathroom. She set my bag down on the big armchair in front of the fireplace. "Let me know if you need anything. Cane goes to work in the morning, so I usually sit by the pool or read. Maybe we could have lunch?"

"Yeah, that sounds nice. Thank you for letting me stay here. The room is beautiful." It was just as nice as the one I had at Carter's place, the room I never slept in. I sat on the edge of the bed and felt the Italian sheets under my fingertips.

"It's our pleasure," she said. "Carter said you were uncomfortable staying alone." She was in denim jeans and a black blouse, her thin figure noticeable in the way her clothes fit her. She had fair skin like snow, looking much different from her son. With painted red lips and mocha-colored eyes, she didn't look Italian, but she was definitely beautiful. I saw Carmen in her expression.

"Yeah, that house is just so big, and I get paranoid sometimes…" I didn't want to elaborate since I couldn't tell her the truth. "When Carter's there, I feel safe. He's the kind of man that can handle himself. But alone…I feel powerless."

"Do you know how to use a gun?" she asked bluntly.

I'd never fired one in my life. "Actually, no."

"Let me show you tomorrow. You're welcome to stay here whenever you want, but learning to handle a gun might give you peace of mind. I know Carter has guns around the house, so if you ever need one, you'll be prepared." She didn't dismiss my fears as ridiculous and offered a solution to the problem.

I shouldn't be surprised that she'd made such an offer. I shouldn't be surprised that she knew how to handle a gun. If she was married to Cane, it only made sense. They seemed to be a powerful family, gauging from my short interaction with Griffin. "Yeah, that would be great."

She nodded. "I'll let you freshen up before dinner. We take it in the dining room."

"Alright. Thank you."

After she left, I pulled out the phone Carter gave me and searched through it. His name was stored in the contacts, along with every other member in his family, even people I'd never met. I had his family tree right at my fingertips.

I joined them downstairs twenty minutes later.

Cane pulled out the chair for me before I sat down. Then he took the seat beside his wife and poured me a glass of wine. "Anything else we can get you, Mia?"

"No, thank you." I ate my dinner, enjoying Carter's mother's cooking as much as she'd enjoyed mine. It was quiet for a while, since we didn't know each other very well.

His mother kept looking at me, staring at my expression like she was searching for something. "How do you like working for my son?"

"Carter is great," I said honestly. "He's been very good to me."

"I'm glad to hear that," she said. "When he told us he was moving back to Tuscany, I could hardly believe it. It was such a change, and then he brought you along too. It seems like my son is growing up, changing his priorities without even realizing it."

It was difficult to lie to someone's face, especially when you were sitting in their house, eating the meal they prepared for you. I was tempted to come clean, to tell his mother the truth. But since this wasn't my lie to tell, it would be wrong. I kept my mouth shut. "I started working for him in Milan. After Conway moved here, Carter told me how much he missed him, along with everyone else. I think that had a lot to do with it." No, it was all because of me. I asked him to save me—and he did.

"That makes me very happy," she said. "Cane and I have been so lucky with our children. They're both amazing in their own ways. Having both of them so close is a blessing. I have a few friends who have had kids who've moved away...and it's so heartbreaking to hear. We've been very fortunate."

"Yes, the Barsettis are nothing short of wonderful." Carter battled with the darkness he possessed, but he never allowed it to pull him under. He had extreme kindness in his blood, and even his darker moments were nothing close to evil. It actually made me like him more.

After dinner, I sat in the living room and watched TV with them. They sat together on the couch, his hand resting on her thigh. They continued to enjoy their wine, still happy and in love.

When it got late, I said goodnight and retreated to my room. The phone was on the bed where I'd left it, and I looked at the screen to see if Carter had called or texted. But the phone was blank. I shouldn't expect anything from him, not when he didn't owe me anything. He was a man I was sleeping with and nothing more. I shouldn't worry about him the way a woman worried over her husband. It was the first time we'd ever been apart, and I missed him immediately. I'd been sleeping by his side for a long time now. Would I be able to sleep in this large bed alone?

I pulled my shirt over my head and unclasped my bra, my back to the door. I brought one of Carter's t-shirts to sleep in, knowing his parents wouldn't see me in my sleepwear. It was the most comfortable thing to wear, much better than pajamas.

A knock sounded on my door and made me jump.

I quickly pulled the shirt over my head and turned around to see Mrs. Barsetti.

She was still in her jeans and blouse, and the friendly expression she usually wore was absent. Her fair skin looked even paler than it did before. She kept one hand on the open door as she stared at me, speechless.

I wasn't sure what had just happened. Maybe she was appalled by the fact that I was wearing Carter's t-shirt. It would be impossible to know for sure that it belonged to him, so I wasn't sure why she would assume. "Everything alright, Mrs. Barsetti?"

When I asked the question, she seemed to snap out of her mood. "Yes…I brought you some water." She held up the plastic bottle in her hand and came toward me. Instead of getting close to me like she had earlier, she kept distance in between us as she placed the bottle in my hand. "Sleep well."

"I will. Thank you…"

She forced a smile before she walked out.

When I was alone, I looked at my phone again, hoping Carter would call.

He never did.

CANE WAS GONE when I woke up in the morning, so it was just Mrs. Barsetti and me. I went downstairs and joined her for breakfast, but I was met with the same strange attitude she gave me last night, like I'd done did something wrong.

The silence was deafening, the tension palpable.

No amount of small talk could fix it.

She drank her coffee and glanced at me from time

to time. She picked up the newspaper and scanned it, but her eyes were shifting back and forth so quickly it didn't seem like she was even reading it. Her breathing was abnormal, and I could feel the hostility in the room. Carter spoke so highly of his mother, so I was surprised by the inhospitable environment she was creating with her silence. His father had been nothing but warm to me. "Mrs. Barsetti…did I do something?"

She lifted her gaze from her newspaper, the guilt in her eyes. "No, of course not." She folded the paper and set it on the table beside her.

"When you came into my room last night, it seemed like I'd done something wrong. The t-shirt I was wearing was Carter's, but I put it into my bag by mistake. I was doing laundry, and it must have—"

"Honey, no." She held up her hand, silencing me with the gesture. Guilt burned in her eyes, as if she knew exactly how she was behaving. "You didn't do anything wrong. I apologize for acting so strange. I just…I'm not sure how to handle this."

"Handle what?" I whispered.

"I know it isn't my place and I should mind my own business, but when I see this kind of thing, I can't ignore it."

Now I had no idea what she was talking about.

She lifted her gaze to look into mine. "Your back… all the scars."

The second she spoke the words, everything made sense. She wasn't appalled that I was wearing her son's clothes. She was disgusted by the scars on my back, the violence that had been inflicted upon me in my past life. They weren't the kinds of marks that happened naturally. Judging by the lines and colors, they were obviously inflicted by a whip. Anyone could see that. "Oh…"

She ran her fingers through her hair as she considered what to say. "Please tell me that my son—"

"No." I wouldn't even let her finish the sentence. Carter liked to hurt me, but not like that. The pain he caused was tame, even felt good at times. He was never brutal in his violence. "Carter would never do something like that."

She leaned back in her chair and closed her eyes for a moment, inhaling a deep breath to clear the pain in her chest. "Oh, thank god." She ran her fingers through her hair again, opening her eyes once more. "Because if my son did that, I would do something worse to him."

I believed her. She seemed like a fighter, like his father. "Carter has never been cruel to me." I wanted to explain my story so she would understand, but I knew Carter didn't want her to know. I kept my mouth shut.

"May I ask what happened?" She watched me with soft eyes, not pressuring me.

I didn't mind sharing my story, but I didn't want to incriminate Carter. "It's not something I like to talk about…"

She gave a slight nod, her disappointment obvious. "Those things are hard to talk about…especially with someone you barely know. As time passes, it gets easier. But since the scars are permanent, you can never forget."

My eyes watched her carefully, feeling something significant in her vague words.

"So, I understand, Mia. That's all I want you to know."

Carter never mentioned something terrible happened to his mother. If she'd experienced something similar, it seemed like he would have mentioned it to me. That meant he had no idea. "I was in the wrong place at the wrong time. A man captured me, turned me into his slave, and I was in his captivity for three years." I could share my story without mentioning Carter at all. Since she'd seen my scars, she already knew something was off anyway. Didn't make sense to hide it. "He was brutal and cruel. There were times when I considered taking my own life, but I never did… because I have a son."

Her eyes immediately watered, feeling the pain from my past even though she hardly knew me. "I'm so sorry…"

I looked away, unable to handle her compassion.

"He's eight?" she whispered, her voice cracking slightly.

"Yes. I missed three years of his life while I was a prisoner. I'm supposed to get him back soon."

"You haven't seen him yet?" she whispered.

"No. But when Carter gets back, my son will be living with us."

"That's terrible, Mia…"

It was easy to feel sorry for myself, but since I was so happy to be free, it didn't make sense to feel anything less than joy. It would be an insult to the time I lost. "It was the worst time of my life, obviously. But instead of letting that define me, I've moved forward. My son and I will have a good life together. I'll raise him to be a good man, someone who would never hurt a woman. And we'll be happy."

"That's a very good attitude," she whispered. "I admire it."

"Thank you."

"My son plays into this story, doesn't he?"

I didn't say anything, not wanting to betray him. After what he'd done for me, I couldn't throw him under the bus. I was loyal to him, would take a bullet for him.

Mrs. Barsetti watched me with twinkling brown eyes, not offended by my silence. "I thought it was strange that he had a maid when he'd never seemed interested in having one before. And the fact that you have a son who will be living there, I also thought was peculiar. I don't want to put you in a position you don't want to be in. But if my son is helping you…" Her eyes watered again, the tears growing so thick, they slid down her cheeks. "I would be so proud of him."

Watching her eyes tear up made mine do the same.

I did my best to keep my emotions in check, refusing to cry in front of anyone but Carter.

She cleared her throat. "Carter doesn't know anything about my past. We agreed to keep it from him, from both of our children. I'll share it with you now, but if the time comes, I want to be the one to tell him this story. The purpose in me telling you is...so you understand that you aren't alone. That there is hope...and there is a happy life to be lived."

I nodded, agreeing to keep her story a secret from Carter.

"My story is nearly identical to yours," she said quietly. "I'd just graduated college when I took a trip to Greece with a friend. We got in the wrong taxi, and that's when we were taken. We were bought by the same monster, and to get me to cooperate, he threatened to hurt my friend. I was his prisoner for a while... It seemed like a lifetime. I was so young, and that made it so much worse. Cane was doing business with my captor. That was how we met. The second I looked at him, I knew he was different. He wasn't a clean-cut man without a dark past, but he was nothing like the monsters that surrounded me. He may have bad intentions sometimes, but he has a heart of gold. They made a deal for some weapons... and I became collateral. Cane took me home for a month...and in that time, we fell in love. The rest of the story doesn't matter. But in the end, Cane saved me. He freed me from that monster by killing him.

We married shortly afterward and lived very happy lives."

I listened to her heartbreaking story that mirrored my own, and I was appalled by what I'd heard. Why was something like this so common? Common enough that two women had almost the exact same story? It was disgusting. "I'm glad Cane killed him."

She wiped away a single tear that had fallen. "Me too. He's a good man…the best."

"The apple doesn't fall far from the tree."

"All of that pain fades over time. I never think about it anymore. This is the first time I've thought about it in years…because I saw the scars. I have similar ones."

"I'm so sorry." I suffered so much, and it hurt to know that Carter's mother went through the same thing. "I'll keep your secret. But I think you should tell Carter eventually. It will hurt him a lot, but he'll admire you even more than he does now. He always speaks so highly of you…and now I know why."

"He does?" she whispered, a smile spreading across her lips.

"Of course."

"He's tough like his father, but also sweet like his father. I've considered telling him, but I wanted to wait until the right time. Pearl told her daughter about her past, and it seemed to bring them closer together."

I didn't ask what that past was, assuming it was none of my business. "I told Carter I was afraid my son would hate me…or not remember me. He told me my son will be proud of me, for surviving something like that. So, I suspect that will be Carter's reaction when you tell him."

"He's such a good man," she said with a sigh. "We really did get very lucky with him."

"He's very brave." Now I knew Carter had nothing to fear telling his mother the truth. He'd risked everything to get me out, but he was exactly like this father… and he had no idea.

"Since you don't have your son back, I can only assume you recently left your captor."

There was no way to maneuver away from the truth. "Yes."

"And that means…my son saved you."

I didn't want to lie to this woman, not when I respected her so much. "Carter didn't want anyone to know. Didn't want anyone to know he took a risk saving me. If he knew what you'd been through, he would probably tell you the truth."

Her eyes watered again, but this time in a new way. "My son is so good…to do that for you. He's reuniting you with your son. Maybe it was dangerous. Maybe it was foolish. But what kind of life is this if we don't help each other? I've never been prouder of him, for helping a young woman like you."

"You should be…he's very selfless." She didn't need to know about our attraction to one another. Now that she knew the truth, she probably assumed it, especially since I wore his shirt to bed.

260

"I think I'll confront him when he gets home. I don't think I can be in the same room with him without telling him how I feel…how proud I am. There are very few men out there who would do what he did. I've come to realize there are far more evil men out there than good men. That means we need to treasure the good ones even more, appreciate them."

"I agree."

She stared at me with newfound affection in her eyes, the gloss from her tears still shiny. "I'm happy you're getting your son back."

"I've practically been holding my breath until I see him again."

She moved her hand onto the table and rested her palm on mine. The touch was maternal, making me think of my mother who died before Luca was born. The Barsettis were different from everyone else. Not only were they loving, but extremely generous. I hardly knew his parents, but they'd already been so kind to me, made me open up to them in a way I never did with anyone else. I never felt judged or persecuted. I just felt accepted…because she'd experienced the exact same thing. Now I had a special bond with his mother, a relationship I could never describe to Carter. "You won't have to hold your breath much longer."

TWELVE

Bones

When I woke up that morning, I watched the sunlight drift into the room and hit Vanessa's face. With messy hair and rested features, she looked just as beautiful asleep as she did when she was awake. Her thick eyelashes and full lips made her look like a model beside me, her olive skin gorgeous in comparison to the white sheets that covered her body. I usually made love to her before she was even awake, but that morning I was content staring at her.

She breathed a deep sigh as she started to wake, her slender arms gently stretching. Her eyes opened slightly, and she took in my features. The green color was even more brilliant in the summer morning light. She focused on my gaze for a few seconds before her lips formed a soft smile.

I didn't need to touch her to make love to her. Drinking in her appearance was enough for me. I'd never stared at anyone with the intensity that I stared at her. It wasn't just her obvious beauty, but the brilliance of her soul. "So fucking beautiful." I said the same words to her while she'd slept in her childhood bed. We saw each other through the screens of our phones. Any time of day she was beautiful, but when she was asleep, she possessed an angelic glow.

"Not as beautiful as you." She pressed her lips against my chest, her luscious lips grazing over my ink. Her hand slid across my abs, her fingertips brushing against the valley between the muscle. "But if I'm so beautiful…why aren't you making love to me?" Vanessa wanted me as much as I wanted her. No matter how hard I fucked her on a daily basis, she could keep up with me.

"I wanted to watch you sleep."

"You don't seem like the kind of man that watches a woman sleep."

"I'm not." I'd hardly shared my bed with anyone, and I certainly didn't snuggle to keep them warm. Vanessa and I didn't need a king-size bed because we only took up a small part of it together. "But you aren't a woman—you're my woman."

She smiled again, the affection moving into her eyes. "Get on top of me." Her arm circled my shoulders, and she kissed my neck, her leg hooking over my waist. She was naked from the night before, so she was ready for me right away.

"I'd love to, but I have to head to work." I hadn't

mentioned anything to her because we got home late last night. I wanted her to be wide awake when I told her what her father and I had decided on.

Her lips stopped against my neck, turning immobile before she pulled away and stared at me. "Work?" Her eyes narrowed, assuming the worst. "You said you were done with that life, Griffin."

"I am, baby. I'm starting a new profession."

"And what profession is that?" She propped herself up on one elbow so she could look down at me. "You've been retired for less than a week. You've already started something else?"

"You know I'm not the lazy type."

"I'm realizing that. You could stay home and take care of me. We both know I can't cook." She rubbed my chest, her slender fingers stroking me gently.

Staying home all day wasn't my style. I had to be on my feet, doing something productive with my time. "I think you'll like this idea more."

"Alright. What is it?" Her face hung above mine, her dark hair reaching down to touch my skin.

"Your father asked me to join him at the winery."

Surprise stretched across her face, her green eyes glowing.

"He said he wants to retire someday, but none of the children want the business. Wants to keep it in the family, so he asked me to take it over when that day arrives. I'll run it, and when we have our children, we can hand it off to them. It's something Crow can give his family even when he's gone. In the meantime, I'll learn everything about the business."

The emotion burned in her eyes instantly, becoming shiny with moisture. Her hand moved across my chest, and she broke eye contact, overwhelmed by the information that hit her hard. "That was very sweet of him to offer. And very sweet of you to accept."

"I didn't like the idea in the beginning. But he made a good point, saying that I didn't have any passions in life, not like the rest of the Barsettis. Working somewhere or owning a business just for the hell of it didn't seem like a good idea. The winery is a family business, and since I'll be family someday, I can take care of it— for you. That's why I agreed."

"That's so… I don't even know what to say."

"I told him I wouldn't accept payment until he retired. Then the profits would come to us, but only because he's at home enjoying his time off. So, I'll be working for free, but we have so much money that having more money doesn't even make sense anymore."

"We do?" she whispered. Vanessa never asked me about my wealth. She knew I had money, but she never asked what my salary was or how much cash I had stored at the bank. It never seemed like she cared.

"Yes." Women were impressed by my wealth, but their opinion never mattered to me. Impressing Vanessa was the only thing I cared about. I wanted to share my estate with her, to cover her in expensive jewels and designer lingerie. I wanted to put her in a big mansion, the queen of my home.

"So you're going to work with my father and uncle every single day?" she asked, mildly surprised.

"Yes."

"Five days a week?"

"Yes."

"You really think you can handle that? You do so much for me, but I want you to know that you don't have to do anything you don't want to. You've buried the hatchet with my father, and that's more than enough. That's all I ever wanted. You don't have to work with him every single day. You could do anything you want, Griffin." Vanessa was always selfless when it came to me. She never asked me to do something I didn't want to. She always remained objective between me and her family. She never asked for more than I could give.

"I want to, baby." When Crow painted that picture for me, I wanted to be involved. I wanted to protect the family business so it could be handed down to the next generation, whether it was my kids or another Barsetti. I'd been appointed the protector, the best person to keep that business untarnished. Crow honored me with the request, showed that he meant every word he said. He trusted me with something he built with his own hands, trusted me to carry out his legacy when he was gone.

Her eyes softened again. "Then that makes me really happy."

I leaned in and kissed her on the forehead. "You can spare me every single day?"

"Yes. It's much better than what you were doing before."

"You'll be alright with me being twenty minutes away every day?"

She rolled her eyes. "Griffin, please."

I smiled, loving that response. "That's my baby." She could handle herself just fine. She didn't need a man to make her feel secure. She had a passion that fueled her energy during the day, and when I came home at night, a different passion would fuel her. Fearless and powerful, she was a woman who matched my strength.

"If I'm your baby, prove it." She yanked on my arm and pulled me on top of her, her head hitting the pillow and her eyes brightening with desire. She used to tease me for needing to fuck her every single morning, but she clearly needed it as much as I did.

"You want me to be late on my first day on the job?" My muscular thighs separated her legs, and I folded her knees toward her chest.

"Yes." Her hands glided up my chest until they gripped my shoulders. "Because you've got to complete your first job of the day before you move on to the second one."

"My job, huh?" My fists sank into the mattress, and

I pressed my head to her wet entrance. With a gentle thrust, I was inside her, slowly sinking into the delicious flesh my cock called home. "What is my job, exactly?"

She grabbed my hips and pulled me deeper inside her, break into a satisfied smile when she felt all of me. "To love your woman every morning." Her lips parted, and she released a sexy moan that filled the entire bedroom.

I buried myself to the hilt, stretching her small cunt wide apart. No matter how many times I made love to her, her pussy remained as tight as ever. My thickness stretched her as far as she would go, but her body always snapped back. That's what made us so good together, so perfect. "I take my job very seriously, baby." I thrust into her slowly, making love to her just the way she wanted. Sometimes she was in the mood for a hard pounding, when I grabbed her by the neck and forced her face into the mattress. Sometimes she wanted me to fuck her on the kitchen table, to fuck her so hard it seemed like she meant nothing to me. But first thing in the morning, she wanted that slow burn, those soft kisses and gentle scratches. She wanted me to tell her I loved her, that I would die for her. She wanted fifteen minutes of pure love to get her day started. Hot breaths, gentle caresses, and soft lovemaking that made her shudder, usually more than once.

She fisted my short hair and kissed me, breathing into my lungs with her deep fire. Her legs shook, and her pussy tightened over and over, enjoying me so much it was obvious in every movement she made. "I know you do."

I PULLED up to the winery twenty minutes late. I left the truck in the parking area then headed to Crow's office in the main building. When I stepped inside, I saw the paintings on the wall. My artistic eye caught Vanessa's handiwork. Images she'd painted of the landscape around the property. I didn't know shit about art, but I recognized Vanessa's soul in her work. I could point out her picture in a sea of others because I knew her so well. That asshole she dated before might appreciate her work, but he didn't know her the way I did.

No one did.

"Griffin?" Pearl's voice came from behind me. "So happy to see you."

I turned around to see her in jeans with a white blouse tucked in. She had a slender figure the way Vanessa did, and her nude pumps made her look elegant with the beautiful landscape of the property. Pearl had natural class, a woman with dignity and respect that she'd earned despite a difficult life. It didn't matter that she was beaten and raped. She still came out on top, a queen like her daughter. "Hello, Mrs. Barsetti. I apologize for being late."

She rolled her eyes before she hugged me. "No such thing as being late around here. When Cane doesn't come in, he doesn't even tell us. He lets his absence explain it." She kissed me on the cheek before she stepped back. "My daughter is okay sparing you five days a week?"

"She can take care of herself." Vanessa was smart and fast. If something ever happened, she knew where the guns were. She had perfect aim and wouldn't hesitate to pull the trigger. I knew from personal experience.

Pearl smiled at my words. "You're right about that."

"She was happy when I told her. Thrilled, actually."

"And we were thrilled you accepted. I've been wanting to do some traveling, but Crow is pretty much glued here. When he retires, I told him I want to see the world. He promised he would take me—and I'm making him keep that promise."

"Crow is a man of his word."

She smiled. "I'm glad you realize that." She moved her hand to my back and guided me down the hallway.

"How's Reid?"

"Doing well. Cries a lot, and almost exclusively in the middle of the night," she said with a sigh. "But I miss taking care of someone, and it's so nice having a baby around. I rock him to sleep and feed him so Sapphire and Conway can rest."

"You're a good grandma."

"Grandma...I guess I am. I like the way that sounds." She knocked on the office door before she opened it.

"It suits you."

Crow looked up from his desk, wearing a suit and tie. He usually wore jeans and a t-shirt, but he must have more professional business to take care of. I'd never seen him in a suit before, and it was amazing how much more intimidating he seemed.

I hated to wear suits.

"Griffin." He rose from behind his desk and walked around to give me a hug. "Glad you're here. We've got lots to do today."

"Should I change?" I asked, looking down at his slacks.

"No, you're fine," he said. "I have a meeting with some vendors. I want you to sit in and just watch. Observe and learn."

"Sounds easy enough."

Pearl moved into her husband and kissed him on the mouth. "I'll see you later."

"Alright, Button." He gave her ass a gentle spank as she walked away.

She shut the door and left us.

Crow grabbed a folder off his desk. "We're moving to the conference room. Save your questions for later." Like the leader he was, he immediately issued orders.

I didn't respond to people telling me what to do, but this time, it didn't bother me. Reminded me of Vanessa, actually.

"I'm guessing Vanessa was happy when you told her?"

I nodded. "Very."

"I wasn't sure how she would feel about you being gone all day."

Even her own family underestimated her. "Vanessa doesn't need me. She has her own passions and her own responsibilities that don't involve me. She needs her own space and her own ambitions. It's a part of her life I have nothing to do with, and I should have nothing to do with. She needs me the way a woman needs a man, but that's it. The rest of the time, she doesn't need me for a damn thing."

Crow looked at me, a slight smile on his lips. "Well said, Griffin."

THIRTEEN

Vanessa

———————

A part of me missed having Griffin right upstairs. When I took my lunch, I could spend it with him, eating and screwing on the dining table. Or if the gallery was slow, I could close early and spend the afternoon with him. But having him work directly with my father every single day was a dream come true.

It was all I ever wanted.

I'd dreamed of having a husband my father would embrace like a son. Now they were friends, two men who respected each other. They had their own relationship, commonalities that had nothing to do with me.

It was perfect.

Spending my day painting in the gallery and running the business was the best utilization of my time. The day passed quickly, and I enjoyed every second of my line of work. When I painted in the gallery, customers walked inside to see my brushwork with their own eyes. They were usually impressed by the images I could create from memory, and after conversation back and forth, they usually took home one of my pieces.

It was a dream job.

A dream that only happened because Bones believed in me. He told me to drop out of school and bought me this gallery. He believed in me more than anyone else, even my parents. His faith was probably based on a mixture of love and obsession, but that didn't change anything.

I sat at my desk and looked out the window, seeing the empty sidewalk at the hottest time of the day. It was humid in Florence, so most of the tourists were in the museums or eating gelato.

I noticed the blacked-out car across the street, with completely tinted windows and unusual rims. It wasn't a small car that usually traveled down these narrow streets. Bones's truck stuck out like a sore thumb because those kinds of vehicles weren't common in the city. The fact that the windows were completely blacked out was disconcerting as well. A dread grew inside of my heart, and that sensation immediately reminded me of Knuckles, the man who broke in to my apartment and kidnapped me.

Or was I just being paranoid?

I didn't consider myself to be a paranoid person. I only worried about things when danger was looking me straight in the face. I turned back to my computer, not trying to make it obvious that I was suspicious.

A few minutes passed, and another car just like it parked on the side of the road.

There was no way that was a coincidence.

My heart started to race in my chest. My palms grew damp with sweat. The adrenaline associated with fear spiked in my blood. There were no guns in the gallery. All I had were random objects and my fists.

The front door on the first black car opened, and a man dressed completely in black stepped out. In a black leather jacket and with a terrifying demeanor, he looked like bad news. Other men got out as well.

"Shit." I only had time for one phone call, so I skipped calling the cops.

The phone rang twice.

"Griffin, pick up!" The doors to the second car opened, and another series of scary-looking men appeared. If they were there just to take me, it seemed unnecessary. They must be prepared for Bones to show up.

He finally answered. "Hey, baby. I'm in the middle—"

"Shut up and listen. Eight men are about to walk into the gallery and take me." I blurted out everything as fast as I could. "They're all armed and all dressed in black. They're headed right this way. I have less than thirty seconds."

Instead of panicking like anyone else would, Bones

spoke with a calm voice. He didn't pause longer than a second before he spoke. "Don't fight them, Vanessa. Be quiet and cooperative. Don't be scared because I promise I will get you."

"I know you will, Griffin." They were almost to the door. "I love you."

"I love you too. Tell me everything you can about these guys before they get to you."

"Two black Mercedes. Blacked-out with tinted windows. Eight men altogether. The man in front has a scar underneath his left eye. They look foreign, maybe Middle Eastern." I watched the first man open the door of the gallery and point a gun right at my face. "I have to go."

"Baby, I love you—"

I could have left the phone on, but I didn't want Griffin to hear what would happen next. I hung up and set the phone on the desk. The gun was pointed at my face, but I refused to show fear. Bones told me not to fight them, and I would listen, knowing I was outnumbered and these men were seriously evil.

The guy walked right up to me, snarling like I'd done something to wrong him. He kept the barrel trained right on me, his finger on the trigger. "Get up."

I looked straight down the barrel, just the way my father did when he was on the ground and outnumbered. Just because I couldn't fight with my fists didn't mean I couldn't have dignity. "He's going to kill all of you." I slowly rose to my feet, meeting his gaze with defiance. "If I were you, I would take this opportunity to walk out with your lives."

The corner of his mouth rose in a malicious sneer. "If he wanted peace, he shouldn't have killed my father."

FOURTEEN

Bones

———————

The second I hung up the phone, I walked back into the conference room where Crow was meeting with one of the biggest wine distributors in Europe. It was a big contract, something that would increase the reach of the wine by ten times. It was a huge client to land, and it seemed like Crow had it in the bag.

But I was about to ruin it. "Crow, I need to talk to you. Now."

Crow flashed me an annoyed expression, but once he saw how deadly serious I was, he dropped his attitude. "Please excuse me for one moment." He left the folder behind and followed me into the hallway.

I didn't let the door shut before I started talking. "Vanessa has been taken. It just happened. I was going to drive back to Florence to retrieve my gear, but there isn't time for that. I need everything you have, guns, ammunition, vests, everything."

All the hostility and anger left his face immediately, replaced by such sorrow it seemed like he'd just lost his world. He couldn't even speak because the air had been ripped out of his lungs. Agony like no other entered his features, turned him from a man to a corpse.

I couldn't give him the time he needed to process this. "I know who took her. I promise you, I will get her back." I wouldn't stop until she was in my arms and all those men were dead. On top of that, I would kill their families too. They crossed a line coming after Vanessa. It was my turn to cross the same line. "Crow, where are your weapons?"

He snapped out of it, finally. "At the house. Let's go." He walked with me down the hallway and pulled out his phone. He called Cane. "Meet at the house. We have an emergency. Don't ask any questions, and just do what I say."

We left the building and ran to the truck. "What about Mrs. Barsetti?"

"We don't have time for that. Drive."

WE PULLED up to the house and darted inside. On the third floor next to his office was where he stashed all his weaponry. He handed over everything, his pistols, shotguns, and rifles. I took everything I could carry and secured a vest around my chest.

I couldn't afford to get shot this time.

"Who are these men?" Crow had changed into jeans and a t-shirt, and he secured a vest over his chest.

"They're from my last hit. I killed my target, but the son caught me in the hallway. I shot him, but I guess I didn't kill him. Now they want revenge." I should have shot him twice to make sure. The rest of the palace had been searching for me, and I didn't have time. How they figured out who I was and understood what Vanessa meant to me was a mystery.

"Do you know where they are?" Cane asked.

"They're probably taking her back to Morocco." There was nowhere they could go where I wouldn't find her.

"How certain are you?" Crow asked.

"Based on Vanessa's description. We spoke before they ambushed her."

Another jolt of pain moved into Crow's eyes. He did his best to fight it, but he struggled.

It broke my heart, so I couldn't watch. This was all my fault. If I'd left the job sooner, this wouldn't be happening right now. "I'll get her back. I promise you."

Crow wouldn't look at me.

Cane looked at his brother, the same throbbing pain in his eyes. He didn't comfort his brother because there wasn't time, but he certainly felt the same agony.

I put what I needed in a bag and walked out, heading back to the entryway. I set my bag on the doorstep then pulled out my phone. Several months ago, I put a tracker in her ankle just in case she tried to run off. After she went out drinking one night, she'd made the idiotic decision to walk home alone. The only reason I knew that was because I'd been watching her tracker like crazy. Now I used it again, hoping they hadn't found it.

It was still working.

And as I feared, they were headed straight for the airport.

Crow and Cane joined me outside where an SUV was parked. Blacked-out and ready for battle, it was just as good as a tank.

"They're headed to the airport. No way to make it on time."

"How do know that?" Crow asked.

Now wasn't the time to hide my mistakes. "I have a tracker on her. They haven't found it yet."

Crow didn't react to the statement. "Let's hope they don't find it. You're certain they're going to Morocco?"

"No doubt." I was willing to bet my life on it. They were arrogant enough to assume I wouldn't figure out what happened to her since I wasn't there. They'd obviously been watching the place, and when I left, they made their move.

"Alright." Crow carried the leather bag over his shoulder. "We have a chopper that can take us to Northern Africa. We'll have another team on the ground with the equipment we need to go the rest of the way."

I would also call Max and bring in the boys. "Alright. Let's get moving."

Conway came out of the house, wearing sweatpants and a t-shirt. "Father, what's going on—"

"Son, I don't have time. I'm sorry." He ran up to him and gave him a quick hug. He kissed him on the forehead before he turned away. "I love you. Tell your mother I love her too."

Speechless, Conway watched him go, terror written all over his face.

We jumped into the SUV and took off.

———

EVERY MINUTE that passed was torture.

I was terrified, more terrified than I'd ever been in my life.

I'd been shot more times than I could count, and I'd stood on the doorstep in front of the pearly gates more than once, but I'd never been afraid.

This was real fear, raw and heavy.

I feared what they were doing to her. I feared...

I couldn't even think it.

I called Max when we were on the chopper. "I need a favor."

"You just retired, and you already need a favor?" he asked, thinking this was all a joke.

"Max, Vanessa has been taken."

He turned quiet.

"I thought I killed the son in Morocco, but he must have survived. He's the one behind this."

"You're sure?"

"No doubt. I'm in the chopper now headed to Africa. Vanessa's father and uncle are with me, and they have a group of men meeting us on the ground with vehicles and artillery. But I need more help than that."

"What do you want me to do, Bones?"

"I need you and the guys. I'm sorry to ask, but I've got to get her back."

"Bones…you aren't part of the team anymore."

"I realize that—"

"And we already put our asses on the line for her just two months ago."

"I get that—"

"I can't help you, Bones." He spoke with pain in his voice, like he hated denying me. "Shane is on a mission right now. I have to run operations from the office. I can't turn my back on him."

"Shit."

"I can send you some extra men, maybe a dozen, but that's the best I can do."

"I'll take it, Max." I thought my boys would be there for me, but if they were in the middle of a mission, there was nothing that could be done. I was on my own.

"I'm so sorry, Bones. I know this must be…" He fell silent, unable to say anything.

"I'm gonna get her back, Max."

"I have no doubt you will."

"I'm not sure how they figured out who I am." I didn't accuse Max of anything, knowing he covered his tracks better than anyone I knew.

"I don't either. I can look into it for you."

"Please." I wanted to know if I had any other enemies creeping around behind my back.

"Do you have a plan?"

"No."

"Is her tracker still in place?"

"I just checked it five minutes ago, and it still has a signal. She's on a plane headed right toward Morocco."

"I bet they're taking her to the palace," Max said. "That's my best bet."

"I agree. They're being sloppy, assuming I wouldn't figure this out."

Max was quiet for a long time. "Or this is exactly what they want…"

To lure me into their territory—so they could get revenge.

"Coming after you in Italy would be stupid. But taking Vanessa gives them the advantage. You're running out of time, so you're going to follow them as quickly as possible, not preparing fully for the war. This is exactly what they want, Bones. They want you —not her."

If they wanted me, they could have me. If they just let my woman go…I would give them my head on a silver platter. "You're right."

"That's good news for you…but also bad. If they can have both of you, that's ideal."

"They aren't getting both." Vanessa was my priority, and I would do anything to gain her freedom. But I had to do my best to survive too, because losing me would kill her anyway.

"I hope you're right, Bones. I'll get that team together and have them meet at the rendezvous point."

"Thanks, Max."

"Good luck, man."

"Yeah…"

He hung up.

Crow and Cane both stared at me, waiting for the details.

"Max will send a dozen men our way to help. They'll give us some equipment too."

"Are your men joining us?" Crow asked.

"No. They're in the middle of a mission." I was disappointed, but I couldn't be angry. Max couldn't turn his back on Shane. That wouldn't be the right thing to do.

"Shit," Cane said as he dragged his hands down his face.

I was ashamed that we were in this situation, that I was the reason Vanessa had been taken. I'd promised to protect her, but now she was in the hands of men who wanted to hurt me. If they laid a single hand on her…I would kill their entire family line. "They want revenge for what I did. If I can't save her, I should be able to trade her."

"Your life for hers?" Crow asked.

I nodded.

"And will you do that?" Crow asked, his eyes filled with a pain he couldn't defeat.

I was offended he even asked. "In a heartbeat."

Satisfied with that answer, he turned away.

FIFTEEN

Vanessa

I was chained to a chair on a private plane.

The men spoke Arabic, which I couldn't understand.

I was dead quiet, keeping my eyes averted and trying to disappear. I didn't want them to even know I was there. Now I was en route to an unknown destination, and the fear started to kick in. I was stuck on a plane, and there was no way Bones would be able to save me now. They could do whatever they wanted to me.

All I had was myself.

I truly believed Bones would save me. But he couldn't stop the events that happened in between.

And I didn't want to go through the same thing my mother went through…

The thought alone made me more afraid than I'd been in my entire life.

There were two guards watching me at all times. They all carried rifles, guns that were too big for their hands. They kept looking at me, like I would do something unexpected at any moment.

The man in charge sat up front, drinking with his men and speaking in the language I couldn't understand. Whoever these men were, they were excessively wealthy and obviously powerful. They were able to board a private plane with dozens of weapons without anyone even glancing at them.

Who the hell were they?

I kept looking out the window, doing my best to remain calm. If Bones weren't around, I believed my father would find a way to save me, but knowing Bones was out there gave me more comfort. He was capable and trained for this. On top of that, he loved me. He would never stop until I was rescued.

I believed in him with all my heart.

BASED on the landscape around me, I figured out I was in Morocco. The famous bazaar with the gathering of thousands of people told me where I was. Bones had just been in Morocco for a hit, and it seemed like the most likely destination.

Bones mentioned he killed the target and was discovered by the son.

That must be the man who took me.

So this was all for revenge, not money.

But if they really wanted revenge, the best way to do that was to kill the person Bones loved most…which was me. And if they didn't kill me, they would torture me. Worse, they would rape me.

I closed my eyes as I sat in the back seat of the car, doing my best to remain calm in the most terrifying position in my life. This was far worse than Knuckles, a single man who only wanted me for one thing. This was an entire organization of terrorists, all carrying enormous guns and enough ammunition to destroy an entire city.

I was just one person—who was handcuffed.

I hoped Bones was one step behind me. He'd probably figured out what was going on. And if the tracker was still active in my ankle, he would be able to trace me right to the spot I was in. As long as that was working, I would be saved.

It was only a matter of time.

They drove up into the Atlas Mountains and along the windy roads that hugged the cliff. Nighttime had descended, so visibility became even worse. We approached a three-story palace on the left, the white walls up leading to circular ceilings decorated with bronze and gold.

Once we arrived, I didn't know what would happen.

I had to prepare for the worst.

They yanked me out of the car and dragged me through the entryway. The first room was three stories tall, the staircase wrapped around the three walls. There were enormous pots and elegant furniture right in the walkway, along with huge paintings that took up all the space on the walls.

If I weren't so afraid, I would find the place beautiful.

The men spoke to each other in their language, glancing at me from time to time.

I wanted to say something, to demand my freedom, but my sassiness wouldn't help me this time. The best thing to do was be quiet, to seem as unthreatening as possible. Bones was coming for me, so there was no point in irritating them.

The two men eventually escorted me up the stairs and into one of the bedrooms. It had a single bed with nothing else in the room. It wasn't elaborate like the rest of the palace, so I knew this room only served one purpose.

To house prisoners like me.

They guided me to the bed then handcuffed my hands to the metal bar at the top of the frame. They spoke to each other for a few minutes before they stepped out, closing the bedroom door.

It was the first time I'd been alone since they took me, and I immediately looked out the window that showed the mountainside. There were bars over the window, making it impossible to escape that way.

But it didn't matter because I was secured to the metal bar above the bed.

All I could do was sit there—and pray Bones came fast.

I'D FALLEN asleep throughout the night, the quiet lulling me into a false sense of safety. I told myself to remain calm, that Bones would be there any moment. Instead of panicking for hours on end, sleeping was the best way to pass the time. There was no immediate danger, not while the bedroom door was closed.

But then I heard the lock click.

My eyes opened in the darkness, the moon shining a light through the window. I'd just been asleep, but since danger lurked around me, I was instantly awake. My eyes focused on the door and watched it move inward as one of the two men who were guarding the door came inside. His gun wasn't with him this time.

That wasn't good.

He shut the door behind him then slowly approached the bed.

His intentions were as obvious as words on a billboard. He'd come into my room in the middle of the night for one thing.

One thing he wouldn't get. "Don't." I pulled my legs toward my body, my hands automatically yanking on the bar overheard even though escape was impossible.

He halted when he realized I was awake. He didn't say a word before he started to undo his pants.

No.

I couldn't let this happen.

I refused to let this happen.

"I'm warning you," I whispered. "Don't do this."

Maybe he didn't speak English, or he just didn't care. He pushed his pants down along with his underwear, revealing a penis that was pathetic in comparison to Bones's. Covered in dark hair, it was the most disgusting thing in the world.

"When I tell Bones what you did, he won't stop with you."

He halted, his dark eyes looking into mine.

"He'll kill your wife. Your parents. Your kids. He'll kill everyone—and I won't stop him. You know what he's capable of. He's the biggest assassin in Europe, a man who's killed more people than you've even met. If you do this, there's no going back."

Just when he seemed to be listening to me, he moved in again. He grabbed one of my legs so he could remove my jeans.

That was when I started to fight. I kicked him as hard as I could, hitting him right in the side.

He turned more aggressive, using his size to pin down my legs.

So much adrenaline. So much fear. "I'll make a deal with you. Don't do this, and when Bones comes, I'll tell him not to kill you. I will protect you. He'll kill everyone else in this palace just the way he killed your leader—but you'll be the one to walk away. You'll take the power. You'll be the only one left standing."

He kept his weight on my legs, but he stopped trying to remove my jeans.

I held his gaze, my heart racing so much that it hurt with every beat. "You know he'll come for me. You know how vicious he will be. I will be the only person who can protect you. Spare me, and I'll spare you."

He stayed on top of me, his eyes locked on mine. An entire minute passed, and nothing but silent eye contact ensued. He deliberated to himself, obviously understanding every word I said.

Even now, Bones was protecting me. His power made lesser men falter, made them cower in fear.

The man moved back, pulling his weight off my legs. Then he pulled up his pants.

I almost started to cry because I was so relieved. Bones protected me. Even when he wasn't in the room with me, he protected me. "You made the right decision. I give you my word that he won't touch you when he gets here."

SIXTEEN

Bones

_____

We assembled on the ground and prepared to move out.

Crow ignored every phone call he received. It was probably Pearl wanting to know what was going on.

But he didn't have the strength to tell her.

The tracker showed that she was in the palace I'd infiltrated just a week ago. She was on the second story in a bedroom.

I didn't want to think about what might be happening to her at that very moment.

"I'll move in with my team. The two of you stay back."

Crow looked at me like I'd just said something incredibly offensive. "All three of us are going in there."

There wasn't time for an argument, but Crow and Cane wouldn't blindly follow orders like the others. "The two of you stay back with the other men. I know the palace better than you do. I already researched the

299

place before I hit it the first time. I know how the patrols work. I know where the guards are. I'm gonna hit them hard. But I need to go alone. Because if I don't make it…then you need to move in. It'll catch them by surprise."

Crow still looked pissed, like he didn't like that idea one bit. "We should give it everything we have."

"This is my fault, and I'm taking responsibility for it. Vanessa is my woman, and I will get her out of there. I'm not going to risk either of you unless I absolutely have to."

"Griffin, Cane and I aren't concerned with our lives right now—"

"Trust me." I held his gaze, needing him to back down. "Vanessa isn't my wife—she's so much more than that. I will get her out of there. They can shoot me as many times as they want. Those bullets won't stop me. Let me get her out of there and back to you. You can take it from there."

Crow still wore his enraged expression but didn't say anything more.

"This is personal now. I want to slaughter every single one of those men until that palace is a grave-yard. I don't want to be worried about you behind me. I don't want to be concerned with anything else other than murder. This is what I do best. No offense, but you have no idea what you're stepping into." I'd killed more men than Cane and Crow combined. I was half their age but had decades of more experience under my belt. "This is my fight. Let me fight it."

Cane turned to his brother, allowing him to make the final decision.

Crow took thirty seconds before he gave his answer. "Get my daughter out of there, Griffin."

That was exactly what I was looking for.

I turned away without saying goodbye and proceeded on foot with the team of six men. Most of them were snipers, and they would take their positions and cover me as I entered the grounds. Two of them would come with me, covering my back so I could focus on my front.

We moved through the darkness and approached the entryway to the palace, which sat on a cliff and overlooked the valley. I had a shotgun slung over my back, a pair of Uzis, and two of my favorite blades.

The blades weren't for effectiveness—but for blood.

I snuck over to the entryway, moving through the bushes and getting past the front guards. They were on either side of the door, both wearing rifles and oblivious to the threat under their noses. They looked at the mountain, missing the brigade of men hiding to the left.

I pulled out my blades and stabbed the first one in the neck, making his throat fill with blood so he could barely make a shriek. His heavy body started to fall just as I descended on the second guard. He was quicker than the first, but not quick enough. He pointed his assault rifle at me but didn't pull the trigger.

Because I sliced his throat so deep I hit the bone.

He crumpled at my feet, his gun clanking against the ground.

Other men heard the sound of their fallen comrades, and that's when the war truly started. Gunfire erupted from both sides.

The men could handle the perimeter, so I dashed inside, coming face-to-face with more men who were prepared to blow my brains out. One man fired right at my chest, hitting the vest that protected me. The momentum of the bullet made most men jerk, but it didn't stop me at all.

I pulled out my pistols and began the bloodbath.

I shot two men in the head, not wasting any bullets by missing my mark. Then I grabbed my shotgun and moved to the next group of men.

I dashed up the staircase and got into a gun battle with five men. They all aimed their bullets at me, but the bullets flew past, destroying the painting on the wall. I peeked over the rail and fired down in return, hitting the two idiots that were out in the open. I took them down with a few rounds and then proceeded to the last three.

When another man ran through the entryway, he had the best shot at me.

I shot him first, hitting him in the hand so his gun flew across the room.

He shrieked and gripped his wrist, holding his now-deformed hand. Blood poured from everywhere, and he moved to his knees, in too much shock to respond.

I took the stairs one at a time as I approached him, my gun lowered.

"Mercy…" He fell back as I came closer to him, slipping on the blood from his hand.

"Sorry, I don't speak English." I didn't waste a bullet, and instead, stabbed him in the neck, killing him viciously like injured game that was being gutted.

His cries died away the second my blade sliced his throat in half.

I moved to the second floor as I heard the gunshots continue outside. Vanessa was down one of the hallways. I knew exactly where she was because I'd memorized the map. But there were other men here by now, men who would attempt to relocate her or ambush me.

I was right. They ambushed me.

Three men came out with rifles. I picked up the grenade from my belt and tossed it down the hallway.

The explosion was enough to make the ground shake. It wasn't close enough to Vanessa to hit her, but she certainly would have felt it.

One of them jumped out of the way before the explosion could touch him. He was crawling away, coughing as he reached for his gun.

I pulled out the knife again, preferring a clean death that saved my ammunition. I stabbed him in the back, right through the heart and lung.

He collapsed, slowly suffocating and bleeding to death.

I left him there instead of putting him out of his misery.

I turned down the hallway and proceeded to Vanessa's room, so much rage in my body that I could barely think straight. All I wanted to do was kill everyone in that palace, kill their wives and children. I wanted to wipe out this entire organization, make their enemies laugh at them for the poor decision they made. "Baby, I'm coming!" I kept my pistol out, ready for anyone who might jump in my way. I didn't care about giving away my position anymore.

I wanted them to know exactly where I was.

I found her door and tried the handle, but it was locked.

"Griffin!" Vanessa's terrified voice shouted through the door.

"Baby, I'm here." I pointed the gun at the lock and fired until the metal snapped apart. Then I kicked the door down, finding one of the men huddled in the corner, practically pissing himself. I pulled out my knife and came at him, watching him scream.

"Griffin, no! Leave him." Vanessa tried to sit up, but she couldn't move, not with the handcuffs that secured her to the bed. "Not him."

I didn't know why she was defending this man, but there wasn't time to ask. I moved to the bed and tugged on the chains, trying to free them with my strength.

"I have a key…" The man from the floor pulled out a silver key and tossed it on the floor.

I kicked his rifle away and grabbed the key. I unlocked one handcuff then handed her the gun. "Watch my back, baby."

"Okay." She held the gun with her right hand, keeping her eyes on the door.

I worked the second lock until I finally got it free.

Vanessa pulled the trigger, and a body collapsed to the floor behind me.

I didn't turn around to check. "Good shot, baby." I finally yanked the cuff from her wrist, enraged when I saw how red both of her wrists were. There wasn't time for kisses or tears. Pandemonium spread all around us. I had to focus on getting her out of there before I could celebrate.

I pulled her to her feet then unfastened my vest.

"What are you doing—"

"Shut up and listen to me." I tied the vest around her and secured it, even though it was too big. I put the gun in her hand. "Stay behind me."

"I'm the one with the vest—"

"Baby." I burned her with just my gaze alone.

She shut her mouth.

I moved first into the hallway, my shotgun raised. "Crow, I have Vanessa. I'm gonna take her to the front. Pull up so I can throw her in."

"Copy that," Crow said, the sound of relief in his voice.

I led the way, my shotgun raised and loaded. I listened to Vanessa behind me; she was breathing loud but kept her gun up the entire time. I moved down the hallway I'd just walked along, and when I reached the entryway, I fired at the two men on the ground floor. I shot the first one dead.

Vanessa got the second one.

We moved down the stairs and out the front door. There were still gunshots everywhere. "Stay behind me, Vanessa. Crow, how far are you?"

"Forty-five seconds."

I grabbed the loaded rifle from the dead man I'd killed earlier. "We're ready."

"Approaching," Crow said.

I saw the blacked-out SUV approach, and I knew we had to make our move now. "Let's go. Stay behind me." We moved out the front door, hustling fast so the gunmen wouldn't notice us right away.

The SUV stopped, and Cane opened the back door.

I practically threw Vanessa inside. "Take her out of here."

Vanessa turned around when she was inside, the blood draining from her face. "Griffin, no!"

"Get your ass in the car," Cane said. "You got your revenge."

"No. Not even close." I grabbed the door.

Vanessa was about to jump back out of the truck. "Griffin!"

I slammed the door shut and turned away, heading

back into the palace to finish this once and for all. I wouldn't be able to sleep at night until every man in that palace was dead. Only when every single one of my enemies was eliminated would I find peace. They all deserved to die for what they did—for taking my woman.

Every. Single. One.

THE SON WAS on his knees in the middle of the room, his guard of men dead around him. Brains splashed across the tile, and men continued to bleed from the holes in their chests. He was bleeding from the mouth where I'd punched his teeth out. His face was so discolored from my punches, he was barely recognizable.

I stood behind him, watching the life leave his body. "I'm going to slit your throat just like I did with all your other men. And when I'm done…" I circled around him, moving to his face so I could stare at his black eyes. "Your wife and two sons will be next."

"Please…"

"If you wanted to keep them safe, you shouldn't have touched my woman."

The fight returned to his gaze. "You killed my father!"

"Who was a murderer and a terrorist. If I didn't kill him, it would have been someone else. Vanessa was an innocent person. So don't give me that bullshit."

"Not my family…"

"You shouldn't have touched mine, then." I pulled out the blade, the knife that had killed most of his men that night. "And I will kill them exactly the way I'm going to kill you, the way I executed all the men who surrendered. I put them on their knees, yanked their heads back, and sliced their throats down to the bone. You're next, asshole."

He started to shake. "Don't. Touch. Them."

"What are you going to do about it?" I kneeled in front of him, holding the bloody knife in my hand. "Huh?"

His jaw was clenched tight as the blood poured down his chin.

"That's right," I said. "Nothing. You will do nothing because you're my bitch now. You will die in the room that used to be your throne. You will be powerless to protect the ones you love. I will never be powerless. Any man who ever touches my family will pay the full price in return."

"Mercy…"

"You forfeited mercy the instant you touched my woman."

"Please…" He started to cry, tears running down his face. "My oldest son is only five…"

I didn't feel any pity in my heart, none at all. "It's sad that an innocent child will die because his father became too arrogant. You really thought this stupid plan of yours was going to work? I'm a hitman. I'm paid to kill people. It's nothing personal. But asshole, you made this personal." I pointed the knife at him.

He no longer seemed afraid of his own death, just for the safety of his family. "Not my children…not my wife."

"You touched my woman."

"And I'm sorry for that…"

"Oh, you're sorry?" I cocked my head to the side. "She was chained up in a room like a goddamn slave. For that reason alone, I'll kill your entire family. Your mother is still alive, so I'll throw her in there too."

"No!"

"Enough with the small talk." I pressed the edge of the blade right against his throat. "Last words?"

He held my gaze as he breathed hard. Acceptance slowly entered his puffy eyes, along with the resignation. "My family is innocent. Please—"

I sliced his neck and let him fall to the floor.

I wiped my blade on his shirt then returned it to the sheath before I walked away. The gunfire had stopped because the war was over. All the men in the palace had been killed, and most of my men had survived. Any backup that might have been coming to the son's aid had driven away, knowing there was no one to save.

I walked past the graveyard of bodies, kicking aside limbs when they got in my way. Vanessa had been saved, and I'd killed everyone who remained behind. But my blood lust wasn't satisfied. He took my family away from me, the most important person in my life. She was my whole world—and he touched her.

I wasn't finished yet.

I would track down the rest of his family—and burn them alive.

I walked to the entryway of the palace and found the last man that I hadn't killed, the one Vanessa asked me to spare. I never had a chance to ask why he was worth saving. Since I didn't know what her reason was, I let him live.

He stared at me, visibly starting to shake now that every man in that palace was dead. He slowly crept away, his hands in the air in the form of surrender.

It was hard for me not to kill him, almost impossible. But I didn't pull my knife because my woman had requested that he live.

She better have a good reason.

I stepped outside as Crow spoke into my ear. "Griffin, are you there?"

I'd turned off the headset during battle, knowing he would just try to talk me out of staying. "I'm here."

"Are you alright?"

"More than alright. Everyone is dead."

He sighed over the line. "I'm glad you're okay."

"How's Vanessa?" I hadn't even gotten a chance to kiss her.

"She's staring at me right now, crying because she knows you're alright."

I wanted her tears to soak into my t-shirt. I wanted

to taste those tears on my tongue. I wanted to wrap my arms around her and tell her I would never let anything happen to her again. I wanted to apologize…for everything. "Tell her I love her."

"She knows, Griffin. You just proved it."

And I wasn't done yet.

"We're at the rendezvous point with the chopper. We'll wait for you before we take off."

"Don't bother."

Crow was quiet for a moment. "Do you have other arrangements?"

"I'm not done here. There's some business I have to finish. When I'm done, I'll head home."

"Griffin, what business?"

"I killed the man who started all of this. But I promised I would kill his family—because he touched mine." I'd never been a moral man. Life and death were boring to me. Everyone experienced both, so if death came prematurely, it didn't matter to me. I'd never killed a man's family in my life, not out of vengeance. But this man crossed a line no one else ever had. They touched my woman, the person who should be untouchable. They took her when I wasn't there, knowing they wouldn't have been able to get to her through me. It was pathetic—and it pissed me off even more. If I'd been there, Vanessa wouldn't have had to go through this at all. I wasn't sure what the men did to her, and I wasn't even prepared to think about it.

"Griffin," Crow said gently. "I understand you're angry—"

"You don't know the half of it."

"But killing his family isn't right," he said.

"They took Vanessa."

"Which was wrong. But don't kill an innocent family—"

"I don't care, Crow." I'd made up my mind, and I wasn't going to change it. "You can keep talking to me, or you can go home back to your wife. I suggest you do the latter."

Crow was quiet for a while before he spoke again. "Vanessa wanted to talk to you." He handed the radio over.

I was staring at the mountain from the front of the palace, the sun rising in the distance and casting the landscape in beautiful colors. The Atlas Mountains started to come alive as the smell of blood rose into the air.

Her beautiful voice sounded over the line, heavy with tears. "Griffin…"

"Baby." My heart softened slightly, but not like it did before. I was still too livid to think rationally, to love her the way I usually did. "Are you alright?"

"I'm fine. They didn't hurt me."

"Good." But that didn't change my rage.

"Don't do this…"

"I have to, Vanessa."

"No, you don't."

I wasn't going to change my mind. Fear and respect were the same in my world. If I wanted no one to fuck with me ever again, I had to scare them shitless. "It's how it is, baby. Go home with your family. I'll see you when I get back."

"Griffin…" Her tears were heard over the phone. "I don't want you to do this."

"I love you, baby. But I don't care what you want." I was being harsh to the woman I loved because I couldn't think clearly. I was so enraged by what these people had done to us. If they'd tried to kill me, I would have brushed it off without caring. But to touch my woman…was an idiotic move.

"Griffin, you killed all the men there. That's enough. Don't hunt down a woman and her kids. You took your revenge and protected me, but going after innocent people will just make you a monster."

"Maybe I want to be a monster."

"No, you don't."

"They took you. It's only fair."

"Don't be like them, Griffin. You're better than this. This isn't you…"

"Maybe you don't know me that well." All I wanted to do was kill and kill some more.

"I do know you," she whispered. "I know you better than anyone. You're still angry right now, as you have every right to be. But this doesn't solve anything. You killed the men who crossed us. You accomplished your goal. Now come back to me so we can go home and be happy together. Killing innocent people isn't going to make you feel better. It'll only make you feel worse. Not right away, but eventually."

I stared at the mountain, silent.

"Griffin, please. I need you right now. I need you to hold me and kiss my tears away."

I breathed hard, my chest rising and falling as I greeted the rising sun.

"If I'm the most important person in your life, then you need to listen to me. I'm telling you that I need you. I'm telling you not to hurt those innocent people. I'm telling you, commanding you, to get your ass over here so we can go home. Don't make me tell you again." Sassiness mixed with tears came over the line, sounding like the woman I fell so hard for.

But I still wanted to keep killing.

"Don't you want to marry me?" she whispered.

The odd question caught me off guard. "Yes."

"Then prove it. Come home with me, and let's do it."

"They deserve to die…"

"No, they don't. And if you do kill them…I won't love you the same way. The man I love is hard and vicious, but only when he needs to be. The rest of the time, he's loving and devoted. He's protective of the less fortunate. Don't turn into someone else, someone I didn't fall for. You're better than this. I know you are. So don't make me ask again. Come to me now—and let's go home."

I'd accomplished the impossible by slaughtering all the men in that palace. I only spared one man and butchered all the others. But the reason I did all of those things was because of the woman I loved. She fueled my rage as well as my joy. If this was that important to her, then I needed to let it go. I had to remember why I did all of this in the first place—to save my woman.

"Griffin?" she whispered.

I resisted the rage burning in my blood and focused on the woman asking for me. She needed me, and killing more people wouldn't give her what she wanted. I folded, subdued by the need in her voice. "I'm coming."

SEVENTEEN

Vanessa

———————

We waited on the outskirts of the border, the chopper ready to take us away the second Bones showed up. I was still disturbed by what he told me, that he wanted to kill the wife and children of his enemy. He butchered everyone in that palace and accomplished the impossible. I didn't want bloodshed, but I understood it had to be done.

But to hurt the family was a line I wouldn't cross.

I couldn't let him do it, regardless of how angry he was. He was a different man when I spoke to him, his rage clouding his judgment. The second those men took me, Bones turned into another person. He regressed back into the man he used to be, the man I originally met. The second I was taken from him, all his civility was gone.

My father stayed by my side, keeping his hand on my shoulder to comfort himself more than to comfort

317

me. When I was back in his arms, he didn't hide his tears. He told me he loved me, squeezed me as he wept, and showed a vulnerable side to him that I'd never witnessed before.

It broke my heart.

He squeezed my shoulder, keeping his hand on me like he might lose me. "You did the right thing, *tesoro*. He would have regretted it."

I looked across the desert, waiting for a car to appear with Bones inside of it. "He wasn't thinking clearly." I had to believe he would have come to his senses on his own, that he wouldn't have murdered innocent people.

"When it comes to the people we love, we never think clearly. If the same situation happened to your mother...I would probably do the exact same thing."

"I really hope not."

"It's hard to understand, *tesoro*. But when a man wants to protect his woman...he'll stop at nothing."

I would stab a man in the heart for hurting Bones, but I would never stab his wife. I crossed my arms over my chest as I waited, wanting to touch the man who'd saved me. I was never afraid he wouldn't come for me, but I still wanted to feel him, see that he was safe without bullet holes in his flesh. "I hope all of this doesn't change your opinion of him..."

He lowered his hand and followed my gaze across the horizon, watching the sun rise. "No. He got you back. That's all that matters. He quit that line of work, so this should never happen again."

"No, it shouldn't."

"I was so scared, *tesoro*. But I also felt better knowing he would stop at nothing to get you back. He's a strong man, one of the strongest I know. If anyone could save you, it would be him. I know he'll protect you for the rest of your life."

"He will." My eyes narrowed at the horizon when I finally saw a black vehicle in the distance. Dust kicked up into the air as the wheels propelled the SUV forward. It approached quickly, covering the distance rapidly because it was driving as fast as it could. "That must be him."

Father walked away and shouted to the crew. "Get the chopper ready. We need to leave as quickly as possible."

The rotors started to circulate, and my hair began to fly in the wind.

The SUV finally arrived, and Bones hopped out of the driver's seat. He looked like he was in perfect condition, not a drop of blood anywhere on his clothes. His eyes appeared to have sustained the most damage, the pain and rage still throbbing from my kidnapping. He closed the door then marched toward me, the same look in his eyes as when I shot him in the snow. His shoulder took the bullet, but my insanity only made him want me more. With nostrils flared and a fire in his eyes, he closed the gap between us then grabbed my face with both hands. He kissed me hard, just the way he did right against the van in the middle of the snow. Indifferent to my father and uncle standing right there, he embraced me like we were the only two people in the world. With crushing force from his mouth and a tight grip with his hands, he held me so fiercely, it seemed like he would never let me go. Words failed him, and he expressed himself the only way he knew how—with his touch.

Once I felt him hold me like that, all the fear I'd held for the past twenty hours evaporated. I knew he would save me, but now that we were together, I felt at peace once more. He annihilated everyone who wanted to do us harm so there was no one left to haunt us.

He pulled his mouth away and looked into my face, still possessing that maniacal gleam in his eyes. He breathed hard as his fingertips dug into my neck. He moved his lips to my forehead and kissed me as he wrapped his arms around me and held me close. His heavy breaths fell against my skin, and he gripped me so tightly I could hardly breathe. His palm moved to the back of my head, and he cradled me like I was fragile. "Fuck. I'm so sorry, baby." He rested his chin on my head, his chest pressing against my body every time he took a deep breath. "I'll never let anything happen to you ever again. You have my word."

"It's okay—"

"It's not okay." His voice broke, the emotion entering his words and forcing him to stop speaking.

I knew he didn't want me to look at him like that, so I kept my face against my chest. I remembered the day he'd left me, the way his eyes glistened and turned red. He was a man of limited emotion, preferring anger and rage over anything more vulnerable. But with me, he wasn't the same man. "I knew you would save me, Griffin. I knew you would come."

"Doesn't matter."

"It's over now." I pulled away and lifted my chin to look into his face.

His eyes were so wet, a tear formed and dripped down his cheek. He maintained a serious expression, his mouth still and his eyes unashamed. He couldn't combat the emotion, but he didn't let it increase either. The tear made its way to his chin.

I kissed it away.

He closed his eyes at my touch, and when he opened them again, the emotion was cleared away. "I slit their throats. Every last one of them."

I didn't want to hear this, but I didn't interrupt him.

"I didn't go for the quickest kill. I forced them all to their knees, and one by one, I put a knife to their throat. They pissed and shit themselves. They begged for their lives, but I didn't flinch. They took you away from me—and I made each one pay the price."

"I know, Griffin," I said gently.

His hand cupped my cheek again, and he stared into my eyes. "That will never happen again. This, I promise you."

"I know."

His thumb brushed across my cheek, and he sighed quietly under his breath. "Did they hurt you?"

"No."

"Don't lie to me."

I held his gaze, showing my sincerity. "I'm not, Griffin."

"Did they…?" He took a deep breath because he couldn't finish the sentence. The thought pained him too much, more than the idea of them hurting me.

"No." Thankfully, that didn't happen. But if Griffin had taken an extra day to arrive, I probably wouldn't have been able to give the same answer. "That man I asked you not to kill…"

His eyes shifted back and forth as he looked into mine.

"He tried…but I told him I would protect him if he stopped. I told him you would come for me, and when you did, I would make sure you spared him. So he didn't do it. He changed his mind…because of you. Even when you weren't in the same room, you protected me. That's how powerful you are, Griffin."

He closed his eyes and stepped back, unable to swallow the grief that filled his body. Crisis had been averted, but the fact that I had to leverage my freedom still killed him inside.

"Whether we're together or apart, you always protect me, Griffin." I pressed my hand to his cheek and willed him to open his eyes again. "We're together now. Everything is alright. Let it go."

He refused to look at me. "Losing my mother was the second worst thing that ever happened to me. She never came home, and until I was taken by the orphanage, I didn't understand what had happened to her. It wasn't until years later, when my classmates had birthday parties and celebrated holidays, that I understood what I was missing…that my mother should still be there. The worst thing that ever happened to me was losing you." He opened his eyes and held my gaze, the fury deep within the look. "I can't go through that again, baby. If I couldn't save you…I would have put a barrel in my mouth and pulled the trigger."

"Don't say that—"

"It's true." His fingers moved into my hair. "I never would have forgiven myself. And I certainly couldn't live with that guilt, with your memory haunting me. I will protect you as long as I live, because whatever happens to you, happens to me too. And I promise that I will never let anything happen again. Never."

"I know…"

"It shouldn't have happened at all. I should have listened to your father sooner. He was right."

"It doesn't matter now. It's over." My hands wrapped around his wrists. "Everyone we love is safe. All our enemies are dead. So let's go home…and have that quiet life we've always talked about."

He pressed his forehead to mine. "You're forgiving me too quickly, baby."

"There's nothing to forgive. No matter what happens in our lives, I know you will always save me. I'm not afraid of anything. Why would I be when I have you?" I closed my eyes as I felt him, felt the connection between both of our souls. "Now take me home."

He kissed my forehead before he finally released me. The emotion that was in his eyes was gone because he quickly bottled it up inside, refusing to show that kind of weakness to anyone but me.

My father walked up to him. Instead of carrying resentment for the man who had caused all of this in the first place, he wrapped his arms around Griffin and hugged him tightly, treating him the way he would Conway. "I'm glad you made it back okay. Was worried there for a minute."

"Don't ever worry about me, Crow."

Seeing the way Bones interacted with my father always brought tears to my eyes. The two men I loved most in the world were close now, and that gave me such happiness. It was what I always wanted, for them to have their own relationship.

"Not possible." My father pulled away and gripped his shoulder. "You're my son. I will always worry about you."

Bones held his gaze and couldn't hide the hint of emotion in his eyes. Those words clearly meant the world to him, even if he wouldn't say it out loud. I recognized his slight movements, the subtle cues he naturally emitted. He said nothing, at a loss for words.

"And thank you for saving Vanessa," my father continued. "I knew you would get her out of there."

"Don't ever thank me for that," Bones said quickly. "It's my fault she was there in the first place. I should have listened to you. I should have walked away from that job a long time ago—"

"It's in the past. Leave it there." My father lowered his hand. "It's time to bury the past for good. It's time to move forward into our new lives. It's time for peace and quiet. It's time for the next stage in all our lives." He shook his head slightly. "It took me forever to listen to my own advice, to not live in the past. You can beat yourself up over this, or we can go home and start over. What do you want to do?"

I hooked my arm around Bones's and rested my face against his shoulder. I could feel the guilt in his heart, feel the anger in his limbs. He blamed himself for all of this, but he shouldn't. We were walking away from that life. We were finally getting everything we wanted. It was time to focus on that—not the people we used to be.

Bones didn't make another argument and only gave a slight nod in return. "Let's go home."

EIGHTEEN

Carter
_____

After I picked up Mia from my parents' place, I drove back to the house fifteen minutes away. I took her bag and greeted her with a simple look, treating her with a hint of indifference. Naturally, I wanted to wrap my arms around her and let my lips brush against her hair. That affection was bottled deep inside. "How was it?" I had one hand on the wheel, the other resting on the center console.

"It was nice." As if she couldn't resist touching me, she placed her hand on mine. "I missed you."

I interlocked our fingers and squeezed her hand. "I missed you too." I'd stayed at Conway's penthouse in Milan and spent all my time working. I didn't go out at night like I normally would. I didn't jerk off either. Didn't seem appealing. When I had Mia waiting for me, all my other options didn't seem like options.

"Your parents are wonderful. They made me feel

right at home. Your mother is really sweet, and your father is nice too. And they're so in love…it's cute."

I shrugged. "I'm glad I didn't have to witness any of that."

She rolled her eyes. "It makes you happy, and you know it."

"From a distance, yes." I turned onto a different street and passed the golden fields down the road from the house we both shared. "What did you think of the cooking?"

"Amazing."

I smiled. "I miss my mama's cooking."

"She knows how to work the kitchen, that's for sure."

I passed through the gates and drove up the long driveway to the house, watching the metal gates close behind me. We inched toward the building and pulled into the garage on the side of the house. "I'm glad you were comfortable there."

"It was a good decision. I wouldn't have been able to stay here alone, even with all your security."

"I need to get you a gun and show you how to use it. Maybe that will make you more comfortable."

"I know how to pull a trigger."

"Handling a gun is more complicated than that. If you master the weapon, you might have more confidence."

"I don't think I want any guns in the house with Luca here."

I hadn't considered that. My lack of experience with kids was becoming more apparent. "Mia, I have a lot stashed around the place. But not having any guns isn't an option, unfortunately." We had to be protected in the unlikely event of an attack. It would take ten minutes for my family to get here to help, and I needed a way to protect us.

"Could you lock them away somehow? That way he can't get to them."

I guess I could carry a key around my wrist at all times. If something happened, I could unlock any door and get what I needed. "I can do that."

"Thank you. He's only eight years old…which means he'll be curious."

"I understand, sweetheart." I still couldn't believe I would be sharing the house with a child. When I made the offer, it didn't sound like an issue, but perhaps my ignorance would make this new lifestyle difficult.

"So…any news on Luca?" Her voice came out weak, like she was afraid she was annoying me by asking the question all the time.

"He'll be here on Thursday." We got out of the car and walked into the house.

She stopped in the hallway, and her loud sigh echoed against the walls. She gripped her chest like she couldn't handle the air that left her lungs. "Thursday… that's only two days from now."

"Yes." I walked into the kitchen and set my bag on the floor. "Two days from now, you'll have Luca."

She leaned against the wall and cupped her cheeks with her palms, having a slight meltdown right in the kitchen. She closed her eyes as she focused on her breathing. Seconds later, her eyes welled up with tears. "Two days…"

Pity rose in my heart, like I was responsible for her pain. I imagined my mother's reaction if someone took me away from her. She would be an even bigger mess, unable to do anything until she got me back. Taking a child away from its mother was the worst kind of torture you could inflict. At least Egor didn't hurt the kid. I wouldn't have put it past him. "Yes, sweetheart. Two days." I stepped in front of her and gripped her shoulders, comforting her in the only way I knew how.

She blinked her tears away then lowered her hands. "I'm so happy… I'm sorry that's not more obvious."

"You never have to explain your emotions to me." My palms cupped her face, and my thumbs wiped away the two tears that dripped down her cheeks. "I know you're happy." My hand moved to her heart. "But I know you're broken at the same time. I promise when you get him back, no one will ever take him away from you again. I'll make sure that never happens." This woman made me pledge my loyalty without even asking. I wanted to make her happy, give her the entire world. She'd earned my respect and my affection, but she'd earned so much more too.

"I know, Carter." She moved into my chest and wrapped her arms around me. She held me close, her cheek resting against my chest. "You're a great man, Carter. The greatest man I've ever known."

Before Mia came into my life, I was selfish, motivated by greed and sex. I was one-dimensional, uninteresting. If I'd known what I was getting myself into with her, I probably would have turned down the offer and kept my hands clean. I wasn't a hero by any means. But now, I wouldn't go back and change anything. This woman clawed through the armor around my heart and forced me to feel something, something I'd never felt before. She forced me not to be selfish, forced me to care about something other than myself. I thought I was a man before she came along, but now I felt like a bigger man than before. "I don't know if I agree with that, but thanks anyway, sweetheart."

She pulled away then grabbed my bag from the floor. "I'll put this away and make you some lunch. Do you have a request?" Once she dropped her affection, she returned to the professional relationship we had during the day.

But I wasn't in the mood for professional. I had been gone for almost three days, sleeping alone every night and working nonstop during the day. My hands got dirty from working on an engine, the pads of my fingertips were sore from gripping the pencil so tightly as I worked on the schematic in my office. Now that I was home, staring at the woman I owned indefinitely, I didn't care about lunch or my bag. "You." I pushed the strap off her shoulder, making the bag fall to the ground with a loud thud. "I don't want lunch." I stepped closer to her, my face slowly inching toward her beautiful face. "I don't want you to do my laundry. I just want you." My hand fisted her hair, and I yanked her face back slightly, making her lips perfectly accessible.

All the emotion left her gaze once I handled her that way, made my erotic demands that she had to fulfill. I kept her in my house because I wanted her to take care of my home—but I wanted her to take care of me too. Her other responsibilities could wait.

"I want you too…sir."

AT THE END of the night, when dinner was finished and the dishes were done, Mia came to my room, wearing the lingerie I'd picked out for her in Milan. With a see-through bra that showed her hard nipples and garters on her beautiful thighs, she looked like the fantasy I had every time my hand was wrapped around my dick. Her long brown hair was curled around her face, her eyelashes were thick, and she looked like a woman who was about to be seriously fucked.

I sat up in bed with my back against the headboard, my dick already hard just from thinking about how she would look. Now that my eyes settled on her tanned skin and feminine curls, my cock twitched noticeably.

She approached the bed, the sound of her heels muffled by the carpet underneath her feet. She was naturally sexy without even trying, her fingers running through her thick hair and her eyes shining brightly despite the darkness in the room. She stopped at the edge of the bed, the arousal in her eyes matching mine.

Impatient, I grabbed her and yanked her on top of me, forcing those long legs to straddle my hips. Her heels were still on, but I didn't mind in the least. I yanked on the front of her bra and forced her tit out, my mouth immediately engulfing her nipple and sucking hard. My fingers gripped her cheeks, and I gently moved her hips up and down, forcing her clit to drag against my shaft through her panties.

Within a minute, I could feel the moisture rub against my skin. Her pussy was already wet for me, so wet she was soaking through the panties and onto my length. I made this woman want sex after everything she'd been through, and that made my ego explode. I pulled her panties to the side and pointed my head at her entrance.

I slid inside so smoothly.

"Oh my god…" She gripped my shoulders as she inhaled, taking my entire length with a shaky breath. Her nails clawed into me, and her mouth opened, parted so a little of her tongue was visible.

My hand cupped her cheek, and I brought her mouth to mine for a kiss. Once her lips were on mine, I felt the fire spread throughout my entire body. She was naturally sexy without even trying. Most women worked hard to please me, hoping to get something more from me, like a relationship with my wallet. But Mia only wanted me for me…never cared about my money. Her entire body stiffened at my kiss, like my mouth was all she could think about, even though my enormous cock was inside her.

I gripped her hips and guided her back and forth, showing her how to ride my cock the way I liked. Slow and gentle was how I moved, so I could kiss her at the same time. After being away for a few days, I thought I would want something darker, kinkier. But now I just wanted the slow passion that satisfied me, the intimate pleasure between our bodies.

She loved sex this way, loved it slow and easy, appreciating every inch of my length as it moved in and out. And she loved kissing me above all else, loved feeling our lips move together with heavy breaths. Her nails clawed into me even more, and her pussy became even wetter, even tighter. She submitted to me because she knew I enjoyed it, but she enjoyed this down to her core.

And that made me enjoy it too.

She came shortly, barely lasting a few minutes before her pussy clenched around my length with the strength of a python. Cream built up around my dick, pooling at the base. She kept going, rocking onto my cock, harder as her hips naturally bucked.

My arms circled her waist, and I yanked her down onto my length, forcing her to finish with my entire dick inside her.

She kept her mouth pressed to mine but didn't kiss me, unable to because the pleasure stole all of her focus. When she finished, she looked into my eyes again, the coffee color of hers so warm it reminded me of an espresso on a winter morning. "I've never come like this in my whole life…"

I started to move her again, knowing my turn was just around the corner. "Me neither."

———

THE NEXT DAY, I fell back into my regular routine. I worked out in the morning, had breakfast, and worked from my laptop and had a meeting with my team remotely. Being five hours away really hadn't made much of a difference in my productivity, except when I had to commute back to Milan for important events.

Mia continued to do her job around the house, keeping it clean and preparing all of my meals, but whenever she was quiet, her gaze would focus on the distance and she wouldn't say a word, obviously thinking about Luca.

He would arrive tomorrow.

"Sweetheart?" I called to her from the dining room.

"Yes, Carter?" She came to my side, wearing the pink apron I got for her. She was always dressed in one of the outfits I put in her closet, designer dresses and separates. She had an affinity for nice clothes, something I didn't know about her until I saw her wear everything in her closet.

"Could you make me an espresso? I'm dragging a bit today."

"Of course." She gripped my shoulder, flashed me a pretty smile, and then walked away.

I liked to ask for things just so I could be the recipient of that look. She was happy to wait on me, happy to give me whatever I wanted. Her gratitude never faded away. It reminded me of my parents, the way my mother would take care of my father the second he came home from work. She always had dinner ready along with a smile. Taking care of him seemed to be her greatest joy.

Mia did the exact same thing.

She came back a few minutes later, a hot cup of espresso on a saucer. "Anything else? What about a biscotti?"

"No sweets." I didn't allow that stuff in the house. "Do we even have biscotti?"

She tried to suppress her grin. "I guess I have a bit of a sweet tooth…"

Since she looked so cute as she said those words, I let it slide. "Well, you enjoy those. I'll pass."

"You never eat sweets?" she asked. "Maybe once in a while?"

"On my birthday." My mom usually made me a cake along with dinner.

Both of her eyebrows rose to the top of her face. "You eat sweets once a year?"

"Sweetheart, I can't look like this if I eat sweets more than once a year." I patted my hard stomach, my eight-pack visible right underneath the shirt. I ate mostly proteins and some carbs, making my body run efficiently, like one of my expensive cars.

"But is it worth it?" She placed her hand over her stomach, where she had a small hint of a belly. "The second I moved in here, I started to gain some weight. You think I care? Nope. Life is short—eat the damn cake."

"It's different for women. You look sexy no matter what size you are. An overweight man isn't attractive."

"Not true," she argued. "I would still think you're sexy with a belly."

I laughed because there was no way in hell I would ever allow myself to have a fat stomach. "We'll never find out."

She walked back into the kitchen so I could get back to my laptop. I sipped my coffee while I heard her work in the kitchen, doing the dishes and placing them in the dishwasher. That was where she spent most of her time throughout the day, other than when she did laundry.

The doorbell rang.

Only family members had access to the gate code, so I assumed it was someone welcome in the house.

"I'll get it," Mia called from the kitchen.

I was in my sweatpants without a shirt, but since this

person had dropped by without announcement, I didn't rush to pull something on. They were disturbing my day, so I didn't care.

Mia's voice came from the other side of the house. "Hello, Mrs. Barsetti. How are you?"

My mom was here?

Their voices grew louder as they approached the dining room.

I stood up to greet my mother, wishing I had something to put on now that I knew it was her.

My mom walked through the archway. She wore a slight smile on her face, but her eyes were heavy like something was on her mind. She didn't make a comment about my bare chest and hugged me. "Hey, Carter. Are you busy right now?"

"Not at all." I hugged her back before I shut my laptop. "Everything alright?"

"I came by because I need to talk to you about something." She was a foot shorter than me and lean like my father. Her dark brown hair was still lustrous and beautiful, and her brown eyes sparkled naturally.

My mother came all the way to my house to speak to me in private—that wasn't good. Since Mia had just stayed with them for a few days, I could only assume that was what this discussion would be about. "Sweetheart…I mean Mia. Could you grab me a shirt, please?"

"Of course, Carter." Mia walked away.

"You don't need to do that, son." Mom sat in the

chair across from me. "This is your home, and I dropped by unannounced. Don't worry about it." She pulled her hair over one shoulder and hardly made eye contact with me.

Was she ashamed of me? Did Mia tell her everything? Would she betray me like that?

Mia returned with the t-shirt. "Can I get you something, Mrs. Barsetti? Iced tea?"

"That would be great," Mom answered.

I pulled the black t-shirt over my head, hiding my nakedness from view. She said it was perfectly fine, but it felt disrespectful to me.

Mia returned with the iced tea along with a plate of cookies. "Let me know if you need anything." She excused herself from the room and walked back into the kitchen, visibly uncomfortable by the tension in the room. It seemed like she knew exactly what my mother wanted to discuss.

So my mother probably knew everything. Now she was going to slap me until I saw stars. I wasn't afraid of the pain, just the disappointment. I was an almost thirty-year-old man who had disappointed my mother. I should have grown out of that phase by now. Now I sat there in silence and waited for her to shake her head and purse her lips.

Mom watched me, her chin propped on her palm.

Like a guilty party put on trial, I exercised my right not to speak. I didn't want to incriminate myself even more.

"Carter, this isn't easy for me to talk about. Your father was going to join us, but I thought it would be better if it was just the two of us. I'm sorry to drop this on you at this moment, but it's been weighing me down since Mia stayed with us."

I wasn't that angry that Mia had told my mother the truth. There was no way to know what the context of the situation was. But I was livid that Mia didn't give me the decency of a warning. After everything I'd done for her, it seemed cold.

"I went into Mia's room one night to check on her. Her back was turned to me, and she was changing. That's when I saw the scars on her back…"

I held my mother's gaze, seeing the picture she wove in my mind.

"Carter, I've seen scars like that before. I know how they got there. I know how much force it would take to leave scars so deep and painful. They marred her back so severely that it's obvious they were created over an extended period of time."

The pain welled up inside my chest when I realized where this conversation was going. "It wasn't me. I would never do something like that—"

"I know that, Carter." She raised her hand to silence me. "The thought never crossed my mind."

I shut my mouth, relieved that my mother didn't think I was a monster.

"But I put the pieces together and realized Mia isn't just some woman you hired to clean up after you.

You've never been the kind of person to have help around the house, and Mia is so young to be in that line of work. Coupled with the scars and her timid behavior, I knew there was more to the story. So I asked her about her scars…and she didn't give me an answer. So I told her my story first…"

Her story first? What story did my mother have to tell? A blank expression must have come over my face because my mother sighed and looked away. "I don't understand…"

"I wasn't sure when I was going to share this story with you. I wanted to wait until you were older, but you're nearly thirty years old…so you've been an adult for a long time. It'll be hard to hear, even harder to process. But since you've helped Mia, an innocent woman who deserves a better life, I think it's time."

So Mia did tell her. And now my mother was going to share another story with me.

"I was in my early twenties when I was captured. I was with a friend at the time, and we were both enslaved by the same master…" She kept looking at the table, unable to meet my gaze.

The second she began her story, the surface of my eyes coated with moisture, and I couldn't blink it away. I'd never been an emotional man. I was like my father, hardly capable of feeling anything real. But I had a soft spot for my family, particularly my mother. She was so strong and so loving. She didn't deserve anything bad ever to happen to her.

"The details of the imprisonment don't matter," she continued, raising her gaze to meet mine. "But Mia and I aren't so different. We've experienced the same kind of torture. I was better off than she was because my enslavement didn't last nearly as long. Your father saved me. He killed the man who held me captive. And he gave me a wonderful life."

Even though I was exposed to this kind of cruelty all the time, hearing my mother speak of it on such a personal level made me ache all over. I should have said something in response to the tale, but I simply couldn't. My mother had been raped and tortured, and my first response was to kill the man responsible for it…but my father already took care of that. I sat in silence, speechless at the revelation and deathly heartbroken over it.

My mother watched me for a long time, practically holding her breath as she waited for me to say something.

But I couldn't. I was too broken.

Mom continued. "Mia told me that you took her away from her master and gave her a new life. She told me how kind and compassionate you are. She told me this not to betray you, but because I pressured her for her story. And Carter…I'm so proud of you. It brings tears to my eyes to think of what you did for this woman. Most men are cruel, but you're good just like your father. Without you, where would this woman be? How would her son be without her? You're a hero, son. I don't care if you risked your family to get her out of that situation. You did the right thing…and I'm so lucky to have you as my son."

My mother had just praised me, the kind of thing I lived for. All I wanted was for my parents to be proud of me, to know raising me had been worth all the time and frustration. But now those compliments meant nothing to me because of everything she'd said before that. "Mama…I'm so sorry." Without even realizing it, tears sprang into my eyes. I felt them glide down my cheeks toward my chin. My chest hurt so much, like I was having a heart attack. "I'm so sorry." I didn't know what else to say, how else to express the way I felt. Knowing someone hurt my mother like that brought me so much pain I didn't know how to absorb the agonizing truth.

"I know…" She rested her hand on mine. "But, Carter, it was a long time ago. I've been very happy for a long time. I never think about that period of my life. There's no need to feel bad for me. I've let it go—and I want you to as well."

I quickly wiped away the tears with my hand and cleared my throat. "Father saved you?"

"Yes. He did." A smile spread across her lips. "He risked everything, even his own family. You two are more alike than you ever realized."

"Were you together before you were captured?"

"No. After. He was doing business with the man who captured me when we met. And the rest is history."

I leaned back in my chair and dragged my hands down my face, shaken by what I'd just heard. It didn't matter that this man was dead. That wasn't good enough. I wanted to torture anyone he ever loved—the way he tortured my mother. I stared at the surface of the table and tried to combat the severe pain that throbbed everywhere. I didn't think less of my mother for what she'd been through. But it was hard to accept that it happened before I was even born.

My mom watched me for a while, being quiet. "Take all the time you need, Carter. I know this is difficult."

She was being patient with me when she was the one who'd suffered the way Mia had. I saw firsthand what Mia had been through, had spoken to her psychopath of a master who got off on beating her mercilessly. Instead of being patient with me, I should be the one making my mother feel better.

I moved around the table and pulled up the chair beside her. "Mama." I grabbed her hand and held it on the table. "I'm sorry. I wish…I wish I had been there so I could have protected you."

She smiled slightly, but tears emerged at the exact same time.

"I've always respected Father, but I respect him even more now."

"He's a good man." She squeezed my hand. "And you're just like him."

I shook my head, knowing my motivation to help Mia was also selfish. I saved her because it was the right thing to do, but also because I wanted her for myself.

"Please don't pity me, Carter," she whispered. "It was a long time ago. I've made my peace with it. I hadn't thought about it much until I saw those scars on Mia's back. I recognized the same abuse I'd endured."

When I reflected on my past, I realized I'd never seen my mother in a swimsuit or clothing that revealed her back. She'd kept those scars concealed from me her entire life. "You've hidden your scars from us…"

Mom nodded. "Yes."

"You don't have to hide them anymore. You shouldn't have to hide them at all." I looked into her eyes. "You're a survivor, not a victim. You lived through that and made a happy home for your family. Not very people could do that, could be strong enough to carry on after something like that. I had no idea…"

Her eyes softened.

"I don't think less of you. I think you're a fighter, Mama. I'm proud of how strong you are." I admired Mia for the exact same qualities, for never giving up and remaining positive. She was willing to jump out of my car and fight me with a knife because she was so determined to get back to her son. I never viewed her as weak for being captured, but for being strong since she continued to survive.

"Carter…thank you." She squeezed my hand again. "I knew you would say that…since you've taken such a liking to Mia."

"Mia is an incredible woman. I admire her. Most people would have taken the easy way out. She never did. She never gave up because she had to get back to her son. Moments like that really define who you are. Mia is a fighter…and she earned my respect."

"And your heart."

I looked at my mother, unsure what she meant by that. "Mia and I aren't romantic."

"So you're letting her live here with her son just because?" Mom smiled as she asked the question, like she knew something I didn't.

"She doesn't have anywhere else to go. She doesn't have any money or any way to support her son."

She kept grinning. "You're very wealthy, Carter. If you really wanted her out of your hair, you would write her a fat check and let her disappear. You let her live here because you want her here."

I couldn't argue with that because she was absolutely right. I bought this new house in cash at the snap of a finger. I hadn't even sold my other place yet, but that didn't change anything. With more money than I knew what to do with, I could make anything happen.

When I didn't respond to the claim, Mom continued to talk. "She thinks the world of you."

"She does?" I whispered, knowing I shouldn't care.

"Yes. Couldn't run out of good things to say about you."

That shouldn't make me feel good. It should make me feel like shit, considering the offer I originally made with her.

"I can tell she adores you…respects you…even loves you."

Maybe some of that was true, but not all of it. "Her feelings for me aren't that deep."

"I don't agree."

"She talks about me finding someone else all the time. She knows what we have isn't forever. It's just… what it is."

Mom studied my face, reading my emotions like a book. "And that bothers you."

"I never said it did."

"But it does."

I angled my face away from hers, trying to make it difficult for her to read me.

"Carter, don't forget who you are. You're the kind of man that speaks his mind and isn't afraid to say what he wants. If you want this woman, tell her that. If you want this woman to love you, make her."

"Make her, huh?" I whispered.

"For someone like you, it must be easy."

I wasn't sure if I wanted Mia to love me at all. "She has a son… I'm not sure how I'll feel about that."

"Why would that change anything?"

"I've never had a girlfriend before. Jumping into a relationship this complicated sounds like a bad idea. The only kid I've ever been around is Reid, and since he's only a few weeks old, that doesn't count. I'm not ready to be a father, let alone a stepfather."

"But you're going to live with both of them?"

"It doesn't change anything. He's her responsibility —not mine."

Mom pulled her hand away. "It sounds to me like you don't want commitment, but you want everything else."

"Maybe."

"I think it's inevitable, Carter. Just accept it—it's not so bad."

I pulled my hand off the table and considered what she said. "After what Mia has been through, I don't think she's looking for love. She said she wants to raise her son and focus on him. She doesn't trust men."

"Except you. Like I said, she couldn't say enough good things about you."

"I'm not good enough for her..." She was in my captivity for a month, and I never tried to save her. The only reason I did was because I got attached to her, enjoyed sleeping with her. She was the one in a bad situation who never gave up. She was a much stronger person than I would ever be.

"You saved her, Carter. You reunited her with her son. Sounds like you're the only man who's worthy of her."

"No offense, Mama, but you're blinded by love."

"No." She rested her hand on my arm. "I know you better than you think I do. I know that Mia would still be a prisoner if it weren't for you, that she would have died without seeing her son ever again. You're her savior, the only man brave enough to do the right thing.

Any other man she meets will never compare to you. Maybe you don't see it right now…but you're the only man she's ever going to want."

───────────

AFTER MY MOTHER LEFT, I went to the second floor where Mia's bedroom was. Since she was nowhere to be found, I assumed she was purposely avoiding me, knowing I would be angry that she told my mother the truth about our situation.

I tapped my knuckles against the door, giving her the option to deny me if she wished. It was the kind of freedom she didn't have before, and since it meant so much to her, I never infringed on it—even though this was my house.

"Come in."

I stepped inside, seeing her on the couch in her private living room. She was in the same dress she wore earlier, her feet pulled up to her knees. She stared at me with trepidation, like she didn't know what might happen now that we were face-to-face.

I slowly approached her, seeing the fear on her face. I stopped and stared at her, saying nothing.

She didn't say anything either.

I kept looking at her until she lowered her gaze.

"I'm sorry I told your mother. But she saw the scars on my back and pretty much pulled everything out of me."

"I'm not angry."

She lifted her gaze again. "Then why do you look so angry?"

"She told me what happened to her…" My mother assured me she was fine, that it was so long ago that it didn't matter anymore. She made her peace with the past and moved on, finding happiness with my father and the family they made together. If my father hadn't saved her, I never would have been born.

"Are you okay?"

"Not sure yet." I lowered myself onto the cushion beside her, my eyes still slightly puffy from the tears I'd shed earlier. "My chest still hurts, and I can't remember the last time I shed tears. But when she told me, I couldn't help it. My mother didn't deserve that."

Mia scooted closer to me, her hand resting against my back and her face close to mine. "I'm sorry…I know how much it must hurt."

"It was a long time ago and she seems fine with it, but…it kills me inside. I want to kill the man who did this to her. He's already dead because my father took care of that, but that's not enough justice."

"It's not."

"She was the one comforting me…when I should have been the one comforting her. I told her I was proud of her for being so strong, for not letting that experience sabotage the rest of her life. She refused to let that evil defeat her. Most people don't have that kind of strength."

Mia smiled. "I'm sure that meant a lot to her."

"I think it did. I'm proud to call her my mother, even more than I was before. But it still kills me inside."

She rubbed my back. "I know."

"I wish I had been a man then like I am now. I could have protected her. I could have made sure nothing ever happened to her. If something were to happen today, I would mutilate the guy stupid enough to try."

"I'm sure she knows that, Carter."

"It'll take a while for me to get over this…"

"That's understandable."

I stared at the carpet beneath our feet, feeling this beautiful woman comfort me with her touch. "She said she was proud of me for helping you. Said it's exactly what she would have wanted me to do."

"She should be proud of you," she whispered.

I didn't tell Mia everything else that was said, keeping that to myself. I wasn't sure how I felt about Mia, and I wasn't entirely sure how she felt about me. She was affectionate with me, but that didn't mean her feelings went deeper than that. She certainly didn't expect anything from me, always said I would end up with someone else.

"I'm glad you aren't angry with me. I was afraid of what was going to happen when you walked into the room."

"I was angry at first, but after our conversation, I understood. Talking to my mom seemed to make everything better, bring us closer together." I turned toward Mia, seeing the pretty brown hair frame her face. "She really likes you."

"We have a lot in common. I really like her too."

Mia was the first woman I had slept with to have ever met my mother. I wasn't sure if that meant anything or meant nothing at all. My hand moved to her thigh, and I gave it a gentle squeeze. "I'm going to bed. I'll see you in the morning."

"It's not even five yet…"

"I know." I rose to my feet. "I just want to be alone right now." I couldn't digest everything my mother said without feeling like I'd been punched in the stomach. I walked to the door, eager to get to my stash of scotch in my bedroom.

"Are you sure?"

I turned around at the sound of her hurt voice. I saw the concern in her eyes, the overwhelming sadness she felt toward me. "I understand if you want to be alone… I just thought I could be alone with you."

I thought back to what my mother said, that Mia's feelings for me were similar to mine for her. It was more than just simple affection and sexual attraction. There was a deeper connection between us, unexplored feelings that neither one of us touched. "You want to be alone with me?"

She stepped forward, the emotion burning in her eyes. "More than anything else in the world."

THE HOURS PASSED as we lay together in my bed. There was no sex and no talking. She was in her panties and bra, and I was stripped down to my boxers. Despite the sight of her nakedness, I wasn't in the mood to drag the strap off her shoulder and reveal that perfect tit.

I wasn't in the mood for anything.

Mia didn't speak, knowing I preferred the company of silence. But she ran her fingers through my hair, rubbed my sore muscles, and comforted me with her feminine touch. Her perfume surrounded me, and my hand brushed against her thigh a few times. Sometimes I would drink my scotch. Sometimes I would light up a cigar.

She didn't protest either one.

I knew I shouldn't be depressed over something that happened decades ago. I hadn't even been conceived yet. It didn't seem like the past still had any hold over my mother. It was so long ago that she'd made her peace with it.

But could I make my peace with it?

If I'd known the truth before I met Mia, I knew I would have behaved differently.

Now I hated myself for the way I acted. I got Mia out of the situation eventually, but that was only because I was screwing her. My first instinct should have been to save her, not trick her into trying to escape so I could have her, so I could hurt her.

I was ashamed of myself.

Was I any different from Egor? Any different from the man who hurt my mother? The revelation changed everything, changed how I viewed myself.

Mia must have picked up on my mood because she addressed it. "Everything alright, Carter?"

"Yeah." I stared across my room, my empty glass on the nightstand beside me.

She rubbed my chest, her eyes focused on my profile. "Seems like your mood has darkened."

She could read me better than I realized. "I regret a lot of things. I should have saved you the second I realized what kind of monster Egor really was. I shouldn't have looked the other way. I shouldn't have participated in it. I shouldn't have tricked you into escaping so I could hurt you…I'm not any different from Egor. I'm not any different from the man who hurt my mother. If my mother had told me this sooner…it would have changed everything."

She rubbed her small hand across my chest. "You're nothing like Egor, Carter. Despite your worst mistakes, you're nothing alike. Remember, when I said no, you listened. You were always kind to me, always friendly. You gave me far more respect than Egor ever did."

"I still didn't help you…"

"Then how am I here? In your house?" She leaned down and pressed a kiss to my shoulder, her soft lips feeling like rose petals.

"Because I was sleeping with you."

Princess in Lingerie

"Not true. You weren't going to save me until I told you I had a son." Her hand halted against my chest, her small fingernails digging into my skin. "You knew you wouldn't be able to live without your own mother. That was why you helped me, Carter. Because it was the right thing to do. You know what Egor did? He left my son orphaned. He destroyed my body so I couldn't have any more children. Don't you dare compare yourself to Egor—you're nothing like him."

My hand rested on top of hers, and I squeezed her fingers. "Maybe that's true. But I still could have been better... I could have treated you better."

"Carter, if you didn't treat me well, I wouldn't be in this bed with you. I wouldn't be kissing your warm skin. I wouldn't be bedding you every night. I have the freedom to walk away, but I don't want to." Her hand moved to my chin, and she directed my stare onto her face. "I'm here with you because there's nowhere else I'd rather be." She leaned into me and rubbed her nose against mine, her soft strands of hair brushing against my skin. She leaned closer then pressed her mouth over mine, giving me a soft kiss. "You're the only man I want, Carter. You're the only man I trust." She kissed me again, her breaths filling my mouth and lungs. Her fingertips dug into the pectoral muscle of my chest. "You're the only man I can kiss this way and mean it."

My hand cradled her head, and my fingers dug into her soft hair. I brought her in for a deeper kiss, my cock coming to life in my shorts. All my self-

355

loathing disappeared when I listened to this woman applaud me, watched this woman want me. My mouth probably tasted like scotch and cigars, but that didn't halt her desire. I maneuvered on top of her and positioned her underneath me, her head hitting the pillow and my body covering hers like a blanket. Just when I'd positioned her legs around my waist, the doorbell rang.

I pulled away and stared into her face, seeing the warmth of her eyes stare back at me. Whoever was at the door must be family again. Otherwise, they wouldn't be able to get past the gate. I gave her a final kiss before I moved off her and pulled on my clothes.

"Do you want me to get the door?" she asked, sitting up in bed.

I pulled on my jeans and my t-shirt. "No. I already know who it is."

"Who?"

"My father." I left the bedroom and hurried down the two flights of stairs to the ground floor. I jogged to the entryway and finally made it to the front door. Without checking to see if it was really him, I opened the door.

As I expected, my father stood there in a black t-shirt and jeans, his hands tucked into his pockets while his car was parked in the driveway behind him. He stared at me with a hard look, bottling his emotions so I couldn't see them.

I knew exactly why he was there, so I didn't ask.

"Come in." I shut the door behind him, and we walked farther into the house.

He walked beside me, his hands still in his pockets. "Your mother told me you were pretty upset…"

I halted beside him, taken aback by the comment. "Did you expect me to react differently?" I wasn't ashamed of my tears. I wasn't ashamed of my heartbreak. The woman who raised me had been raped and tortured. Was I just supposed to brush that off?

"She's worried about you. That's all."

"I'm not the one she should be worried about." I faced my father, feeling a hint of rage I couldn't combat. I wanted to kill the man who did this to her, but he'd been gone for over thirty years. There was nothing else for me to do besides let it go.

His gaze shifted away as he sighed quietly. "I told her we should never tell you. I didn't think any good would come of it. It was a very long time ago and has nothing to do with our lives anymore. We've been very happy for a long time."

"No, I'm glad she told me." Even though it hurt so much, I needed to know the truth. I needed to know what my mother had been through so I could respect her even more, so I could decide what kind of man I wanted to be. "I'm just heartbroken over it."

"I understand, son. It used to kill me too. But seeing her happy for all these years makes me forget about it."

What would my mother have done without my father? Would she have died in captivity and I never would have been born? Would she never have had the freedom she deserved? "She told me you saved her?"

He nodded. "And your uncle Crow too. When I saved your mother, it started a war. Your aunt was pregnant with Conway at the time, so Crow sent her away to keep her safe. It was just the two of us and a few of our men…until we got the Skull Kings involved. The man who took your mother kidnapped Crow, so I didn't have any other option but to ask for their help. In exchange, they wanted my arms dealing business. Of course, I handed it over so I could get Crow out of there. I killed the man who hurt your mother—shot him in the face. And that was the end."

If my mother had never met a powerful man, she couldn't have escaped. My father was a hero. "Thank you…"

His eyes softened, and he rested his hand on my shoulder. "Don't thank me, Carter. I would have gladly given my life to save her. She's the only woman I've ever loved. She's the only woman who's ever meant anything to me. I would do it again in a heartbeat…because I love her more with every year that passes." He lowered his hand. "I know this is difficult to process, but remember that this is all in the past. Your mother has been safe and happy for a long time."

"I know, but it shouldn't have happened in the first place."

"That's the reality of the world we live in. You shouldn't dwell on the past, Carter. You should be grateful that your mother escaped and got a second chance at life. She got to be a wife and a mother. And being a mother has been the greatest joy she's ever known."

I already knew that without being told. "I don't want to be like him."

"Like who?" Father asked.

"The man who did that to her. I don't want to be like Egor either. I didn't treat Mia the way she deserved, and now I'm ashamed of myself. She told me I'm nothing like him, that I'm not cruel and brutal, that I have a kind soul and a soft heart. But I didn't rescue her the way you rescued Mom. I was self-ish...greedy." I lowered my gaze, unable to look at him.

He was quiet for a long time, a sigh filling the silence a moment later. "Carter...don't be so hard on yourself. Not everything is as it seems. If it weren't for you, that woman might be dead right now. You've given her a second chance at life, another chance to be with her son. I told you I was angry you risked all of us to save her, but I'm also very proud. It takes guts to do what you did, to save this innocent woman. How could I not be proud of that?"

I lifted my gaze to meet his, seeing the sincerity on his face.

"You're nothing like those men, Carter. If you were, Mia would already be gone by now. That woman adores you. I see it every time she looks at you. She's very happy here, Carter. She's never going to leave unless you make her."

"Maybe I don't want her to leave…"

Father's eyes lightened noticeably. "Then don't let her."

NINETEEN

Mia

I couldn't focus on anything that day.

I took a cold shower because I was too distracted to realize the water crashing down on me was cold, not warm. Only when Carter joined me did I realized it was ice-cold against my skin. When I got ready, I tried to pull a shirt over my dress. I wasn't paying attention to what I was doing all morning, so none of my actions made sense.

All I could think about was Luca.

He was coming today.

I didn't make Carter breakfast or lunch because I couldn't think straight. Luca's bedroom was ready to go, along with his toys and clothes. I made sure everything was perfect before he arrived, but I still didn't know what I would say to him when I saw him again. How would I explain my absence? How would I explain the last three years?

Carter didn't give me a hard time about my poor job performance. He gave me the space I needed to process what was about to happen. Our evening last night had been difficult because he was still digesting the truth about his mother. But now all I could think about was my son.

I stood at the dining room window because it had a great view of the path that led down to the gate. Since I couldn't concentrate on anything else, I stood there and waited, hoping to see a black car pull up to the gate.

Carter came up behind me and gripped my shoulders. "You alright, sweetheart?"

"I'm terrified. I can't breathe. My chest hurts. No, I'm not alright." What would I do when Luca got out of the car and had no idea who I was? He was only five when I disappeared. Three years had come and gone, critical years for his development. He could have a completely different personality now. He could be bitter about the orphanage he'd lived in, angry about the teachers and other kids. Or maybe he was happy…and wished he were there instead of with me. "So many things could go wrong. He might hate me. He might not remember me. I've been waiting for this moment for so long…but now I'm afraid it'll blow up in my face."

He circled his arms around my waist and rested his chin on my head. "It's going to be alright, sweetheart. None of those things will happen."

"You don't know that…"

"I know that a boy always loves his mother, no

matter how old he gets." He shifted his arms around my chest, circling my petite frame with his strength. I was cocooned in his embrace, the muscles of his arms acting as a natural heater. It was a hot summer day, but my trepidation made me ice-cold.

We stood together in front of the window, but my heart wouldn't slow down. "When will be here?"

"Within thirty minutes."

"Oh my god…" This was really happening, and I was getting light-headed thinking about it. I'd never known love the way I did with Luca. Nothing in my life had ever been more important than him. When I was being beaten and raped every single day, I contemplated suicide all the time. I found ways to make it happen, to make it as quick and painless as possible. But Luca always steadied my hand. If there was any chance I could get back to him, I had to try. I couldn't give up and take the easy way out. Now, I was standing at the window, counting down the minutes until the car pulled into the driveway.

Carter held me in his arms as we waited together. He didn't say anything else to make me feel better, just gripped me tightly and comforted me the only way he could. His cologne washed over me as well as his natural scent. I was used to it now since I slept in his bed every night. Now that Luca would be back in my life, Carter would become an afterthought.

A black car appeared on the horizon and approached the gate along the road.

"He's here…" I left Carter's embrace and ran to the front door, my heart pounding in my throat. I couldn't wait to set my gaze on my son, to see my own eyes in that adorable face. My arms ached to hold him, to feel with my bare hands how much he'd grown.

Carter followed behind, taking his time as he joined me by the front door.

I opened the door and walked outside onto the front patio and saw the black gates swing open and reveal a black car that slowly made its way up the driveway. Tears already formed in my eyes before I even saw my son. My hands were shaking so much I couldn't keep them still.

Carter came up behind me and placed his hand on my shoulder.

The car pulled up to the front of the house, all the windows tinted so nothing could be seen inside. The car was shifted into park, and the engine turned off.

Now, I couldn't breathe. I stared at the back seat and waited for something to happen.

The driver came around and opened the back door. "We're here, Luca."

A small boy shuffled out of the car, and his shoes hit the concrete. The man was still in the way, so Luca's features were impossible to make out. He grabbed something from the back seat, probably a backpack. "Where are we?" His voice was soft and quiet, full of shyness.

The second I heard his voice, I knew it was him. "Luca…"

The driver stepped out of the way and finally revealed my son. Half my height and far skinnier than I wanted him to be stood the boy that I loved with my whole heart. His brown hair was overgrown because he always hated getting his hair cut. His coffee-colored eyes were identical to mine, warm and beautiful. He wore jean shorts, black shoes, and a dark blue t-shirt. He had my skin tone, an fair color he didn't inherit from his father. He was just as perfect as I remembered, a healthy and handsome boy.

I held my breath for nearly a minute, my eyes locked on to his.

He stared at me for a while, as if my face were familiar to him. It'd been a long time since he'd seen me, and he didn't have any pictures of me. My features hadn't changed, but a five-year-old didn't have the sharpest memory. But he continued to stare at me like there was a hint of familiarity.

I squatted down so we were closer to being eye level. "Luca…" The tears fell like a waterfall, and I couldn't stop myself from crying. I started to sob before I even held him in my arms. "Little Bear…" When he was a baby, bears were his favorite animal, so I gave him the nickname. He might have been too young to remember.

But his eyes flashed with recognition, like that name meant something to him. He slowly came toward me, ignoring Carter behind me.

I wanted to stay back so I wouldn't startle him, but now I didn't have the patience. I walked toward him then kneeled in front of him, so close to him that I could hear him breathe. "Little Bear…it's me. It's Mom." My hands rested on his small arms, feeling his slightness as well as his growth. He was several inches taller than he was the last time I saw him. He hadn't even started school yet. Now he was three years older, three years bigger.

"Mom?" he whispered.

"Yes." I nodded then wiped away my tears with my hands. "It's me. I'm so sorry, Luca. I'm sorry I've been gone for so long."

He watched the tears roll down my cheeks, his features stoic.

"I'm sorry I left you…but I didn't want to. I'm here now, and I'll never leave you again." I squeezed his arms, feeling my son in my hands for the first time.

Luca kept staring at me, silent.

I didn't want to rush him, not when he was uncertain and probably afraid. "I know you're confused right now. That's okay. Take all the time you need. I'm going to be taking care of you from now on. Nothing will ever happen to you again. I promise." Just as I did when he was little, I grabbed both of his hands and kissed them with my lips. I used to do it every night before I tucked him in.

He watched my movements, and finally, he had some kind of reaction. "Mommy?"

"Yes, Little Bear. It's Mommy."

That's when his eyes started to redden, the moisture forming in his gaze. "You left…and I was scared."

"I know. I know."

He moved into my body and hugged me, wrapping his arms around me.

I gripped him tightly and cradled the back of his head with my palm. I wept into his shoulder, my tears soaking into his clothes and leaving stains everywhere. I squeezed him hard and held him for a long time, never wanting to let go. My little boy was back in my arms, and nothing would ever take him away from me. He was my whole world, my whole life, and here he was. "I love you, Little Bear. I love you so much. I'll never leave you again."

"I love you too, Mommy…"

That was the moment when my heart gave out—when I heard those beautiful words.

I TOOK Luca to his bedroom on the second floor, which was decorated with a dinosaur theme. He'd loved dinosaurs before I lost him, and I hoped he still felt that way. He took a look around and sat on the bed, his feet dangling over the edge.

I sat beside him and ran my fingers through his hair, unable to believe I was really touching him. My son was right beside me after all the horrible years

367

we'd been apart. His hair felt the same way in my fingertips.

"Mom?"

"Yes, Little Bear?"

"Where did you go?" He turned his gaze and looked up at me.

He was way too young to know the truth. He was incapable of understanding it. Carter was an almost thirty-year-old man, and the truth about his mother nearly destroyed him. "I had to leave…but I didn't want to. I never would have left you if I'd had a choice."

Luca didn't ask any more questions, but he obviously didn't understand my explanation.

"How was the orphanage?"

He shrugged. "I didn't like it. Food was bad, and the kids were mean."

My hand paused in his hair, my heart aching. "I'm sorry…what about school?"

"That was okay too." He looked around the bedroom. "Is this my room?"

"Yes. Do you like it?"

He nodded.

"I'm right next door, so you know where to find me."

He rested his hands on the edge of the bed and kicked his legs forward and back. He used to be more talkative before I was taken from him. He was probably nervous, unsure what to say to me because it'd been so long. He was too young to understand what was happening. "This house is bigger than the place I stayed at before…"

"The orphanage?" I asked.

"Yeah. You live here by yourself?"

"No, not by myself. I live here with…" I didn't know how to explain this to Luca. I didn't want him to think Carter would be his stepfather, but I didn't want him to assume he was a stranger either. "This is where I work. The man who owns the house is my boss."

"You work here?" he asked.

"Yes. I'm the maid. I cook for him, clean for him, and keep up the house."

"So he's really rich?"

"Yeah, I guess. But don't say that to him. It's not polite."

"Okay," he said quietly.

"He's a very nice man. He's a good friend of mine. You'll love him, Luca."

"This place is really cool. I can't believe he has it all to himself."

The only reason Carter bought it was so all three of us could be comfortable living together. He was hard on himself for not saving me sooner, but he more than made up for it with his generosity.

"Is there a pool?"

"Yes."

It was the first time he showed me that boyish grin. "Really? Can I play in it?"

"Of course. But only when I'm there, alright? No swimming alone."

"Okay, Mom." He spoke with resignation, just the way he did when I told him what to do when he was young.

I'd missed that so much. "There's toys in the chest over there. I'll cook all your meals for you. I enrolled you in the school down the street. I'll pick you up and drop you off every morning."

"A new school?" he asked.

"Yes. It's a very nice school. You'll like it."

"I don't want to make new friends…"

"Starting over is hard. But remember, when you make new friends, you can have a swim party over here."

His eyes widened. "I can?" His voice hit a new pitch of excitement. "Really?"

"Of course, Little Bear." I ran my hand through his hair. "So make lots of friends, alright?"

"Okay, I'll try."

Carter tapped his knuckles on the doorframe. "May I come in?"

Carter had been standing there when Luca arrived, but no introductions were made. I was focused on my son exclusively, disregarding both Carter and the man who brought him to me. Just last night, Carter was the number one man in my life. But now he had been forgotten. "Yes."

Carter stepped into Luca's bedroom and walked

toward us, his eyes on my son. He gave him a friendly smile before he squatted on the ground so they could be at eye level. "Hey, Luca. I'm so happy you're here. Your mother talks about you all the time."

Luca was immediately tense again, shy and uncomfortable around this man he didn't know. He'd been that way as a child, and now that he'd been on his own for the past three years, he was even shier. "She does?"

"Absolutely," Carter said, still smiling. "She loves you very much. Tells me every day."

Luca looked at the ground, as if he was embarrassed by that.

Carter kept talking. "I wanted to introduce myself. My name is Carter." He extended his hand to shake Luca's.

Luca extended his left hand and then awkwardly tried to correct it.

Carter kept smiling. "I'll show you a trick. Always use your right hand." He grabbed Luca's right wrist then directed it toward his palm. "Grip tightly here. Touch my wrist. Up and down once." He completed the handshake then pulled away. "Perfect. You got it."

"Carter?" Luca asked, repeating his name.

"Yes, that's my name. You'll see me around the house a lot. My bedroom and office are on the third floor."

"And the third floor is off-limits to you, Luca," I said, knowing I had to be firm so Luca would understand. "The second floor is where you and I live. We have everything we need, including our own living room and dining room. So when you're home, hang out up here."

"Okay, Mom," Luca said. "Um, Carter?"

"Yes, little man?" Carter asked.

"Can I use your swimming pool?"

Carter grinned wider, amused by the request. "Anytime. As long as your mother is watching. Do you know how to swim?"

Luca shook his head. "No…"

"We'll need to work on that first. How about we give it a try now?"

Luca stiffened in excitement. "That would be great! I would love to." He hopped off the bed, so excited that he couldn't sit still.

Carter chuckled. "Luca, don't forget to ask your mother if that's okay."

"Oh, sorry." Luca turned to me. "Mom, can I go swimming with Carter?"

I watched my son ask for permission, and the tears filled my eyes with unstoppable force. This was exactly what I wanted, to be a mom. I wanted my son to ask me these things, to turn to me as his parent. It was so normal, something mothers did on a daily basis, and I missed it so much. "Yes. I'll join you."

CARTER WORKED WITH LUCA, teaching him to kick

and use his arms to pull him forward through the water. Luca was so thin that he didn't have much buoyancy, so Carter had to hold him most of the time. He held him by the stomach and carried him across the pool as he asked him to kick. He headed toward me as I stood on the other side of the pool.

Luca kicked hard, splashing water everywhere and getting Carter's hair wet.

"Good," Carter said. "Keep kicking." He carried him to my side of the pool and to the ledge.

Luca grabbed on so he could hang in the water and catch his breath. "Did you see me, Mom?"

"Yes, I did. You were great." I grabbed him by the hips and carried him to the stairs so he could touch the bottom. "Let's take a short break and try again."

"Okay." He sat on the top step and held on to the metal pole of the railing. "I'm hungry."

"I'll make us something," I offered. "What do you want, Luca?"

"Grilled cheese."

Not having me around seemed to have destroyed his manners. "Grilled cheese, please."

Luca lowered his voice. "Please…"

I got out of the water and dried off with a towel.

Carter stared at me, watching the water drip off my body in the bathing suit. He didn't seem to care about looking at me while my son was around. "Is it okay if I keep showing him?"

I knew Carter didn't have any experience with kids,

but I trusted him. He took care of me, and I had faith he could take care of my son. "Sure. You want some lunch too?"

"Please." He waggled his eyebrows, showing manners the way I'd just taught Luca.

"Coming right up." After I was dry, I walked into the kitchen and whipped up lunch. I came back fifteen minutes later to see Luca swimming back and forth across the pool by himself. I set the lunch on the table under the umbrella along with a pitcher of lemonade.

"You got it, little man." Carter stood in the deep end of the pool and watched Luca on the other side. "One more time and then we'll eat."

"Mom, watch!" Luca let go of the ledge and swam across the pool toward Carter. He kicked hard, splashing water all over the concrete as he made his way to the other side. When he reached Carter, he turned around and swam back the opposite way.

"Wow." I clapped my hands. "That was great, Luca." The afternoon was the best day of my life, and it was so ordinary that no one would understand the feeling inside my chest. My imprisonment seemed like a lifetime ago now that I had Luca in my life again. We were living the life that we deserved, enjoying the sunshine and the pool. And none of this would be possible without Carter. "Now, let's go out and have some lunch."

Luca climbed up the steps with Carter and got water all over the concrete. Like Carter had done this before, he grabbed a large towel and wrapped it around Luca to dry him off. He rubbed the fabric into his skin and hair to make sure he was completely dry before they both walked to the table. Carter did the same to himself next, drying off his muscular physique with the towel.

My natural impulse was to stare at him, to watch the drops slowly roll down the grooves between the muscle, but that seemed inappropriate while Luca was there, even though he was far too young to notice things like that.

We sat together at the table, and Luca ate his sandwich quietly, kicking his legs and looking at the acres of land of the backyard. Luca had never experienced anything luxurious like this before, so this must be especially impressive to him. It was obvious he was already comfortable with Carter because he was being himself, eating quickly and resting his elbows on the table. He must be comfortable with me too because his shyness was gone.

Carter ate the garden salad I made for him, topped with grilled chicken and light dressing. "Thank you for lunch, Mia. It's great."

"Yeah," Luca said. "Thanks, Mom."

I didn't care about Carter's compliment, but my son's words nearly brought me to tears again. "You're welcome." It was such a regular day to an outside point of view, but for me, it was one of the greatest days of my life…and I would never forget it.

WHEN IT WAS BEDTIME, I read Luca a story. I used to do that when he was younger, but when I picked up a book and lay beside him in bed, he didn't object to it. Sometimes I forgot so much time had passed and he might not be interested in that anymore, but he seemed to enjoy it.

I read for fifteen minutes and noticed Luca had closed his eyes. He was beside me with the dinosaur sheets pulled to his shoulders. He was used to sleeping alone, but I didn't want to move from his side.

It was so nice to lie there, to listen to him breathe.

I stared at his cute face for a long time as I held the book against my chest. With thick eyelashes and soft cheeks, he was adorable and innocent. So small and helpless, he managed to survive a severe life change. He lost his mother and was put into the system, but that experience didn't destroy his boyish curiosity.

Now that I had him back in my life, I loved him even more than I could have imagined. He was my whole world, my entire purpose for existence. I could never let anything happen to us ever again.

But I'd learned the hard way that I wasn't strong enough to protect us both. No matter how hard I fought, I couldn't escape. I couldn't give my son the protection he needed. The second we left Carter's home, we would be vulnerable all over again.

I never wanted that to happen.

TWENTY

Carter

———

I didn't spend any time with Mia over the next few days.

I made my own coffee and meals before I worked in my office. She was spending all of her time with her son, taking him swimming or playing with him in their bedrooms. She took him to the grocery store with her, along with everywhere else she went.

Every time I went to her bedroom at night, she was sleeping in his bed.

I never thought I would be jealous of an eight-year-old.

But I was jealous. Extremely.

I hadn't seen her for more than a few minutes at any given time. But I knew I couldn't be selfish right now. She'd missed three years with her son. Now all she wanted to do was get that time back, get to know him again.

I wouldn't take that away from her.

Laundry piled up, the dishes weren't done, and there wasn't a hot meal on the table—but that was okay. When he went back to school, everything would return to normal. Besides, her son was a pretty cool kid. He was easygoing, easy to talk to, and he was excited about everything. He seemed to like me too. Anytime he saw me, he greeted me with a handshake.

It became a special routine we did.

I was in the kitchen making a sandwich when Mia walked inside, glowing brighter than the sun. Her eyes were full of happiness, and she smiled bigger than I'd ever seen her. Her joy was infectious, reaching every single corner of the room. "Hey." She walked up to me and kissed me on the cheek.

It was the only affection I'd gotten for days. "You two are having fun?"

"So much fun. I took him shopping to get some school supplies. He wanted all dinosaur stuff. I'm so glad he's still interested in that."

"Dinosaurs are awesome. I'm still interested in them."

She chuckled then looked down at the sandwich I was making. "I'm so sorry I haven't been working like I was before—"

"I understand, sweetheart. I'm glad the two of you are spending time together."

"It's so amazing. Just the way it used to be…but better. I don't know how to thank you for what you've done for both of us…" She grabbed my wrist and gave me a squeeze. Her affection immediately made me warm, her touch lighting a fire inside me. Nothing about it was sexual, but it made me want her so much. "He starts school tomorrow…and I'm trying to keep myself together."

"What's the problem? It's a great school."

"I know it is. I'll just miss him all day. I'll be able to get back to work, but I'll be counting down the hours until I can pick him up again."

"At least I'll have you in my bed for a few hours of the day."

She turned her gaze on me, smiling slightly. "I've been sleeping with Luca every night."

"Yes, I've noticed."

"I'm sorry," she whispered. "I just—"

"You don't need to explain anything, sweetheart. You just got him back. My turn will come again." My hand moved into her hair, and I tucked her hair behind her ear as my eyes moved over her lips. "I just have to get used to sharing you…and I will."

Her fingers wrapped around my wrists as she looked into my eyes. "He's the only man you'll ever have to share me with."

"I'm okay with that." Now I only had a small fraction of her heart because her son had everything else. He had her heart, her spirit, her soul. But that was exactly how it should be, exactly how my mother loved me.

"What do you think of him?" she whispered.

379

I grinned. "What do I think? He's great. Sweet kid. Now he shakes my hand every morning when he sees me…pretty cute."

"He is cute."

"He's great, honestly." I didn't have any experience with kids, and I'd thought having one around would just be a nightmare. But I retreated up to the third floor when I needed my own space. "He has your spirit. I see it every time I'm in the same room as him." Some of his features were inherited from his father, but I pretended otherwise. That man didn't step up when he should have, so he had no claim as Luca's father. As far as I could tell, the boy was completely hers. My thumb brushed across her bottom lip, and I missed the days when I would lift her onto the counter and take her then and there. Now we shared the house with a third person, a little man who'd changed our lives forever.

"I'm glad you like him. It seemed like you two were connecting."

"I didn't realize kids could be so cool."

"Well, Luca is amazing. I know I'm biased because I'm his mother, but he really is. He's grateful for what he has and wears his heart on his sleeve. He's the kind of boy that will catch a spider in the house then let him go outside. He's sensitive…"

"I'm sure he gets all of that from you."

She shrugged. "Maybe."

I leaned in and kissed her on the mouth, unable to resist an embrace. It'd been so long since I had that mouth on mine, been the recipient of those fiery kisses. I wanted to take her to bed upstairs, but I had no idea where the little man was. So I made the passionate kiss short, knowing I would have to finish it later.

When she pulled her lips away, her eyes were lit up with desire. Her hand moved up my chest, and she gripped the fabric of my t-shirt, like she wanted to keep kissing me. Her fingers were always demanding, gripping me the same way I gripped the back of her neck. She licked her lips then nibbled on her bottom lip for a second.

I nearly kissed her again.

"Carter?" she whispered.

"Yes, sweetheart?" I knew whatever she was going to ask me was serious, based on her tone. "There's something I want to ask you. I just don't know how to ask it. I'm not sure what I'm trying to say."

"Try and we'll figure it out." My arm rested around her waist, hugging the curves of her hips. My chest was pressed to hers, and I could feel her plump tits. This woman had the kind of body that drove me wild. Fantasies popped into my mind, all involving her tits and ass.

"Alright…" She broke eye contact for a moment, staring at my chest before she lifted her gaze to meet mine again. "Now that I have Luca back, I never want anything to happen to him again. Knowing he was in that orphanage all alone still keeps me up at night. I want him to be safe, to grow up without being afraid of what might happen. I've always considered myself to be a strong woman because of everything I've accomplished, but being Egor's prisoner just showed me how incapable I really am."

"That's not true, sweetheart."

"It is true," she whispered. "I'm not strong enough to protect Luca. If someone wanted to cause us harm… I wouldn't be able to do anything to stop it. That thought terrifies me, not because of what might happen to me, but what might happen to my son."

"What are you asking me, Mia?" I wasn't sure where this was going. I told her she could live here as long as she wanted and continue to work for me. As long as she was under my roof, she would never have to worry about stuff like that.

"I…I don't know. I see the way you are with him, and I see how powerful you are. You're the reason we're both here. You're the reason we're safe…from everything. I always got the impression that you weren't interested in relationships or commitment, marriage or a family. But you and I seem to have something special… a unique connection. Unless I'm wrong?"

Now was the time to tell her otherwise, but I kept my mouth shut. I didn't pretend that there wasn't something here, that she didn't make my heart beat to a special rhythm. "Yes, we have something…" I'd never bedded one woman this long before. I'd never gone through so much work to have a woman. I'd never risked my neck for someone else the way I did for her. I constantly bowed to this woman, moved mountains to give her whatever she wanted. It didn't matter that she'd been beaten and raped. My attraction to her never waned. I didn't think about what happened to her before I came along. I only thought about the two of us.

She was quiet as she tried to figure out what to say next. "We would love to spend the rest of our lives here, to be protected by a powerful man like you. No harm would ever come to us with you around. I could raise my son and live a peaceful life."

"And that's something I've already offered to you. You know I'll protect you."

"I know," she whispered. "But…I guess I want more. I want a powerful husband who will keep us safe at night. I want a man my son can look up to. I want to give him the best life possible. I never want to be afraid of the evil and cruel men out there."

I hardly listened to anything else she said because all I could focus on was the word husband.

"I will give you anything you want in return. Not only my body, but my devotion and commitment. I already care deeply for you, Carter. I'm so loyal to you…would do anything you asked. You can have you own flings in the background and keep your personal life how you want it, but I can fulfill the other part of your life. I can be a wife to you, make you a home, and if you want to have children…I'm sure we could make that happen. I could raise them and do all the work so you don't have to…if you'll protect us for the rest of our lives."

I stared at her blankly, unable to believe what she'd just said. "Did you just ask me to marry you?" I blurted out the words in a harsh tone, shocked that this woman put that kind of offer on the table.

"Yes…" Redness entered her cheeks, her embarrassment turning her into a tomato. "Not exactly, but yes. It's just an idea. I didn't mean to offend you. Just forget what I said. I just—"

"You want me to be your husband?" I asked, still incredulous. A woman like her could have any man she wanted, regardless of her past.

"Yes. Me and every other woman in the world." She rolled her eyes. "I was under the impression you weren't looking for something serious from anyone. So, with me, you can have both. You can have a family and have your legacy continue, while keeping the life you have now. In exchange for your protection…I thought it would be a fair trade. But forget I said anything, okay? It was a stupid thing to ask."

I stared at her without focusing on her features. I knew I wanted this woman to stay, to live in my house indefinitely. I could have paid her off and gotten rid of her a long time ago. I wouldn't have spent so much time with her son if I didn't care about her. I wouldn't have been faithful to her for so long unless there was something here. I wanted to keep her forever anyway, but I felt like shit forcing her to do that. Now she was doing it freely, giving me exactly what I wanted.

I never wanted to let this woman go. "Yes."

"Can we just forget about it?" she asked. "I was just —" Her eyes widened when my answer sank into her bones. "Wait…what?"

"Yes." I watched her reaction change, watched the relief enter her gaze. "That sounds like a fair trade to me." I wanted this woman by my side every single day, even with a kid of her own. I never wanted her to leave, and by agreeing to her terms, I could have her for the rest of my life. She was creating her own sentence, committing to a lifetime of being with me. I'd never wanted to get married anyway. I didn't want to find a woman who would love me for me and not my money. Why would I waste my time doing that when I already had that woman right here?

Mia wanted me for me.

Still shocked, she stared at me with a stunned expression. "I guess I wasn't expecting you to say yes right away…or say yes at all."

"Me neither." My hand cupped her cheek, and I looked into her gaze, seeing a woman who'd stolen my obsession from the first time I looked at her. It was like an arranged marriage, something of convenience for both of us. I could have her for the rest of my life, have her fill the role I wanted, and she could have a powerful man to protect her and her son. It would be simple, uncomplicated with all the emotions that accompanied romance. And I could also have a family without having to deal with diapers and vomit all the time. It fixed all my problems. I was about to turn thirty, and I wasn't getting any younger.

"Wow…I don't know what to say."

I rubbed my nose against hers. "I have one stipulation."

"Alright…"

"You have to sleep in my bed every night. Not his."

TWENTY-ONE

Bones

———————

The gate was left open for us, so we followed the dirt path around the manicured gardens until we reached the two-story Tuscan home with the two large pillars in front. With a lush front yard and an even bigger back-yard, it was a piece of property slightly bigger than my place near Lake Garda.

Vanessa eyed the house as it came into view, speaking quietly under her breath. "Whoa…"

I parked near the front of the house then hopped out. The place caught my eye because of the large stone wall that wrapped around the property. Walls had restrictions in the region, and they couldn't exceed seven feet in height, but since this property was consid-ered to be a historic landmark, the walls were double that height. Since the walls were covered with beautiful green ivy, it didn't seem like the place was surrounded by concrete. The extensive landscaping along the wall, the thick trees and lush plants, made the wall even more invisible.

Vanessa walked up to the front of the house, studying the historical building with her arms across her chest. The paint on the walls was weathered and beaten, standing the test of centuries.

I watched her figure as I came up behind her, eyeing that dark hair as it reached down to the center of her back. "It was built in seventeen hundred."

"Really?" she asked in surprise. "It looks old, but wow…"

I wasn't sure if Vanessa would like it or not. The only reason I picked this place was because it seemed to be the safest. The walls were thick and tall, and it was impossible to see the house from the street because of the extensive landscaping. If someone wanted to target us, it would be very difficult even to figure out if we were home. After what happened, safety was all I cared about. There was no way in hell I was letting anyone take Vanessa away from me again.

We headed inside, seeing the downstairs parlor with the small tile and wallpaper. The place was charming, filled with timeless architecture that didn't exist in other residences. Her family's estate was about a hundred years old, making it far newer than this place.

Vanessa explored the house, looking at the kitchen, the dining room, and then taking the stairs to the second floor. There were five bedrooms there, the master bedroom having the most space, along with an

enormous closet. There was also a small room that must
have been an office, which overlooked the backyard. It
would be a perfect place for her to paint.

I hovered behind her, waiting for her opinion on the
piece of property. I wanted to buy it, but she had the
final say in the matter. If she didn't like it, I would have
to find a new place that was just as safe. If nothing like
that existed, I might have to build something.

She went into every room, touching the old paint on
the walls and inspecting the dirty windows. It hadn't
been inhabited for a long time, and now it was on the
market to cover debts to the government.

Vanessa was usually vocal about her opinions, so her
silence told me she didn't like the place. Her thoughts
were always transparent to me, but now she was closed
tighter than a clam. She headed down the stairs again
and looked into the backyard, where the lush backyard
stretched for another acre before it hit the wall. With
her arms crossed over her chest, she examined the
bright flowers against the greenery of the grass
and trees.

I came up behind her, my chest reaching her back
and my hands moving to her arms. I rested my lips
against the back of her head, the smell of her shampoo
heavy on my nose. My fingers gently grazed against her
soft skin. "Baby." She still hadn't said a single word
to me.

"I love it…"

My fingers froze in place. "You do?"

"Yes." She moved into the dining room. "We can have our family dinners here. The kitchen is big enough to make holiday meals once in a while. The backyard has lots of room to play. We might have to put a pool in, but I guess we can go to my parents if the kids want to swim." She moved to the bottom of the staircase. "There are five bedrooms, so that's enough room for three kids and an office. It's a little bigger than I wanted, but I think it's what we need. It's also very private…"

Within forty-five seconds, she painted my whole life in that house. She showed me the three kids I would have, the afternoons I would spend with her parents by the poolside, and the dinners I would be cooking since she couldn't work a pan. It was a family life I'd never wanted, but now that it was here, I could see it so easily, so vividly. Seeing the excitement on her face chased away all my fear. I'd never intended to love a woman, but when I met her, that was all I wanted—to love her fiercely. Now my purpose in life was protecting her and making her smile. It was a big responsibility, but I loved every moment of it.

She turned back to me. "What do you think, Griffin?"

"Let's get it."

She smiled as she returned to me, her hands crawling up my chest. "You love it, then?"

"Why do you think I showed it to you?" It didn't matter where we lived. All I wanted was something safe, a fortress where I could keep her and the kids hidden away.

"I love that it's old. It has so much history, so much character. I love my parents' place, but it seems modern compared to this."

"It's a historical landmark, so I'm not sure if getting a pool is possible."

"That's okay," she said. "My parents will love having us over every summer."

I imagined they would have us over every season of the year. "Then let's do it."

She jumped into my chest and wrapped her arms around my neck. "Our home."

I held her against me easily, her body lighter than air. "Yes. Our home."

———

I HADN'T RETURNED to the winery since we'd come back from Morocco. I wanted Vanessa in my line of sight at all times. Now that I had her back, it was impossible for me to let her go. Now that someone had laid a hand on her, I couldn't let her slip through my fingers again. I accompanied her to the gallery every single day. Instead of being helpful by assisting her customers or handling the shipments, I just watched her the entire time. Sometimes my gaze turned to the windows to see if anything suspicious was out there waiting for us—but there never was.

A couple left the gallery, leaving the two of us alone together. Vanessa walked up to me, wearing a blue dress that made the swell of her tits look incredible. Her hair was curled, and her gold hoop earrings hung from her lobes. With sun-kissed olive skin, she was gorgeous, even when she wore the angry expression she did now.

I gave her the same look I always gave her—like I might rip off her clothes and bend her over the desk.

She crossed her arms over her chest. "It's time for you to go back to work."

I'd agreed to take over the winery for her father, but that was twenty minutes away. It would be impossible for me to protect her when there was distance between us. I didn't care about the commitment I'd made to her father, not when I had a more important commitment to fulfill. He hadn't asked me when I was returning, probably because he knew exactly why. I stared at her with the same seriousness, disregarding her cuteness.

"You're chasing away my customers."

"I'm not doing anything." I hovered in the background like a statue.

"You're brooding in silence like a gargoyle. It makes people uncomfortable."

"Tell them I'm security."

"Why would a gallery need security?"

Because men broke in and took my woman just a week ago. I held her gaze without rising from the chair, being difficult on purpose. "If they don't like it, they can leave."

"And they are leaving," she hissed. "I need to sell this stuff, Griffin."

"We have plenty of money."

"That's not the point, and you know it." She walked over to me, her gold sandals slapping against the floor as she walked. "It's time for you to go back to work with my father."

I shook my head slightly. "This is where I belong."

"You're really going to sit there and watch every little thing I do?"

"I'm not watching you." I watched everything around her, from the way customers interacted with her to the way the men stared at her as they walked past the windows.

"Griffin, this is unnecessary."

I didn't want to argue with her, not after what we'd been through. All I wanted to do was cherish her, live our lives in peaceful bliss. "I will decide what's necessary. Go back to work and ignore me."

"Excuse me?" Her hand moved to her hip as she shifted her weight. "You'll decide what's necessary? This is a partnership. We're a team. We decide things together."

"Yes." I'd always believed Vanessa was a capable woman who could handle herself. But then my whole world crashed down around me and scared the shit out of me. "But it's my job to protect you. I'm not letting anyone take you away from me…ever again." I didn't want to sit in the gallery all day when I could be lifting weights or doing something more productive, but Vanessa was my responsibility.

Her eyes softened slightly, but she still seemed angry. "I get that, but the threat has passed. It's over."

It was over, but I was still afraid. "I'm not ready."

"Not ready to what?"

"Walk away. I can't be twenty minutes away from you."

"Griffin." She stepped closer to me until she sat across my thighs. Her arm hooked around my neck, and she looked into my face, her feet dangling above the floor because she was too petite. "I understand you're scared. I was scared too. But we have to move on with our lives. If we keep living like this…they win." Her hand cupped my cheek, and the second she caressed me like she loved me, I turned soft. "My art is what I'm most passionate about. I need to paint, and every time I sell a piece, it gives me this amazing joy. My artwork is going to hang in someone's home…it's such an honor. I can't stop doing that because I'm scared."

"I never asked you to. That's why I'm sitting here." I never asked her to give up her dream. I simply put my life on hold so I could keep an eye on her. If anyone wanted to hurt her but saw me standing there, he'd run for the hills.

"You can't stop living either, Griffin." She angled my face toward hers, making me look at her. "You belong at the winery with my father. That's your legacy.

And this is where I belong. When the afternoon is over, we go home to each other—every day."

Everything she said was rational, but I wasn't thinking rationally. "I can't let anything happen to you." When I'd finally gotten her back in my arms, I broke down again. This woman was my whole world. If anything happened to her…I never would recover.

"I know." Her fingers moved into my hair. "But one of the reasons why I love you is because you believe in me. You know I'm a fighter. You respect my strength and my intelligence. You know I can handle myself."

"Yes…to a certain extent." But when eight men came at her all at once, there was nothing she could do. Only I could have saved her.

"You killed all those men. There's no one left to hunt us."

I'd retired from my job and didn't leave any stone unturned. It seemed like my past was buried for good. There was no reason to look over my shoulder when there was no one following me. The promise I gave to her had been fulfilled.

"So there's no reason to protect me anymore."

"I will always protect you, baby." I would protect her from everything, from all the horrible things that could possibly hurt her. I would take all the bullets, all the punches, and make sure she was left untouched.

"I know. But there's nothing to protect me from anymore. I have a pistol in the desk if I ever need it. But a group of men is never going to burst into this gallery again. No one is going to rob me because all my transactions are digital. There's no one out there who wants to hurt either of us. So let it go, Griffin. Let me do my job and stop scaring away all my customers."

"What am I doing that's so scary?"

"Staring people down like a hungry bear."

"I'm not doing that. That's just how I look."

"Whatever. It makes people uncomfortable." She ran her fingers through my hair as she sat on my lap, her sexy lips close to mine. With her legs crossed and her dress hiked up to her thighs, she was artfully seducing me. Her perfume entered my nose, making me soften like a wilting flower. "Griffin, go back to work."

I growled quietly.

She smiled. "And you say you don't act like a bear…"

"I act like a bear with you. That's it."

She kissed the corner of my mouth, her bright lipstick leaving a gentle stain against my mouth. She breathed new life into my lungs, gave me a sense of peace no one else could bring. She had me wrapped around her finger, and she knew it. "Griffin."

I closed my eyes and savored the feeling of her lips against mine, treasuring it as a special memory even though I received those warm embraces on a daily basis. She cast a spell on me the moment we met, and the effects had never worn off. "Alright. I'll go back to work."

WHEN I ARRIVED at the winery in the heart of
Tuscany, I pulled up my phone and checked the tracker
on the screen. Seeing Vanessa exactly where I left her
gave me the strength to walk into the building and enter
Crow's office.

Vanessa was right. I couldn't watch her every single
moment of the day. We would have to sacrifice both of
our lives to make that happen, and it seemed unlikely
that someone would bother us again. I'd butchered
every single member of the crew that tried to steal
Vanessa, so there was no reason to look over my
shoulder.

I needed to leave it in the past.

I tapped my knuckles against the office door before I
stepped inside.

Crow was behind the desk, wearing a black t-shirt.
He was signing a stack of papers, his black wedding
ring a perfect complement to his dark skin. With a
structured jaw and brilliant eyes, he was the embodi-
ment of the strength that all the Barsettis inherited.
"Griffin." He dropped the pen and rose from behind
the desk, slightly surprised to see me. He moved around
the desk and approached me, a grin coming onto his
face. "I wasn't sure when I would see you next." Instead
of greeting me with a handshake, he hugged me the
way he hugged his son.

I hugged him back, embracing this man like a

father. I used to despise him with every fiber of my being. I used to want to slit his throat and watch him die. I used to want to murder his wife for revenge. But now…I couldn't imagine my life without him. "That makes two of us."

When he pulled away, he continued to smile. "Vanessa made you come back to work?"

I nodded. "Apparently, I was scaring away all of her customers."

Crow laughed loudly, the chuckle coming from deep in his chest. "I can picture that pretty clearly."

"She said I stared people down like a hungry bear."

He tapped his fingers against his temple. "A very vivid picture. But I'm sure she made you realize you can't watch her all the time. I used to be the same way with my wife. I realized it was unrealistic to keep her on a leash for her safety. She claimed I was taking away her freedom, making her a prisoner all over again."

Vanessa would always be my prisoner—whether she realized it or not.

"I'm sure there's nothing to worry about, Griffin. You know how much I love my daughter, and if I'm not worried, you shouldn't be either. If those men were your only enemies, you dealt with them. As long as you live a peaceful life, there shouldn't be anything to be wary of."

All of that made complete sense, and there was no argument against it. "I guess I have PTSD because of it." When Vanessa slipped through my fingertips, it gave

me the worst feeling in the world…helplessness. I'd
never been so afraid in my life. I'd never panicked the
way I did in that moment. I'd never been so hateful.
"Everything else I've dealt with in my life has just been
problems…problems with simple solutions. But losing
Vanessa…wasn't some kind of problem. It was the
worst moment of my life, a moment I can't look back
on without feeling powerless all over again." I didn't
look her father in the eye as I spoke, slightly embarrassed by the emotion swelling inside my chest. "It's
gonna take me some time to get over it."

Crow watched me, a sympathetic look on his face.
"It'll pass—in time. The best thing you can do is go
back to a normal life. As the weeks pass, your fears will
pass. Then you'll stop thinking about it altogether."

I was certain Crow knew exactly how I felt, after
everything he'd lived through. "I'm surprised you don't
hate me because of what happened."

"Hate you?" he whispered. "You got my daughter
out of there."

"I'm also the reason she was there in the first place.
I should have listened to you when you told me to quit.
I didn't listen…and I almost lost the most important
thing in my life."

He gave a quiet sigh before he turned around and
grabbed the bottle of scotch sitting on his bookshelf. He
picked up two short glasses and filled them with the
amber liquor.

I took my cue to sit in the chair in front of his desk.

He set the glass in front of me before he moved to his chair. "You can't play that game, Griffin. If you do, you'll always lose." He took a long drink of the liquor, licking his lips as he set the glass down on the surface of his desk. "You can think about the past and wonder why you didn't make better decisions, but in the end, what does that accomplish?"

I'd never been a man who lived with regret. I stood by my decisions and didn't question them. Vanessa was different because I'd never been in this situation before. I'd never loved someone the way I loved her. She was the single most important thing in my life—more important than my own life. I used to be selfish before she came along, but now I was completely selfless.

"It's difficult to see straight when someone you love is involved. When I first got married, a part of me missed my life before Pearl came along, not because I wanted to be single again, but because life was just simpler. I didn't care about anyone but myself, so my decisions had little consequence. But once she became the most important thing in my life, she turned into baggage. I constantly had something to protect, something valuable that could be stolen. It created a huge headache."

I understood the feeling all too well.

"You can hate yourself for not listening to me about retiring sooner, but you couldn't have done it any other way. You had to be loyal to your team, and loyalty is important to Barsettis. In the end, you're capable of protecting my daughter, and that's all that matters."

"And what if something happens again?"

He shrugged. "You'll be there for her. I have no doubt of that."

He used to wish me dead, but now he had so much confidence in me.

"Conway would be dead right now if it weren't for you. I would be too. Probably my brother. Then they may have moved in after my wife and sister-in-law next. But you changed the course of the future. Then you ended that feud permanently. When Vanessa was taken, you destroyed your enemies. Frankly, the safest place for Vanessa is in your heart." He pointed to my chest. "Safest place in the world."

I WALKED in the door and found Vanessa in the kitchen. She was still in the deep blue dress she wore that afternoon. I already knew she was home on my drive back to Florence because I checked her tracker every fifteen minutes. Without that little device, my anxiety would be insurmountable.

She poured the milk into her cereal before she noticed me. "How was your first day back?"

I tossed my keys on the table as I slowly walked toward her, amused that this perfect woman continued to make cereal for herself for most meals rather than learn how to cook something. "Cereal for dinner?"

"It's a snack. I figured you were making dinner." She looked up at me, that beautiful smile just for me. Her eyes glowed in a special way that didn't happen for another person. Without even touching me, she treated me in a way she never treated anyone else.

"I spoil you too much."

She shrugged. "Can't argue with that." She rose on her tiptoes and kissed me on the mouth.

I kept my eyes open and watched her, watched her visibly melt for me. Her hand was pressed against my chest for balance, and her tits looked incredible from this angle.

When she pulled away, that same light was in her eyes. "So, you made it through the day?"

"Yes. Your father talked me down."

"Ohh…one of those lectures. Been there, done that." She left her bowl of cereal on the counter and kept her attention on me. "I'm glad he made you feel better. He's very wise…when he's not being annoying."

"Yeah."

She turned back to her bowl and finally scooped a bite into her mouth. "I got a lot more customers after you left."

I dug into my jeans and pulled out the set of keys that I'd gotten from the real estate agent. I placed them on the counter beside us and stared at her.

She glanced at the keys, immediately recognizing

they weren't ours. They were made of brass, and they were big and ancient, not like the keys we had to the apartment. There was a slight hint of rust on the metal. "What's this?"

"The keys to your new home." I waited for her to explode, for her to jump into my arms and scream with joy.

"You're being serious?" She dropped the bowl back on the counter, the milk spilling over and rolling toward the microwave. She snatched the keys and felt them in her fingertips before she clutched them to her chest. "We got it."

"It's all ours."

"Oh my god." She launched herself into my arms and wrapped her arms around my waist, her dress immediately popping open to reveal her sexy skin in her black thong. "I can't believe it. It's ours!" Her arms hooked around my neck, and she hugged me tightly. "Thank you. Thank you for buying it for me."

I carried her toward the dining table, the place where I made love to her in the middle of our meals. "You're welcome, baby." I sat her on the wood and yanked her straps down to reveal her perfect tits. My hands pulled her thong down next before I positioned her at the edge of the table.

"You want me to show you my appreciation?"

I dropped my jeans and boxers and prepared to thrust inside her. "I expect you to pay for half with this perfect pussy." My hands gripped the backs of her knees, and I pinned her down against the table so I could fuck her good and hard.

She gripped both of my wrists and looked at me with fire in her eyes, her sexiness incredible. With her hair all over the table and her green eyes so bright, she looked like a fantasy I couldn't even make up. "That sounds fair to me."

I WORKED in the warehouse most of the day, marking the products that had been produced that week. Barsetti Vineyards just acquired a new client with a large demand for a chain of restaurants, so our production had increased. I noted everything had been shipped out and took care of the shipment. I wasn't moving crates and boxes around like I did before since Crow had hired someone to handle those things. Now I took care of the paperwork, traveling from one vineyard to the next before I came back.

It wasn't as exciting as my old profession, but at least it was something meaningful. It would protect Vanessa's legacy so she could pass it on to her children. Even though I spent eight hours there every single day without getting paid, it was a good utilization of my time.

And I checked Vanessa's tracker every hour.

She was never where she shouldn't be. Sometimes at lunchtime, she was in a restaurant, probably with

Carmen. But she never deviated from the two-mile radius around the apartment. The rest of the time, her dot was inside the gallery.

It always brought me a sense of calm that got me through the rest of the day.

At the end of the day, I returned to the main winery and headed to Crow's office. My heart was beating so hard in my chest that I couldn't stop my hands from shaking. The nerves were getting to me, making my spine tighten against the muscles that flanked my back. This uneasiness was new to me. Even when he'd hated me, I never felt this way.

But this was something I'd never done before.

I stepped inside his office and saw him standing behind his desk.

"Hey, how'd it go?" Crow powered down his laptop before he shut the lid.

"Got it all right here." I placed the reports on his desk so he could look at them tomorrow.

"Great." He placed the stack inside his desk.

"We're making good time. Should be able to fill the order. Cane had to move some stuff around at the second location, but we made it work."

"Excellent." He walked around the desk and placed his phone in his pocket. He wore dark jeans and an olive green V-neck. There was a prominent vein in his neck and along his forearms. He wore a shiny watch on his left wrist. He was a simple man who cared about the bare minimum. He only wore suits for meetings and wore jeans and boots the rest of the time. "You're doing great work, Griffin. Adelina has been happy that Cane is home early every night. Same thing goes for Pearl. Maybe we'll retire a little sooner than planned…"

The compliment didn't mean anything to me, at least, not in that moment.

Crow noticed the tension in the silence. His eyes scanned back and forth as he looked into my face, trying to gauge my emotions based on my coldness. His hands slid into his pockets, and he stopped before me in front of the leather chairs that faced his desk. "Everything alright, Griffin?"

I wasn't nervous because of his response. I was nervous for a million other reasons. I'd never been good with feeling emotions, let alone expressing them. The only person I could talk to was Vanessa, and that was because she understood me so well. I was a man of silence, and that had always been fine for her. She seemed to know what I wanted to say without hearing me say it. "I don't know how to do this, so…" I dug into my pocket and pulled out the small box I'd kept stashed there since this morning.

The second Crow saw it, he took a deep breath and ran his hand through his hair. "I knew this was coming." He returned his hand to his pocket then lifted his gaze to look at me, this time his expression softer than before. "But I'm still not ready for it."

I extended the box so he could take it.

He eyed it for a moment before he took it. He

opened the lid and stared at the three-carat diamond that immediately caught the light coming through the window. The main stone was in the center, beautiful and big, and smaller diamonds wrapped around the band halfway. I bought the highest clarity diamonds because I wanted it to sparkle constantly as she moved her hands, whether she was painting or working in her gallery. Crow took a deep breath before he let out a long whistle. "Jesus, Griffin." He took the ring out of the box and examined it closer. "This is one hell of a ring."

Anytime she wore it, I wanted every man who looked at her to know she was claimed—and not by an ordinary man. I wanted that fifty-thousand-dollar ring to ward off any asshole who thought he might have shot with her. "It's bug repellent."

Crow chuckled lightly before he put the ring back in the box. "It's beautiful."

"Thanks."

He closed the box and handed it back to me. "She'll love it."

"Yeah…" I cleared my throat as I shoved the box back into my pocket. "Mr. Barsetti, may I have your blessing to marry your daughter?" I'd never been the kind of man to ask permission for anything, and the only reason why I did it now was because it was important to him. But when I saw his eyes soften even more and a new wave of emotion enter his expression, I didn't mind asking the question. I saw the love for his daughter in the difference that came over his composure, the way his daughter changed him from being a strong and hard man to being a father who loved his children more than anything in the world. She was his weakness, but he wasn't ashamed of that vulnerability at all.

He didn't say anything, not because his answer would be no, but because words left him in that moment. He ran his hand through his hair and blinked his eyes quickly, combating the tears that flooded his gaze. He took another deep breath like he didn't know what else to do. "I'm sorry…"

"It's alright." I looked away from his gaze, giving him some privacy.

"Of course, you have my blessing, Griffin." He moved toward me and placed his hand on my shoulder. "I know you'll love my daughter, provide for her, and protect her. Besides, you're already a son to me." He gave me a gentle squeeze before he dropped his hand. "And I appreciate you asking me."

I gave him a slight nod.

"So…when are you going to ask her?"

I wasn't a romantic guy with romantic ideas, but I knew how I wanted to ask her to marry me. I knew what would make her the happiest, what would bring her to tears as she gave me the answer I wanted to hear. "This is my idea…"

TWENTY-TWO

Vanessa

_____

We spent the afternoon with the movers, getting everything into the house. I went on a shopping spree that week and picked out everything I wanted for the two-story house. Since the house was hundreds of years old, I specifically selected furniture with that antique style, keeping the tone the same.

Two of the guest rooms were filled with antique furniture and king-size beds. I picked tones of blush, gray, and white to fill the rooms, bringing light colors to capture the subtle beauty of the home.

I left the third guest room empty on purpose.

Bones and I hadn't talked about it much, but within the next year, I wanted to be pregnant. I wanted to have a baby and put the crib and furniture into this room. Didn't make sense to fill it with furniture only to replace it in a year.

When Bones didn't ask why I kept it empty, I assumed he knew exactly why.

My family came over for dinner that night, a housewarming party to break in the new home. I didn't help Bones in the kitchen since I pretty much couldn't do anything anyway, and I took my family on a tour of the house.

"It's so beautiful," Mom said, and Aunt Adelina nodded. "And it's so you. I can see the two of you growing old in this house."

"What about this room?" Carmen asked, stepping into the empty bedroom.

"That's the baby's room," I explained.

Carmen's eyes immediately darted to my stomach. "What?" she shrieked, her voice becoming high-pitched in no time. "You're pregnant?"

"No." I covered her mouth so she would be quiet. "I just mean, when we have a baby…this is the room." I lowered my hand and rolled my eyes. "You're going to make everyone freak out."

"Sorry," Carmen said with a laugh. "It seems like you're preparing for a baby…just assumed."

"I just didn't want to fill it with furniture and then replace it all in less than a year." I pictured myself being pregnant, a belly that slowly got bigger until I had to stay home because I couldn't drive or work anymore. Bones would stay home and take care of me, his large hand resting on my belly.

"Less than a year?" Carmen asked. "Does he know about this?"

I shrugged. "I think he does."

"I wonder if he's going to ask you to marry him soon." Carmen moved closer to me and my mom. "I've been waiting for it for a while."

I wanted to be married, but having a ring on my finger wasn't that important to me. "Whether we're married or not, we're committed to each other for the rest of our lives. I don't care if he's my husband when we start a family. Being in this house makes me want to fill it with children, and that's something he already agreed to."

Mom wrapped her arm around my shoulders. "That's a good perspective on love. When you're really in love, the specifics don't matter. As long as you're togeth-er." She rubbed my back before she stepped into the hall-way. "And the fact that the man cooks makes him a keeper. Your father may get a bull's-eye every time, but he doesn't know the difference between a pan and a pot."

We headed back down the stairs and into the back-yard. Sapphire was sitting on the patio furniture with Reid resting in her arms. Conway was beside her, his arm draped over her shoulder.

My father was in the kitchen with Bones, drinking scotch while he watched him prepare dinner.

The doorbell rang from the other side of the house. "That must be Carter." I walked to the front of the house and opened the door, coming face-to-face with my cousin, who looked a lot like Conway.

But he wasn't alone.

Mia was with him—along with a young boy.

"Mia?" I blurted, surprised to see her at a family event. "How are you?" I ignored my cousin and hugged her first.

"I'm great," she said. "Better than I've ever been. When Carter told me you were having a get-together, I asked if we could come along. It's been so long since I've seen you."

"We're happy to have you here. And who's this little guy?" I already knew he was her son, based on the things she'd told me about him. I kneeled down in front of him, giving him a friendly smile to make him feel welcome.

The boy was shy, giving me half a grin before he waved. "Luca."

Carter placed his hand on the boy's shoulder. "Luca, this is my cousin, Vanessa. Show her what we learned."

Luca extended his right hand to shake mine. "Nice to meet you."

I chuckled as I shook his hand. "Nice to meet you too. Please come in."

Carter walked inside with Luca, keeping his hand on his shoulder. "I've got a few other family members here I want to introduce you to."

"Anyone my age?" Luca asked.

"No," Carter answered. "But I have a new cousin that's a baby."

Luca shook his head. "I'm not friends with babies."

Carter chuckled as he guided him farther into the house. "Alright, let's start with my dad. He's pretty cool."

Mia watched the two of them walk away, emotion and joy in her eyes. She sighed as she watched them leave the hallway and join the rest of my family on the patio. Like she forgot I was there, it took her a few seconds before she turned back to me. "I hope we aren't intruding—"

"Absolutely not." In that short interaction, I gleaned everything I needed to know. Carter seemed to help Mia in the beginning out of the goodness of his heart, but based on this, there was nothing just friends about their relationship. Carter took Luca under his wing like a son, and Mia looked on as she watched the two men she loved get along so well. "You guys are family too."

She turned back to me, her eyebrows slightly raised.

"I'm very happy for you." I didn't need to ask what had changed to understand the scene right in front of my eyes. There was a connection between the two of them, something that bonded them so close together that Carter, an infamous playboy, had taken a young boy under his wing. That was not something he would do for just anyone.

"Thank you."

TWENTY-THREE

Carter

My parents had no idea that Mia and Luca would be joining us that evening. My invitation had been spontaneous, but since these two were so important to me, it seemed like they should be there. I didn't want to leave them at home like they were some kind of dirty secret.

I walked up to my father with my hand resting on Luca's shoulder.

"He seems scary," Luca whispered.

Because he could be terrifying. "He's not. Nothing to be afraid of."

My father turned to me from where he stood next to my mother on the patio. His eyes were on me for barely a second before they flicked to the small boy beside me. An innate kindness entered his eyes, knowing exactly who the child was.

My mom smiled immediately, moisture entering her gaze. "Luca…" She kneeled down and extended her arms to him. "I know exactly who you are without ever seeing your face. Come here, sweetie."

Luca left my embrace and moved into the stranger's arms. He didn't say anything as he hugged her back, but he probably figured out she was my mother. "Hi…"

Mom hugged him tightly and patted the back of his head. "You're so cute. It's so nice to meet you. I'm Adelina, Carter's mother."

I looked at my father as Luca and my mother became acquainted.

He turned to me, a slight smile on his lips. "Cute kid."

"Yeah, he is."

"You two seem to get along pretty well."

I never knew anything about kids or cared to spend time with one, but when I met Luca, everything clicked. We swam in the pool together, watched TV together, and when he went back to school, he asked me to help him with his math homework. "Yeah…we do. I never knew kids could be so cool."

"They can be. You were, at least."

"But not Carmen?" I teased.

He chuckled. "She was great too."

Luca pulled away from my mom and turned to my father next. He extended his hand. "It's nice to meet you…Carter's dad."

My father chuckled before he shook his hand. "You've got a strong grip there. Where'd you learn that?"

Luca glanced at me. "Carter."

"I taught him how to give a good handshake. I'm glad he passed that down to you." My father dropped his hand then kneeled down so they were at eye level. "You can call me Cane, by the way."

"Cane." Luca nodded. "Got it."

"So, how are you liking time with my son?" my father asked.

Luca glanced at me again. "I love it. He's the coolest guy I've ever known…taught me how to swim."

"Aww…" Mom looked at me, her eyes soft. She ran her fingers through his hair, cradling him just the way she used to with me. "You're such a sweet little boy."

"Uh, thanks," Luca whispered.

Mia joined us a moment later, wearing a beautiful yellow dress that was perfect for the end of summer. She came to my side and watched my parents interact with her son. "Quite the social butterfly, huh?" She rested her hands on his shoulders and looked down at him, smiling as a strand of hair came loose.

"Yeah," Luca said. "These are Carter's parents."

"I know," she said. "I've met them before."

"Let's meet everyone else." My mom took Luca's hand, and together with Mia, they moved around the party and made their introductions. Conway knew about Mia but had never met her before.

When my father and I were alone together, he gave me a knowing look. "The three of you mix well together."

Ever since Luca came into our lives, my sex life had taken a serious hit. I was lucky to get some alone time with Mia during the day while Luca was at school. But once he was home, she was closed for business. Ironically, I didn't mind. "Yeah, we do."

"Doesn't seem like she's going anywhere."

She wasn't going anywhere ever again. "No, she's not." I didn't tell him what we decided on, since it didn't seem like the best time. We were there to celebrate the new house Vanessa and Griffin had moved in to. It was a housewarming party, and it would be distasteful to announce our upcoming nuptials.

Father turned his stare on the two of them as they talked with Conway and Sapphire. "Being a father figure is serious business, Carter. That kid looks up to you. It would be devastating to get close to you only to lose you."

"I understand that."

"Alright," he said. "It's one thing to break a woman's heart. It's another to break a child's heart."

I loved that kid even though I hadn't known him that long. The second he was in my home, we immediately clicked. It was difficult to picture my life without him, without that smile and zest for life. "That's the last thing on my mind."

Father finally dropped it. "Alright. Looks like your mother and I might have a grandson."

"Yeah…I think you might."

TWENTY-FOUR

Vanessa

———————

The dining room was surrounded by windows, so everyone had a great view of the changing colors from the setting sun. Bones carried the big plates of food to the center of the table, and I uncorked the wine bottles and filled all the glasses, giving Luca apple juice. All thirteen of us gathered at the table, Bones taking the seat at the head.

"This is impressive, Griffin," my mother said. "Everything looks so good. I couldn't even make all of this without Lars for help."

"I took a few bites in the kitchen," my father admitted. "And it's good too."

My hand moved to Bones's on the table, touched that he went to all this effort for me. I told him I wanted to have my family over for dinner, to celebrate the last few days of summer before fall arrived. This was all I

419

ever wanted, to share my family with the love of my life —and vice versa.

Bones pulled his hand away. "Thank you, everyone. There's actually something I wanted to say…"

I was about to grab my glass of wine when I turned back to him, surprised he would address my entire family at one time. He wasn't much for words, and cooking for everyone was more than enough.

Bones was quiet for a while, like he was trying to think of the right words to speak. "As you all know…I don't have a family. I lost my mom at a very young age. I can barely remember her face, but I've never forgotten her spirit. I feel it again when I'm with all of you… because it feels like I'm with family again."

I stopped breathing because I couldn't believe Bones said something so heartfelt. He said it to a group of people he had once hated. He barely expressed his private thoughts to me, let alone a room full of my cousins and parents.

He continued. "I didn't know how much I needed this until I had it again. I know things weren't good in the beginning…when Vanessa first brought me around. It was intense and difficult, but somehow, we ended up here. Now all of you mean a lot to me…because you mean so much to Vanessa." He turned his gaze on me, like he was only speaking to me now. "You've given me a reason to live. You've given me happiness. You've given me everything that I've been missing…and I love you with all my heart."

I wished he hadn't said this in front of my whole family because it brought tears to my eyes. The emotion was too strong to ignore, and the tears pooled on the surface of my eyes until they became too heavy and dripped down my cheeks. "Griffin…"

He kept the same gaze, unaffected by my emotion like the statue he was. He wore the same intense expression I saw him wear the night we met. He wasn't transparent like most people were, keeping his thoughts and feelings buried under those pounds of muscle. He kept his hand on mine and gave me a gentle squeeze, his skin warm to the touch. "Despite everything that I was, you still loved me. Despite all the odds we had stacked against us, you still fought for me. You asked your family to accept me even though there was no chance that was going to happen…but you also remained loyal to them. Now that I know them so well, I understand why you're so committed to them…because family is everything. And I'm honored to be a part of yours."

More tears fell, and I didn't understand why he was doing this to me. He was making me feel a million things at once as my family sat there and watched me cry.

"The moment you put that bullet in my shoulder, I was yours. You're a fighter, the strongest woman I've ever met. You put me in my place more times than I can count. You hold your own in a fight and do more damage than you receive. I fell in love with all those qualities, but it took me a long time to figure out where they came from. They're Barsetti traits...traits you inherited from a wonderful family."

This speech was longer than I anticipated, but I didn't ask him to stop. I didn't ask him to stop making me cry.

"You will always be a Barsetti. I accept that because I'm willing to share you." He pulled his hand away from mine and then moved to his knee on the floor.

"Oh my fucking god!" I covered my mouth with my hands when everything clicked into place. Carmen squealed from the other side of the table, and my mom and aunt did the same. I watched him move to one knee and pull the small box out of his pocket. "Shit, this is really happening." I thought I would wake up one morning, and there would be a ring sitting on my finger. I never expected Bones to actually ask because he wasn't the kind of man that asked for things.

He opened the box and pulled out the ring.

A ridiculously huge ring with glorious diamonds everywhere. "Holy shit, that's big."

Bones didn't crack a smile as he grabbed my left hand and slipped the ring onto my finger. The rest of my family stood up so they could watch the events unfold. "I asked your father's permission. I asked your family's permission. But I refuse to ask for yours. Marry me." He was true to who he was, never giving me a choice because that wasn't his style. He gave my family the respect I wanted because it was important to me, but between the two of us, it was different.

It was exactly how I wanted him to ask me— not to ask me at all. "Yes." My arms circled his neck, and I moved into his chest on the floor, letting those powerful arms wrap around me. That embrace would be there every single day for the rest of our lives. He was the only man I'd ever loved—the only man I would ever love.

My family clapped and cheered, their applause filling our new home with happiness. They filled the silent corners with memories, bringing a new energy into the home where we would start our lives. The house had been sitting there for hundreds of years, but now it was starting over—with us.

Bones pulled his head back so he could look at me, his palm cupping my cheek. His thumb brushed away the tears that streamed down my cheeks. He'd only showed his emotion twice in our relationship, both times was when he almost lost me. That emotion wasn't there now, but I knew that didn't mean he wasn't happy. He kissed a new tear that just fell from my eye. He gathered it on his lips before he moved to my other cheek and kissed me again.

"I wish I would stop crying...I can't help it."

"You know I like it when you cry," he whispered so only I could hear. He finally kissed me on the mouth, giving me a PG kiss that was appropriate for the rest of the family to witness. "You're mine...for the rest of your life."

"Even if you gave me a choice, I would still want to be yours for the rest of my life."

He finally gave a slight smile. "A man doesn't give his woman a choice. He loves her without permission. He protects her without her watching. And he remains faithful to her when she's not looking. You're my prisoner…but I'm glad you're a willing prisoner."

TWENTY-FIVE

Carter

I woke up Sunday morning with Mia beside me, buck naked and beautiful. I was on my back with her pressed into my side, his leg hooked between my knees. Her arm was draped around my torso.

She was all over me.

Luca fell asleep early last night on the couch, so Mia tucked him into bed before she joined me in my bedroom upstairs.

And I'd made love to her all night long.

My eyes had barely been open for a few seconds before there was a knock on the door. "Mom?" Luca's gentle voice came through the door on the other side of the room. "Mom?"

I sighed and pulled Mia tighter against me, not wanting to give her up so soon. It wasn't even eight in the morning, and Luca was wide awake.

Luca knocked again. "Mom?"

Mia finally woke up, no longer able to ignore the sound of her son's voice. "I'll be there in a second, baby."

Luca's footsteps finally trailed away as he ran down the hallway.

She sat up in bed and ran her fingers through her messy hair.

"Does that mean we're busted?" My hand reluctantly let her go, my fingers aching for her the second she was gone from my embrace.

"He's pretty smart for an eight-year-old. I think he already knew."

"Is that a problem?"

"No." She stood up and pulled her clothes on from the floor. "He'll have to get used to it. He likes you, so I'm sure it's fine."

"Has he ever met any of the other men you've…" I couldn't finish the sentence because I got jealous just thinking about the other men she'd been with. I'd slept with more women than I could count so it was hypocritical of me to care, but I couldn't help it. Now that she was mine, I didn't want to think about anyone else who had been before me.

"No. Luca has never seen the other men I dated. I always kept them separate."

"So I'm the only man he's ever seen you with?"

She leaned over the bed and kissed me before she headed to the door. "Yes…egomaniac."

I smacked her ass before she got too far away. "I like that."

"I'm going to get breakfast started. You want the usual?"

"Sure."

She smiled before she walked out.

I lay in bed a little longer, knowing she would want to have Luca brush his teeth and get dressed before he went downstairs to the kitchen. Now that Mia and I were more open about our relationship, it didn't make sense to keep them on the second floor. If something bad ever happened, I would be too far away to do anything. Perhaps I should move Luca's bedroom across the hall from mine that way they could both be close by.

I got dressed and headed downstairs. Before I descended the final floor, I could smell the coffee and bacon. I headed into the kitchen and saw Luca sitting on one of the barstools at the kitchen island with a coloring book in front of him. He was coloring in a large T-Rex.

"Hey, little man." I rubbed his head gently as I looked down at his drawing. "Pretty cool."

"Thanks, Carter." He handed me a crayon. "You wanna try?"

"Maybe after breakfast." I moved around the kitchen island and came to Mia's side as she stood at the stove. She was whipping up French toast, eggs, and bacon. "Something smells good."

"Are you talking about the food or me?" She flipped the bread in the pan.

I grinned. "Both."

She scooped the food onto a plate and then placed it in front of Luca. "Eat up. All of it. You didn't eat your dinner last night."

Luca must have been hungry because he didn't make a complaint.

She came back to me and poured me a cup of coffee. "Breakfast will be ready in a few minutes."

"Alright." Instead of walking into the dining room, I remained beside her and sipped my coffee.

"You're just going to stand there?" she asked, amused.

"Yep." I kept drinking my coffee. "It's my kitchen. I can do whatever I want."

"I can't argue with that… thought maybe you could read the paper or something."

"That sounds boring. I'd rather watch you work in my kitchen." I glanced at Luca on the other side of the kitchen, where he was focused on his coloring book.

"So…did your family think it was strange that you brought me along last night?"

"Did they act like it was strange?"

"No…but maybe they said something to you."

"Not at all. They love you. Luca too."

She smiled as she stirred the eggs. "They're all so nice. I just want them to like me. I mean, I already knew they liked me before, but it's different now that we're…together."

"Why would that make any difference?"

"Well…I'm sure no parent wants their child to end up with an abused woman who already has an eight-year-old son."

I rolled my eyes. "Maybe normal people in normal places, but the Barsettis aren't normal. We don't judge people because of things like that. My father and uncle taught me not to judge a woman by what she's been through. They taught me a real man will erase a woman's past. He'll make her forget every bad thing that happened to her because he makes her feel so loved. So, no, my family doesn't care, sweetheart."

She paused what she was doing, those words obviously meaning something to her. When she kept moving and placed the slices of French toast on the plate, she spoke again. "So, did you tell them that we're getting married?"

"No. I'm glad I didn't since Vanessa and Griffin got engaged. That would have been the worst time."

"You're right, it would have been."

"I'll tell them soon. Give it a few days."

She dished the rest of the food onto the plate before she handed it to me. "Sounds good. I wonder how they'll react."

"I'm sure they'll be happy."

"Really?"

"They seemed happy to see us together last night." I

didn't tell her that my parents knew I had serious feelings for her. It seemed easier to keep it this way, to keep it lighthearted without any expectations.

"That's different…"

"I wouldn't worry about it. They like you a lot, Mia. And they like the way I am with you."

A FEW DAYS LATER, I stopped by the winery at lunchtime.

My father was talking with my uncle in the tasting room, my aunt Pearl standing with them.

"It doesn't seem like you guys are working much." I saw them gathered around the table with a few empty bottles of wine. It seemed like they were drinking more than actually getting things done.

My father turned around and grinned, knowing I was making a joke. "And what are you doing here? Doesn't seem like you're working either."

I gave my father a hug and did the same with my aunt and uncle. "I never got the chance to tell you congratulations the other night." My aunt and uncle must be thrilled about Vanessa's engagement.

"Thanks," Aunt Pearl said with a smile. "Our daughter is very happy, and that makes us happy."

"Griffin is a strong guy," Crow said. "He'll do a good job taking care of her."

"No doubt," I said. "Where's Griffin now?"

"He's doing work at the other winery," Father explained. "I don't think he'd be too happy to know how much we're slacking off."

"He's a great worker, so we have more time to do nothing," Crow added with a laugh. "He's been a great addition to the team."

"So, is there something you needed, son?" my father asked. "It's unlike you just to show up here."

"I wanted to talk to you about something," I said. "In private."

"Alright." Father walked away with me and headed toward the gravel pathway in front of the cars. "Everything alright?"

"Yeah, everything is great," I said quickly. "It's good news, not bad news."

"I'm all ears." He stopped and crossed his arms over his chest.

I felt strange saying the words before I even spoke. I slid my hands into the pockets of my jeans before I braced myself for the impact. "Mia and I...we've decided to get married."

His expression was blank for five seconds before his skepticism kicked in. "What?"

"We're getting married." I did my best not to smile, but it was difficult to fight the happiness exploding from my chest. "We were talking last week, and she kinda asked if that's something I would want to do. She said she needs someone to protect her and Luca, and in return, she would make me a home and raise any kids I want to have…" As I said the words out loud, I knew how they must have sounded to my father. It didn't make any sense from an outside point of view.

He continued to give me the same look. "So, you're getting married because it's convenient?"

"I guess you could put it that way," I said with a shrug.

My father wasn't the least bit happy. He rubbed the back of his neck, sighed in disappointment, and then gave me a bitter look. "You're a nearly thirty-year-old man who knows what he's doing. You started your own company the second you were out of the house because you're so damn smart. So I don't understand why you're being so stupid right now."

"You think marrying Mia is stupid?" I asked, surprised by his frankness.

"No. But I think the two of you are stupid."

I raised an eyebrow, unsure what that meant. "What?"

"Why can't you just tell each other that you love each other? Why do you have to make some bullshit excuse and say it's for convenience? It doesn't make any sense to me. If you want to get married, fine. But at least be honest about why." He smacked me upside the head, something he hadn't done since I was young. "Where's that brilliant brain of yours?"

"Look, it's not that straightforward. I know how I feel about her…but I don't think she feels the same way." I'd never admitted that truth to myself or out loud. It was the first time I'd ever truly acknowledged my feelings.

"You're kidding, right?" He cocked his head to the side, looking furious. "She just asked you to marry her?"

"She didn't propose to me. She kinda just talked about it."

"Whatever. You think she would do that just for a place to live? You already said she could stay there and be your maid. There's something more here. I'm ashamed you're too afraid to actually admit it."

"I'm not afraid," I said defensively.

"Then you need to clear the air with her. Be honest. Tell her you love her and listen to her say it back. Then move forward. Because what you're doing is some pathetic form of what it should really be. I don't understand why both of you would be acting this way."

"What makes you so certain she feels the same way? Wouldn't she just tell me?"

"Think about it, Carter. She's a victim of rape and abuse. Maybe she thinks you would never love her that way, so she doesn't want to say anything and risk losing you. What if she did tell you she loved you, and you didn't say it back? Wouldn't you kick her out?"

Assuming I didn't love her, those feelings would create an awkward situation.

"It's too risky for her. So she did this instead because she has something to offer you."

"But if you know how I feel about her, why doesn't she?"

He shrugged. "Sometimes we only see what we want to see. Now, go home and talk to her about this. When you approach your mother about this, that is the story you're going to tell her. That you two love each other and want to be together. Don't tell her the idiotic story you just told me. That's not gonna make your mother happy or proud."

"Alright…I'll talk to Mia."

He clapped my shoulder. "Be straight with her. The Barsettis aren't afraid to tell people how they feel. Make me proud."

SUMMER WAS ALMOST OVER, so Luca was enjoying the pool as much as he could. He'd finally become proficient at swimming, but Mia always sat at the edge of the pool and kept a close eye on him.

I walked outside in my swim trunks, noting the way Mia looked at my bare chest when I emerged from the house. My towel was over my shoulder, so I tossed it over the back of the chair before I approached Mia.

"You're gonna swim, Carter?" Luca asked as he kicked toward our side of the pool.

"Yep." I moved to the spot beside Mia. "Wanted to enjoy the last of summer while I can."

"Cool! Watch this!" Luca turned around and swam by himself to the opposite end of the pool.

I already knew he could that since I taught him

everything he knew, but I still clapped when he gripped the opposite edge. "Great job, little man."

Mia was in her black bikini beside me, her long hair pulled into a bun and shades sitting on her nose. It was the first time I'd seen her wear a piece that didn't cover the scars on her back. She didn't seem to care anymore.

Which was good.

I'm sure Luca would express his curiosity about the scars eventually, but she would come up with a reasonable explanation.

Those marks used to turn me on because I fantasized about hurting her. But now, it was difficult for me to acknowledge them, when the sight of them caused me so much pain. She deserved a better fate than what she'd had to experience. No one should ever have to suffer through that.

"Everything alright?" Mia's light voice entered my ear as she stared at her son.

"Yeah. Why?"

"You just got really quiet all of a sudden."

I liked being honest with her. The transparency was refreshing. "Your scars."

"They bother you?" she whispered.

"No. Just make me sad."

She turned her face toward me, but her eyes were impossible to see through her dark shades. "I thought you liked them?"

I shrugged. "I guess my tastes have changed." Our vanilla lifestyle seemed to be enough for me now. We made love quietly so Luca wouldn't overhear us. There were no whips or chains, and there weren't even screams. But that didn't make me feel like I was missing something. It was the most satisfied I'd ever felt.

Luca had a few pool toys on the opposite side, water guns and inflatable tubes. He grabbed one of the guns and clung to the floatable raft as he drifted around and squirted the ants that crawled up the side of the concrete.

"How's he liking school?" I asked, watching him concentrate on the insects.

"He really loves it," she said with a sigh. "He's already made friends, and he likes his teachers. Says he loves it here far more than the orphanage. I haven't asked him too many questions about that because I don't want to know the details." She didn't care about her own suffering over the past three years, just what her son had to go through without her.

Her selflessness made me adore her even more. "It doesn't matter where he was before. He's in a good place now. He's happy."

"Yes…very true." She kept watching Luca, a slight smile on her lips.

And I kept watching her.

LUCA FELL asleep on the couch downstairs, his toys spread out across the rug in front of the fireplace. Mia scooped him up into her arms and then carried him up the stairs to put him to bed.

"You want me to do that?" Luca was a skinny boy, but she had a long walk ahead of her.

"No. I love doing this." With his head pressed against her shoulder and one of his arms hanging by his side, she carried him to the bottom of the staircase.

"Can I expect you in my bedroom?" I asked, hoping she would put Luca to bed easily then sneak off to be with me.

"Yes." She turned to look at me before she moved onto the first step. "You can always expect that, Carter." She ascended the stairs and moved to the second floor.

When she was gone, I retreated to my bedroom, pleased to have the alone time I'd been craving all day. I left my boxers on the floor and got into bed, knowing I wouldn't need them for what was about to happen next.

Fifteen minutes later, Mia entered the bedroom. She approached the bedside and slipped out of her jeans and t-shirt before she crawled into bed. Instead of moving to the spot beside me, she straddled my hips and positioned herself on top of me.

My hands went to her hips, and I moaned as I felt her point my head at her entrance. She slowly lowered herself with her tits in my face, and I pulled on her hips to make her move a little faster down my length. When she had all of me deep inside her, I squeezed her ass cheeks. Talk about perfect pussy.

Her quiet breaths filled my bedroom and got louder

as she moved up and down. She pressed her hands against my chest for balance as she shifted back and forth, riding me a little harder with every thrust.

My feet dug into the mattress as I pushed myself up and deeper inside her, feeling her slickness grow as we continued to move together. My thumbs dug into her hips, and I watched her tits shake right in my face, the scene so erotic I could barely keep my bullet in the barrel. I sat up on one of my elbows and kissed those sexy nipples as she continued to fuck me, to smear that cream up and down my base.

Her nails dug into my shoulder, and she moved into me harder, thrusting her hips and driving herself to the finish line. When she came, she bucked slightly, her moans uncontrollable and loud.

I watched her sexy performance, my dick remaining at full mast so she could reach her high. My fingers dug into her luscious cheeks, and I fought the fire that started in my balls, the burning sensation before blastoff.

When she finished, she stopped on top of me, her face just inches above mine. Her hair fell against my chest, soft and smooth. She caught her breath as she let the final waves of pleasure rock through her. Her pussy still gripped me with tremendous force, and she slowly slackened around my length.

I guided her hips up and down again, ready to enjoy her in the same way. Now that she had gone first, I didn't hold myself back from the pleasure she'd just received. I pulled her up and down harder and gave her every inch of my length, wanting to fill her as much as possible. When I hit my trigger, it was like flipping a light switch.

I immediately exploded.

And filled her with so much come. "Sweetheart..." I understood what Conway was talking about when he walked away from his bachelor life. He traded in kinky sex and threesomes for vanilla sex like this.

But vanilla was my new favorite flavor.

It didn't matter how slow we moved together. It didn't matter how much foreplay was involved. I would much rather watch this woman ride me then pick up any other woman. I would much rather teach her son to swim than spend a night out on the town. A simple life was something I never wanted, but now it was the most peaceful bliss I'd ever experienced.

She took all my come then kissed me softly on the lips, her pussy still surrounding my length. Her hand moved into my hair, and she deepened the kiss, like the climax wasn't enough for her. She wanted me for more than sex, for more than protection.

She wanted me for me.

She slowly moved off of me, my softening dick slipping out of her with resistance. She cuddled into my side and draped her arm across my waist, exactly what she did right before she went to sleep. It was her position of choice, the way she liked to sleep every night because it made her feel most safe.

I could have let her drift off to sleep, but I didn't. I stared at the ceiling for a few minutes before I broke the silence. "Sweetheart?"

"Hmm?"

I'd been thinking about my father's words all week, knowing he'd been right about everything. That man never seemed to be wrong, even though I would never admit that to his face. "There's something I want to talk to you about."

When she realized this conversation was serious, she propped herself up on her elbow so she could look down into my face. "Alright."

"I've been thinking about this whole marriage thing…"

Her eyes immediately dropped in sadness, like she expected me to tell her I'd changed my mind about the whole thing. It wasn't a look of just sorrow, but one of profound devastation. She normally covered up those reactions, but this time she couldn't.

I liked that response—even though that made me a jackass. "I haven't been honest with you, sweetheart. I haven't been honest with myself. But after talking to my father, I realized I couldn't live a lie anymore."

"Okay…" Her voice shook with fear.

"The reason why I said yes was…because I love you." It was the first time I'd said those words to a woman besides my mom. I suddenly felt different, like that confession changed my entire life forever. It surprised me how easy it was to say. Everything that happened in the past few months suddenly became clear. I'd risked everything to save her from Egor, thinking I was doing it for my own selfish reasons.

Now I knew that wasn't true.

I saved her because I had to—because I loved her.

The sorrow in her gaze disappeared instantly, but her eyes still retained the heartfelt emotion. She was tense and still, unable to move or breathe. As if my words were the last thing she'd ever expected me to say, she couldn't react.

I waited for her to say those words back to me, and the longer the silence lasted, the more afraid I became. What if I'd just ruined the beautiful thing we had? After Luca's father abandoned her and Egor tortured her, perhaps being in love was the last thing she wanted. Maybe I'd just ruined the greatest thing that ever happened to me.

I wished I could take it all back.

Finally, her lungs responded, and she took a deep breath. "I wasn't expecting you to say that…"

Instantly, all the joy in the world was stripped away. I hid my disappointment as much as I could, but there was no way I could erase all of it. Maybe I shouldn't have let my father get to me. Was I an idiot for thinking a woman like her would ever love me? After the way I'd treated her, she deserved someone better.

"You've been so good to both Luca and me. Neither one of us would be here without you…"

I turned my gaze away, hurt by the soft rejection she

was giving me. It was just an explanation of why she couldn't return my feelings—but I didn't need an explanation. This was my first time being rejected—and it hurt as bad as everyone said it did.

"I never thought I would ever trust a man ever again. I never thought I would want to have sex again. I never thought sex could even be that good…but you showed me otherwise. I've never felt safer than I do sharing this house with you. You're such a special man, Carter. Hearing you say that…leaves me speechless."

I used my arms to scoot my body up so I could lean against the headboard. "I mean it, sweetheart. And it's okay if you don't feel the same way. After the way I treated you, I wouldn't blame you." I might have pulled her out of that horrible situation, but I hadn't been a gentleman while she was in my captivity. I'd tried to trick her just so I could fuck her. I chained her up in a bedroom and forced her to slice open her ankle just to pull the tracker out. I wasn't proud of the man I was at the time. Just because I was good to her now didn't mean I was absolved of my previous crimes.

"Don't feel the same way?" She looked at me, her eyebrow raised.

I turned my gaze back on her, seeing the slight smile on her lips.

"Are you kidding me?" she asked with a faint laugh. "You're the sexiest man I've ever seen. Anytime you walk around the house in just your sweatpants, it's like torture. You're incredibly successful on your own merit.

You make me feel beautiful, make me feel special. With you, I feel so safe. And you're so good to my son…have been more of a father to him than anyone else we've ever known. I'm surprised you didn't already know how I felt about you. I guess I thought it was obvious…"

My heart started to race once I heard her confession. The sting of rejection left my body and was replaced with genuine happiness. "No, it wasn't obvious."

"Asking to marry you wasn't obvious?"

"I thought you were just looking for protection."

"I was. But I was also looking for a piece of you for the rest of my life…even if I had to share you. Luca loves you so much, and I don't want him to lose you. You're an incredible role model for him, and you're a dream man, the kind of man who only exists in made-up stories." She inched closer to me, her hair trailing along my skin. "Of course I love you, Carter. I just didn't think you would ever love me…"

My hand tucked her beautiful hair behind her ear, and I leaned in and kissed her on the mouth. "You're the most beautiful woman I've ever seen. That was the first thought that popped into my head when I laid eyes on you. Then when you jumped out of my car…I thought you were the bravest woman I've ever seen. Even when the odds were stacked against you, you never gave up. That's the hottest thing I've ever seen. It doesn't matter if I was in a better position than you were. You proved just how powerful and strong you are.

You're an inspiration…to everyone." I didn't see her as a victim of rape and torture. I saw her as someone who overcame every obstacle that came her way. I saw her as a light in the darkness, a burning candle that refused to flicker out in the wind. "I'm the luckiest man in the world if you think I'm good enough for you."

Instantly, her eyes watered, the light reflecting off the pools of moisture in her eyes. The second she blinked, the tears cascaded down like two small water-falls. "That's…the sweetest thing I've ever heard."

I wiped away a tear with my thumb. "I mean it, sweetheart."

She wiped away the tears from her other cheek. "I've been through so much. I've known depression so intimately that suicide seemed like a dream. If I didn't have my son, I would have taken my life a long time ago. Now that I have you…it seems like God is rewarding me for not giving up. He's given me a second chance at life. He's making up for all the horrible things I had to suffer through. It's more than I ever could have asked for, to be loved by a man like you. You don't think less of me for what I've been through…"

"Never." I kept brushing the hair from her face, doing my best not to get emotional at the sight of her tears.

"You saved my life. You saved my son."

"Best decision I've ever made."

"You've restored my faith in people. I'd only been exposed to assholes, and then I met you and your family…and I see there are good men out there. There is hope in this world. There is love. And if you'd never shown that to me, I don't know what kind of example I could have been to Luca since my spirit had been crushed. But you've given me new life."

She'd never said those things to me before, so I didn't understand the depth of her gratitude. I'd always known she was grateful, but these confessions were on a much deeper level. "It makes me happy that you're happy."

"I'm so happy, Carter. I want to be with you forever. I want to stay by your side as long as I live. I've been in the real world, and I know what's out there…nothing but cruelty. This is the first time I've ever felt like I've been home. You've given us something no one else ever could…not even me. It's a dream come true…being loved by you."

I knew most women wanted me for my money and the security I could provide for them. They wanted fancy cars, expensive jewelry, and the best seats at the opera. They were impressed by my wealth, not the man underneath the suit. But Mia loved me for my other traits, for my kindness, gentleness, and bravery. She loved me for being good to her son, for saving her from the cruel man who tortured her. Now she was indebted to me forever, looked up to me like I was a god. She loved me because of everything we'd been through together.

That made me love her more. "Sweetheart." I

PENELOPE SKY

wrapped my arm around her waist and pulled her closer to me, so our faces were just inches apart. "Marry me. Let me be your husband. Let me be a father to Luca. Let me be everything to you…since you're everything to me." She deserved a real proposal, not a quick conversation in the kitchen when her son was in the other room. She deserved something deeper than that, to know I loved her.

The tears started up again, making her eyes puffy and red, glistening with moisture. "You know my answer."

My hand cupped her cheek, and my fingers dug into her hair. I directed her gaze on me, loving the way she cried for me. "I want to hear it anyway."

"Even if I may not be able to give you children…?"

"We'll figure out a way, sweetheart." There were procedures we could do, or we could adopt. Worst-case scenario, we had Luca. He already felt like a son to me, and I knew that love would only grow in time. "Now say yes."

She smiled through her tears. "Yes…"

TWENTY-SIX

Vanessa

—————

The sparkle of my ring caught my eye every time
I moved.

The diamond acted as a prism of colors, a beautiful
rainbow that flashed across the flawless diamonds, glit-
tering like newly uncovered treasure. When I hung up a
painting in the gallery, I noticed it. When I sat at my
computer and typed, I noticed it too.

The diamonds were excessive, especially the large
one in the center. I never cared for expensive jewelry
and had always been fond of my mother's wedding
ring, which was just a button molded into a metal band.
It seemed oddly cheap for a woman so wealthy, but it
had so much character and clearly meant something to
both of my parents.

But Bones wanted something bold and flashy—and
he delivered.

I would have loved anything he gave me, but I did

447

love this ring in particular—even though it was pretty heavy.

As I worked that afternoon, I floated like a cloud. I couldn't stop smiling, couldn't stop thinking about the way Bones, the most stubborn man in the world, got on one knee in front of my whole family and asked me to marry him.

Well, told me to marry him.

I'd never been so happy in my life.

The front door opened, and someone stepped inside. "I can't tell what's brighter—that ring or your smile."

"Me neither, Father." I turned around and saw him walk inside my gallery, wearing the same happiness in his eyes that I wore in my smile. It didn't seem like this moment would ever arrive, not after he hated Bones so much in the past. But here we were…with a diamond on my left hand. I moved into his arms and hugged him. "Maybe it's a tie."

"No." He kissed my forehead before he pulled away. "That diamond can't compare with that smile." He stepped to the side and slid his hands into his pockets before he glanced at the new painting I had just put on the wall. He gazed at it for a moment before he turned back to me. "I'm glad you're happy, *tesoro*. I don't think I've ever seen you this radiant."

"Wait until the wedding."

He chuckled. "Good point."

"So, how is he?"

He shrugged. "Haven't seen him today. He took the day off."

I cocked an eyebrow because Bones left that morning as usual. "What?"

My father's smile slowly faded. "He told me he needed a personal day. I assumed he would be down here."

Bones didn't actually lie to me. He didn't tell me he was going to work. He didn't say anything at all, actually. "That's strange…he left the house in the morning like normal."

"Hmm…" My father didn't try to make a guess about his whereabouts. "I wouldn't worry about it."

Bones would never betray me in any way, so I wasn't concerned what he was doing. When I saw him next, he would tell me. "I'm not. So, what brings you here?"

"I had a meeting in town, so I thought I would stop by." He moved to my desk and leaned against the counter, his arms crossing over his chest. "Want to get some lunch?"

"I would, but I just ate."

"Oh well. I guess I should head back to the winery since your uncle is doing everything today…but I like making him work, so maybe I'll stall a little longer." He grinned slightly, being playful but serious at the same time.

"I'm sure he's done the same to you."

"Oh, he has," he said with a chuckle. "And payback is a bitch. You're lucky you're the only operator in your business. You never have to worry about things like that."

"I thought you liked working with your brother?"

He shrugged. "I like seeing him all the time, but we butt heads a lot."

"Never noticed," I teased.

"The winery was my own business when we were younger. I brought him in because we lost our other business, and he didn't have anything else. But he made it grow, so we have a few different vineyards now."

"That was nice of you."

"He's family…" He looked at the other paintings on the wall.

"And it was really sweet of you to give it to Griffin…" Before Griffin asked me to marry him, my father had already accepted him like a son. He brought him into our legacy and gave him a business he spent most of his life cultivating. It was a gesture that spoke louder than words.

"No one else better, *tesoro*." He lifted his gaze and looked into mine. "He'll do a good job. I have no doubt."

I smiled at him. "That still must have been hard for you."

"Not really, actually. He's not the kind of man who will allow someone to take advantage of him. He'll protect everything I built with my bare hands."

"But he'll also scare away your customers with that scowl…"

He chuckled. "People respect him for it. I respect him."

My father had been wrong when he treated Griffin so coldly, but he more than made up for it. "I appreciate everything you've done for him. He has somewhere he belongs...and I know that means a lot to him, even if he doesn't say it in those words."

He nodded. "I know he does. I told him I love him like a son...because I do."

"And I think he loves you like a father."

"If he doesn't, maybe he will someday." He gripped the edge of my desk. "We've got plenty of time. Look how far we've come in a single year."

It was hard to believe I'd loved Bones for almost an entire year. It seemed like he'd been in my life forever... not just a short time.

"So, any plans for the wedding?"

"Uh, we haven't talked about it much." We haven't talked at all, actually. Ever since he put that ring on my finger, he'd been hunting me down around the house and making love to me on every single piece of furniture we owned. His possession increased tenfold. That dark look he gave me with those piercing eyes became far more intense than it'd ever been before. And when I took off my ring to shower, he looked at me like he might slap my ass so hard I wouldn't be able to walk again.

My father didn't say any more about it. "He asked me in my office at the end of the day. I knew the moment was coming, but I wasn't ready for it. I've been dreading this day since you were born, and it was a relief when I gave him my blessing and really meant it. There's no doubt in my mind that man loves you…loves you the way I love your mother."

I knew this was hard for my father, and he was doing such a good job handling it. "I know he does." I gave him a slight smile, feeling the emotion bubble up inside my chest. "He'll be a good husband. He'll be a good father. And he'll be a good son to you."

"He already is. We've come a long way. When I look back on the past, it's hard to believe that stuff ever happened."

"Me too." I'd been through so much heartbreak, but it'd all been worth it to end up here.

My father's eyes darted to the window as someone walked inside. "Looks like we're about to find out what Griffin did with his personal day."

I turned around and saw Griffin enter my gallery, his thick arms stretching the gray color of his t-shirt. His nice arms were covered with black ink, and with his short hair and intense stare, he looked like the most terrifying man on the planet.

I guess I had a thing for scary men.

He looked at me, those bright blue eyes the only soft feature about him. As if my father wasn't standing right there, he turned his possessive gaze on me, glancing at my ring to make sure I was wearing it. "Baby." He bent his neck and gave me a short kiss on the mouth, but judging by the way he gripped my waist so tightly, he had to restrain himself from kissing me as hard as he really wanted.

"Griffin. Care to give me an explanation of where you've been all day?"

He cocked an eyebrow, shooting me a flash of annoyance. "If I asked you that same question, I'd get slapped."

But you love getting slapped. "What happened to your hand?" I noticed the white gauze wrapped around the ring finger on his left hand. There wasn't a sign of blood, but it seemed like he had a bad injury.

Griffin didn't glance at it. "If I'm not working today and you aren't either, what does that mean?" He turned to my father and ignored my question.

Father shrugged. "Cane is busting his ass —for once."

Griffin gave a slight smile. "Good."

I looked at his hand again. "What happened?"

He pulled his hand to his chest and carefully pulled the gauze off his finger. He tossed it into the garbage can by my desk and held up his left hand, showing the black ink that wrapped around his finger and formed a thick wedding band. It contrasted against his fair skin, being just as obvious as the diamonds I wore.

It took me a second to process what I was looking at. "You want a tattoo as a ring…"

"We both know I'm not a jewelry kind of guy." Griffin lowered his hand. "I don't even wear a watch."

"But we aren't married yet," I said with a chuckle. "You're supposed to do that after we get married."

"After?" he asked, not caring about having this conversation in front of my father. "We are married. I asked you last week, and you said yes."

"That's not how it works." His ignorance was adorable at times. "There's no way you don't know that. We're supposed to have a wedding and—"

"That's not us." He silenced me with his ferocious look. "Our bond started long before I put that ring on your finger. Signing a piece of paper isn't going to make that more true. This ink represents a lot more than matrimonial love. It represents my eternal commitment to you. So I can get this ink anytime I want, whether I'm your husband or not."

My father's eyes shifted back and forth as he looked at us, clearly uncomfortable with the intimate conversation we were having. It was something he shouldn't stand there and witness. He cleared his throat then slowly drifted away. "I should get back to the winery..." He let himself out, his shoes tapping against the floor until he was gone.

Bones never took his eyes off me. His chest rose and fell with his deep breaths, and he looked at me like he'd never been angrier with me.

"Griffin, I'm not angry that you got that tattoo. It's sweet, actually."

His breathing decreased slightly, along with his aggression.

"I just thought you did it prematurely. We may not have a wedding for a year…"

Now he was pissed off all over again. "You've got to be kidding me."

"It takes time to plan a wedding, Griffin. My family knows a lot of people, so there will be a ton of guests."

He looked like he could pick up my desk and throw it out the window. "I don't want any guests at our wedding. I want it just to be us and a few people. There's no goddamn way I'm waiting a year to marry you. Is this a joke?"

"Then what were you expecting?"

"Tomorrow."

Both of my eyebrows rose up my forehead. "Tomorrow?"

"Or the day after. What about today?"

"Are you crazy?"

"No, baby. You're the one who's crazy. How could you possibly want to wait a year to be married to me?"

"It's not that I want to wait," I argued. "It's just… It's stupid."

"Tell me."

Like every other woman on the planet, I'd dreamed of how I wanted my wedding to be. "I've always wanted to wear a wedding dress. If we do it at the court, I can't really do that. And I know my father wants to give me away. So…we need to have a wedding, Griffin."

His eyes watched me for a long time. "We can still do that."

"Then we need to wait."

"You can get a wedding dress in a day or so."

"But then it needs to be fitted—"

"What the hell is Conway for?" he snapped. "That's what he does for a living."

Sometimes I forgot my brother actually had talents besides being annoying.

"And we can have a small ceremony—just family. We'll do it on Saturday."

That was only a few days away, but when Bones described it that way, it actually sounded pretty perfect.

"You wanted to start a family right away?" he asked, the tension in his eyes slowly dying away now that he was getting his way.

"Yes…but I thought we would talk about that later."

"Well, we need to be married first."

I rolled my eyes. "Our relationship has never been conventional, so let's not start now."

"When I asked your father if I could marry you, I promised I would take care of you. So if you want to start a family, I want to do it the right way. I want to be your husband. I want to get you pregnant in our bed, our rings on our hands."

It was one of the sweetest things I'd ever heard him say.

"And don't expect me to wait a year for that to happen."

"So…you really want to start a family with me?" I knew I wanted children. I'd known since I was a little girl. But when I mentioned it to Griffin, he didn't seem interested at all.

"I thought I didn't have a choice in the matter."

"But I would hope that you would have changed your mind on your own..."

He looked down for a moment, considering his answer carefully before he gave it. "I love you more than anything else in the world, and the idea of something happening to you...is my worst nightmare. So the idea of having babies...having a daughter who looks like you...just scares me even more. The more people I love, the more I have to protect. The more I have to lose. That's what scares me." He grabbed my hand and surrounded it with both of his palms, like he was protecting my hand with his. "In that regard, I don't think I'll ever be ready."

I brought his hand to my mouth and kissed his knuckles. "You already are ready, Griffin. You're a protector. And you'll always be the best protector I know." I held his gaze as I kissed him before I moved into his chest.

He wrapped his powerful arms around me and rested his chin on my head. "Marry me on Saturday."

Now I wanted to marry him that very moment. "Saturday."

TWENTY-SEVEN

Carter

I watched her sleep beside me, treasuring the final moments before Luca woke up and pounded on the door. Her hand rested on her chest, and her hair was all over the pillow. When she was asleep, she was even more beautiful.

A few minutes later, she finally woke up. She opened her eyes first, released a relaxed sigh, and then turned her gaze on me. She focused on my face for a moment before the smile crept onto her lips. "Morning."

"Morning, sweetheart." My hand went to her stomach then drifted to her hand. I placed my hand on hers, the weight of my palm bringing attention to hers.

Her hand moved underneath mine, and that's when she flinched. She turned her gaze to her left hand and narrowed her gaze on the diamond ring sitting on her left ring finger. As if she couldn't understand if this was a dream or not, she still didn't react. Only when she brought her hand closer to her face did she understand. "Oh my god." She jerked upright and gripped her hand with the other, examining the enormous rock I'd picked out for her. It was a beautiful ring, sleek and simple. When she took Luca to school yesterday, I'd slipped out and headed to Florence to pick it out. "It's so beautiful…" She brushed her thumb over the diamond. "It's perfect. Yes…a million times yes."

I tried not to chuckle. "You already agreed to marry me."

"I know, but now I want to marry you even more." She cupped my cheeks and kissed me, the metal band touching the skin of my cheek. Her fingers moved into my hair, and she slowly positioned herself on my lap.

I rested my back against the headboard and pulled her closer to me, my body immediately anxious for hers. That ring looked perfect on her, and it would look perfect for the rest of our lives.

Just when the passion heated up even more, Luca came to the door and knocked. "Mom?"

She sighed into my mouth, frustrated.

"Mom?" Luca repeated.

"I love my son," she whispered. "But I hate him right now."

If I didn't love Luca so much, I would probably be just as annoyed. But I found the interruption almost comical since it happened almost every single morning. Morning sex wasn't common for us anymore. Only when Luca was asleep did we have our fun—but we always made the best of it. "You can make it up to me later."

She cupped my cheek and kissed me again, her tits right against my chest. "And I will."

MIA ALREADY TALKED to Luca and explained what was going on, that I would be her husband in a short amount of time. Luca never had a father figure in his life so it wasn't clear how he would react to it, but he seemed fine with it.

But I decided to talk to him on my own.

I sat across from him at the kitchen table. He just finished his after-school snack, and his homework was spread out around him. Math was his worst subject, but since it was my best, I was able to help him.

Luca put down his pencil and looked at me, his brown eyes identical to his mother's. "What did you want to talk to me about?"

"Your mother."

"What about her?" he asked.

"I know she told you that she and I were getting married."

Luca stared at me blankly, like that information didn't mean anything to him. Maybe he didn't care about any of this at all. After living in an orphanage, he was probably used to changing circumstances.

"I thought we could talk about that a little bit…just the two of us."

"Okay…"

Normally, when I spoke to Luca, it was easy. But then again, we were talking about math homework, swimming, or dinosaurs. This kid was just eight years old. There was so much he didn't understand. "Do you know anything about your dad?" Mia had told me she'd told him, but I wasn't sure if he remembered.

He nodded. "He left when Mom was pregnant with me. She never saw him again."

"And that was wrong of him. Thankfully, your mother didn't need him in the first place. She's strong and capable, and she loves you so much." I only wished I'd been there to help her. I never would have turned my back on her. What kind of man did that?

"I know she does," he whispered.

"I want you to know that's never gonna happen with me. I'm never gonna disappear, Luca."

He fidgeted with his pencil and avoided my gaze for a while. "You aren't…?"

"Never." It was wrong to make a promise like that to a child unless you were going to keep it. But I was definitely going to keep it. "I love your mother very much, and I will treat her right. And I also love you…" The words flew out of my mouth so easily. I'd become attached to this young boy so easily because his joy was infectious.

"I love you too, Carter." He looked up at me again.

Instantly, my eyes began to water. I wondered if this was how my father felt about me, if his heart skipped a beat when I said things like that. "So…it's okay if I marry your mom?"

"That means we would live here with you?" he asked. "Like…forever?"

"Yeah."

"That sounds good to me. My mom seems happy here. She smiles a lot."

I knew I wasn't the reason for that. Luca didn't understand that he was the source of all her joy. I made her happy to a certain extent, but Luca would always be everything to her. I would always come in second— which was fine with me. "Yeah, she does."

"So, that means you're my dad now?"

"Uh, if you want me to be. You can keep calling me Carter. But if you ever wanna call me Dad…you can."

"Cool." He picked up his pencil again. As if a serious conversation had never happened, he went back to his homework.

Talking to kids was a lot easier than talking to adults sometimes.

I STOPPED BY MY PARENTS' place in the evening. Now that I'd straightened things out with Mia, I was ready to tell my parents the news. My father already knew, but at least now he was getting the news delivered the way he wanted.

My mother opened the door, both happy and surprised to see me standing there. "Hey, son." She hugged me and kissed me on the cheek. "Are Mia and Luca with you?"

"No. Just me." I stepped inside and hugged my father, who was already smiling like he knew exactly why I was there.

"Everything alright?" Mom asked.

"Yeah. More than fine." I placed my hands in my pockets before I looked my mom in the eye and told her about Mia. "I asked Mia to marry me. She said yes." I couldn't keep the grin off my face, couldn't hide the thrill of happiness it gave me. She was so happy with the ring I gave her, happy with the life I offered her.

Father smiled. "Wow, that's really great news. Congratulations, Carter."

Mom took a second longer to react, but that was because her response was a million times bigger. "Oh my god, that's so great!" She cupped her mouth with her palms and screamed into her hands before she jumped into my arms. "That makes me so happy, Carter. Mia is absolutely lovely, and so is her son."

"Yes, they both are."

Mom cupped my face and kissed my cheek before she stepped back. "It's been such an exciting week for the Barsettis. We're so lucky."

I definitely felt like the luckiest man in the world.

"Thanks for being so understanding about this. I know most parents wouldn't be too thrilled about her past… but you guys raised me to be better than that."

Mom smiled. "We raised you to be an incredible man…just like your father." She moved into his side and fit under his arm as Father wrapped his arm around her shoulders. "We couldn't be happier."

"Since tomorrow is Vanessa's wedding, I thought we would keep this to ourselves." I didn't want to spoil her day with my engagement, not that she would care about anything else besides Griffin.

"Carter, no one is gonna care," Mom said. "We're all family. If Mia and Luca are part of our family, then they need to be treated that way. Don't make her hide her ring. That would be wrong."

Since they thought it was okay, I decided I would be honest about it. "Looks like Carmen is the last one, then."

"Oh, don't worry about her," Mom said. "She can have any guy she wants. She's just taking her time finding him."

Father continued to wear his smile, but it faltered slightly. "Or, she could move back in here and just live with her parents forever…"

Mom hit him playfully. "Carmen is a grown woman. You need to get it over it, Cane."

"Not possible," Father said. "Look how long it took Crow."

"And you better have learned from his mistakes."

Mom left his side and came back to me. "Why didn't you bring her over here with Luca?"

"I wanted to talk to you alone first," I said. "Give you some warning."

"Warning?" she asked, bewildered. "This is the greatest thing ever to have happened to you, Carter. There's nothing better than having a family. Money and ambition are important, but only for so long. Eventually, those things don't matter…only the people you love. I'm excited to see Mia, my new daughter…and my new grandson."

CONWAY and I shared a drink together in the study at his father's home. Sapphire and Aunt Pearl were with Reid in the living room, and Crow was working on the yard outside preparing for the wedding tomorrow.

"Did you get the house?" Conway and I didn't spend as much time together anymore, not since his life changed with a wife and kid. Now that I had Mia and Luca, I understood how much priorities shifted.

"We did." He drank his scotch then licked his lips. "We'll get the keys on Monday."

"You must be eager to get out of here."

He shook his head slightly. "Not really. It's been nice spending time with my parents since I've been living in Milan for so long. Sapphire loves it. Honestly, she would want to live here forever if she could have her way."

"Really?" I asked, surprised since Conway was such a solitary person.

"My mom has been doing a lot with Reid, and that's really made it easier on both of us. Sapphire adores my parents. I can tell she sees them as parents… sees them as the family she never had. That's made me more patient about living here."

"Uh, what about sex?"

"My mom takes care of Reid, so that's not a problem. Since we're on different floors, we have our own privacy."

I loved my parents, but I could never live with them again. Even if Mia and I had a baby, I wouldn't want my mom to move in with us to help. "It's a shame we don't hang out the way we used to. We're two miles apart, but we never see each other."

"It is a bummer. But in a few months, it'll be easier. Reid needs a lot of attention right now."

"That's fine. You should treasure this time with him."

"And I do." He poured more scotch. "I love that kid so much. I didn't think I'd love anyone more than Sapphire, but I do. I'd take a bullet for him in a heartbeat. Sometimes I can't sleep at night because I worry about him…even though he's perfectly safe with my mom. Fatherhood was never appealing to me, but once he was here…it all clicked."

That was exactly how I felt about Luca. "I've fallen hard for Mia's son. Nice kid."

"Yeah, he seems like a sweetheart."

I finished off my glass before I told him my news. "So, there's something I want to tell you."

"You knocked up Mia?" he asked, dead serious.

"No. I asked her to marry me." I watched his expression, unsure what he would think about my quick engagement. I hadn't known Mia that long, but it seemed unlikely I would ever feel something for another woman again. Mia was special in more ways than I could express.

"You're serious?" He slowly lowered his empty glass to the table, his eyes stunned.

"Dead serious."

"Jesus." He slammed the glass onto the table. "Why didn't you lead with that?"

I shrugged. "We haven't talked in a while, so wanted to break the ice a bit."

"I can't believe it. Carter Barsetti takes a wife." He ran his hand through his hair, his eyes showing his surprise but his lips showing his smile. "I've seen you ass-fuck two women in one night. Now you're marrying someone—with a kid."

"Yes…pretty crazy. And do me a favor and don't mention that story to Mia."

He rolled his eyes. "Like she would be surprised, man."

"Whatever. I don't tell Sapphire shit. That goes both ways."

"Like I'd ever sell you out. But she'd love you

anyway. It doesn't matter what kind of nasty shit we did before we met them. When you meet the right woman, it's like that stuff never happened."

"Yeah, I'm sure you're right." It wasn't like Mia hadn't seen the worst of me in the past. She loved me anyway, despite my horrendous crimes.

"So, what about Luca?"

"He's okay with it. We've gotten pretty close over the last few weeks."

"That's great, man. Looks at us…all grown-up."

"I can't believe it either." I shook my head before I refilled our glasses with scotch.

"When's the wedding?"

"Not sure. It'll be something small, something simple and quick. Maybe just a courthouse type thing."

"Our wedding was small but perfect."

I nodded, remembering how elegant Sapphire looked on their wedding day. And I'd never forget how happy my cousin looked. "Regardless of what we do… you'll be my best man?" Conway was more of a brother to me, a best friend. Cousin didn't describe us appropriately. We'd been through a lot together, our ups and downs, and we carried the Barsetti name with pride. We'd made our parents proud, and now we were starting a new generation, a new legacy for all of us.

Conway looked at me differently, clearly touched by the question. He took a deep breath before a slow smile crept onto his lips. He brushed his nose with his thumb, sighed, and then responded. "You know I will."

TWENTY-EIGHT

Vanessa

———————

Mama ran her fingers through my curls, making sure my soft hair hung down my back perfectly. I considered hiring someone to do my makeup, to put fake eyelashes on my eyelids and blush on my cheeks. But when I remembered Bones loved me the way I was, made love to me the way I was, I realized he wouldn't want me to look like a different person. So I kept everything light, subtle eyeshadow, lipstick, and foundation.

Something more natural.

Mama looked at my appearance in the mirror as she stood behind me. "You look perfect, sweetheart." She grabbed the back of my train and adjusted it behind me, making sure it looked just right.

"Thanks, Mama." I picked a formfitting dress, pearl white with sleeves made of lace. The color contrasted against my olive skin, and the diamond necklace my mother loaned me sparkled. I didn't wear heels, choosing to go barefoot so I could feel the grass underneath my feet as I walked to my future husband.

My mother gripped both of my shoulders then kissed me on the cheek. "Griffin is a very lucky man."

"And I'm lucky that he thinks so."

"Are you nervous at all?" She walked to the window and peeked out onto the lawn, seeing the white rose petals on the ground and the white arch my father built with his bare hands. It was the same place where my parents got married, my brother as well. Now it seemed to be a family tradition.

My dress felt tight against my stomach and my heart rate wouldn't slow down, but that was mere excitement. "No. There's not a doubt in my mind he's the man I want."

She smiled at me. "I didn't ask if you had doubts. Just asked if you were nervous."

"Were you nervous when you married Father?"

"Yes," she answered immediately. "But your father is an intense man. It seemed like I couldn't walk to him fast enough. He was always disappointed with how slowly I was moving. Being loved by a man like that can be difficult, but very rewarding. Griffin seems to have a lot of the same qualities."

Bossy. Controlling. Possessive. Yes, he had all the qualities that made him a little crazy. "He does."

"So be nervous as long as you can. It's the happiest day of your life—and it's one of my mine."

Father came in next, wearing a black suit and tie. His gaze moved up my dress until he settled on my face. A slight smile appeared on his lips, along with a hint of pride. "You've never looked more beautiful, *tesoro*."

"Thanks, Father…"

He kissed me on the cheek then wrapped his arm around my mother's waist. "I think we did a good job, Button."

"Yes," Mama whispered. "Couldn't have asked for a better daughter."

The three of us stood there together, cherishing the final moments when I would be just their daughter, unmarried and without a family of my own. Once I left the house with Bones, I would be having my own children, and things would never be the same. They wouldn't be worse, probably better, but never the same as they were now.

Mama cleared her throat and moved from Father's embrace. "We're getting started soon. I'll see you guys down there."

Father kept staring at me, like he wanted to say something but couldn't find the words. He'd never been an emotional man when I was growing up, but ever since Bones came into the picture, he'd become much softer.

"You'll never lose me, Father."

His eyes narrowed slightly on my face, touched by my words.

"I'll always be your daughter…even when you're

pushing eighty and I'm forty." I repeated the words back to him, trying to make him feel better.

He finally smiled. "Yes…you'll always be my daughter. The only thing that's changing is I'm getting a son, a very noble young man. I know I'm not myself right now, but I am happy, *tesoro*…even if it doesn't seem that way. A father's job is to make sure his daughter ends up with a good man… I did my job. It's something I'll never have to worry about again."

"No, you won't," I whispered. "How's he doing?"

"Quiet. He's been drinking with me and Conway all day. Seems anxious."

"I'm sure he is."

"Not that I can blame him…when you're the most beautiful bride I've ever seen."

"Father…" My eyes watered, and I immediately blinked my tears away, not wanting to ruin my makeup.

He came to my side and extended his arm to me so I could take it. "Let me give you away to a man who's earned you, *tesoro*."

MY FATHER GUIDED me down the steps and to the grass at the end of the porch. He used his frame to support me the entire way, even though I was barefoot and had no trouble.

Had no trouble walking to the man I was meant to be with.

The sun was setting, and there were white rose petals everywhere.

I lifted my gaze and met Griffin's. Piercing blue like the ocean, his eyes were glued to me with the same intensity I expected every single day. He made me his before I even reached him, claimed me from dozens of feet away with his enormous presence. He watched me like my father wasn't right beside me, guiding me to him.

I didn't even make it halfway before I started to cry.

I'd lost this man once before, and it was the hardest thing I'd ever had to go through. I knew I would never love anyone the way I loved him. Boys came and went, but he was the first man who could handle me. He loved me the way every woman dreamed of being loved. He didn't care about the women who stared at him everywhere he went, oblivious to them because I was the only thing ever on his mind. He told me he loved me without skipping a beat, laying his feelings in the open without a hint of hesitation. Strong, powerful, and confident, he was exactly what I'd been looking for…my entire life.

That was why I couldn't stop crying.

Because I loved this man so much.

He wasn't what I was looking for. When I met him, I despised him. But when I had the chance to kill him, I couldn't do it. The second he was on top of me, the game was over. I was his long before I told him I loved him.

We'd been through so much together, overcame all the obstacles that seemed insurmountable.

Because he never gave up on me.

He was one hell of a man.

Dressed in a black suit that Conway had tailored for him, he looked so handsome, the shadow of stubble on his chin. Despite the beautiful color of his eyes, his expression was more intense than I'd ever seen it—like he wanted to yank me out of my father's hands. The wait was unbearable. I could see it in the way he looked at me.

It was the only time I'd ever seen him dress that way —so handsome.

We finally reached him, a lifetime later. My father grabbed my hand and placed it in Griffin's. "I give you my daughter—because you'll take care of her." He squeezed my hand one last time before he left me go.

Bones kept his gaze on me, but he shut his eyes for a long moment, like he was at war with himself. Then he turned back to my father and moved his hand to his shoulder. "Always, Mr. Barsetti."

My father gave him a slight nod before he stepped away, leaving me to marry the man I loved. He moved to the seat beside my mom, who was crying into a tissue. He wrapped his arm around her, the tears glistening in his eyes.

Bones looked at me again, taking both of my hands and facing me. He didn't say a single word, but he didn't need to say anything at all. He could always tell me how he felt without moving his lips. Right now, I was the most beautiful thing he'd ever seen, and while he loved my dress, he'd rather see it on the floor of our bedroom.

He directed both of my hands against his chest, where I could feel his strong heartbeat against his black suit. Thump. Thump. Thump. It was slow and steady, like he could have been sleeping. This beat was calm and true, like this moment was bittersweet.

I took a deep breath and did my best to stem my tears, but it seemed useless. I didn't want my makeup to be ruined, to look ugly on my wedding day because I couldn't keep my emotions under control. There was so much feeling in that moment, so much pain, love, and joy.

"Baby." He rubbed his hand across mine as he kept my palm against his chest. "I love you."

"I love you too."

He didn't show tears the way I did, his face stoic like any other day. He did a better job of keeping his feelings under control, but his calmness didn't stop my tears. "It seems like we've been waiting a lifetime for this."

"Yes…"

"As my wife, I give you my heart. It'll be your lullaby when you sleep. It'll always move into my throat every morning when I look at you…when I look at you now.

When I die, it'll lie next to you. We'll be together always, our souls dancing on the wind for eternity…our heartbeats as a faint drum in the distance."

Bones had never said anything so beautiful. He was a man of few words, but when he did say something, it always blew my mind. He struggled to express himself, but that made his words so much sweeter. He meant every word, every syllable. "Griffin…"

"Baby, I will love you every day for the rest of my life. I will be your husband, and I will be the best damn husband the world has ever seen. When you sleep beside me, you'll never be afraid of what happens outside our walls. Our children will be safe…and we can keep having as many kids as you want until you cut me off…because I will give you anything you ask for as long as you continue to love me, to continue to be the greatest thing that ever happened to me."

I wanted to wipe my tears away, but I didn't pull my hands from his chest.

"You will take my name, but I know you will always be a Barsetti. I'm not the kind of man that shares, but I will share you with them…because they're my family too. I will provide everything for both of us, take good care of you so you'll always have what you need. You'll spend your days painting and raising our kids, never worrying about earning a penny because that's my job. I will worship you every day, kiss the ground you walk on, and make love to you every night because I want to enjoy you as long as

I can until our time runs out…because one lifetime just isn't enough."

I didn't even care that he said that in front of my whole family. It was beautiful and honest…his trademarks. He didn't care what anyone thought of him. Never had and never would. It was why I loved him so much. "I…I wrote my vows, but I just…" I closed my eyes and willed myself to stop crying. But no matter what I did, the tears wouldn't stop.

Bones was patient as he waited for me to gather myself. He waited, squeezing my hand against his chest.

"I'm sorry. I love you…nothing else is coming out."

"That's okay, baby. I'll say them for you." He squeezed my hand. "I know you love me because it goes without saying. When I walk into the room and you look at me…it's special. You try not to smile, but it's impossible. As I come closer and closer to you, your body stiffens in different ways. Once my hands are on you, all that tension releases…and you turn into melted butter in my hands. You love me the way a real woman should love a man, fearlessly, wholeheartedly, and with everything you have. You're a fighter, the kind of woman that stands her ground against a man twice her size, and I know you would give your life for mine in a heartbeat…even though I would never want you to. You love me despite my flaws, saw past my darkness and saw the light. Only a woman like you could handle someone like me…and I know we both believe that we're meant for each other. You love me for working my ass off to earn your father's approval, and you will always be loyal to me for that. We both know I earned you…and that's the kind of man you want…one earns his woman."

I nodded slightly, agreeing with everything he'd just said. He ripped the words out of my mouth, reading my heart as well as he could read my eyes. "Yes, that's how I love you."

When we were done, the priest finished the ceremony. He turned to Bones, who slipped the ring onto my finger. "Do you take this woman—"

"Yes." His deep voice shut up the priest, his hard eyes glued to mine.

The priest kept going. "And do you take this man—"

"Yes."

For the first time, Bones showed the softer emotion he rarely let anyone see—even me. Emotion tugged at his eyes, a beautiful softness that showed the vulnerability of a summer flower about to wilt in winter. His hand relaxed against mine, and he tilted his head slightly, my fast response meaning more to him than everything else I said. He couldn't wait to marry me— but I couldn't wait to marry him even more.

"I now pronounce you husband and wife. You may—"

Bones grabbed my face and kissed me hard, kissing me harder than he ever had in our lives. One hand dug into my hair without caring about keeping it nice. His other hand cupped the back of my neck slightly as he moved deeper into me. Applause and whistles rang out around us, but neither one of us cared. I was officially his wife, and that meant he didn't give a damn what anyone thought of us.

His arm hugged my waist, and he pulled me hard into his thick body, gathering me in his arms and smothering me with his love and devotion. His lips moved against mine, and he cherished me the way he promised, loving me deeply and passionately.

When he pulled away, he kept his gaze close to mine, ignoring everyone else around us.

That's when I saw the distant tears in his eyes, the emotion that reflected my own.

We were standing under the olive tree, the place where my parents wed after the horrible scars they suffered. The blood war seemed like an ancient myth, the hate diminished because of the love that washed it all away.

The moment in time would only last an instant, but that spot would always be marked by our love. Centuries would pass, but there would always be an energy here, a sign of the powerful love that ended a war.

Bones scooped me up into his arms, one arm behind my knee while the other was behind my shoulders. He supported me with ease then carried me down the aisle where our friends and family clapped and cheered. His eyes were only on me, as if no one else was there. "You're one hell of a woman, baby. Thank you for being my woman."

My arms circled his neck, and I kissed him as he carried me across the grass. "Thank you for being one hell of a man."

Also by Penelope Sky

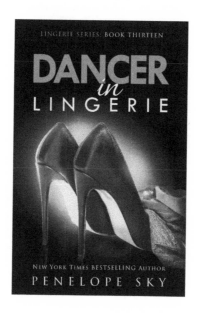

Order Now

CPSIA information can be obtained
at www.ICGtesting.com
Printed in the USA
LVHW041814140319
610673LV00002B/246

9 781725 918221